LEMON & MALICE

A FANTASY ADVENTURE

Acknowledgements

Thank you, to my family. Especially to my husband, Chris, for believing in my dreams when I didn't, and for being patient with me through all the ups and downs. This book wouldn't have happened without his help. *I love you*.

Special thanks to my editor, Brandy. She put time into my work, in a way I had only dreamed of before I found her.

For my father. For the nights you sat by my bed, reading to me about lost monkeys, fifth dimensions, and hobbits.

PROLOGUE

The daylight waned over Beacon City; the sun making one last stand against the evening's shadow. A stray beam of brilliant light shone through the stained glass of the city's temple, casting red and yellow fractals of light on Gespar Fairchild where he stood in the inner sanctuary. Gespar fiddled with the talisman hanging from his belt as he stared at the window contemplating the importance of patience, particularly for a holy warrior.

He turned instantly at the first popping hiss from the brazier behind him. The flames burned as they always did, more golden than a natural fire, but otherwise normal. But, after a few moments, blue sparks flickered around the yellow wisps. The popping became more persistent, and the blue sparks pulled together as a glowing orb in the center of the pit.

As soon as the parchment solidified, he reached into the flames to grab it. Thanks to his talisman, the flames licked harmlessly around his hand. Even after years of carrying it, the divine magic still left him in awe.

He broke the Triad seal and unrolled it, revealing the soft, sweeping script within.

Paladin Fairchild

You were right to wait for guidance before proceeding. We would remind you again of the importance of this task. Bring the Stone to us immediately. Whatever material or monetary support you need to successfully deliver the relic to the Grand Temple is at your disposal.

We must insist upon your discretion. To that end, your request for a support team from the church is denied. Do not give information on this job to any of the clergies or seek help from any Faithful or your fellow Paladins. Any aid you require should be discreet and minimally informed.

We await your arrival. The gods smile upon your quest.

The seal at the bottom of the letter consisted of three names: Lestra, Arthur, and Diana. It was a missive directly from the Blessed Leaders. The only authority higher would be the Gods themselves. The direction itself was somewhat unusual, but then again, this assignment had been different from the start.

He folded the letter up and placed it in his satchel on his way towards the door. Leaving the inner sanctuary, he crossed into the main hall, attracting curious glances from a cleric and a few loitering Faithful, the lower tier of holy servants. He acknowledged them with a shallow bow, but left the temple without a word.

Out in the city streets, the temple's silence gave way to the steady roar of evening activity. Gespar set out with purpose and more than a little excitement. Such an opportunity was truly a blessing. Aware that his many blessings demanded gratitude, he viewed every mission as an opportunity to prove himself worthy and repay the kindness shown by the Empire and the Gods.

The Beacon Temple was at the northernmost peak of the city, which by no coincidence was the nicest part of town. Beacon was the third-largest city in the Empire, though it was packed just as full as Central. It hugged the bay on its shore-facing side, curving southward and fading from high-class luxury to slums as it went until the city was nothing more than filthy huts and shady docks spilling into the sea at its southernmost point.

Where Gespar had stepped outside, his feet had landed on intricate paving stones laid in decorative patterns with explicit attention to detail. Now the streets were giving way to carefully crafted, smooth brick. He was headed to an inn in the Middleton Market district, on the nicer side of rowdy. The place attracted a variety of travelers and locals, the perfect starting point.

The Paladin's years of training made him highly capable. The Empire had honed him into a well-sharpened tool, but he was also wise enough to know when he needed help and humble enough to admit it. Failure wasn't an option, and if this Stone was as powerful as the evidence seemed to suggest, then the Empire wasn't the only interested party. Luckily for Gespar, Beacon city was teeming with minimally informed help for hire.

ONE

Beatrice Lemon was not a genius. Her mouth, however, was smart enough that she was usually able to convince people that she was relatively clever. Unfortunately, that also meant it had gotten her into trouble on several occasions.

This was shaping up to be one such occasion.

"I'm just saying that while you are exceptionally well qualified for door-guarding duty, letting us in seems more like a *business* decision. So maybe you should ask someone that can make business decisions," she said to the man blocking her path.

They stood in one of the seedier alleys in Beacon. This particular back street housed the entrance to the den of one of the top trades-men in the city, 'tradesman' being a forgiving title for the criminal ringleaders one might go to if they needed goods or services they couldn't obtain through legal means.

The man held a torch against the night, illuminating his own sallow face and the others gathered around him, as well as the broken down cobblestone at their feet.

"Claw said specifically *not* to let you in," he doubled down. She could hear the annoyance hidden in his tone growing, though he fought to suppress it. He was trying to strike a balance. Rude enough to deter her, but not rude enough to bring wrath upon himself.

The men behind him, another human and a lizard-like draken, held steady eye contact with her. This might have seemed strange or threatening, but she knew it was less about where they were looking and more about where they were trying not to look- at the looming shadow over her shoulder.

"Word is you're hot after what happened in Drell. Boss doesn't need you around if you're gonna attract attention."

"What happened in Drell?" Beatrice asked, feigning surprise. The man squinted his already narrow eyes at her.

"You know. That guard that fell out the window. Everyone knows there was a girl and a..." his eyes darted to the looming figure standing behind Beatrice for just a moment. "An orc... ain't many pairs like the two of you runnin' around."

The Orc in question snorted and Beatrice smiled sweetly, attempting to feign some sort of comradery with the lackey before her. "Listen, Paul. It's Paul, right?"

"It's not."

Beatrice acted as though she hadn't heard him. "You said it yourself, Pete. That guard fell out a window. That's all there is to it. Maybe we were there. Maybe it was a different orc and a different lovely young woman. But it doesn't matter because we're here now and we didn't come empty-handed."

Right on cue, her companion held up a delicate chain weighed down with a green-tinged gemstone the size of a large coin and several smaller ones that climbed up the chain on one side, all uncut and asymmetrical. The stones caught the light from the torch, scattering it back across the faces of the onlookers with an uncanny brilliance that made the men squint. After a long enough pause for the visual to inspire the proper amount of awe, Beatrice spoke again. "So, I'm guessing Claw is going to want to see us after all. Or... we can just take this somewhere else, and you can tell him why."

The man was silent for several seconds. He shook his head, tapping a finger in erratic bursts against his torch. He looked around to his colleagues for some sort of opinion. The large human shrugged, taking another step backward towards the door. The draken, a dark teal male with lanky limbs and a flicking tail hissed, "He's going to want that."

Another long silence stretched out as the guard weighed the options. Beatrice wasn't above forcing her way in, but it hardly seemed worth the trouble this time. Instead, she waited, with false patience written on her face.

Finally, the answer came, "Fine. But if he wants you gone, I'm dragging you back out myself." And he stepped aside.

"Of course you are, naturally," Beatrice conceded, bowing before walking through the creaking wooden door.

The orc followed at her heels, taking one swift lunge as he walked past, causing all three of the guards to flinch like spooked children. He was well over seven feet tall and as wide across as two smaller men standing shoulder to shoulder. Beatrice didn't even reach his shoulders and walking ahead of him in the dark hall of Claw's den she was almost lost in his shadow.

The entrance hall was narrow and the lights dim, with small rooms branching off at irregular intervals. Most were empty, or shielded from view by tightly drawn curtains. In one or two she could hear labored breathing, the cause of which she tried not to imagine. Passing another she glanced a dwarf wearing comically large goggles, portioning an unnaturally red liquid out into small glass bottles. As he looked up, his magnified eyes flashed in the lamp light, and he winked. She broke eye contact quickly, knowing better than to pay any attention to the happenings in this establishment.

At the end of the hall, a chamber opened up. The room was lit with a large brazier in each corner and littered with crates of various sizes stacked among expensive-looking cushions and chairs. Walking into this room they passed two identical blonde elven men. Dressed head to toe in black leather, both gave the distinct impression of snakes braced for strike in the shadows.

"Evening, gentlemen," Beatrice greeted them with a grin.

"Welcome home, Lemon... Malacar," one responded. The other reached for his weapon.

A perturbed growl on the far side of the room drew their attention to Claw where he sat behind his massive mahogany desk. The change in the old orsen's countenance as he watched them enter was only a minor shift from mild disinterest to mild annoyance. His midsection, soft from years of directing more work than he did himself, hardly left room for the thin elf-woman that sat on his lap. She didn't stop her repetitive stroking of the fur on his temple, where silver grey shot through his otherwise deep brown coat.

"Well," he spoke, his voice a growling baritone. "If it isn't Beatrice Lemon and Malice Malacar."

"Evening, Boss. I hear you missed us while we were away," Beatrice said.

"I seem to remember telling Percy not to let you in here. Or, did he fall out a window as well?"

"Everyone seems stuck on that. That guy really did fall out a window," she answered. The devil was in the details, and it didn't matter a lick if he'd gotten a little nudge from some meaty grey hands. The guard had been the grabby sort, with a bad attitude and a power complex.

"I just think it's funny," Claw went on, though he didn't sound amused at all. "I offer the pair of you hit contracts that you refuse because you 'aren't assassins', but you have no problems killing Faithful guards of the Triad in a tavern brawl."

"You won't find a soul in Drell mourning that loss, besides his mother perhaps. Even the other guards seemed relieved," Beatrice returned. She was tired of the subject.

"Not that we had anything to do with it. Of course," she added as an afterthought. "Can we talk about business now? I know you haven't forgotten that you sent us to Drell for a reason."

Claw grunted his assent. Malice again produced the necklace, and with a nudge Claw gestured for the elf to fetch it. She hopped to her feet without a sound, nearly losing her garment, which Beatrice realized was nothing more than a large bedsheet. The woman didn't miss a step however, pulling the covering back around her momentarily exposed form as she approached.

Malice looked down at her holding her hand out in expectation but didn't hand it over until Beatrice gave him a permissive nod. The elf hurried back over to the orsen, who grabbed her about the waist to pull her back up to her perch on his knee before taking the chain from her.

As Claw examined it, he grumbled to himself, a growl that could easily have been annoyance or approval. The gems once again caught the low light cast off by the fires and reflected it back out, putting out more vibrancy than it took in. The room glowed, looking small and dusty in the sudden exposure.

"The Fires of the Depths, they're called. Very rare stones. It is impressive, isn't it?" he finally mused.

Impressive is an understatement.

Beatrice nearly told him as much, but thought better of it. "So, that's that. I believe we agreed upon eight platinum."

"Where's this one?" Claw pinched an empty casing on the chain.

Beatrice didn't bother answering.

"There's a stone missing, *Beatrice,*" the orsen growled. "Did you think I wouldn't notice?"

"That's how it was when I found it. You wanted the necklace with the gemstones and I got it! There was no mention of tracking down stones that weren't included."

"So let me get this in order." Claw narrowed his black eyes. "I send you to Drell to fetch these stones. You draw attention to yourself by killing a city guardsman, and then you don't even bring me back the full set. You've disappointed me terribly."

Seeing where this was going Beatrice crossed her arms over her chest. "Six then?"

Claw laughed a low rumbling sort of laugh that would've given a small child nightmares. "Four."

"You hairy, stinking cheapskate! That's unacceptable, and you know it!" Beatrice took an angry step forward before she realized what she was doing, and of course, Malice followed her lead. She was brought back to her senses by the cold sound of the elven twins at the door unsheathing their weapons.

Claw stood up with a loud bark, hardly waiting for the elf to scramble to her feet. His fur bristled and his dark eyes burned as he glared at them, his nose wrinkling. "Don't you dare forget who you're dealing with, girl. Take your four platinum and get out before I change my mind."

Beatrice did a lightening fast visual sweep of the room, running the odds in her head. Between herself and Malice they would probably have no trouble with the twins, but Claw himself would be a challenge. His consort probably wasn't as soft as she looked either. There was also no telling who or what or how many were in the side rooms.

She relaxed her stance, nodding once in resignation. Claw bent at his desk, using the ring on one of his furry hands to unlock an intricate metal box. He counted out four large coins and handed them to the elf maiden, who strutted over to them once more, handing over the coin and giving them a glare that communicated quite clearly where she thought they ought to shove their platinums.

"Oh, and Beatrice?" Claw interrupted as they moved to leave the den. "Don't bother coming back."

-

Two

Less than an hour later Beatrice and Malice stomped toward the 'Knightcap', their favorite haunt and unofficial home base. The street the inn was located on was bustling with the usual energy of the city at night. A tired merchant stood half-asleep at his cart, hoping to sell a few more of the day's meat pies to the revelers still out for the evening. Another was selling potions for a 'good time', concoctions that would only have their consumer feeling good until the splitting headache set in tomorrow morning. A busker played a melancholy tune on a pipe while the people rolled past him. Malice Malacar pretended not to notice the performance, keeping his eyes fixed ahead and his ears on Bee's chatter.

"He's a cheat. A slime ball," she had been repeating with varying vocabulary. "Telling *us* not to come back? Maybe we weren't planning on it. It would serve him right if we didn't."

They stepped through the threshold of the inn. Brighter, warmer, and louder on the inside. The gentle roar of a crowd of the sixty or so people on the ground floor was a welcoming sound. Reminded him of his clan days. Benny the bard played a jaunty song on an out-of-tune piano in the far corner. She was self-taught and based on the evidence she wasn't a great teacher.

The mismatched pair slid up to the bar. Berta, the barkeep and owner of the establishment, was near at hand, and they could overhear her dealing with a few drunks from out of town. "I don't care who says the customer is always right, sometimes the customer is a damn idiot."

Beatrice pulled the fresh coins from a pocket on her belt and handed two of then over to Mal. "Better than nothing, right?"

"Hrrmph." *Better than nothing. Not better than the eight plats they were promised.*

Berta approached from the other side of the counter, heavily setting two tankards down in front of them. Malice immediately reached for the one containing warm goat milk, leaving the ale for Beatrice.

"So?" Berta inquired, looking down at Bee over a knobbed nose. "Was this the big one? You got enough to fund my retirement this time?"

In place of an answer, Beatrice slid the two remaining platinum across the counter to the old woman. "One of those back in gold, please."

Berta nodded, taking the coins and walking away. "Maybe next time then."

The unspoken understanding was that the other would be applied to their open account. Berta was a notorious grouch, but she liked Beatrice and Malice well enough. They were loyal customers and had finished more brawls in the Knightcap than they had started. As long as they kept coin coming in her direction on a fairly regular basis, she kept a small auxiliary room for them in the basement and kept their mugs and bellies full.

As they silently sipped at their mugs Malice mulled over the trip to the Den. It *would* serve that ass of an orsen right if they didn't go back. He *was* a cheat and a louse. But that hadn't stopped them from taking his jobs yet.

Malice was tired of it.

A sudden fit of piercing female laughter from the other side of the room drew him out of his thoughts.

The epicenter of the noise was a stranger. He had attracted a small group of admirers and curious onlookers and he was basking in the attention. His clothes hinted that he was a traveler. Not unusual for this establishment, but his garb was too showy for this side of town and his personality seemed to match. His ears came to the familiar elven point where they poked out from the black hair tied in a loose bundle at the back of his head, but he wasn't as thin and wiry as the full-blooded elf folk usually were.

"Not bad to look at, is he?" Beatrice mused.

Malice produced something like a choked cough in response. The pair watched the stranger for a moment as he punctuated whatever lively conversation was taking place with surreptitious arm gestures.

"Some sort of traveling performer?" Bee wondered out loud.

"Obviously." With that Mal turned back to the bar, rapping his heavy knuckles on the counter before taking a sloppy swig of his drink. Eyeballing strangers wasn't going to get them their next pay. Beatrice shot him a sidelong glance he could feel on his temple, but she didn't speak.

"What's the plan now, Bee?" he finally asked her.

Beatrice drained her tankard.

"Another round and an early night? Gods know we could use the rest."

"You know I wasn't talking about tonight. We got no new jobs coming in from Claw and four plats won't last us long," Malice clarified, even though Bee knew what he was thinking.

"Specially with the way you drink," he added as she flagged down Berta for a refill.

The barkeep delivered her drink along with the ten gold in change, and Beatrice pocketed them as she spoke. "No plan. Claw will be back. We're the best he's got. That cranky old bear will be begging us to take a job in no time."

"What if 'no time' takes longer than you think?"

Beatrice waved away the comment. "If funds get too low we can always sell this."

She pulled a chain from under her collar, revealing a green-tinged gem carefully secured at the end. As it caught the light of the nearest lamp it flashed, and Beatrice quickly palmed it and dropped it back underneath her shirt before anyone took notice.

"Although," she added, "I hope it doesn't come to that, I sort of like it."

For fucks sake. He shot her a scolding glare, and she shrugged.

"You had that the whole time? Why am I surprised?"

"I figured Claw was going to try to cheap-out on us. This was just a little insurance," she shrugged again. "I was right, and now he's one gem and two good thieves short."

"This could be an opportunity," Malice prodded, trying his luck, "to work with someone who doesn't cheat us on every job. We could take on some mercenary work, from one of the tavern boards uptown or even the consulate."

"I don't know, Mal. The jobs you don't need a recommendation for pay coppers, and building a reputation in that circle would be like pulling dragon's teeth."

"Ha! Doesn't sound that hard to me!" He sat taller, pounding his broad chest with one massive fist.

"Easy for you to say, you're four hundred pounds of green muscle and I might as well be your mascot."

"I like it," Malice declared, bringing his fist down onto the bar with a dramatic thud. "Malice The Great, and his dancing monkey."

She gave him a quick, painless jab in the arm. Pushing past the jokes, Mal pressed the matter.

"Really, Bee. You have skill beyond sneakery. We could make it. Easy."

He watched as she swirled her drink idly, staring into its depths as if it stretched on forever. "It's an option. I guess. Let's just see what happens."

The conversation died, leaving them the only silent company in the room. He let Bee sit in her thoughts. He didn't much care how they made their coin, but they were stagnant. An orc had his limits.

"His coin purse looks fit to burst," Beatrice finally spoke, her attention having turned back to the elven stranger. She pointed out the fat purple pouch hanging from the man's belt. "What do you figure then? Some sort of musician? Flute player perhaps?"

"Hmph, he's probably had his lips around a flute or two."

"Haven't we all."

Malice took the bait, turning his own gaze and appraising the man.

"Magician."

Fuckin' magicians, Mal thought. They always thought they were so damn smart.

"No!" Beatrice laughed at the accusation, "You can't be serious!"

"Magician." Mal repeated.

"Look at him though! The clothes? The coin? You don't make that kind of money as a magician."

"You do if you're doing the right kind of magic." Malice tapped the side of his nose with one thick finger. "Street games. Sleight of hand. Something about him just feels..."

Mal shook his head, trying to drop the subject.

Beatrice feigned shock. "You aren't suggesting this mysterious stranger made his fortune through trickery and hustles?"

"I would bet on it."

Beatrice perked up at the words, amusement burning in her round brown eyes. She shot him a challenging grin, the kind that roped in whoever she aimed it at. "Alright, I'll take that bet. Let's see what our new friend is all about."

Bets with an orc, much like most things with an orc, are not about the money but the competition.

She finished her second tankard of the night with three quick gulps and stood up, taking a moment to stretch her limbs as she looked around the room. "You handle introductions, I'll take the long way around."

Mal nodded, watching her as she wandered off into the crowd in a seemingly random direction.

He waited only a moment before stomping straight across the tavern floor towards the man and his cluster of admirers.

Malice couldn't help being conspicuous as a greyish boulder amongst the sepia spectrum of humans and elves. Though his size alone would've been enough to intimidate most, the square-set and sharp features of his face gave an impression of stern menace. Between his charcoal eyes and an angular jaw heavy enough to crush a small building, he was either glorious or terrifying depending on the observer. He had attracted the attention of the group before he reached them. But, that was part of the plan after all. The girls, with emotions ranging from confusion to fear, broke away and dispersed back into the crowd. The elf though, stood looking up at him. If he was the slightest bit perturbed by the interruption it didn't show.

"You're new here," Mal started.

"Yes," the elf confirmed, though it hadn't been a question. "There aren't many orcs this far south. I imagine you have a few good stories behind you."

"Uh-huh, more than you could guess." Malice was not impressed, even if the flattery had caused his chest to inflate ever so slightly. "More interested in you though. Me and my friend have a sort of bet going about what it is you do."

"Your friend? The young woman you were with at the bar?" The stranger's brow shot up, and he glanced back at the bar expectantly. "It seems we both couldn't help but notice the other, and I was actually wondering the same about the pair of you. Where is this friend now?"

Malice looked around the crowd, eyes settling on Beatrice standing not so far away. She was casually talking with an old carpenter that was a regular patron of the tavern. She caught his eye and nodded almost imperceptibly. She had finished whatever mischief she had been up to.

Mal made a show of waving her over and Beatrice made a show of walking to them, bumping past a few shoulders along the way and excusing herself as she went. She gave a polite nod in greeting. Malice wasted no time getting back to the topic at hand. "So, what are you?"

For a moment the stranger stood staring at Malice, and while the smile never left his face his brow furrowed and he stuttered slightly before answering.

"Well, I'm half-elf if that's what you mean. From Cestian originally, but I stay on the road," he started.

"No," Mal shook his head. "What do you *do*, half-elf?"

Something like relief washed over the elf. "Of course, your 'bet'. My name is Lemry, and I am a storyteller." He bowed low, extending an arm with a flourish as he went. "I travel the world collecting the finest tales I can find, and then share them with those I am fortunate enough to meet along the way."

"You tell stories? Like a nursemaid? To make a living?"

"Something like that, though many of my stories wouldn't be fit for a child's bedside."

"You're sure you're not a magician?" Malice gave the man another once-over.

"Uh, well," He looked confused, but still amused. "I'm not, but I know a trick or two."

The man turned an overcooked gaze on Beatrice, offering his hands to her. "May I?"

"You may." Beatrice placed her hands in his own.

"You see," he began, opening Bee's hands gently and turning them upward, "a little trick or misdirection can add something to certain tales." He copied the gesture with his own hands, showing that they were empty. "and I must say," He went on, reaching up to give Beatrice's cheek a playful brush with his thumb "The most interesting characters in any story are the ones..." he swept her wild brown hair behind her ear, pulling back to reveal a copper pinched in his grasp "that are hiding something."

Malice groaned. The only thing worse than a magician was the sort of man that fancied *himself* the mysterious one.

"Bravo, sir." Beatrice took the copper that he still held out and after examining it she pocketed the coin and leaned in closer. She was matching the man's mannerisms now. Playing his game.

"I wonder then if you're hiding something yourself?" she asked.

Lemry was enjoying the game. A mischievous fire burned in his eyes as he whispered, "Perhaps you'll have to dig a little deeper? Uncover all my secrets?"

Beatrice nodded as if considering the suggestion before perking up and dropping her smolder. "Nope, I already found it."

"Pardon?"

Bee reached out to his ear. Instead of a single coin in her hand, she revealed an entire coin purse, purple and heavy. Recognition flashed across Lemry's face and his hand felt at his belt. She gave the pouch a little shake, jingling the contents playfully before offering it back to its rightful owner.

"Beatrice Lemon," she formally introduced herself, leaving her hand extended for a shake after Lemry had retrieved his purse. "I'm not a magician either."

"It's my pleasure, Miss Lemon, I'm sure."

As Beatrice shook the man's hand, Malice couldn't help but to inspect his large tattoo. A black snake wound around the full length of his arm, crisscrossing itself at several points. It ended in a spade-shaped head on the inside of his forearm, its tail in its mouth. It was the most interesting thing about him, and he had led with *storytelling*.

"And, this is Malice Malacar." Beatrice diverted her eyes, gesturing to her companion.

"This means I lost," Malice stated. Now that he no longer held stakes in this interaction he searched the room for other company. Other seats. Anything. He knew all he needed to about Lemry.

"Well, I was wrong too. He isn't a musician either. So no one lost."

"Or we both did." Malice shot a glance as sharp as daggers at the storyteller.

"How about I buy us a round of drinks?" Lemry chimed in. "Then we've all won- you, a free drink and myself, some good company."

"How could we say no to that?" Beatrice accepted, and their new friend sauntered off towards the bar.

Malice hardly waited until he was out of earshot before speaking matter-of-factly. "He likes you."

"You think so?"

Malice shook his head. "I don't think he likes you the right sort of way. He makes me uncomfortable. There's something sneaky about him."

Beatrice shot him an incredulous look, but the orc only shook his head again. "Not sneaky like you. It's like he's sneaky about being sneaky. I can't figure him out. You should be careful."

Malice went quiet. He had said all he needed to. She wasn't a fool, and it would at least have her thinking.

It was true that on a typical evening she was more likely to attempt stealing a man's attention than their valuables, but that was as far as it ever went. Beatrice spoke of romantic attachments with a salted tone, and he knew the reasons for it were best left in the past. He'd never met a man good enough for her anyway, and this flake sure as hells wasn't it.

Her flirtations with the handsome young men they met around the Empire didn't bother him, but maybe their recent adventures in Drell had him on edge.

He hoped it wasn't going to be a repeating event.

"I can take care of myself, Mal... at least most of the time," she spoke, aware of his thoughts. "You're not completely wrong though. At the very least he had more money than a storyteller ought to."

"I bring gifts, friends!" They were interrupted by Lemry's return. He gracefully wove through the crowd, carrying three cups as if it were nothing. "The barkeep was kind enough to help me with your preferences, so..." he held out a mug to Mal. "Hot milk for the muscle." Next, he bowed, offering a cup to Beatrice, "and the house ale for the lady."

Beatrice laughed at his dramatic presentation as she took the drink, but caught herself at the weary glance from Malice. "Thank you, Lemry." She raised the drink high in the air. "To a new friendship, fit for the most legendary tales."

It was Lemry's turn to laugh, and all three drank heartily from their cups.

Bee found a seat at a nearby table and sat down heavily. "How about it then, storyteller? Do you have a tale for us?"

"How about a classic? When's the last time you heard the tale of how the realms came to be?"

Beatrice shrugged. "When I was a child, probably. And certainly, we've never heard it from a professional. Go ahead."

"Gladly. It is my favorite, after all." Lemry paused as if preparing himself for the feat of telling the tale. He looked from Beatrice to Malice with a dramatic pin-point stare, and then he began.

"Before there *was*, there was the One Creator. Every idea before its conception. Existence incarnate. To be such, was to be chaos. And it was to be lonely. So, the One began to take themselves apart.

They poured the chaos from their mind and it formed the first of the Divine Realms. Seeing the lands of order and chaos barren and empty, they made Nered to rule that realm. And so the first of the divine beings came to be."

"Easy there." Beatrice looked around to see how many others were listening to the elf talk. "The hard Triad folks would say 'demon'. You might want to know your audience for this tale, Lemry."

Malice shifted uncomfortably. Neither of them cared about the terminology, but they had heard the rumors of people arrested as demon worshippers for such simple mistakes. The last thing they needed was the church on their ass.

Lemry lifted his hands as if surrendering the point. "My apologies, I learned the tales in Cestian and seem to get some of the details mixed up when I tell them in the Empire. It's one of the dangers of the trade."

"No harm done, really."

"Right…" Lemry smiled, before easing back into the story slowly.

"Next, the One blinked, making the realm of the Light and the Darkness. Crepus was born to rule over their new creation.

The story goes that the One looked over these first two wild, primal Realms. Seeing what they had made, their heart swelled at the beauty and ugliness of it all. Those feelings sprang forth into the 'demon' Ludus, and the realm of love and hate.

Then there was the realm of the first of your *gods*, Vedett, protection and deception.

The realms began to boil and fill with Shades and spirits formed by the thoughts and emotions that had formed their very landscapes.

And with this new population rolling across the lands, the One saw fit to make a new realm, ruled by Gerra- the realm of War and Peace.

Finally, or so they thought, the One poured these powers of conception into the Realm of creation and destruction. Sald was created to rule this realm, and the One believed Sald would be their greatest companion, the one that best understood the plight of being omnipotent, of being a creator.

The realms though, were flawed. Each encompassed the full spectrum of their being, both sides of a coin, but even separated into their separate Realms, the Divines... and demons- were drawn to each other, struggling with each other, for eternity.

And so, the One began to see the errors they had made in their creation. The first error was that eternity was far too long for any balance to last, and so the realm of life and death was formed. Din, the 'demon' of life and death was made, and with his existence, the final flaw and ultimate failure of the Divine Realms was made apparent to the One Creator.

Looking across all seven of the Realms, they saw the truth of their misguided creation- the separation of their parts did not solve the confusion. Instead of fragmenting their existence, the answer lay in how the parts were mixed- diluted. So, the one took all that remained and made the Earthen Realm. All that had made the Divine Realms was blended into this final domain. Instead of an all-powerful leader, the One made the mortal races, like different combinations of the ingredients that made the whole. There was no magic left in the Creator's bones, their power was drained and used in the final creation, and the very heart of the One formed the center of this realm."

Lemry was stretched out in his chair, his arms spread wide at the conclusion of the tale of creation. His audience was silent.

"Now, the last bit of this tale varies depending on where you're telling it.

The Triad Temple teaches that Sald saw the Earthen Realm, powerless and orphaned. She loved it as though it were her own creation, and allied with Gerra and Vedett to serve this new Realm and protect it from the Demon Lords that saw to exploit it to feed their own appetites.

The orcs though, might end it differently?" Lemry gestured to him.

"I guess, yeah." Malice hardly looked up from the task he had taken up when they sat, polishing the same spot on his hammer continuously. "I guess the Clan Lore-Keepers would end it the same way as any story. Gerra ends all. Meaning that it doesn't much matter which other gods or demons are involved, any situation you're in will always end up finding you peace or finding you a fight."

"And in Cestian," Lemry added, in a lower voice. "They would say that all the Divines have a place in the Earthen Realm, that it is where all other Realms meet."

"Bravo." Beatrice clapped. "Now, how about something we haven't heard a hundred times?"

"Difficult to please, are we? Perhaps the lady would like something with a touch of romance?" Lemry's spring-green eyes flashed as he leaned toward her.

Beatrice smirked at him but leaned back in her chair, creating distance between them. "Relax, friend," she said pointedly. "I'll *hear* your romance tale, not re-enact it"

"Noted, my dear."

Lemry rolled into another tale, of a Cestian princess whisked away by a dwarven noble. He proved to be a mediocre storyteller, furthering the mystery of his abundant coin. He was animated though, and loud, his deep, rolling voice had attracted a small crowd by the time he reached the end of the tale. As the story concluded, the princess confessing her love to the man who had, essentially, kidnapped her and the pair living happily forever more, the crowd dispersed and many of the tavern patrons began to work their way out into the street or up to their rooms.

Malice was growing tired. His shoulders were heavy, and he slumped forward in his seat. It may have been their days on the road, or their business with Claw that had drained him, but he blamed Lemry in part. The elf's energy and animation were slowly wearing on the orc.

Beatrice was deeper in her cups than was typical for her, and while she wasn't a sloppy drunk the intoxication was beginning to become apparent. "I know what story I want to hear next," she announced, a mischievous tinge in her tone.

"And what is that, my dear?" Lemry leaned towards her yet again.

Malice rolled his eyes with as much exaggeration as he could manage, Beatrice heard it loud and clear. She reined in her enthusiasm, but continued her request.

Beatrice reached out, tapping the inked snake on his arm with her forefinger. "Tell us about this."

Lemry sat back in his chair, looking around the room thoughtfully as if considering the request before responding, "Here's the thing, sweet Beatrice. I've talked an awful lot this evening, but I haven't heard a single story from you yet. And I just know the pair of you must have some interesting tales."

At that, Malice stood up. "You make me tired. I'm going to bed. Are you coming to the room, Beatrice?"

"Not yet." Beatrice waved him off. "I'll indulge good Lemry in a tale or two."

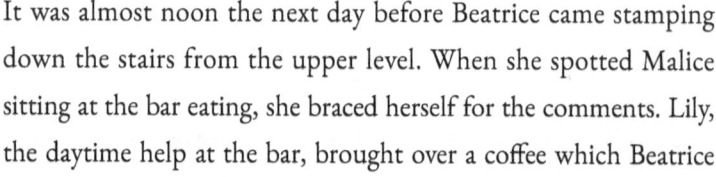

It was almost noon the next day before Beatrice came stamping down the stairs from the upper level. When she spotted Malice sitting at the bar eating, she braced herself for the comments. Lily, the daytime help at the bar, brought over a coffee which Beatrice accepted with a grateful nod.

"Sausage?" Malice held a fat link dangerously close to her nose, causing her to recoil instantly.

"Don't, I think I'm going to be sick."

"It was that bad, huh?"

"No."

"That good?" He asked, doubtfully.

"No. Honestly, I don't really remember." Beatrice leaned over her cup as she spoke, resting her head in her hands and letting the scent of the warm coffee block out the other smells around her.

"How much did you have to drink last night?"

"Evidently, enough to make me forget the actual amount."

"And your new friend?"

"Dunno. He was gone when I woke up," she said, rubbing at her eyes before sipping delicately at her drink. "The thing is Mal, I'm not convinced anything... happened. I woke up fully dressed, and as far as I can remember he really did only want me to tell him stories."

"I told you he was strange."

"Well, you weren't wrong," she allowed, knowing it was an admission he would hang on to for days.

"How many stories did you tell him?"

Bee's stomach churned noisily. "A lot."

Malice huffed.

She continued, thinking out loud, "His stuff was still in the room. He'll be back."

Whatever may or may not have happened, she didn't much feel like talking about it, least of all with Lemry himself.

"We could find something else to do for a few days," Malice offered, all too helpfully.

"Something like a merc contract?" Beatrice asked.

"What a great idea." Malice gave her a toothy and triumphant grin.

Beatrice snatched a sausage from his plate and bit into it reluctantly.

"Fine."

THREE

Walking through the bustling city streets, Malice attracted the typical amount of attention. To be more precise, he caught enough stares from the curious passersby that both he and Beatrice were aware of it, but not enough that either of them gave a damn. He certainly wasn't the only orc in Beacon, but they were rare enough to stand out, which was only exacerbated by their stature.

The brunt of Beacon's population, like the majority of the Empire of the Triad, was made up of humans, elves, and all possible mixtures of the two. The orcs, orsen, and dwarves trickled down from their respective homelands to the north and were more common the further north you ventured. In contrast, the cold-blooded, lizard-like draken, came from the tropical Sun Spot Isles across the southern sea and while they were quite common in southern harbor cities they rarely ventured further north than Central City.

They had left the Knightcap almost twenty minutes prior and had been heading in a general uptown direction without having determined a destination.

"So, what do you think?" Malice finally asked.

"Lot's of things. All the time," Beatrice retorted. "Sometimes simultaneously, it's a real problem."

"It's not your only problem. Not your worst either. But what do you think right now, about finding a job? Where do you wanna start?"

"Well..." Beatrice hesitated a moment.

This was exactly what she had been thinking about, but she wasn't particularly pleased with her own answer.

"I figure we go to the consulate first. We won't have many options and it'll pay less than nothing but if we do one or two throw-away jobs we'll have a little rep started and we can start looking for a private contract with a higher pay rate. "

"Good, yes!" Malice thumped his chest enthusiastically.

"Well, I figure if we're going to do this we better do it right." Beatrice didn't match a fraction of his enthusiasm. "Don't get too excited there, Big Guy. We'll probably be getting kittens out of trees to start with."

"I feel the start of something on the wind, Bee. We leave the shadows for the life of a warrior! For glorious battles! For honor!"

"Yes! And increased risk of physical harm, and moderate pay, and a saturated talent pool!"

Malice was unperturbed. "It will just make our success even sweeter."

"Yeah, yeah. Let's go then."

The consulate was situated in the Ivory district, the nest for empirical business and a meeting ground for the noble families and the church rulers of the Triad. One service offered by the church was the handling of work for hire. Local jobs were brought before a Cleric, mostly by noble families and businesses, but occasionally by concerned citizens. If the job was not so important as to be assigned to a paladin or an appropriate faithful servant, it was offered out as contract work. It didn't pay as much as private contracts, but the consulate was at least a reliable employer.

They also kept good records, meaning that an up-start mercenary could build a traceable reputation. The 'traceable' part gave Beatrice pause, but a reputation would be necessary if they planned on doing anything more than a one-off stint in the mercenary world, and especially so if they wanted any of that work to be lucrative.

Private work usually required a well-known and respectable citizen to write a letter or sign the contract for the mercenary, serving as a show of faith and an honorary recommendation. Obviously, Beatrice and Malice didn't have that.

The pair very rarely made it this far uptown, and though she wouldn't have admitted it Beatrice was feeling a little out of place as they moved down the streets.

The houses looked more like art pieces, each with its own walled-in garden and large enough that its occupying family would hardly have to share space with each other if they didn't want to. She knew exactly what those fine houses were like on the inside. Childhood memories of stuffy parties in scratchy dresses danced around her mind as they passed the rows of picture-perfect homes.

The consulate building itself was a sight in the mid-afternoon sun, constructed of the finest white stone, and framed with intricately carved pillars and large arching windows. It was out-shined only by the Triad temple on its left, standing proud and piercing the heavens with a massive spire.

They climbed the shallow steps to the consulate entrance, and though the Faithful posted at the doors eyed them quizzically they didn't stop their entry.

Inside, a draken female directed them towards the proper office, and quicker than they had expected, the pair found themselves sitting in the office of a bearded and bespectacled man that called himself Gerald Grimer.

Gerald sat across from them, hands clasped and eyes tracking between Beatrice and Malice as if he wasn't entirely sure what he was looking at. Malice scratched at his chin uncomfortably. The large clock on the desk counted off the seconds at what seemed to be a deafening volume.

Finally, Beatrice realized the man wasn't going to be speaking on his own any time soon.

"So," she prompted. "Do you have a job for us?"

"What?" He looked taken aback by the sudden speech. "Oh! Yes, a job. Of course."

"Of course," she mimicked, careful not to sound *too* snide. *Claw may be an ass,* she thought. *But at least he's not a halfwit.*

He smiled back at her. Shaking his head as if clearing it, Gerald pulled two books to the center of his desk and flipped through both of them before pulling a quill from its stand. "Your names?"

Beatrice hesitated to answer. Perhaps they should have considered setting up with an alias. It could work, if they were consistent and-

"Malice Malacar, Clan Killer, and the Great Hammer-wielder."

"Clan killer?"

"And I'm Beatrice." She raised herself slightly from her seat to lean over the large desk for a handshake, flashing her most winning smile. "Beatrice Lemon."

"Yes, well…" Gerald flipped through a few pages in the smaller book. "And this will be your first contract with the consulate?"

"Yep!"

Finding a fresh page, he began to write. "That's alright. Do you have any letters of recommendation?"

"Nope."

"Alright… Previous job experience?"

"Well, no." Beatrice was careful to keep her tone upbeat. She stretched her neck as much as she thought she could manage without it being noticeable, attempting to catch a glimpse at the notes the man was taking on them. His handwriting was shit though and upside-down it looked like a child's mindless scratch.

Gerald paused his scribbling, looking up at the two with the first hint of doubt in his eyes. "And you're sure this is something you want to do?"

"Honestly?" Beatrice started. A low, quiet growl rolled in Mal's chest like thunder.

"Honestly, yes we're very sure," she finished, slumping in her seat.

"Right." Gerald took down one more note in the small book before setting down his quill and turning his attention to the larger tome. "That is quite alright. Everyone does have to start somewhere after all. Let's see what I might have for you."

The man began flipping slowly through the book, humming and hawing to himself over the various pages. Finally, he flipped to a page that seemed to please him, he flattened it carefully with his palm and patted it excitedly. "Now, isn't this just perfect! Here's one for a few promising up-and-comers like yourselves!"

Beatrice and Malice perked up at this, leaning forward in their seats.

"Now see here," he began dramatically recounting the contract as if it were an epic adventure. "The Lord Tracy's prized dog seems to have run off and is lost somewhere in the Western countryside! Upon his safe return the Lord offers fifty gold as a reward!"

Beatrice sat back again with a dramatic thud, raising an eyebrow at Malice. One benefit of the deep and tested comradery between the pair was the uncanny ability for one to know exactly when the other was thinking 'I told you so', without the words ever actually being said out loud.

'How about not that," Malice answered. "You've gotta have something better."

"Better?" Gerald scratched his brow, looking over the page again as though he had missed something important.

"Better. As in more good than a lost dog." Malice stood up, speaking slowly and carefully as if perhaps Gerald was having a hard time keeping up, and maybe a good shaking would get him up to speed. "And no kittens."

"Kittens?" Grimer looked as though he wasn't sure if this was a joke or the appropriate time to panic.

"Alright, Mr. Grimes," Beatrice interjected, attempting to reel the room back into the realm of order. "What my colleague is trying to say is, despite our apparent lack of experience we are more capable than we look. And I mean..." she pointed at Malice hulking over the desk. "Just look at him."

"It's Grimer, actually," the man said, looking up at the towering Orc.

"I'm almost certain that's what I said. The point is, we're good. Very good. We're almost certainly a blessing sent to your office by the gods themselves, and we want to *help* you. So, maybe we can start with something a step above a lost dog?"

"Well," Gerald began after a long pause, still looking at Malice intently. "You do look quite... capable. And I do have a contract that I need taken care of rather quickly. But, I really couldn't put this on someone without a proven reputation."

"How about," Beatrice returned, pressing her hands together and smiling at Gerald carefully. "You tell us what the job is, and we'll tell you if it's something we can handle."

The man tapped on his book noisily, mulling over the idea for a moment before pulling a roll of parchment from his desk drawer. "It's bandits. A small group of them has set up a camp on the east road to Bay, about a day's journey from here. They've been terrorizing travelers between the two cities non-stop, and they're spreading their reach. With the Divine Gathering coming up in Triad City all the Paladins are engaged elsewhere and can't deal with something like this."

"We can handle it," Malice said flatly.

"You say a 'small' group?" Beatrice asked.

"Yes, relatively small."

"We can handle it."

"Relative to what exactly?"

"Relative to a larger group of bandits," Gerald said, helpfully.

"We can handle it," Malice said again, this time turning to Bee.

"Alright, fine. We'll take care of your bandit problem. We can handle it," she conceded.

"Outstanding. The pay will be four platinum upon successful resolution of the contract. In the event I don't hear from you in two weeks we will begin offering the contract up to other mercenaries again. Any questions?"

"I guess not."

Gerald quickly copied down the details of the contract on a piece of parchment, signed the bottom with a flourish, and stamped it with a Triad seal before handing it to Beatrice. "Best of luck, my friends. May Gerra guide your sword. May Vedett shield you. May Sald craft your destiny well."

"Yeah," Beatrice waved without looking back as they exited the room. "You too."

FOUR

A skip in the step of anyone over about six feet has a distinctively different effect than intended. As might be imagined, a skip in the step of a seven-foot orc looks remarkably like a rampage in progress. This is perhaps why Beatrice and Malice were drawing more looks from the upper-class citizens of Beacon City now than they had on their way to the consulate building.

"Happy?" Beatrice asked as they walked along as if it weren't obvious.

"Mm." Malice nodded contentedly. "This is good. Smash some skulls, kill some bandits. It's going to be a good time."

This drew a smile from Beatrice despite herself. "I bet. The most fun a girl can have without a ball gown."

Despite Beatrice's lack of enthusiasm earlier in the day, she also found herself in higher spirits on their walk back through the city. It wasn't terrible, really. And at least it was straightforward.

Reaching the open market, they parted ways. Malice headed back towards the Knightcap to retrieve their road-packs since Beatrice wasn't too keen on going back yet. Bee headed down the market street until they were to meet back up near the city gates in a few hours.

Today the heat was laying heavily on Beacon with the humidity of the coastal air, but it didn't slow the throng bustling through the streets. The people moved through the stalls and shops like sand through a sieve, filtered out by the brightly colored stalls as they went.

As was always the case when she didn't have a massive grey lunk by her side, Beatrice found that she was quickly lost in the crowd, a mass of wild brown curls dressed in unremarkable leathers. As a thief, anonymity and the ability to hide in plain sight were some of her most important tools. As a head-strong young woman who had more dreams of glory than she would ever admit to, it wasn't ideal.

She had grown up in Central city, the daughter of a prominent merchant and his socialite wife. Beatrice had been one of seven siblings, including three beautiful and bubbly older sisters. She had been middle of the pack in age, intelligence, looks, and almost all of the factors that feel like they define your personal worth in your formidable years. Life had not been hard, or tragic, or even particularly uncomfortable. It had simply been unremarkable.

Misguided though it may have been Beatrice had begun to see her perceived obscurity as her one defining characteristic. At fifteen, instead of waiting for the scraps left over after her older sisters married the most handsome, wealthy, and influential bachelors, she left home. Her head had been full of the popular stories of the time, of heroic rogues that found fame and fortune with their wits and wiles. Almost immediately she had fallen in with a band of young thugs with similar dreams, and heads just as full of romance and adventure.

That, in a roundabout way was how she found herself here as a thief-for-hire in Beacon city, always just shy of some big break. Always just shy of remarkable.

She stopped at a stall that was selling jewelry. They had a small collection on display, and a hair ornament caught her eye. It was a golden comb, fashioned to look like delicate leaves and inlaid with tiny blue stones. She ran her fingers gently across the metal, admiring the detailed textures no one would see once it was in place.

"A beautiful bauble for a beautiful lady? It would suit you."

The merchant watched her with a kind smile.

"It is beautiful. But too fancy for this outfit, don't you think?" Beatrice said.

"Your friend disagrees, I'm sure. Perhaps he would like a gift for you?"

Beatrice smiled back at the old man. Being careful not to show any unease, she turned around. A tall, blonde elf tipped his chin at her. One of Claw's.

"I doubt the thought had crossed his mind," Beatrice joked with the merchant. The old man began to protest, but she was already nodding politely to dismiss herself and walking on down the street.

The elf had fallen in to step with her and was walking with her as naturally as if they had been shopping companions the whole afternoon.

The elven twins, Dart and Paz, had worked for Claw much longer than Beatrice and Malice had. They were lithe and shared the same pointed features and piercing blue eyes. Handsome but stern. It was good they had ended up in their line of work, Beatrice thought, because no one would have bought from such intimidating fish-mongers.

She knew well enough that Dart found her rather amusing, but Paz was not a fan. Unfortunately, she never had gotten particularly good at telling which one was which, and therefore she wasn't sure where she stood at this exact moment.

"I thought for sure you were going to pocket that comb," he spoke.

"I had absolutely no reason to do that."

He shrugged. "Has that ever stopped you before?"

"Wouldn't you like to know?" she retorted, but was careful to keep a playful smile on her face. "Where's your brother?"

"Close. Waiting," he answered simply. "What about yours? "

"Waiting."

He acknowledged with a nod, "Shall we get this over with then?" He gestured about a hundred feet ahead, where the other twin stood at the door of an empty storefront.

This wasn't looking particularly promising. Even ignoring the fact that Claw hadn't been happy with her the day before, it was incredibly out of the ordinary for him to seek her out like this. Regular business would have seen her summoned to the den. Beatrice felt her stomach flip.

"Actually, are we in a rush? I haven't had much to eat today." She watched his face carefully.

He hesitated, looking down the street towards his brother. *Not a flat-out refusal. Must be Dart.*

"Look." She pointed at a sweets stall just to her left. "Not out of our way, just give me a moment?"

He seemed unsure of how to answer her. Taking the opportunity, Beatrice veered towards the stall. "A sticky bun, please."

She reached for her coin purse, trying to scope out as much of her surroundings as possible in the meantime. She didn't see any other familiar faces lurking in the crowd, but that didn't mean they weren't there. With so many unknown variables, running for it was a long shot.

As she pulled a coin from her pouch, Dart's own long and elegant fingers were already placing a copper in the palm of the baker. He received the bun, and then passed it gracefully to Beatrice.

"Thanks."

"Don't mention it. Seriously. Can we go now?"

Beatrice hesitated. "Any chance you'd just let me reschedule this little meeting?"

"No can do." Dart took the opportunity to take hold of her left arm, gently but insistently guiding her towards their destination.

Beatrice bit into the warm bun in her other hand, despite her appetite having fled completely. "Do you figure I'll need to hurry to finish this so my blade arm is free?"

Dart sighed. His words were careful, still patient despite Bee's pushing. "I certainly hope not, Beatrice."

As they reached the door of what appeared to be a long-abandoned tailor's shop, Dart dropped her arm. Paz looked impatiently down his nose at her and then raised an annoyed eyebrow at his brother. "You lured her in with sweets?"

Dart shrugged.

"You know how it is, Paz. Catch more flies with honey," Beatrice said, then surreptitiously she widened her eyes as if something had just occurred to her. "You probably want some too, don't you?" She held the half-eaten bun out right under his nose, where it was promptly swatted from her hand.

As it rolled across the floor, Beatrice clicked her tongue with disappointment.

"This isn't a tea party." Paz shot his brother a sharpened glare and reached to grab for Beatrice, clearly having already lost all patience.

Side-stepping his grasp, Beatrice walked inside of her own accord, and the twins followed closely behind, blocking her path out.

The interior was dim, only drawing enough light through the dingy partially boarded windows at the front of the shop to give shape to the bare walls and the half a dozen human-shaped mannequins scattered about. Even in the faint light, Claw's broad form was unmistakable. Beatrice approached him, careful to stop just out of reach of his deadly hands.

"You're sending mixed messages, Claw." She fought off the urge to rest her hand on the hilt of her dirk where it hung at her hip. "You told me to stay away, and now less than a day later, you're tracking me down? Makes it hard not to flatter myself."

"Don't," Claw growled. "I'm not here by my own choice, Beatrice. I've found myself in a unique situation. I need you to take a job."

"Oh, too bad. We've already taken one."

"Another job? From who?" A slight possessiveness colored his tone.

"C'mon, you know you aren't the only game in town."

"It doesn't matter. Drop the job. This is more important and more profitable for us both."

"Then why give it to me?" Beatrice crossed her arms across her chest, her guard still high.

"The client asked for you by name. Said it had to be you."

"Who is it?"

"Didn't use a real name, said we could refer to him as Din."

"Din? As in the demon lord of death? Sorry, I don't know him," Beatrice tried to make light. Claw exhaled heavily and she took it as a cue to refocus. "Alright. Anonymous client. What's the job?"

The orsen considered her before speaking. "A paladin knight posted an urgent contract for mercenary security in delivering an object to Triad city. The job has already been accepted on behalf of Malice and yourself. Your real job is to steal the object before that delivery is made. Any information you can get on what the church's plan for the object is and how they got it will be a bonus to the client."

"And what is it I'm stealing?"

"I don't know. Some sort of stone. A church relic. Whatever it is, it's worth fifty platinum to you."

The amount was more than enough to elicit interest for Bee. That was a lot of coin. *Too much.* "And, what if I'm not interested?"

Claw nodded as if he had expected as much. He gestured with one claw. "Paz?"

Beatrice turned quickly, only to catch a fist square in the lips that sent her head reeling backward.

Fighting to clear the shock from her mind Beatrice managed to unsheathe her blade with lightning-fast reflexes, despite the stinging in her mouth and the ringing in her ears. Whipping her foot-long blade out in front of her, Beatrice felt Dart's long arms closing around her. She threw an elbow backward, making contact, though she wasn't sure where. It was enough to loosen his grip and for a glorious moment, she thought she was free. But, as quickly as she had squirmed away, his hands found her arms again, grabbing tighter and locking her in place.

"Don't, Beatrice," Dart cautioned. As well-meaning as the whisper in her ear might have been, Beatrice was beyond hearing it. She lashed in his grasp, a cornered animal ready to fight.

Paz came at her again, full power this time. His fist found its mark on the right side of her gut.

The pain immediately radiated through her middle, and an airy groan escaped involuntarily as her legs gave out beneath her. His grip on her still firm, Dart slowed her fall, easing her down to a stupor on the hard floor before releasing her.

"Understood?" Claw growled.

"Fuck."

"You see, I'm not asking. This is a high-profile gig and a lot of coin. If all I've got to put on the line is your life, that's fine by me."

Beatrice glared up at the orsen.

"You have three choices; Turn down my offer and we kill you now, and then we find Malacar. Leave here and try to make a run for it, and I'll put out a contract on your heads worth more than you ever were alive. Or," Claw paced the floor. "You take this job, earn the biggest paycheck of your life, and stay alive a bit longer."

Beatrice wiped the blood from her puffed bottom lip, taking her time before speaking again. "Well, when do we start?"

"Today. It's already arranged, and this paladin expects you to meet him at the Reveler's Respite."

Beatrice sighed, standing carefully. "The plan isn't great. I don't make a habit of introducing myself to a target before stealing their stuff."

"You've got to find out what it is you're stealing, Beatrice. I've given you a generous place to start. After that I don't care what you do, just do it."

"Fine. Let's say we pull this off. What the hell are we supposed to do once we're at the top of the Triad's most wanted list?"

"You would be amazed how many problems you can work through with enough money. Frankly, I don't give a damn what you do. Take a vacation to Cestian for a few months and then come back as Lady Lemoncurd Talks-a-Lot. Not my problem."

"That's a stupid name."

Claw ignored her. "Once you have the relic, the client says they'll make contact."

"Steal an unknown item with an unknown purpose for an unknown client, to be delivered at an unknown time and place? And that didn't stink to you?"

"What can I say, he paid half my handling fees up front." Claw bared his teeth in what might have been a smirk. "All I had to do was get you the Paladin's merc job. The rest is on you, Beatrice. I'm willing to take that risk."

"Of course you are."

Claw handed her a parchment with the mercenary contract details, signed by the Paladin and one 'Lord Vespan'. Without another word he moved towards the exit. Dart and Paz followed.

At the door the orsen turned back. "Paladin Fairchild. The Reveler's Respite, this evening. Don't fuck this up, Beatrice."

FIVE

Malice was growing restless as the evening drew closer. He sat on the ground, leaning against the large public well located near the main gate into Beacon.

The trip to the Knightcap had been uneventful. Their gear had been fetched, a milk had been had and all without a single storyteller in sight. Now they could get on with business, and it was going to be good indeed.

He wasn't worried about Beatrice. After nearly six years, he figured he knew Beatrice better than she knew herself and he was certain she needed this even more than he did. She was clever, brave, and loyal when it counted. Sure, she saw herself as a rogue, but she was harder on the outside and softer on the inside than she gave herself credit for. In short, she was more orc-like than she would like to believe. If only she wasn't just so damn small and squishy.

Mal had seen plenty of the mercenaries that came through the major cities. The majority of them were the sons of farmers, bored with their lot in life. You had the veteran soldiers and lifetime mercs too of course, but they were only the top layer of the business. There was more than enough room for the likes of Beatrice and Malice to flourish.

It was to their benefit that their background had made them more dangerous than any common bandit. They were going to make quick work of this contract, and the next one too. He knew Beatrice and knew she was going to get a rush from the sudden abundance of coin and glory. It would only be a matter of time before they were the top mercenaries in Beacon. Malice was ready.

The minutes ticked past, and there was still no sign of Beatrice. Malice watched the people trickling in and out of the city, searching for her face in the crowd. Incoming were traders from the villages in the countryside and the cities beyond. Farmers from outside the walls wandered in for drink, goods, or simply an escape from the monotony of country life. A caravan of dwarves pulled in a cart draped in deep green linens and laden with spices from the north. Outgoing he watched a Triad cleric escorted by a paladin and two Faithful leaving with full road gear and all dressed in the scarlet markings of Gerra, the Triad god of war and peace. They were most certainly headed to Triad City for the fancy church gathering being held there.

A small human boy stepped into view, only a few feet away from Malice's seat. He must have been about ten years of age, dressed in dingy linen country clothes that hung loosely on his small frame. He clung with both hands to a rope tethered to a silky brown goat.

The boy looked around at the crowded buildings and busy streets with a mixture of awe and terror, his mouth drooping open and eyes wide. His mouth snapped shut as his eyes landed on Malice, and the two stared at each other intently for a moment.

Malice waved at the boy. "Nice goat."

The child looked back at the animal, absentmindedly rubbing one of its soft ears. "Her name is Darcy."

Darcy stared into the pits of oblivion with large vacant eyes that were unblinking, either taking in everything around them or nothing.

Malice nodded approvingly. "I like her."

"Me too. She's the nicest goat." The corners of his mouth tugged downward slightly at the words. "But Mama says we have enough goats, and the coins would do us better. I'm supposed to sell her."

"Have you ever been to the city alone before?"

The boy shook his head wearily.

"Why didn't your Ma come to sell Darcy?"

"There's a new baby..." his voice trailed off. Darcy slowly blinked a single eyelid.

"I think I would like to have a goat," Malice mused. "How much are you asking?"

"Mama says if I bring home less than five coppers she'll whoop me good."

Considering first the goat and then the child, Malice reached a fast conclusion. "Alright," He pulled a gold from his pouch and handed it over. "I'll buy Darcy."

The boy gawked at the coin in his hand but hesitated as he went to hand the orc the goat's rope. "You aren't going to eat her, are you?"

Mal shrugged, taking the rope. "Don't think so. Not unless I have to."

"What's this then?"

Beatrice had finally arrived, and had walked right up to the odd collection before being noticed. She eyed Malice, the boy, and the goat in turn.

Malice eyed her right back, immediately noting the hint of a bruise over the right side of her mouth and the split in her lip, not to mention the uncharacteristic tension in her mannerisms. "You look like shit."

"Thanks for that."

"What happened to you?"

Beatrice shifted her weight, looking away from Malice. "We'll get to that. What's with the goat?"

The boy looked on, his interest clearly outweighing his unease. Malice stood tall, presenting the goat as if it was his own firstborn. "This is Darcy. She's my goat now. I bought her from my friend here."

Beatrice closed her eyes, pressing a thumb firmly to the space between her brows as if her brain had suddenly sprung a leak. The seconds ticked by with only the sounds of the city around them.

It was the child who broke their silence. "She's the nicest goat," he told Beatrice reassuringly. She opened her eyes to look at him carefully before turning back to the orc.

"Mal, what are you going to do with a goat?" she asked, finally.

"Milk it," Mal answered confidently, but seeing Beatrice's unconvinced gaze he added, "Take it for walks?"

"No, Mal. Just no," she spoke, standing to her full height as if it added authority to her words despite her head hardly being level with Malice's chest. "Now is not a good time for this."

"When is there ever a good time for a goat with us?"

"Exactly."

Malice hesitated, wringing the rope in his thick hands. With a heavy sigh, Beatrice turned her attention to the boy. "How much is the goat worth?"

"Well, five coppers I guess but he-"

"Ok," Beatrice interrupted him, pulling coins from her belt purse. "I will pay you five copper right now," she flashed the coins at him and reached over to grab the rope from Malice. "To turn around and take this goat back home with you."

She pressed the rope and five coppers into the boy's hand and smiled at him conspiratorially. He wavered, looking uncertainly at Malice for some sign of what to do.

"Now, c'mon," Beatrice urged her friend, taking a few steps up the street. "We've got a meeting uptown."

"Uptown?" This was enough to catch Malice's attention. He reluctantly began to follow.

"Wait!" the boy called after him, holding out the gold in his small hand. "Here's your money back, Mister."

"Keep it," Malice said, waving at him over his shoulder.

The pair had moved well out of earshot before speaking again. Walking side by side through the streets, Malice watched his partner with a keen eye. She could feel his annoyance at the change in plans as though it were burning into the top of her head.

"Wanna tell me what's going on now?"

"Well, I've got good news and bad news." As she spoke, Beatrice looked ahead intently.

"Bad news first."

"Claw's put us on a job. The mandatory kind. We don't do it and we get a contract on our heads."

Malice exhaled loudly through his nose.

"Good news is it's technically another merc job. You've got two in one day, Mal."

"*Claw* is forcing us to take a merc job?"

"Well... I guess there's more bad news. We're supposed to steal something from our new employer." She paused. "He's a Triad Paladin."

"Shit Bee, we can't do that."

"Did you miss the part where I said it was our heads if we don't?" she snapped.

"We do this wrong and we're dead. We do it right and we'll have more money than we've ever seen in one place."

Neither of them spoke for a long stretch as they walked on.

"Mal," Beatrice spoke up. "Maybe you could sit this one out. No use in both of us getting into trouble with the church. If you don't think you can handle it..."

"You asking me to back down?"

"Nah, of course not." She relaxed slightly.

"But..." Bee added. "It sounds like a pretty big deal. If we do this right, it could open up a whole new world for us."

"So could a few good merc jobs."

Bee ignored him.

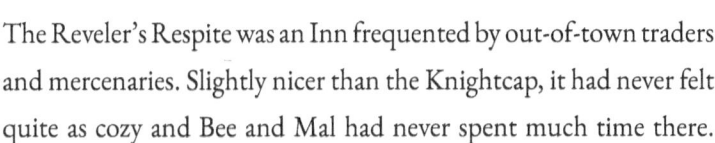

The Reveler's Respite was an Inn frequented by out-of-town traders and mercenaries. Slightly nicer than the Knightcap, it had never felt quite as cozy and Bee and Mal had never spent much time there. They exchanged a glance before stepping into the inn.

It was quiet, still too early for the usual crowds. Three men sat at the bar, though the barkeeper was nowhere in sight. As Beatrice and Malice walked in all eyes turned their way. This included the eyes of a young man, sitting at a table in the far corner. His armor and yellow cloak gave him away as the paladin immediately.

"Well. Shit."

Upon seeing him Beatrice muttered under her breath, attempting to keep her face void of any reaction. "I was imagining something a little more 'servant to the gods' and not so much 'actual god'."

"He is pretty," Malice agreed, "but a bit too... sunny for my taste."

Sunny was a rather apt description, as all his features shared a golden tone that gave him a warm glow. The paladin, though bulky with the muscles of rigorous training and physical exertion, held himself with a certain lightness. It was hard to say if his posture came from confidence in himself, his ideals, or just a byproduct of his upbringing. His sandy hair wasn't grown out long as was popular for the current male aesthetic. In fact, it barely hung down over his forehead. This flattered his features quite nicely, though his face didn't seem to need the help.

Paused in the doorway to take in the sight of the paladin, they realized somewhat awkwardly that he was looking back at them as well. The look in his eyes wasn't hostile, just a guarded curiosity. The other patrons looked at them with a similar half-suspicious glare. Beatrice wiped the dumbstruck look from her face, attempting a non-threatening smile. Luckily Malice did not attempt the same, as any smile from an orc tends to feel at least a little threatening.

The eyes of the other men followed them as they approached their mark. The sound of their boots seemed deafening in the otherwise tense silence.

"Paladin Fairchild?" Bee spoke, "I believe you're expecting us."

"I am?" He seemed genuinely surprised by this, his bright eyes raking across them and his neat brows creasing gently.

For a moment Beatrice felt her gut flip uncomfortably. Malice shifted his weight next to her. If Claw had already screwed them she would give him a piece of her mind. Right up until the moment they gutted her for it.

Beatrice produced the contract from her satchel, and the paladin's eyes widened, with a sudden and violent realization. "Oh, of course! Please, forgive me."

He stood quickly, extending a hand first to Beatrice who hesitantly and delicately offered her own. A soft flush colored his cheeks as though he had embarrassed himself and Beatrice found something about it made her own face warm to match.

"I must say I'm not used to doing business this way, and neither of you are quite what I expected. "

"Well—" She couldn't think of the proper response to such an admission, and instead finished with a lame nod.

"I am Gespar Fairchild, Paladin Knight of the order of Vedett." Releasing Beatrice he offered his hand to Malice. "You must be Beatrice Lemon and-"

He was interrupted by Mal's booming voice. "Malice Malacar, Clan Killer, The Great Hammer wielder, *and* Consulate mercenary."

"Impressive. Well met, Mister Malacar."

Beatrice stared at her companion, trying to convey her horror at this spouting of real information without alerting the paladin of the problem. Trying to compose herself, she turned her attention back to the man.

"Guess-Par, was it?

"Yes, ma'am. I look forward to working with you both."

The sunshine smile wielded by Fairchild hit Beatrice just as hard as the fist she had taken to the face earlier.

"You do?" Lost in the golden-brown eyes looking at them so earnestly, Beatrice suffered a temporary lapse in mental clarity before remembering who they were and why they were there. "Maybe we should talk about the job then?"

"Of course," Gespar gestured to the other seats at his table, waiting for Beatrice and Malice to take one before reclaiming his own. "As advertised, we will be making a delivery to the Grand Temple in Triad City. You will act as bodyguards to myself and the object we are delivering. This has all been kept incredibly quiet, so I don't anticipate trouble. That said, I can't risk needing aid and not having it. Our cargo is too precious."

"Well then," Beatrice returned. "When should we plan on setting out?"

"Ah," Gespar faltered momentarily. "I was hoping we could leave this evening... The more immediate the better."

This was met by a marked silence.

"What about the bandits?" asked Malice, a tinge of aggravation in his deep voice.

"Pardon?"

"Mal, please," Beatrice tried to cut the subject short, but the orc plowed on, speaking now to the confused paladin.

"We have another contract to take care of. Some bandits on the road to Bay."

"This is *clearly* the priority now," Beatrice said, pointedly.

"But what about-"

"If I may?" Gespar interjected, pulling them from the brink of a squabble. "I believe the Gods have smiled upon our journey. We will have to take a detour through Bay for my job anyway. We can deal with these bandits on the way, and I would be more than glad to help."

"There. Happy now?" Beatrice's sarcasm was almost entirely veiled, though that didn't mean Mal wouldn't hear it loud and clear.

The Orc was silent. Perhaps the depth of the situation was sinking in, but Beatrice doubted it. More likely, he was content to move on now that he had gotten his way. Whichever was true, the change in energy was palpable, leaving the group staring around the table.

"Well then, shall we go?"

An adventure is a beautiful thing, something truly special. If it wasn't it wouldn't be called an adventure at all. Sometimes an adventure begins with a crash, spurred on by some extreme circumstance, a spontaneous combustion of fate. Other times they begin with a deep breath and a determined step, after a lifetime of preparation. It appeared that this adventure, however, would start with an awkward silence and the clumsy scraping of chair legs on an old wooden floor.

Beatrice and Malice stood in the street, waiting for their paladin to gather his things.

Beatrice could feel Mal's eyes on her as she paced the space in front of the Respite, but she avoided looking his way. The amused, crooked grin he wore was pissing her off.

"You gonna be able to do this?" he asked.

She turned on him. "Of course, why would I not?"

"Maybe because you can't even remember your name when Mr. Sunshine starts talking, let alone what your job is?"

"Oh, I forget my own name? I'm more concerned with *him* forgetting our names, seeing as how Claw gave him our real ones."

Malice looked relatively unconcerned, shrugging as Beatrice went on. "You realize now that 'Sunshine' is in on it we can't claim that contract on the bandits? What do you think will happen when we show up at the consulate to collect payment after we've just finished stealing from the church? Our best bet now is to get this over with as quickly as possible. We get him away from the city, get our goods, and get out before we find ourselves any deeper."

"Or before you get distracted?"

"I don't know what you're talking about." Beatrice leaned moodily against the stone wall of the building.

"I'm talking about you. You're all about the job, and you get too invested. Then it's personal, or there's something you want for yourself. That's when the job gets complicated. Happens every time. And this time I bet that Paladin is going to be the distraction."

"You're full of shit. That's never happened."

"Never?" Malice reached out, pulling the chain about her neck enough to free the gem from under her shirt. Beatrice snatched it back quickly. The stone's uncanny shine was noticeable, even while the sun still cast light on the city.

"That's not the same thing. This has value. What could that golden-boy paladin have that I would want?"

"Good looks? Charm? A pure heart? The best manners you've ever seen? A big thick-"

Beatrice cut him off with a jab in the side and a glare. "I'm glad you're enjoying yourself. Just don't get so caught up in your delusions that you forget that our lives are on the line here."

Paladin Fairchild came through the door, glowing in the evening sun and giving Malice a familiar pat on the shoulder. "Are you ready, my friend? My lady?"

"Don't 'my lady' me," Beatrice snapped, turning on her heels and starting off down the street.

Six

G espar stayed quiet as he walked through the Beacon streets along with his new companions. He had no reason to doubt their capabilities. They had come with proper recommendations and they certainly appeared to be just the sort he needed. But, the way their temperaments had seemingly flipped in the short amount of time he had left them alone was unsettling.

The orc was walking by his side, and Gespar had caught him sizing him up three times already. There was none of his namesake malice in his stares to be sure. Each time Gespar had looked his way he was met with a friendly if somewhat fangy grin.

Their female associate though, walked ahead of them at enough of a distance to separate herself. She had seemed amiable enough at the inn, but now she walked moodily before them as if she was trying to forget she had the company.

Gespar had been around plenty of capable women during his time with the church. This one was built more like a barmaid than a mercenary, but there was something about her that he couldn't put his finger on. The smiles she had cast when they met had a fire to them, made all the more mysterious by their sudden absence. For each of the few words she had spoken to him her striking eyes held an impression of a hundred more left unsaid. He found himself watching her back intently as they left the city, unable to make heads or tales of her.

A glance to his right made it apparent that his stares had not gone unnoticed, as the orc was watching him just as intently. Quickly suppressing the sudden flare of embarrassment, Gespar addressed his thoughts, speaking low enough that only Malice could hear him. "I fear I've done something to offend Miss Lemon."

The booming laugh he got in response startled Gespar, who didn't see the humor in the situation.

"No," Malice assured him once his amusement was under control. "No, but she might be easier to deal with if you did."

"I'm sorry? What does that mean?"

Malice ignored the question. "You look strong. But young. Have you been with the church long?"

Gespar nodded, reluctantly allowing the change in topic. "I began my training when I was only twelve."

"You left home early then." There was a notable rise in the volume of Malice's voice as if he intended the conversation to be heard. Gespar looked uncomfortably at Miss Lemon, but she continued ahead as if she hadn't noticed.

"I did. As the second son of the Fairchild family, I was promised to the service of the church upon birth."

"Interesting," Mal responded, with added animation now. "And tell me, Paladin Fairchild, do you do any magic tricks?"

"What? No, I don't know any."

"No, of course you don't, Sunshine!" The orc laughed again, slapping him on the back.

For the first time since they had left the inn, Beatrice turned back to them, shooting Malice an icy glare. "Having fun, boys? Getting in some good bonding time?"

"Absolutely. I may like him more than you."

Beatrice's eyes met Gespar's for a fleeting moment before she turned back around and continued further away from Beacon City.

The road led them first northward, crossing through an open land that slowly pulled away from the coastline. Small homesteads dotted the way, spreading further apart the further they got from the city. As night began to settle in, they spotted tree lines for the first time, small patches of forest sprang up and the road began to veer gently to the east.

Eventually, they reached a fork in the road, one path heading north to Central City and the other further east to Bay.

They hadn't been alone on the roads since leaving Beacon but as the sun waned so did the number of people they passed.

Beatrice fell back to walk at Gespar's other side. "So, are we allowed to ask what this special delivery is?"

Gespar had to admit that Beatrice's renewed personable attitude was a relief, and he welcomed the chance to speak with her more. The topic though... "Meaning no offense, the less you know the better."

"Sure, sure." Beatrice nodded at him. At least she was understanding. The trio walked silently for a moment down the now-darkened path.

"It's not terribly heavy is it?" she chimed again, and at a glance from Gespar she added, "Since you don't have any extra boxes or bags, it must be packed in with your usual things. I do hope that if it's heavy you'll trust us enough to share the burden if you need a break."

"I appreciate your consideration, but-" Gespar considered his next words carefully. There was a fine line between being discreet and withholding vital information. The Blessed Leaders surely understood that. "I don't have it yet. That's why we have to go through Bay. We have to... pick it up."

"I see," she spoke again. She seemed to think for a moment, and Gespar saw her look casually at the orc before she nodded and went on. "We could run into our bandits anywhere between here and there. We ought to stop, rest, and maybe come up with a plan."

There was no disagreement on the subject, so the party veered off the path slightly to find a secluded spot past the tree line.

It was decided that a small fire would do no harm and they dispersed for the moment to find kindling and settle in.

———◆◇◆———

Once the Paladin was out of earshot, Beatrice stomped over to Malice.

"What now?" she hissed at him.

"You're asking me?"

She crossed her arms, glaring at him with all the frustration she could muster but Mal only waved a dismissive hand her way. "We go with it. Get rid of the bandits. Go to Bay. Then, if you're still set on stealing this thing we'll take it. No big deal."

"If I'm still *set on* it? I'm set on success, Mal! And do I have to remind you that our lives depend on that success?"

"Yeah, I know Bee. Let's just see where this goes." With that the orc wandered off on his own, putting a stop to any further conversation.

Unsatisfied, Beatrice returned to the spot they had chosen, sat down on the ground, and found herself reflecting on how far out of her control this day had strayed. She was still lost in her thoughts when the paladin came back.

"I brought you something," he spoke, extending a hand awkwardly towards her.

Beatrice's brow furrowed slightly at the sight. Gespar held out a fistful of tiny yellow flowers and a few larger orange ones.

"That's..." she struggled for words, not sure if she should be flattered or annoyed, and instead settled into a flustered confusion.

Seemingly realizing how the gesture must appear, Gespar's cheeks flushed just slightly and he pulled back.

"I noticed you have a cut."

He indicated the split in her lip. "These plants make a good salve that will take the sting out and hopefully close it up faster."

Beatrice successfully pushed down the slight tinge of disappointment this clarification caused, leaving nothing but relief to color her silent response.

"I can show you how to make it if you like," he offered. "Do you have much experience with medicines?"

"Unfortunately, no. I know a stiff drink is relief enough for almost anything, and that's where my knowledge ends."

Gespar laughed as he sat next to her, turning his attention towards sparking a fire. "That would work too, but unfortunately I don't have a good drink to offer you."

"Well then, how about you provide the salve and I'll provide the drink?" She freed a flask from her satchel, holding it out to the paladin with a smirk, which he returned easily as he accepted her offering.

"Something tells me I'm lucky to have found the pair of you," he said before tilting the flask to his lips. Beatrice realized that she was watching this action a little too intently, and looked away. The sip caused him to cough and sputter, and Beatrice couldn't help but laugh as he handed the flask back to her. "That's stronger than I expected!"

"Well, it's a small flask." Beatrice took her own swig, and they fell into a not-uncomfortable silence as Gespar coaxed the flames into existence and then turned his attention to muddling the flowers he had found.

Beatrice watched him carefully as he worked. His hands, though large and better suited for weapon-wielding, worked expertly at this delicate task.

Gespar shot a glance towards Malice, who had situated himself back at the tree line watching the road intently. "You seem close," he pointed out, nodding towards the orc.

"We are. We've been together for years now. "

"Together?" Gespar questioned.

"You're asking me about the nature of my relationship with my orc companion?"

"I meant no offense, though I am curious. You must admit you're an odd pairing."

"No offense taken. You're not the first person to ask. I'll let Malice answer you though, he always gets a kick out of it."

Gespar began to protest but Beatrice ignored him, calling Malice over. The orc approached after reluctantly pulling himself away from his post. "What's wrong now?"

"Our new friend was wondering if we're 'romantically' involved."

If there had been any bandits, predators, or otherwise ill-intentioned folk near at hand they would have been immediately and precisely alerted to the party's exact location by the booming laugh that erupted from Malice at this inquiry. When this had gone on for longer than necessary, and Gespar looked ready to crawl into the fire, the orc finally found words amid his laughing fit. "You want to know if I fuck her," he guffawed.

"Gods, that's not what I-" The Paladin's protests were lost on Mal, who was still enjoying this immensely.

"I mean, just look at her," the orc ordered.

Gespar did look at her, his face turning a violent shade of red that almost made Beatrice regret setting him up.

"I'm sorry," he muttered.

"Gross," Mal laughed. This took Gespar by surprise. His eyes went wide as he looked at her again, searching her as if he had missed something the first time. Beatrice felt an unfamiliar self-consciousness creeping over her as his gaze lingered.

"She's so squishy and ugly," Malice went on.

"I'm not so bad by human standards, thanks."

Malice waved her protest away with a heavy hand. "Look at the size of her! Have you ever seen an orc cock?"

"No!" Gespar choked, clearly horrified.

"They're massive. Laying with her would be like trying to wear a sock as a hat." The orc mimed attempting to stretch what appeared to be quite a small stocking over his large skull.

"Ok." Beatrice interrupted. "That's enough."

Seeing how pale he had become, she handed the flask back to Gespar and he took it eagerly. Malice wiped mirthful tears from his eyes. "Ah, but it doesn't matter. Even if she wasn't so physically unappealing, she's like a sister to me."

"Probably could have led with that," Beatrice suggested as Mal sat down with them.

"I like you, Sunshine. If you're asking because you're interested, you have my blessing."

"Enough, Mal," she warned. This had stopped being funny.

"Oh, I assure you that wasn't my intention. I would never," Gespar insisted.

That stung more than Beatrice would like to admit. She was used to Mal's scathing remarks, amused by them even. But, coming from this handsome man they landed heavier.

"Right, and now that you've both ensured that my self-esteem has been buried for the night I think I would like some rest."

"That's not how I meant it," Gespar's words were hurried. "You're a beautiful woman. I only mean that as a paladin of the Triad I am sworn to purity."

The silence that followed was somehow more awkward than Malice's vulgar display moments before.

"That's real, huh? I mean, you guys really follow that rule?" Beatrice asked.

"I like to think most of us do, yes. It's really not a big deal. I am honored to carry out my duties as a paladin every single day, and I live my life by my title. Something as trivial as... earthly pleasures, is nothing more than an afterthought."

"Nah, it's no big deal bein' a virgin, though I personally would advise that you're missing out. It just seems like a weird thing for the church to force you to do." Malice crossed his arms as he spoke.

"There's solid reasoning behind it. It wouldn't be good to have paladins traveling from city to city defiling the local's daughters. We should be trusted, upstanding citizens."

"If you weren't sworn to purity your first instinct would be to 'defile' people's daughters?" Beatrice asked, hoping that teasing him might lighten the sudden shift in the mood. Gespar shook his head but otherwise ignored her.

"Meaningless romantic attachments are a distraction from our service to the gods. We marry within the church, and the vow is also a promise to our future partner."

The paladin was not flustered anymore. His chest raised slightly as he explained his circumstances. His words came easily now, with the confidence of a well-rehearsed monologue.

"And it's not as if the church asks anyone to give up anything without understanding what is being asked of them. We're allowed an experience before we take our vows."

"Yikes." The word left Beatrice's mouth before she could stop herself. The idea of a church-approved de-flowering sounded decidedly more disgusting than sensual.

"What?" Gespar seemed genuinely surprised by her reaction.

"Nothing." Mal graciously took over for her. "Just sounds kind of like they've got you on some kind of creepy leash. 'Here's a taste of the good stuff, you can have more later, but only if you're a good little boy." Malice shrugged, frowning at the paladin.

"I'm not leashed. I'm lucky enough to be betrothed to a woman of the church, and quite a powerful one at that. She's the only woman I've been with and the only woman I will ever be with. Is that so terrible?"

Malice shook his head, relenting to the paladin's words.

"Of course it's not. Your devotion is admirable and your woman is lucky," Beatrice said, standing up and draining what remained in her flask. "You've got our congratulations, Sunshine."

"Here," Gespar handed her the ointment, as well as the extra flowers he had gathered. He didn't look her in the eyes this time. "Hang on to those, you might need them."

"Thanks..."

The group quieted down, agreeing to rest until just before sunrise before advancing carefully behind the cover of the tree line to try to spot the bandit camp. The fire was extinguished, a watch order was decided, and the three companions spread out and settled in.

Beatrice took the first watch, enjoying the relative silence of the night away from the city. There was no sign of anything larger than a squirrel nearby, and after an uneventful few hours, she went to fetch Gespar for his turn on guard.

She couldn't help but sigh as she approached him. "*Idiot.*"

The paladin was fast asleep, his yellow cloak wrapped tightly in his arms and cushioning his head from the hard ground. His belongings lay two feet away on the ground, entirely unattended. If the item they were after had already been in his possession, Beatrice could have plucked it and whatever else she wanted and been off into the night without a hitch. Such blind trust in his new companions could easily have been a sign of his own tendency toward trustworthiness, but Beatrice was more inclined to believe it was evidence of a severe lack of intelligence, common sense, or maybe both.

She nudged him gently with the toe of her boot. "You're up, Paladin."

He woke gracefully and rose to his feet without the slightest hint of complaint. They exchanged minimal words before Gespar wandered closer to the road.

Seven

Beatrice found herself a spot at a tree near Malice and positioning herself on the side of the tree opposite from Gespar's post, she pulled the necklace from her clothes. Though this was one of the smaller stones from the collection, it glowed with more than enough light for Beatrice to read by in the dark of the woods. She wondered at the way it seemed to catch the faint light of the moon overhead and multiply it. No one had *said* that the gems were blessed with Divine magic, but she couldn't think of any other explanation for how it worked. If it were true, it was highly illegal. Magic of light would come from Crepus. A demon. What she did know for certain was that it *felt* magical, it was hypnotically beautiful, and she would be wise not to let the Paladin see it.

Beatrice woke with a start, she wasn't sure how much later. She hadn't let her guard fall completely until she had heard Malice take over for his turn at the watch, at which point she had given herself over to sleep. She wasn't sure what noise had stirred her, but now she could hear a hushed rustling and whispering voices some distance away.

Silent as a ghost, she rolled to her stomach, peeking around the tree she had stationed herself against. Gespar could be seen, about fifteen feet away sleeping soundly. Further on, where Malice should have been on guard near the road, Beatrice counted at least seven shadows, murmuring amongst themselves and then hunching to lift a large and seemingly heavy shape from the ground. Beatrice was certain the shape was an unconscious Malice.

Beatrice stayed low to the ground, belly-crawling through the dirt to where Gespar lay. She coaxed him awake, placing a gentle hand over his mouth before lifting a finger to her own. The sleepy confusion on his face cleared quickly as he heard the intruding group struggling with their heavy load.

"This thing must weigh as much as two cows. I say we kill him here."

They could make out some of the conversation, though most of it appeared to be pointless jabbering.

"Did you see how strong he was? He'd be good to have on our side. We take him to Mess. *Then* if he ain't friendly we kill him."

Another round of muttering issued from the group. She felt Gespar tense by her side, his arm shooting out for his sword. She grabbed him, trying to convey through barely visible hand signals to be patient.

"Hey, wait," As if on cue, a nasal voice piped up.

Beatrice and Gespar froze in the dirt like startled rabbits.

"Whatya mean 'wait', this is heavy!"

"I *mean*, don't you think it's weird he was alone like that? Maybe we should have a look around."

Beatrice heard Gespar's breathing pause, but she shook her head, willing him to wait a moment longer.

"I think if there's more we better hurry up and get out of here. Let's go."

One more round of mutters rippled through the shadows, and after a moment Gespar and Beatrice were left alone again in the silence of the trees.

Springing to her feet, Beatrice went directly to where the men had taken Malice.

"Those were the bandits we seek, no doubt," Gespar whispered, hastily reapplying the plate armor he had discarded the night before. "They're formidable indeed if they took down our friend so easily."

"Not *so* easily, after all," Beatrice indicated towards a human form, lying dead on the ground at her feet. "Looks like Mal got a hold of this one's neck. I'm guessing the others took advantage of that to jump him. I counted seven of them."

"They're moving slowly. If we hurry, we can catch them on the path."

"And make a stand, two against seven? With no idea of how capable they are? No, I think our best bet is to tail them back to their camp. Once they're there they'll likely spread out and we'll have a much better chance."

Gespar considered her carefully in the moonlight as if weighing their limited options. Beatrice took his hesitation as an opportunity and began walking quietly away. This sealed the plan, and Gespar followed her carefully, creeping silently through the trees.

They caught sight of the bandits almost immediately. The group moved at a crawl, carrying the weight of the orc between them.

Beatrice and Gespar followed at a safe distance, careful not to be spotted now that the sun was rising.

Bee's focus was entirely on getting Malice back from these goons. They had been in plenty of scrapes before, and between the two of them, they had always come through. It didn't matter how many they were up against. Even this job, as large and life-threatening as it was, wouldn't matter one lick until Malice was safe.

After almost an hour of slinking along in this manner, the bandits veered back towards the trees, turning down a path that would have been almost imperceptible to someone who wasn't looking for it. Pursuing at a greater distance, Beatrice and Gespar followed their target until the group reached a makeshift log fence surrounding an encampment.

There were five large tents within the fence, most of which were the generic canvas structures used by hunting parties and caravan travelers. One of the tents was marked with the insignia of a northern trading company, and the largest had the Triad spiral symbol emblazoned in gold on each side.

The bandits carried Malice through the main opening in the fence and into the Triad tent. A few minutes later, five of the seven men exited the tent and went their separate ways.

Beatrice and Gespar watched silently from behind a cluster of thick briars at the base of a tree. From their vantage point, they could see an additional five men around a large fire pit.

"So much for a 'small' group," Beatrice scoffed. "This won't be fun, but if I sneak around to that far side and you come in from over there moving slow we can whittle down their numbers."

"That's a clever thought, but our best bet is to tackle this head-on. If they're this organized there must be someone in charge. We address them directly and force them to submit."

"Yeah, ok." Beatrice laughed this off, but she had barely turned her attention back to planning when Gespar stood to his full height and moved to step towards the camp.

Snatching his arm she hurried to pull him back behind cover. "What in the seven hells are you doing?"

"Exactly what I said I was going to do." Gespar's brow furrowed in confusion, "You agreed."

"I thought you were joking!"

"The situation is a bit too serious for jokes, don't you think?"

Beatrice ignored the comment, pressing her thumb to her forehead. "So, you're going to go give them a stern talking-to in the name of the Gods? And they're going to give us back Mal, and then follow us in a happy little parade to Bay to turn themselves in?"

"Obviously not, but sneaking in is only going to get us caught and killed."

"So our options are to walk in the front and get killed almost immediately, or sneak in the back and get killed less immediately."

Gespar's bright eyes searched Beatrice's face intently. "You're right."

"I know."

"And that's why you're not going in."

This was just unexpected enough to catch Bee off guard. She looked back at him, lost for words.

"I'll go in and try to negotiate with the bandits. There's little hope of success, but hopefully I can keep them from killing Malice or myself while we wait for help." As he went on, Gespar suddenly grabbed her by the shoulders. "You must go the rest of the way to Bay and go to the consulate for aid. I'll do what I can to buy us time."

Beatrice squinted at him. "Is idiocy a prerequisite for being named paladin, or do they train that into you?"

"Excuse me?"

"That's an awful plan. Even if I run all the way to Bay, and the first assholes I run into at the consulate hop right to their feet and run back out here with me, we're talking about an entire day. If you think you're going to last an *hour* in there after telling those guys they've been naughty you're highly overestimating your own people skills."

"I know it's dangerous. That's exactly why I can't let you storm in there with me. There is no use in all of us dying."

"There's no use in any of us dying! You're welcome to carry out stupid plans when it's your own life on the line, but I am *not* leaving Malice to these guys for a whole day."

Gespar straightened his spine, puffing his chest slightly and looking at Beatrice with cool, stern eyes. "As a paladin knight of the Triad *and* as your current employer, I command you to go to Bay to bring aid from the consulate. You will not enter this bandit camp today."

Beatrice looked him up and down slowly before taking a deep breath. "Ok."

"Ok?" He deflated slightly, as if shocked that his order had worked so easily.

"Yes, sir. You're right. I'll do as you say. I'll leave." She gave him her most melancholy smile, going so far as to place a hand on his cheek. "Please don't give up hope. I will be back for you, with an army if that's what it takes."

Gespar nodded gravely. "Thank you, Beatrice."

He reached out, taking her hand in his own. His golden eyes bore into her, full of sorrow and something she couldn't place. Beatrice could have sworn at that moment he was about to say more, and she suddenly felt exposed, nervous but intrigued. Instead, he gave her hand a slight squeeze, dropped it, and then turned and walked towards the bandit camp.

She caught her breath, watching his back for a moment.

"Idiot," she muttered under her breath, before turning and creeping away through the brush.

EIGHT

The Fairchild family were remnants of the past. Like all the noble families in the Empire, they were the legacy of the times before the church had risen to power, brought to their station by the kings and queens of old and money that must have been older still.

Gregor Fairchild had only two sons. The first, Philip, would inherit the lavish manor the family held in Triad City, all the pomp that went along with it, as well as the spice mine to the north and the direct trade partnership with the Church.

As second son, Gespar was the 'extra', and therefore an opportunity. He was promised in service to the church, a sign of mutual loyalty and promise of future influence that flowed in both directions.

As a Fairchild, he could have had almost any position he wanted within the church (short of Blessed Leader, of course). Paladin Knight had seemed an easy choice. Being on the road and serving the Empire and its people in an actionable way suited him better than the more stationary position of a cleric.

As a Faithful knight-in-training, he had been the charge of High Paladin Codrin, along with three other boys. Deacon, Penn, and Carter had been closer to him than his own brother. They were taught together, trained together, and grown into formidable men of the church together.

Penn had been the best of them- the most idealistic, purest of heart, the most devoted, and the most talented. He had come from humble beginnings and proven himself at every turn. Penn was in line for a position at the Grand Temple, promised as husband to the Blessed Leader Diana herself. He was everything a Paladin should be. And then, he was gone.

Penn's death had struck them barely six months before they were set to take their vows and become full-fledged paladins.

The mission was one of their last with High Paladin Codrin. It should have been simple. A village on the west coast of the Empire had sent a nasty letter in place of their taxes, and they were sent to investigate and collect the dues if possible. Instead of an impoverished village, they had found a cult.

The people had fallen to demon worship. They accepted blessings from Ludus, claiming that their village was thriving on love, but their hatred for the empire, and the paladins, burned hot. They had attempted to arrest the village leader, and his woman had lashed out, striking Penn dead.

It was a raw and painful exposure to the realities of the world. The Realms that claimed the most innocent titles, *love, light, life,* were a danger to their own, distorted by their contradictory nature and the demons that ruled them. Hate. Darkness. Death.

Carter had snuck away in the dead of night one week before their vows, without so much as a letter of explanation. They never heard a word of him again. Only Deacon and Gespar had stood before the three Blessed Leaders in that final ceremony.

In times like this- every job for the church, every time that push came to shove, it was thoughts of those brothers that came to Gespar's mind. What would Penn have done? How could he live up to the potential of the man that should have been standing where he was now?

As he walked into the camp Gespar had anticipated an immediate retaliation, or a rush of bandits snatching him. This didn't happen, and Gespar had walked at least fifty paces past the border created by the fence before he stopped, looking around him. The men seated around the fire were engrossed with their breakfast. Three other men were closer to his current location and appeared to be having a heated conversation. No one appeared to care that an armed and armored stranger had just walked into their midst.

"Excuse me?" He called out for the attention of the three closer men.

"Perfect," one of them spoke, noticing Gespar. "An unbiased opinion."

They beckoned him closer, and uncertain of what else to do Gespar stepped towards them.

"This is important. Who's got the best call for signaling in the woods?" Without another word all of the men began making wild animal hoots and howls, attracting the looks of all the others outside.

Gespar watched, baffled and silent while the men shouted wildly at him. The calls eventually slowed and quieted, and when the cacophony had settled, they stared at him expectantly.

"Hey, wait a minute." The man that had just been doing an impressive screech owl impression narrowed his gaze as if just realizing there was something unusual about this stranger. "What are you doing here?"

"I demand to speak to whoever is in charge here."

"In charge? You wanna talk to Mess?"

"If that is who is in charge, yes."

Gespar tried to keep his composure and an impression that he was in control of the situation, though these men made it difficult.

The owl man gestured towards the large tent with the church symbols on the canvas, and then the men turned away, beginning to caw into the air again without another thought to Gespar. A couple of the men moved from their spot at the fire to tail him, but they kept a few feet away.

As he approached the tent, he clenched and unclenched his fists, and taking a deep breath, he assumed the most authoritative quality he could muster.

He gently pushed the flap aside, stooping only slightly to enter the tent. As his eyes adjusted, he saw a large pile of furs pushed to one side of the tent and a large table with four chairs in the center. Three of the chairs were occupied, one of them by Malice. Three other men stood around the tent, watching with disinterest.

"Morning, Sunshine." The orc nodded in greeting and continued eating what appeared to be an intensely dry cut of bread. A task made awkward by the ties binding his wrists tightly together.

The other two seats were occupied by men that watched Gespar with a critical gaze. One of the men was human. His ears were misshapen, the cartilage inflamed and bubbled from repeated damage. The tips looked like they had been cut to a point in a poor attempt to mimic the elven characteristic. His face was sickly and severe, and he shifted nervously in his seat.

The other man showed no sign of nerves, leaning back in his chair as he looked over Gespar. "And who are you? Some hotshot hero?"

He was dwarven, not very old, not quite as tall as a human man but sturdily built. His thick black beard grew down to his middle. Large vertical strips were shaved from it on either side of his mouth but based on the amount of stubble growing in the empty spaces it hadn't been groomed for a while now.

"I am Paladin Knight Fairchild of the order of the Goddess Vedett, and this orc is my charge. You will release him and cease your activity in this area by order of the Triad Empire."

"Ah," the dwarf acknowledged him. "They call me Mess. And I can assure you I'm not doing any of that. Have a seat, Paladin Knight Fairchild."

Gespar made no move to do so, and Mal paused his crunching, looking sideways at their host.

"Sit," Mess insisted this time, and the men around the tent tensed.

Joining them reluctantly at the table, Gespar sat. The silence of the tent was only punctuated by the men cawing outside and Mal's loud eating.

"Are you alright, Malice?"

"Eh? Yeah, I'm fine. You alright?"

Gespar nodded.

"Touching. I love reunions," Mess commented. "Now, you see. We're doing pretty well for ourselves out here. We're not going anywhere. And..." He paused for a moment, thinking hard about his next words. "And, the Empire can eat my ass."

Malice grunted.

Gespar's face tensed, though he tried to remain calm. "If you won't submit willingly the church will respond with force. Your criminal activity will not be tolerated."

"Oh ho, force? They train you up to be pretty capable warriors, right? Look, pretty boy, I was just making our friend here an offer. I'll make the same one to you. Work for us."

"I would never work with you. I serve in the name of Vedett- in the name of protection- and you prey on those that can't protect themselves."

The human man jumped at Gespar's sudden outburst, but Mess took it in stride. "You didn't let me finish, kid. Work for us, and we won't kill you. That's the deal. Pretty good, Malice?"

"Sounds fair." Malice shrugged.

"No." Gespar kept his voice low now. "I will die before dealing with the likes of you."

"Well." Mal spoke again. "If he's out, I'm out."

Despite his words the orc kept eating, moving his attention to some sort of charred fish.

Mess stood up impatiently, toying with a hammer hanging from his belt. Gespar was almost certain that it belonged to Malice. As he paced, the collected dwarf that had sat at the table seemed to melt away, leaving something visibly unstable in his place.

"That is a real shame. A waste. And a dull choice on your part." He turned back to Gespar with a new and suspicious glint in his eyes. "What is your play here? The church sends two souls out here to take us down? I'm offended. Maybe I'm just trying to smooth my hurt feelings, but that sounds like too few. Especially given how sure you both seem."

The dwarf ruffled his beard and walked right up to one of the bandits standing opposite, getting entirely too close for the comfort of anyone present before he turned again quickly. "You're a distraction." He pulled the hammer loose. "A distraction, while the rest ambush us. That's sneaky, even for the church."

The human bandit with the damaged ears, who had been squirming as if something terribly itchy had worked its way into his socks, finally piped in. Gespar recognized his nasal voice from the group that had taken Malice. "If there's an ambush we ought to reverse-ambush them!"

"Reverse ambush!" Mess laughed as if this was either the best or worst idea he had heard.

"You're being paranoid," Gespar accused.

The comment snapped a thread in Mess, and he lunged at Gespar where he sat. "That's exactly what you would say if you were trying to ambush me!"

The paladin turned his face away to avoid the fishy stink of the dwarf's breath. "It's only the two of us," he insisted.

"So, I don't need to send Gumby here out with a group to stage a reverse ambush?" He indicated the jumpy human with the mangled ears. Gespar felt a spike of panic surge through him but stilled himself. Mess's eyes were unblinking, watching his face with dreadful attention.

"You can if you would like. Sending some of you away couldn't hurt our chances here." Gespar's voice was steady. It was a solid bluff, or so he thought. But Mess began to laugh, right in his face.

Then, Malice began to laugh too. The orc's gravely booming laugh filled the tent until it had put a stop to Mess's own mirth.

Something had settled in Mess's eyes, and when he spoke it was with the same calm tones he had used before.

"What are you laughing about?"

"It's just that he's lying, and he's about as bad at it as I thought he would be."

"What's he lying about?" Mess leaned in so close to Gespar's face that he thought their eyeballs might touch.

"We're not alone," Mal said, teasing the dwarf. "There's one more."

Gespar felt his composure falter. *What was Malice thinking?*

"She's gone. I sent her away."

"She?"

"-isn't a threat... And she's long gone by now!" Gespar held his breath, praying his words would land.

"What good is one more going to do you anyway?" Mess asked, shrugging away this new information, relaxing, and pulling away from Gespar's face. "It makes no difference."

"It's going to make all the difference," Mal sneered, bringing his bound hands behind his head in a mocking, relaxed pose. "And by the sound of it, the difference was already made."

A hush fell over the inside of the tent, and although no one could say exactly when it had happened, one by one they realized that the ruckus outside had fallen silent.

A wildfire filled Mess's eyes, though his voice was steady as he spoke. "You lot, relieve Pretty Boy of his weapons and get him good and comfortable. Gumby, go see what's happening outside."

The weasely man jumped to his feet, scrambling out of the tent. Just as quickly, the other three men rushed Gespar. Standing abruptly, Gespar shoved at the man that reached him first, and then the second, but to no avail. As the third man grabbed for him the other two were already recovering. Catching his arms. Pulling roughly. With joint effort, they tethered his hands and snatched the sword from his belt.

There was silence again for several long moments. Gespar felt that the atmosphere was not nearly as tense as the situation called for, as Malice and Mess sat casually staring at each other across the table.

Finally, a crash from outside, accompanied by the cracking splinter of lumber and the scream of a frightened man split the quiet. Malice grinned.

"MESS? Mess!" Gumby called out from an unknown distance. The dwarf stood, looking dangerously annoyed.

"Watch these two." He growled as he exited the tent in a hurry, looking like he was on the brink of a frenzy.

As soon as the tent flaps had settled behind the bandit leader, Gespar turned, imploring the men that guarded them. "If you untie us right now, I will ensure that the church has mercy on you."

The three bandits exchanged a look.

"Begging your pardon, Sir *Paladin*," one of them answered. "But, I would never work with the church. You might say they prey upon those that can't protect themselves."

The other two snickered. Gespar's face reddened with defensive anger, but before he could respond there was another noise from outside. This time the commotion was more confused and rowdier than before. A crash, a clatter, and a jumble of voices- ending in abrupt silence.

Before long Gumby's flushed and sweaty head poked through the tent opening. "Mess says to bring the prisoners out."

Neither of them fought their handlers. They were as eager as they were apprehensive to see what had happened, what Beatrice had done.

A sparse fog had rolled in as the sun had risen that morning, blurring the tree line and giving the campsite the same feeling as an abandoned battlefield. One of the tents was collapsed in on itself in a heap of canvas, and in another spot, a large section of the improvised fence had fallen.

Including the three men that accompanied them, there were only eight bandits out in the clearing. Mess was pacing haphazardly, and Gumby stood behind him wringing his hands. In the center of it all was a dazed-looking brute holding Beatrice tightly around her chest, her arms pinned to her sides.

To her credit, Beatrice looked more annoyed than frightened or distressed.

"Not too shabby. How many did you get, Bee?" Malice asked as they were brought to stand close to her.

"I did alright." She spoke low, watching Mess carefully.

"Ten," the dwarf answered for her. "Ten men were cut down. So, how many more of you are there?"

Mess's voice was calm and steady, a striking mismatch from his mannerisms, which were growing increasingly frantic.

"Sorry, Scruffy. It's just me."

"What demon have you sold your soul to, witch?"

"No demons. No Gods. Just one little lady against your band of assholes."

Mess reared back an open palm, striking her across the face.

Malice growled, and Gespar felt a white-hot anger ignite in his chest. He lunged forward, only to be quickly jerked backward by one of his handlers. The jarring motion pulled at his shoulder sharply.

"If you lay a hand on her again, I will cut you down myself," Gespar threatened, making no attempt to hide his ire.

Mess considered the paladin, a smirk tilting his beard. "Ah, is she yours then?"

Gespar glared at him, refusing to respond. Even Beatrice kept her mouth shut.

"The deal has changed, gentlemen."

"Deal? They get a deal? Why don't I get a deal?" Beatrice interrupted.

Mess ignored her, continuing to address Malice and Gespar. "You can volunteer to cut down this bitch yourself to prove your intent and join me to replace the numbers we lost." He approached Gespar with wild eyes. "Or I can slaughter you like pigs in front of your woman before I let the rest of the men take turns with her."

Gumby cackled behind Mess.

"You bastard," Gespar spat at the dwarf as he spoke. "I will—"

"What is that?" Malice's deep voice cut in, directing all attention towards one of the tents that hadn't been knocked down in the earlier commotion. A sturdy wooden stake was driven into the ground next to the tent, with two ropes tied to it. One of the ropes held a chestnut-colored horse that looked like it hadn't had quite enough to eat in its recent history. The other rope was tethered to a healthy, sleek brown goat. Its eyes glazed over as though seeing something in a different realm.

When he didn't receive an answer, he asked again. "What is that? The goat."

"Are you dumb? It's a goat. Like you said," piped Gumby.

"Where did you get it?"

The man shrugged. "Found it on the road. Like most of our things."

Malice was rigid. "Where's the kid?"

"What kid?" It was Mess who asked, looking from Malice to Gumby with blossoming interest.

"The kid who goes with that goat. Where is he?"

"Why do you care so much?"

"Cause the Orc has figured out what we already know," Gumby laughed. "Boy meat tastes better than goat meat!"

Mess chuckled, eyeing the orc. Under the dwarf's gaze, Malice grinned slowly, letting out a low laugh of his own. It sent chills down Gespar's spine. Had Malice lost his mind? They were at the mercy of men that had none, and he was worried about a goat?

"Now, where were we?" Mess snapped back to a straight face, getting back to business and swinging Malice's hammer in wide sloppy strokes in the air.

"I'll do it." Malice raised a hand. Both hands, in fact, being that they were connected. Mess grinned wickedly at Gespar's furious expression before turning to Mal.

"I knew you were worth something, my friend!"

"Malice, you can't. We are better than these fiends, even in death."

"I dunno. Sounds like somebody's got to go, and I like living pretty well." Malice shrugged.

Mess crossed to Malice, cutting his binds. Malice rolled his wrists, stretching his arms and loosening up his tensed joints.

"Malice, you won't do this. I know you won't. You told me that Beatrice was like your own blood. After all your years together, you wouldn't betray her like this."

"C'mon Mal," Beatrice chimed in weakly. "Don't."

Mess ceremoniously handed the hammer back to the orc before stepping back and gesturing dramatically. "Bonus points if you make it messy."

Malice circled to stand in front of Beatrice, a grave look on his intimidating face. Gespar struggled to break away from the man holding him but another joined the fray, grabbing his other arm and pulling him several steps back.

Gespar watched in horror as the orc sized up his mark. Beatrice was silent, shifting only slightly as if testing the hold the bandit had on her. Her eyes darted around the clearing, finally settling on Gespar for a moment before she looked back to Malice.

"Better make it quick, you big oaf."

And then she *smirked*.

Gespar found himself awestruck. This woman, who could single-handedly wipe out most of a bandit camp now stood smiling in the face of death, and somehow it was the most beautiful thing he had ever seen.

He was brought back to the moment by the sight of the orc nodding, raising the hammer, and bringing it back behind his left shoulder.

"Malice! Mal! Please!" Gespar cried out but was ignored by all except one of the men holding him, who jerked at his arm painfully and chortled.

Horrified, the paladin began reciting a prayer to the Goddess under his breath. A whispered prayer of protection for this brave (if somewhat foolish) woman, and for himself. He knew it wouldn't do any good, but being otherwise completely helpless, it was all he had left.

The amulet he wore was as much protection as he could hope for from the Goddess Vedett. It served as his badge. His mark as a paladin. It was also endowed with a blessing of protection. This could preserve Gespar from exposure, minor wounding, the shield fires used by the church, and even poor luck in some cases, but a direct and fatal wound would strike him as truly as anyone else. In this dire moment, his blessing from the Goddess would do little for him, and nothing whatsoever for Beatrice.

Malice, still holding his hammer aloft, lowered it momentarily to appraise the situation. "Hmm. You're too close." He grumbled at the man pinning Beatrice still. "You're gonna have to let her go or something."

The man hesitated. "But if I just let her go-" he trailed off, looking to Mess for answers.

"I said, or something," Mal clarified.

"Just hold her out." Mess impatiently straightened his arms in front of him. "Out. Away from you. Let's go, people."

Malice raised the hammer again as the bandit awkwardly shifted Bee to hold her at arm's length, clearly trying to stretch his own body as far away as possible. Somewhat ashamed of himself, Gespar turned his head away. He clenched his eyes tightly, bracing himself for the sickening sound of metal and bone colliding. The sound came, but it took longer than he anticipated and was followed immediately by a chorus of shouts, grunts, and motion.

Gespar would regret later that he had looked away, not for any false damage to his bravery or nobility, but because it meant that he hadn't seen exactly how the subsequent moments had played out.

As Gespar had closed his eyes, turning his head away, Malice had raised the war hammer high above his head. Instead of one swift swing, it was two, the main killing blow preceded by a short, stinted swing– a fake-out. Beatrice had been watching intently for this fake-out. At the first hint of a swing she had buckled, turning her full body to dead weight in the bandit's extended grasp, and dropping to the ground. The sudden shift in weight distribution caused the man to lurch forward, which is when the second blow landed, striking him with full force. The man, a burly young buck with drooping eyes, fell in a mass at Beatrice's left side.

Beatrice pulled the sword from his belt in the blink of an eye, jumping to her feet and whipping around to face whoever would come next.

Mess yowled like a wildcat, pulling a dagger and holding it high in the air. "Get these bastards!" he screamed.

Gespar, eyes now wide open, was frantically trying to catch up with the shifted situation.

Malice was wheeling around, fangs barred, a guttural growl issuing from his core, and rage burning in his eyes. Four of the bandits jumped at Malice and Beatrice simultaneously, and the pair stood back to back ready for a fight.

Regaining composure and now fully aware of the situation, Gespar turned abruptly, easily escaping the clutches of the men that had been holding him at bay. It wasn't difficult, as both of them were startled and entirely uncertain of what they should be doing now.

Finding himself loose, he let his training and instincts as a warrior knight take over. He swiftly kicked the closer man. His shin to stun him, his gut to buckle him, and as he stepped back Gespar advanced, clasping his bound hands and bringing them down on the back of the man's head like a mighty club. The bandit dropped.

The second stammered, pausing a moment before charging. Gespar ducked to avoid the dagger that was drawn and swung at him. Stomping on the bandit's foot, he stood back up again, directing all his weight up through his arms as he went and striking at the man's chin. He faltered, and Gespar sucked in a deep breath to prepare for another go. As he made his move, only a moment later, a blow from behind had Gespar reeling, falling into the man he had just struck.

The bandit broke his fall, and as the paladin rolled off the man and onto his own back he was greeted by the wild eyes and waving beard of Mess.

"You pretty motherfucker!" the dwarf growled. "I'm going to tear you apart and eat the slime under your skin. Your gods have abandoned you, paladin!"

Gespar took another deep breath and forced himself to look Mess square in the eyes. He braced himself for the end. A paladin dies with courage. A paladin dies blanketed in his faith. If this was his fate then he would bear it with the grace and courage he had seen Penn exhibit on the day of his death.

As it were, that was not what fate had in store for him that day.

As Mess reared back, the hammer hit him square in the side of the head, knocking the dwarf to the side. Malice didn't stop, bringing the hammer up again and then back down in the center of Mess's chest as a growling shout rolled from his chest. The sound of ribs cracking and flesh breaking issued as Mess coughed a thick splatter of blood.

"Is that messy enough for you?" Malice sneered.

There was no answer. Mess wheezed a final breath and went still.

Malice extended a hand to Gespar, who took it gratefully.

As he stood, Gespar surveyed the area. Two bandits plus Mess lay around him on the ground, and another four lay not too far away, where his companions had dealt with them. Beatrice joined them, and as she did she held up her forearm and Malice did the same. They clasped hands, their arms wrapped gently, and they exchanged a knowing glance and matching nods before turning back to Gespar.

"Not bad, Ges." Beatrice smiled at him, holding her hand out to him next.

Gespar took it, perhaps not as casually and comfortably as Malice had, but he nodded at her all the same and looked into her eyes. She looked back at him with eyes a-fire, but as their gaze lingered her smirk faltered. Quickly she nodded, dropped his hand, and turned away from him.

Gespar did not look away. "You said you were leaving." His voice rose slightly as he spoke. "I told you to go. You said you were! I thought you were safe!"

"Yeah, well I lied." There was a hint of challenge in Beatrice's tone. "Are you going to stand here and tell me I made the wrong call?"

"No," Gespar answered quietly. "You were right."

"I know."

During their exchange, Malice had begun to walk away. He moved towards the goat tethered on the other side of the camp. He crouched down, examining the goat carefully and petting its ears thoughtfully.

"Ah, man." Beatrice's head drooped as she saw what Malice was doing. She approached Malice quietly, her voice softer when she spoke than Gespar had imagined it could be.

"It can't be the same goat, Mal. How could you even know that?"

"It's Darcy," he affirmed. "I know. Look at her ears."

"Yeah..." Beatrice looked at the goat uncertainly. "I didn't really look at it that hard the first time. You're sure?"

"I'm sure."

"I don't understand," Gespar spoke. "You know the goat?"

Malice nodded. "It's my goat. Kind of." He said. "And if the boy that had this goat had pockets heavy enough to make him interesting to these monsters it was our fault."

"Gods, Mal! That's a shitty way to think of it."

A subtle noise behind the closest tent caught the group's attention and they all hurried toward it, clearing the corner just in time to see the bandit Gumby slipping through a gap in the fence.

"Hey!" Malice growled, rushing the fence. "What did you do with the kid?"

Now assured of his escape, Gumby snickered at them, his gait somewhere between a run and a dance as he scurried off. "Nothing worse than you lot did to us, that's for sure," and he began to sprint, into the trees and away into the woods.

Malice snarled, throwing his weight against the fence. It shifted dangerously but required another hit from the orc before it came crashing down. The three companions jumped over the rubble, but there was already no sign of Gumby.

"We won't catch him," Gespar pointed out.

"He's right," Beatrice agreed. "But if he goes much deeper into the trees in that direction he may wish we had. He was headed straight towards the Wander Wood."

While Beatrice and Gespar searched the camp, Malice tended to the animals. Gespar's large sword, marked with the Triad symbol on the hilt, was in Mess's tent, along with a broad collection of stolen goods, mostly linens, and spices, which they packed in a large sack. Beatrice was able to convince Gespar that they should barter the goods in Bay to help offset their travel expenses. The items marked as church property he insisted they would turn back over to the church as soon as they arrived in the city. Beatrice couldn't help but point out to Malice later that evening that these were clearly the most valuable of the recovered goods, and without Sunshine's presence, this would have been a much more lucrative venture.

They knocked down the rest of the tents, dragging the canvas and wooden beams to a pile in the center of the clearing and lit it ablaze. The smoke rose lazily above the treetops as a warning signal to any of the bandit crew that may have been away during their purge. *Don't come back.*

Despite adamant argument from Beatrice that the goat not be brought along, it was. Malice was not going to back down this time. Gespar also decided that the horse should be taken into their care. After a more thorough inspection, he determined that it was a healthy and sturdy creature despite its current state, and with some kind treatment and generous feeding it would be a fine horse. While it felt cruel to make it carry a rider before it had a few good meals, it was at least strong enough to carry the goods the party took from the bandit camp.

He asked if he might claim it if they weren't interested in keeping it for themselves. Malice of course was content with his goat, and Beatrice would rather Gespar claimed both of the animals. And so, they worked their way back out to the main road and made way for Bay City.

The trio was mostly silent as they walked, each caught up in their ruminations on the events of the morning.

Malice was mourning the life of a child he hadn't known. *What kind of scum robbed and murdered children*? That was low, even for bandits. More importantly, *what kind of orc let kid-killing scum get away*?

Gespar was absorbing how close they had come to death, and how close he had come to failure. If they had fallen here, the delivery of the Shadowgate Stone would have been put in jeopardy. It was not lost on Gespar that without Beatrice's stubborn disobedience that may have been exactly what had happened, but he was also aware that they had only been in the situation because of his companions to start with. He couldn't bring himself to regret helping them though, despite the danger or the turn of events. He had learned a great deal.

Beatrice's thoughts weren't quite as dark as her companions, though they troubled her almost as much. She was thinking about the damn fool of a paladin. *If you lay a hand on her again, I will cut you down myself-* As if the idiot could have cut anyone down while bound and helpless. The way he had pleaded with Mal to spare her life, the concern in his eyes when all was said and done... This man was trouble. The sooner they got to Bay and made off with this artifact, the better.

NINE

I f Beacon City was a perfect example of the gradient of the upper class of society to the lower class, Bay was an in-depth study of the lower end and the myriad of ways that the criminal and corrupt can exploit it. The entire city was washed in a dreary grey, and even the section of the city that housed the local temple and consulate looked aged and gloomy beyond its years. The city was smaller in size and population, and the local economy was much more dependent on the fishing trade than Beacon.

There was a large district on the eastern side of town that was comprised of nothing but warehouses and empty workshops. During more prosperous times, it was a bustling center for craftsmen and shipyards. The locals made beautiful ships and the sturdiest boats that sailed the southern seas. Now they stood empty, or worse, housed local organizations and 'businesses' that a wise man would steer clear of.

At the Bay gates, the company found a livery yard. Gespar paid the fee to have the chestnut horse cared for, throwing in a little extra to have her bathed thoroughly and fed as much as she would eat. When he asked if it was the same fee to board a goat, the short old man running the place looked at him as if he had suddenly forgotten the common tongue. Gespar decided on his own to pay the same as he had for the horse, and the man accepted, despite his lingering confusion.

"Be good to Darcy," Malice growled at the man as they left, which seemed to clear up any misunderstandings quite well.

With their hooved companions accounted for, Beatrice, Malice, and Gespar walked into Bay city more downtrodden and tired than any of them could remember being. The city's gloomy landscape certainly did little to lift their spirits.

"There's an inn close to the consulate we've stayed at before. I'd say it's the safest in town," Beatrice offered. "We don't want to spend any more time in the low town than we have to. Bay can be tricky to navigate."

"I'm aware of how Bay can be," Gespar responded. "I'm an idealist, not oblivious."

"You say that as though the two are exclusive, but they actually go hand-in-hand more often than not."

"Alright." Gespar was getting used to Beatrice's manners, and as such he was trying to let her comment slide off. "Typically, I would stay in the Temple Barracks, but I think in our situation an inn would be better. Lead the way."

The Sea Drop Inn must have been a properly cheerful place once upon a time. The couple that ran it did their best to maintain that cheer by keeping the interior well lit by an abundance of mismatched chandeliers, as well as a large hearth that blazed at all hours. Soft yellow curtains hung in all the windows, and a large, colorful tapestry hung on the back wall. The tapestry featured a warm harbor town in brilliant blues and greys, with beautiful red ships floating in the cotton ocean, all under a warm golden sky. It was a depiction of Bay, though it was so unrecognizable as the dismal city outside of the Sea Drop's walls that most visitors never made the connection.

The forced brightness only made these particular travelers more aware of their fatigue as they sat around a table sharing a quiet meal. They may have cleared out the east road bandits like they had set out to do, but it didn't feel particularly like a win to any of them. When Gespar suggested they wait until the next day to tend to their business in the city no one disagreed.

The next morning found them suitably rested. Malice was still slightly out of sorts but the other two were much more inclined to move past the bandit incident.

They dragged the bags of Triad goods to the consulate after a slow morning that had consisted mostly of sulking around the Sea Drop. Beatrice watched with a heavy heart as Ges filled out a small stack of papers and handed it all over. The elf that had taken the paperwork rifled through the things and announced proudly that it must be a plats-worth at least. "Good find, friends!"

Beatrice smiled through her teeth.

Next, they were directed towards the contract office. The man in charge here was no Gerald Grimer. The tall elven man could have been eighteen or eighty, dressed in a velvet suit and large gaudy jewelry the likes of which you might find in a wealthy grandmother's underwear drawer.

"Hello!" He stood, greeting them with a broad grin that flashed a golden tooth. "I don't know you."

"You don't. That's probably fine." Beatrice looked around the office, decorated as flamboyantly as the man himself. She broke eye contact with a stuffed raccoon wearing an expensive looking watch and tiny pants and produced the contract for the bandit job. "We're just here to turn in a contract we picked up in Beacon."

The man took the contract and held it delicately at arm's length to read it over. "The bandits on the road to Beacon?" He snorted, letting the contract drop to his desk with a flutter. He pulled out a book similar to the one Grimer had rifled through and began flipping pages, pausing every few to look up and appraise these 'mercenaries'. Eventually, he shut the book, folding his hands before he spoke. "Well, due to your lack of... paperwork, I'm going to have to send out someone to confirm. Seeing as how all the paladins and faithful are preoccupied on account of the Divine Gathering in the Capital, it might take a while. You're free to keep checking back."

"It might take 'a while'? We don't exactly have free time right now."

The elf shrugged. "You don't have to wait. If you would rather, we can void the contract and you can go about your business."

"Void it? But it's done!"

"But I don't know that, do I?" He flashed his golden smile again. Malice rumbled.

"Enough." Gespar stepped forward. "I am Paladin Knight Fairchild, and I am witness to the contract."

The man's eyes passed over Gespar, settling on his Triad talisman.

"The job is done. Finalize the contract, pay these folks, and send word to Beacon. I vouch for them, and you can write my recommendation in their file."

"Fantastic," was the elf's response. It didn't sound like he meant it.

Twenty minutes later they stepped out of the consulate building. Beatrice folded her hastily scrawled copy of a letter of recommendation signed by Gespar and tucked it into her satchel. Every passing hour they spent with this man seemed to dig them deeper into a web of recognition. Today she hardly had the energy or desire to be upset by it.

Clinking the four plats together in her hand, she shot Malice a glance. He nodded back, in a way that indicated not only that he knew what she was thinking, but also that she shouldn't even have to ask. Beatrice made a point of not sighing audibly and handed two of the platinum coins to Mal before holding one out to Gespar, who looked at it with sincere confusion.

"What is this?"

"A share of the reward from the bandit's contract." She left the 'obviously' off the end.

To her surprise, he laughed. "I hardly earned that, did I? All I did was ignore your plan, get tied up, and then eventually knock out *maybe* two bandits. And you took care of how many?"

Beatrice smirked. "I think the final count was twelve. But, you weren't entirely useless. The way I see it, you were a pretty good distraction."

"Keep it," Gespar reached out, gently wrapping her fingers around the coin in her hand. "And I'll be your distraction anytime, free of charge."

"Well," Beatrice didn't skip a beat, ignoring the way her stomach fluttered at his innocent words. She pocketed the coins, "You don't have to tell me twice."

"What's next?" Malice asked, stepping away from the consulate. "We got a package to pick up?"

The reminder of the larger picture was unwelcome, but perhaps necessary.

"We do," Gespar agreed.

"So, where are we headed, Sunshine? The temple?"

Gespar absentmindedly squeezed at his shoulder, looking up and down the street. Malice and Beatrice waited patiently for a response.

"I need to check up on a few things," he finally said. When his companions still looked at him expectantly, he went on, "You guys head back to the inn. I'll meet you there when I'm done and we'll discuss our next move."

They weren't inclined to argue with him, and so Beatrice and Malice found themselves at the Star Drop Inn, short one golden paladin.

"If he comes back with it tonight, we're taking it tonight," Beatrice spoke in a hushed voice. "It's about time we got this over with."

They were sat at a table in the far corner of the room, eating a stew that managed to perfectly capture the essence of Bay- fish that was a remarkable hue of grayish brown and miraculously bland given how over-salted it was. For good measure, the innkeeper had added a small sprinkle of some dried herb on top to add a touch of color. Beatrice was playing with a lace doily on the table to keep her eyes off the door and wondering how often the innkeeper had to replace them.

"Get it over with," Mal nodded. "Can't stand Sunshine anymore?"

"That's not the point. You know he's plenty nice to be around. Sure, the job would be easier if he was an asshole, or made rude comments, or looked like a goblin... or smelled like a goblin," she paused to let Malice laugh at her a moment. "But he doesn't talk nice enough or smell good enough to change the facts. And the facts are, we've gotta do this job."

"Yeah, ok," Malice conceded a little too easily. "What about that bandit contract though?"

Beatrice pursed her lips to keep from smiling. "Twelve isn't too shabby. By my count, you only got four."

"But I got the big one, that counts for more. Besides, it was a pretty good show." Malice rubbed his hands together.

"You missed the best parts while you were tied up in that tent!" she teased. "We did alright. It was certainly a little more straightforward than any job we ever got from Claw."

"And with that shiny new recommendation from Sunshine, we'll be getting some prime contracts."

"Yeah, I'm sure the postscript where he adds the bit about how professionally and expertly we stole from him will win us some serious favor."

"We could just kill him if that would be easier for you," Malice pointed out.

"We both know you wouldn't kill him now."

"Absolutely not. I like him. You would have to do it."

"Absolutely not!" Beatrice protested.

"We can rock-paper-scissors for it." Malice held out his fists.

"Not a chance, Mal." Beatrice leaned back, amused despite the dark tone of their conversation. Rock, paper, scissors with Mal was a trap. It was his unwavering opinion that because his hands were so much larger than hers it didn't matter what either of them called. His massive scissors always managed to beat her rock.

The evening passed, and they kept the conversation light. Being the safest and cleanest inn Bay had meant that the Sea Drop saw a decent amount of business, and as the ground floor filled up it began to feel almost familiar.

The sun went down and the night wore on. Beatrice's attention began to shift expectantly back to the door, and eventually, even Malice seemed on edge.

A few more hours passed, and the crowd had somewhat dissipated and still, Gespar had not returned. Beatrice stood up abruptly, interrupting Malice in the middle of a remark about goat care.

"Well, that's it. It's over. We shouldn't have let him wander off alone in Bay. He's dead. We're all dead."

"Do you want to go look for him?"

She let this idea simmer for a moment before plopping back down in her seat. "No, I don't."

"Do you think Berta would let me make cheeses in the basement of the Knightcap?"

"What are you talking about, Mal?"

"Goat cheese? Have you even been listening?"

It was a while longer still before Gespar walked through the Sea Drop's door. Only a handful of out-of-town guests were still downstairs, Beatrice and Malice among them.

"Welcome back, Paladin. Did you enjoy your night out?" She had meant the sarcasm to come through a bit sharper. Beatrice couldn't help but notice how tired Gespar looked, the way he slumped slightly under the weight of his armor, and the way his golden eyes were circled with weariness. Though she wouldn't voice any concern for him, she worried the falter of her tone would betray her.

"We were just about to report you missing to the guards," Malice added.

"I apologize for being so late. I had to confirm that my information was still good and do some... research."

"Research? Is that Paladin code for drinkin' and whorin'?"

"I can tell you that for this paladin in particular it is not."

"Well," Beatrice joined, "Did you at least get what we needed?"

"The information, anyways. We have an appointment the day after tomorrow to receive the artifact, and we will leave town first thing the next morning."

"An appointment? Is it just me or is this all a bit strange?" Beatrice asked. *Strange and exceedingly frustrating.*

"We'll use tomorrow to prepare for the *appointment*, and the trip to the Capital."

Beatrice squinted at Gespar but didn't bother asking more questions. "Tomorrow then." She stood, walked away from the men, and headed towards the border's rooms.

"I am sorry if I worried you, Beatrice." Gespar's words were enough to make her pause, and she turned back long enough to acknowledge him.

"Don't apologize. We do what we have to to get the job done." As she turned again to leave she added, with a softer tone, "Goodnight, Ges."

TEN

The next day, Gespar returned to the inn accompanied by a young shop-hand lugging goods he'd acquired for their journey. He instructed the boy on which room to deliver the packages to and keeping one box with him, he joined Beatrice and Malice at what had become their usual table.

At first, he attempted small talk, something along the lines of, "The weather isn't terrible today, it's almost sunny."

He got up, got himself a drink, and sat back down. He drank in silence for nearly half an hour before taking a deep breath and forcing himself to talk.

"I guess you know that tomorrow we've got to start this mission properly. And the first part of that is acquiring the Shadowgate Stone- that's the artifact we're tasked with returning to the Grand Temple."

He paused, waiting for a reaction. With none to be had, he continued. "I haven't shared many details with you up until this point to protect the mission itself, and to protect you, but you can't be of any assistance if I don't tell you what needs to be done."

Genuine curiosity had both Malice and Beatrice drawn to full attention. Beatrice encouraged the paladin to continued, speaking in a muted voice. "And what is it that needs done?"

"The artifact is not currently in the church's possession, and our first job is to secure it. Tomorrow we're meeting with a dealer from the organization that's got it. They work out of an old warehouse in the low town. They call themselves the Harbor Vipers."

Beatrice shot Malice a look. He was already shaking his head.

"What is it," Gespar asked, tracking the exchange. "You're familiar?"

"I wouldn't say 'familiar', but we know the name and the reputation," Beatrice answered. "They're pretty damn low on the list of people you want to work with, Ges. That operation is notoriously crooked and ruthless."

Malice nodded in agreement. "They're the kind of people that kill the guys workin' for them just as often as they do the guys workin' against them."

Gespar sighed, "The intel I've gathered on them paints a similar picture. I wish we didn't have to deal with them, but if they're half as bad as everyone says it's only more vital that we claim the Stone from them."

All three went silent, momentarily absorbed by their individual concerns.

"I've secured a meeting at their warehouse tomorrow, but there's an additional catch."

"Naturally." Beatrice slumped in her seat, crossing her arms prettily and looking at him in a way that Gespar found rather unfair.

"The Vipers are apparently less friendly with the Church than they are with anyone else. I've had to set up this meeting under false pretenses." Gespar paused, half expecting some protest to this information, but receiving none, he went on.

"It appears that they don't know what they have, so we are approaching them as wealthy collectors looking to make a deal. We will buy the Stone off of them, avoid any conflict, and leave town quickly."

"I'm noticing a worrying pattern with you, Ges," Beatrice said matter-of-factly.

"What do you mean?"

"I mean, the only plan in your repertoire seems to be 'walk up and ask for what you want'. What makes you think they'll just sell this stone to you?"

"The fact that I'm willing to pay them whatever they ask."

"That's not the worst plan I've heard," Malice pointed out to Beatrice.

"It's not the best though, is it?" But she didn't bother arguing the point further.

"I also think that you should stay at the inn for this one, Malice. I'm hoping that Beatrice and I can pass as an unassuming couple looking to spend too much money. I worry that bringing muscle with us will make us seem ready for confrontation."

Malice looked at Beatrice expectantly, but instead of remarking on the stupidity of this or telling Gespar why it was a bad idea, she only shrugged.

"So, Beatrice and I will attend the meeting with the dealer tomorrow shortly after mid-day." Gespar was pleased to have at least this low level of cooperation. He hadn't been sure what to expect from his mercenaries.

"And I'll go out to the livery yard and make sure the animals are ready to go," Malice announced.

Gespar smiled at him. "Perfect. Thank you, Mal."

His attention then turned back to the large box he had set on the table.

"It would also be unconvincing for us to show up in leathers and Triad armor, so I picked up some civilian clothing for us. I hope you don't mind that I chose it for you."

He pushed the box gently in front of Beatrice, who was now sitting straight at attention in her chair, though there was a carefully calculated look of disinterest painted on her face. "I'm sure it's fine," she said shortly, but she lifted one edge of the box enough to peek at the mass of soft-looking deeply dyed fabric within. "Looks expensive," she said, replacing the lid carefully.

"That's the idea." Gespar said. He couldn't help but smile at her. He could never say it, but he was rather proud of this purchase. The lady's garment shop had been uncharted territory for him, and most of the choices had been too soft or too dull, lavender and grey dresses that he couldn't imagine Beatrice in. This one though, he had known was right as soon as he laid eyes on it. "And, I believe you'll find the skirts are just full enough that your blade will sit nicely underneath, in case this doesn't go to plan."

"Practical." Malice laughed, and Beatrice shot him a look sharp enough to kill.

"Is there something wrong?" Gespar asked, his cheeks heating slightly at what he assumed was some oversight or offense on his part.

"Look at her," Mal chuckled.

"Shut it, Mal."

Mal ignored her. "All cool and professional on the outside, acting like she doesn't care but you can almost see her squirming like a little girl on the inside." Malice leaned over the table holding a hand to his mouth as if he was about to tell a secret, though he failed to whisper when he spoke. "Our girl here loves a bit of frippery. I bet you've just made her day with that fancy getup."

"Oh!" Gespar was relieved and highly amused. "If I had known I would have picked up some ornaments to go with it," he teased.

Malice grumbled another low laugh. Beatrice's cheeks had gone a lovely shade of pink, but she held her stern expression. "Don't be ridiculous. It would be a waste, just like this heap." She stood, pulling the box close to her body. "After tomorrow it'll get packed away and never worn again. It's not like I'll be sneaking through bandit camps dressed up like some sort of doll."

"If anyone *could* pull that off, I'm certain it's you." Gespar was without a doubt smirking at her now.

Beatrice opened her mouth to retort, but strangely she shut it again without even the slightest smart comment. Instead, she took the box and walked off to her room.

"Was that too much? Is she upset with us?" Gespar asked, somewhat regretting his teasing.

Malice shook his head. "She's fine. I'd bet anything if you walked in on her right now, you'd find her taking that thing out of the box to have a closer look."

The thought pleased Gespar, more than he thought it should.

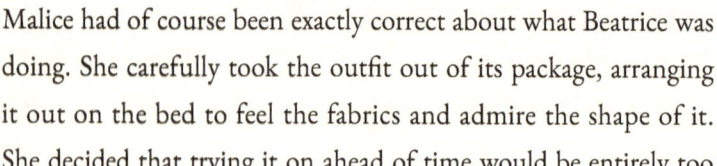

Malice had of course been exactly correct about what Beatrice was doing. She carefully took the outfit out of its package, arranging it out on the bed to feel the fabrics and admire the shape of it. She decided that trying it on ahead of time would be entirely too indulgent, and so she waited until an appropriate time the next morning to put it on.

Setting aside her black blouse and road leathers, she dressed from the bottom up. The brown skirt was only about half as heavy as it looked like it ought to be. There were two brass buttons in the front that could be used to lift and fasten the skirt up high enough to allow for movement, which Beatrice promptly did. She would spare the fabric from the filthy paths of Bay as long as possible. Next was the deep blue blouse, with matching brass buttons and flowing puffed sleeves. The collar came high, but there was enough of a thin plunge before the buttons began that the glowing amulet around her neck peaked through when she moved. This she removed and tucked carefully into a small pouch on the belt at her hips. Finally, she fastened the shapely leather bodice and turned to appraise herself in the dingy mirror. She pouted as prettily as she could manage and wondered if there was a single mirror in Bay that wasn't too weather-worn to see herself in properly.

She fastened her hair in two twists at the nape of her neck like she'd seen some of the ladies from uptown Beacon wear it. Admiring the effect, she decided that she probably could take down a bandit camp looking this way. Or do just about anything else for that matter. She could probably even spend an afternoon with her sisters and their esteemed husbands and not look the slightest bit out of place.

She sauntered out to the tavern with her head held high.

"Well, look at you," Mal remarked as she approached.

"Yeah," she said obstinately. "Look at me. If you've got something to say, say it now."

"Nothing at all. Just that you look pretty, like a real lady." Malice grinned at her.

"Thanks, Mal."

"Yeah. The only thing that could make it more convincing would be a real gentleman on your arm." Malice gestured towards the bar, where Gespar was settling their accounts with the innkeeper.

"Gods, I think I'm going to be sick." Beatrice's eyes rolled at the sight of him but ended their journey back where they had begun, planted firmly on the paladin. "He's going to attract way too much attention looking like that. We've got to get the armor back on that man... and maybe a helmet with a visor on it."

His crisp white shirt gaped open halfway down his broad chest, and it was met by a high-waisted pair of fine leather pants that hugged his body closely down the full length of his muscular legs, where they were tucked away into clean riding boots.

"This is a joke," Beatrice declared. "He's joking."

Joke or not, Malice did seem to see the humor in it.

Beatrice, who had gotten lost somewhere in the rolling landscape of his pectorals, was jerked back to reality by Gespar's voice. "Beatrice?"

He approached, his grin brightening the already well-lit room further. "You are an absolute vision. Beatrice the uptown bride is almost as beautiful as Beatrice the mercenary."

"Bee was just commenting on how you look too... What was it you were saying, Bee? He was—"

"Normal." She cut Malice off abruptly. "Which is good, because that's the look we were going for. You look very normal."

"I wish I could say the same about you. Are you ready?" Gespar offered his hand, beaming.

She grasped frantically for a smart remark. Something clever or biting. "Ready as... ready."

Gespar and Beatrice headed west before circling back around to the southeastern portion of town, to throw off the trail of anyone that might be watching their approach. To the same end, they walked arm in arm down the city streets to reinforce their cover. As she tucked her hand into the crook of his elbow Beatrice bristled, acutely aware of their proximity. Each step down the street became more natural, however. She wondered if she was only imagining it, or if his originally tense arm also relaxed in her grip.

At mid-day, the streets were as busy as they ever were in Bay. All manner of people dribbled down the paths, but the energy and vibrancy one might be used to feeling in the other cities were nowhere to be found. The smell of fish tinged the air wherever they went, not rancid or even entirely unpleasant in some places, but always present.

"What are you grinning about, Mr. Fairchild?" Beatrice shook his arm gently.

"It's a nice feeling to walk through town with a beautiful woman by my side. I would judge by the stares that you have made me the most envied man in Bay, Mrs. Fairchild."

"I don't think they're staring at me. I'm not the one with a full buffet of muscle on display."

"Buffet? You'll make me blush."

I could make you do more than that, Beatrice thought, and unfortunately, the effect was that she instead made herself blush. What she said out loud was, "What is your *real* wife like, Ges?"

What was meant to serve as a distraction from how deeply and suddenly they had lapsed into a dangerously comfortable place, seemed only to attract Gespar's attention to it. He sighed, his brow creasing slightly. "She isn't my wife yet, first of all."

"Your betrothed then."

"She's strong. Smart. Important and influential. My parents nearly cried for joy when they heard that's who I was promised to."

"So, a real winner. Nice. Did you get to choose her?"

"No. Matches are made by High Clerics."

Beatrice nodded. "Well, the high clerics chose her a good husband. I'm sure she's as pleased with her lot as you are."

It was a different, wry sort of laugh that Gespar responded with. "Sure, I'm sure she's just as pleased as she was with the first two husbands."

"She's already been married twice? What happened to the first two?"

"Nothing at all, they live a very comfortable life in the Capital as first and second husband."

She watched an animal scurry across the street some distance ahead of them. It was either the largest rat or the smallest dog she had ever seen. "Gods. I thought only the Blessed Leaders took multiple spouses anymore."

"Yeah, well..." Gespar's thoughts seemed to drift far away for a moment, but he dragged them back to the present, casting a quick glance at Beatrice as they walked. "I know what you're going to say."

"You do?"

"All that talk about purity and promises and only being with one woman, and I'm not even her first husband? It sounds pretty hypocritical."

"I was *not* going to say that... even if I was thinking it pretty hard." She was relieved when he smiled at her words.

"Ges, do you even *want* to marry this lady?"

They walked several paces in silence, and she began to worry she had crossed a line before he finally answered.

"I'm grateful for the honor I've been given. I've been a great deal luckier than many."

"That wasn't what I asked."

"It's not about what I want. It's bigger than that, it's part of being a paladin."

Beatrice tightened her grip on his arm. "You said you were 'promised' to the church too. Did you even want to be a paladin?"

This time his answer came without delay, not halting like a thought in progress but easily put to words like a fact he had learned long ago and repeated to himself many times over.

"So much of what we are is built around what we have to be and what others expect of us. No one escapes from that. So, if I am going to spend a lifetime being what everyone needs me to be, I am going to be the best that I can be." Gespar still smiled softly, but his eyes seemed distant and sad. "I do what I must with pride. But what about you? I may be promised to the church and promised to a woman I love only in the sense that I admire who she is, but I would wager that you've got your own ties. What are you promised to Beatrice?"

A lump seemed to form in Beatrice's throat, and her face grew hot. "You lost me somewhere, I'm not sure I understand what you mean."

He laughed in earnest. "Don't you? I think if you held on to me any tighter it would snap my arm right off."

She dropped his arm as quickly as if the contact had suddenly burned her, creating a healthier space between them.

"Don't look at me with those doe eyes, Bee." He closed the gap between them, though he didn't take her arm again. "I do believe that's the first hint of genuine fear I've seen on your face. I don't think I like it, so how about we change the subject."

Beatrice agreed, but there wasn't much conversation for the remainder of their walk.

As they closed in on the Harbor Vipers' nest, the buildings around them seemed to grow larger. The small shops and houses towards the center of town were replaced by larger workshops and warehouses, and eventually, they had passed a handful of compounds hidden away behind large stone walls. They were packed closely enough that the alleyways between them were completely shadowed from the sun at every time of day except for high-noon.

The largest of these compounds loomed over them presently. The walls were stacked stone, at least ten feet tall, and felt as though they were bulging outward, encroaching on the block of shacks on its right and the warehouse to its left. The opening in the wall was wide enough for a wagon to pass through, provided that it wasn't a very large wagon. They paused for a moment to gather themselves before approaching.

ELEVEN

Devlin Slone adjusted her iron bodice, squaring her wide shoulders.

"Go get two more of those lazy bastards from out back," she told her assistant, Clearwater. "I want everyone on their toes."

She smoothed back her hair as she watched Clearwater walk away, his scaled tail swinging.

"The rest of you," she eyed the four idiots lined up by the outer wall. "Best behavior or I'll feed you to the dogs."

They were a pathetic lot. The dogs were more useful anyhow. And ate less. Even when she first joined the Harbor Vipers she had at least been competent. Motivated. Literate.

At least for today's business, she just needed them to take up space and follow basic directions.

One by one the men looked away, distracted by the pair approaching their gate. The couple slowed as they came close. They were young, well dressed, and too attractive not to be a couple of well-bred uptowners from one of the bigger cities. Easy money. The young man held on to the woman's arm firmly, protectively.

"I would venture that these are our esteemed clients. You two stand out in Bay if you don't mind me saying." Slone greeted them.

"Not at all." The man offered his hand to her without releasing his wife with the other. "Devlin Slone?"

"Indeed. I suppose that makes you Phillip and Misses Fairchild." Slone grabbed the offered hand tightly, shook it once violently, and then dropped it just as quickly, turning on her heels and stepping inside the walls. "Let's go inside and discuss what it is you're looking for."

Inside the walls of the compound were half a dozen wagons and three smaller buildings around the large main warehouse that Slone led them to.

As the heavy door was swung shut and latched behind them, all of the natural light was blotted out.

Her eyes adjusted quickly to the dim torchlight, but she waited a moment for the couple to orient themselves. They looked around at the dozen or so Vipers that Slone had gathered inside the warehouse. She smiled tightly as the couple exchanged a worried glance. *Let them know whose house they're in.*

Rows of crates stacked high lined the walls and segmented the inside of the building. In some areas the boxes were stacked in such a way to separate makeshift rooms within the larger area. In one section stood a collection of life-sized figures cut from fine marble, one of each race, peering coldly around the warehouse.

Slone watched as the young wife jumped, startled by the sound of whimpers coming from the cages crowded together in another dark corner. Mister Fairchild pulled his woman closer.

"Your letter intrigued me, Mr. Fairchild." She sized them up. He looked strong, probably had some sort of training. But he had a weakness, and if they were here, they were dumb to boot. "How did you put it? Unique interests and a large budget?"

"That's correct. We're hopeful that you'll have something that interests us."

Some of her men began moving in closer, like wolves circling weak deer. Mrs. Fairchild shifted uncomfortably, clutching at her skirt. He looked at her with concern in his eyes. They must be newlyweds, the way they hung on each other, looked at each other with big round eyes. Like all those wealthy, spoiled nobles, they would grow bored of each other. Daddy's money could buy you a pretty wife, but it couldn't buy you love. Slone wasn't sure if it made her sick or jealous.

"Let's cut the crap, shall we?" Slone's words were chilly. Hush settled over the other people moving through the warehouse. "People don't just come here to browse. People come here because they've found out that we're the ones that have what it is they're after. So, what are you after?"

"I assure you, I-" Fairchild's words faltered.

"I said no crap."

Clearwater entered the warehouse, the door shutting behind him with a clack. He cocked his head to one side, his tail twitching curiously. The scarred old draken might be the only one with any brains here. Slone held up a hand, signaling him to wait. He nodded and began waving back some of the circling idiots.

Mrs. Fairchild grasped her husband's hand, pulling his attention to her. "Tell her."

The young man nodded.

Interesting. Slone was somewhat impressed. The pretty little wife seemed to hold more power here than she had assumed.

"I have learned you recently came to possess a certain stone- black, carved, and of Cestian origin."

Clearwater hissed so softly it was barely audible.

"Well, well." Slone tilted her head. This was *not* what she had expected. "What would folks like you want with something like that?"

"Seems like that shouldn't matter to you, as long as you get paid."

"That's exactly the answer I was looking for." Slone signaled to Clearwater and turned towards the back of the warehouse. "Follow me, and don't touch *anything*."

This would be an easy enough command to adhere to. The warehouse wasn't exactly inviting, and the types of things they passed weren't exactly the sort of baubles that would tempt these types to reach out and touch. Then again, she wouldn't have expected the Stone to interest them either.

They followed her closely, their hands still entwined. Slone could hear Clearwater close behind them

They weaved through the entire length of the warehouse that way. The musty air made the space feel even more crowded than it was. At the back wall, they stopped in front of an unassuming door. Slone pulled a weighty ring of keys from her belt, and as she found the proper key and placed it in the lock she spoke. "Truth be told, it would be a relief to get this thing out of here. It feels... wrong."

The door clicked open, and the party moved inside a small room. There were a handful of open crates of round yellow fruits that tinted the air with a sweet aroma, something from SunSpot. The bust of a regal-looking human man perched on a stand in the corner. A few closed boxes lined the walls, along with a table with a wooden chest placed carefully at its center. A large window on the far wall was closed with wooden shutters, but a few stray beams of sunlight slid through the slats to light the room.

Slone stepped up to the table, turning to see Mrs. Fairchild *casing the room.* She was subtle, certainly, but the way her eyes scanned every object, lingered on the door, found the boarded-up window- it was calculated. The girl looked back at Clearwater, who had un- sheathed his sword and held it readily at the door behind them, but her face didn't so much as flinch. She simply felt at her skirts again, and Slone barely glimpsed the bulge of a handle concealed in the fabric. Slone was impressed. Of course, they weren't just a few nobles with coins burning a hole in their pockets. They were liars. And Slone loved being lied to. It made the rest of her job more fun.

Now to see if they really knew what they were getting into.

"Is this what you're looking for?" Slone lifted the lid, revealing an egg-shaped stone the size of a human head nestled into a layer of straw. It was smooth and polished so thoroughly that it looked wet. Slone always got the impression that if she reached out to touch it her hands would sink right into its depths. It was intricately carved with spirals of various sizes and thicknesses, intertwining here and there, and hard to follow.

"That's it." Fairchild's voice was hushed and dry.

Slone replaced the lid. It wasn't until the sunlight seemed to reenter the room that its absence even became apparent. There was a sort of collective exhale as if everyone in the room had been holding their breath while the box was open. Slone felt a headache coming on, as she always did after looking at the infernal thing.

The air in the small room had felt stagnant when they had entered. Now it was charged with some unexplainable force.

Mrs. Fairchild looked pale, drained. Fairchild looked at her with those eyes again, wrapping an arm around her shoulder for just a moment.

Slone smiled coldly. So, *that* wasn't a lie. She still had leverage.

"Sixty-Five Platinum." Fairchild said blankly.

The misses gawked, and Slone smiled again. They were showing their cards now.

"One hundred."

The young man didn't wait to answer. "Fine, but I'll have to gather the funds. One hundred platinum, tomorrow."

Slone's thick lips pulled into a tight smile, and she nodded at them and gestured towards the door. "Deal." She said, and they moved back out into the warehouse proper. As she went she gave Clearwater a pointed signal. The woman was the leverage point.

A handful of Vipers gathered around the door waiting for them, just as Slone had ordered.

The couple slowed as they realized something was wrong. Fairchild looked at Slone with a handsomely furrowed brow. "What is this?"

"A little insurance on our part," Slone answered. A few of her men drew weapons. "I'll need the sixty-five you have with you, to ensure that we have a deal and you won't share any information you shouldn't."

"Absolutely not!" he insisted. "It may be insurance for you, but we have no way of knowing you'll keep your end of the bargain."

Slone flicked her wrist at Clearwater. The draken closed a scaly hand around the young woman's arm. She sighed, as if the sudden threat to her life was a simple inconvenience, but it was enough to catch Fairchild's attention. The man bristled at the sight of the knife Clearwater held pressed against her spine.

"I do hope you'll reconsider." Slone sneered.

The muscles in Fairchild's jaw tightened, and he loosened a fat purse from his belt, handing it over begrudgingly.

Slone gave it a good shake. "Good boy. Bring the rest tomorrow and you'll get your stone." She waved her hand, and the men stood down.

Clearwater released the wife, and she took several steps, distancing herself from him quickly. Fairchild reached for her, but she didn't relent, dodging his grasp. "I'm fine. Let's go."

They left the Harbor Vipers' base quickly, and with no further interference. The assembled men dispersed back to their usual routines.

"Do you think they'll be back?" Clearwater asked as he stepped closer to her.

"I'm almost certain they will be." But, Slone almost wished they would stay away. She would take forty more plats off them, happily. And they would deserve it. But, it almost felt like a shame to kill them. She remembered what it was like to be so young.

She considered Clearwater for a moment.

"The dogs?" She prompted.

"Fed. Even bathed them."

"The collections from the wharf?"

"Got them this morning. Already in the safe."

"That recruit with the big mouth?"

Clearwater's pupils dilated slightly in the dim light.

"Gone."

At least someone around here could get things done. The rest of them were no better than dog-feed.

"Good." She said, squaring her shoulders. "I won't be eating in that mess of a hall tonight. Bring my food to my office."

"Yes, ma'am."

"And a bottle of that Cestian wine."

TWELVE

They had crossed all the way back to the upper side of Bay when Gespar finally spoke. "Will you be alright if we split up here?"

The further they got from the stone, the more Beatrice's emotions settled, and her thoughts cleared. Her mind had begun working on new thoughts and plans several streets back. "Where are you going?"

"To the Temple. I'll have to send word to the capital and secure the extra funds for the Stone. When we go back tomorrow, I think we ought to take Malice with us."

"Ges..." Beatrice began to speak but thought better of it. "Just don't stay gone too late this time."

Her chest warmed pleasantly as he returned her smile. And so, they parted ways in the street. Gespar headed towards the Temple, and Beatrice quickly picked up her pace as she headed back to the Sea Drop.

She was still basking in the warm feeling when she bounced through the door to the inn. Her spirits were the highest they had been since before their last job for Claw.

"Hey," Mal's voice came from beside her as if he had been waiting right inside the doorway for her return. "Where's Sunshine?"

"At the Temple, picking up some extra coin. Listen Mal, I've got good news."

"Yeah, I've got news too."

"Ok, but listen. I know what we're after, I know where it is, and we won't have to steal it from Ges."

Malice's eyes did brighten at this, but he persisted. "That all sounds great, but I think you're gonna' want to hear- "

"Mal, this is the best-case scenario for us! We can steal the Stone from the Harbor Vipers tonight. It's actually the *right thing* to do because if Ges goes back there with more plats they're going to kill him and take it." She was speaking quickly, rambling on. "We're keeping ourselves and him alive this way. We steal it tonight, disappear back to Beacon, and he goes on with his shiny Paladin life. Win-win."

"That's great, Bee. Let's do it. Now will you listen to me?"

"Gods, Mal. What is it?"

"There she is. The illustrious Beatrice Lemon!" The voice slid through the air like warm honey.

"You have got to be kidding me," Beatrice hissed.

"I tried to warn you."

"You're a vision! A dream!"

A hand was placed on her lower back, and a kiss was planted in the air next to her cheek. Beatrice smiled tightly. "What a wonderful coincidence. I never imagined we would run into you here, Lemry."

Thirteen

When Gespar finally returned to the Sea Drop, he found the unique blend of travelers around their preferred table having a drink.

Beatrice spotted him first and waved him over with a great deal of enthusiasm. Her smile rounded her cheeks prettily.

"There's Sunshine!" Mal greeted him, and the other two raised their cups at him. As he approached the table his brow furrowed slightly at the sight of the stranger seated with his friends.

"You alright?" Beatrice asked.

"Fine, I'll have to go back to the temple tomorrow morning, but then we're ready to go."

He eyed the stranger again. He was sleek, somewhat exotic in his Cestain clothing. He remembered the way the girls back home would gather in clumps, giggling and admiring the handsome Cestian ambassadors and traders on the rare occasion they attended the social events in the capital.

He glanced at Beatrice again. She was laughing at some off-hand comment he hadn't heard, and seemed to be the most relaxed he had ever seen her.

"Everything ok here?"

"Fine."

"You've made a new acquaintance?" Gespar forced a smile, trying to put on his best diplomatic face as he nodded in greeting at the man.

"Well, not that new..." Beatrice admitted. "This is Lemry the storyteller, our—" She faltered for half a breath and Lemry chimed in to pick up the slack.

"Acquaintance," he finished, standing up to extend a hand to Gespar.

Beatrice smiled, gesturing as if to present him to the Paladin.

"Friend," Lemry continued.

"Good friend," Beatrice conceded, holding aloft the drink in her hand. Gespar wondered how many Lemry had already bought that evening.

"Drinking buddy," the elf said.

"Naturally."

"Confidante."

"Well..."

"And perhaps fated lover, someday."

"Not that one."

Beatrice spoke shortly, and Gespar tried to read her face for assurance, but if it was flat-out rejection it seemed to roll off Lemry like nothing. He smiled as if she had told a joke and addressed Gespar. "And who do I have the pleasure of addressing?"

"Gespar Fairchild, Paladin Knight."

"And, the best employer a merc could ask for. And I'll bet after the day we had you could use a drink too." Beatrice stood, absentmindedly giving Gespar's arm a pat before she headed towards the bar. He watched her go before stretching himself carefully and taking a seat.

"Have you known each other long?" he asked, hoping he only sounded politely interested.

"Not really," Malice answered.

"And not in any of the ways I'm sure you're worried about, my friend."

"I don't catch your meaning." Gespar felt he should take some offense to this comment, and felt even more sure that it shouldn't have pleased him so much to hear it.

"Of course, my mistake." Lemry held his hands up.

Beatrice returned to the table, placing a heavy tankard in front of Gespar and reclaiming her seat.

"We have traveling storytellers at the Grand Temple from time to time. Have you ever been?"

"I haven't. They're very particular about the sort of stories they like at your temples."

"Well, what sort of stories do you tell?"

"All sorts, that's the problem." Lemry chuckled. "I tell stories of regular people, of history, and fantasy, of the Realms and the Gods- Triad and otherwise. I even know a few tales of adventure and thievery."

Gespar tried to ignore the wink Lemry directed at Beatrice with this comment.

"Would you like to hear a tale?"

"It might be a nice distraction." Gespar tried to relax. He was being foolish, probably because of the stress of their trip to the Harbor Viper's nest. "Tell us a story, and your next round is on me."

"Deal." Lemry's pearly white teeth flashed in the abundant light. "What sort of tale would you like?"

"You said you knew tales of adventure and 'thievery'. It sounds like perhaps you had something in mind already," Gespar said.

"The realms," Beatrice interjected. "A tale of the Divine Realms. Seems fitting, right?"

"Less fitting than you would think. But, then again..." Lemry wavered for a moment as if considering the options. "How about a compromise? I have a tale that will fit both your requests quite nicely, and I would dare to say none of you have heard this one before."

"I should hope not." Beatrice sat back to moodily sip at her mug.

"No, dear Beatrice. This is the tale of one Divine that dared to steal from another. The short version though, because I'm thirsty."

Beatrice relaxed in her seat, her pout softening slightly.

"The story begins with Sald, the proudest of the gods- and rightfully so, perhaps. The highest of the Triad, Lord of creation and destruction, and Champion of the Mortal Realm.

Sald cares for little that she did not create herself, but once she had a trinket. A pretty little bauble. And it pleased her greatly."

"What need does a god have for *trinkets*?" Gespar asked.

"Ah, that's a good question. You see, it wasn't just any trinket. Sald saw potential in its beauty, she found inspiration in viewing it. It planted seeds in her mind.

But Nered, perhaps the most cunning of the di-" Lemry caught himself. "*Demons*- Heard of Sald's trinket. What can you expect from the Lord of Chaos, if not an inclination towards troublemaking?"

A young woman who had sat reading at a table nearby closed her book, listening to Lemry with wide, admiring eyes.

"So, Nered hatched a plan. He disguised himself as a worshipper of Sald. And he stole the trinket away, brought it to the Mortal Realm, and hid it where he hoped Sald couldn't reach.

Sald was angry beyond belief. She could not find her trinket but she *did* find Nered, and she cursed the demon, banishing him from the Divine Realms."

"But that would mean—" the girl at the other table caught herself, blushing. Lemry smiled at her, and her blush deepened.

He took up her thought and continued. "That would mean Nered is *here*. Exiled to the Mortal Realm, where even the other Divines can't find him. Some say you can tell when he's near. That he leaves chaos in his wake, wherever he goes."

"And did Sald ever find her trinket?" the girl asked.

"Who knows, my dear. That sounds like another tale."

"You're right," Gespar spoke. "I can honestly say that I've never heard that story, even during all my years of learning in preparation to become a Paladin. You're sure you didn't just make that one up?"

Lemry winked at him. It made Gespar uneasy, and he noticed for the first time how odd the man's eyes were.

"Well, *I* would say that we were promised a fresh round after that story, right Ges?" Beatrice nudged him suddenly, causing him to jump sideways in his chair.

"Hey, I said *his* next round."

As if a trance had been broken, they were smiling again, any tension cleared from the air.

Despite the denial, Gespar followed her to the bar and they returned with drinks for the party. They enjoyed the remainder of the evening in a similar fashion, and it was a rather welcome distraction from their mission. Beatrice and Malice—and admittedly Lemry—were good drinking companions, and he found as they spent more time together that he was rather comfortable in their company.

Even so, it wasn't terribly late when Gespar stood and excused himself from the table. "The day has caught up with me, and I'm afraid I will need my rest for tomorrow."

He patted Malice roughly on the shoulder, then nodded at Lemry. "It was nice to meet you."

He bowed towards Beatrice. "Goodnight." But hesitated a moment, glancing back at Lemry once more before dismissing himself from the group.

Fourteen

eatrice's stomach ached for a moment, as she watched Gespar
walk away. She realized this unceremonious goodnight would
probably be the last time they saw him. With no other way around
it, she let him go and sat quietly for just a moment to quiet her
thoughts.

"Well," Beatrice stood surreptitiously. "I suppose we should get
some rest also."

Malice met her gaze, nodding and standing to join her.

"That is a shame," Lemry sighed. "But I will be in town for as
long as business keeps me here, perhaps we can revel in each other's
company tomorrow evening."

"Perhaps. Goodnight, Lemry."

As they retreated down the hall towards the lodger's quarters,
Beatrice spoke to Malice in a hushed tone. "Meet me in the street in
two hours. And, don't go past our old pal there unless you absolutely
have to. We don't need him telling Ges any more stories."

In her room, Beatrice carefully changed out of her fine clothes.
With a tinge of sadness, she folded the outfit and placed it back in
the box, laying it carefully on the corner of the bed. It wasn't hers to

keep, and besides, what would she do with it anyway? When Gespar came looking for her tomorrow he would find it right here.

Beatrice put her usual leathers back on and made sure that everything else was in her satchel. Then as she looked around the room, her eyes settled back on the box.

She exhaled with stubborn force, and quickly removed the lid and shoved the clothes into her satchel, which bulged uncomfortably, barely able to contain it all. What would he do with a set of nice female clothing? Give it to his fancy church wife? The thought caused her to boil, and she nodded to herself, comfortable with her decision to take it with her.

After waiting the appropriate amount of time, she went to the small window of her room, looking out at the crooked buildings and even more crooked streets of Bay. Throwing out one leg, and then the other, she lowered herself to the ground and quietly made her way to the path in front of the Sea Drop Inn. Malice was only a few minutes behind.

Together, they walked through Bay towards the Harbor Vipers' base. They didn't bother taking the same round-about way to get there that she had taken with Gespar, and so they made much better time.

As they walked, Beatrice filled Mal in on all the details of what had happened earlier. As they came upon the base the pair split, both knowing what to do next, just as two actors preparing to perform a well-rehearsed play.

Malice continued down the street, no stealth, no sneakery- he simply walked right up to the opening in the wall surrounding the

Vipers' nest. There were now only two men standing at the entrance.

"Hey!" Malice started loud, calling to them.

The men looked at each other, each placing a hand on the hilt of their sword.

"Hey," Malice repeated, "You guys the Harbor Vipers?"

There was an extended silence. Finally, one of the men answered, "Who's askin'?"

Malice looked up and down the empty street. "Just me. Unless you see somebody else here. You the Vipers?"

"I *see* that it's you, but who *are* you?"

"An orc. Lookin' for the Vipers. You them?"

The second man had peaked around the corner, summoning over a few more from inside to join them at the entrance. The first man pulled his sword, though he had begun to sweat as he stood before Malice. "Why are you looking for the Vipers?"

"Well, I was thinking maybe I ought to be one."

The man relaxed slightly, looking around for an indicator of what he should do with this new development.

Meanwhile, Beatrice had slid down a dark side street and found herself at the base of the stone wall surrounding the compound. She closed her eyes, trying to picture the layout of the buildings inside, then she picked a spot of the wall she thought would be closest to the backroom of the warehouse.

Scaling the wall was no problem, the stacked stones provided plenty of places for both her hands and feet to grip. She moved slowly nevertheless, careful not to make any noise. Still, she reached the top fairly quickly and peaked over the edge to survey the scene. She could see the gate from this vantage point. The small group there was gathered around Malice, absorbed in whatever distraction he'd thought of. She could hear voices, but not the words that they spoke. Malice did his job perfectly, there was no one around to see Beatrice raise herself over the wall and crawl down the other side just as quietly.

In the forgiving blanket of the night, Beatrice stayed low, moving through the darkness towards the warehouse. The window of the back room was easy to identify and low enough that she would not have to climb to reach it. The shutters were not proper at all, but a collection of well-matched boards nailed straight into the side of the building. Calm and collected, Beatrice looked over the handiwork.

These had been placed quickly, and sloppily, and could be removed in the same fashion. Beatrice slipped her blade from its resting place. There was a notch toward the hilt perfect for catching nail heads for exactly this reason. With one hand holding the wood firmly in place, and the other working as carefully and quietly as possible, Beatrice quickly removed three of the lower boards and set them silently on the dirt.

As she positioned herself to slide through the gap she had created, a cacophony of voices sounded from the gate. She froze, listening. It was laughter. What was more, she could recognize the booming baritone of Malice's grumbling laugh mixed with the rest. Quickly she slid out of the open air and into the small back room.

Without the sunshine outside leaking in to light the space, it was dreadfully dark. Unable to see more than half a foot in front of her face, Beatrice cursed silently. Facing in the direction that she knew she would find the stone, she crept forward, inch by inch, until her foot knocked something in her path. There was the soft thud of the impact, and Beatrice was certain her heart had stopped beating entirely. She stood still, waiting for a louder noise, or a shout, or the sound of people running towards the back room. Nothing.

She again tried to orient herself to face her target and was almost certain that it grew even darker at that side of the room. Moving her foot slightly, she again felt whatever she had butted up against.

"Dammit, if there was just a *little* light in here..." Beatrice hissed. It was then that the thought occurred to her. Carefully, she pulled the chain about her neck, freeing the small stone and with it a barrage of greenish light.

Beatrice jumped back, shocked by the white dead eyes staring at her, almost screaming before her mind recognized it as the stone bust she had seen earlier. Rolling her eyes at her own foolishness, Beatrice side-stepped around the pedestal.

The room was now entirely lit. Entirely *too* lit, in fact. Beatrice tried to cup the necklace to lessen the glow and hurried to the now clearly visible chest. Dropping the chain for a moment, she hoisted the box up with entirely too much oomph, almost propelling herself backward with the motion. Based on size and appearance she had supposed that the stone would be quite heavy, but the box weighed no more than if it was empty. Worrying for a moment that this might be the case, Beatrice set the box down and cracked the lid carefully.

Her blood ran cold. The stone was indeed still there, impossibly dark and ominous. As she watched, the darkness seemed to ooze from the wet blackness of the swirls like ink staining the air around it. She realized, with sudden horror, that the darkness was growing from it, and was about to spill out of the opening she had created. She dropped the lid quickly, cringing at the clap that seemed to echo as it landed.

"Shit." She latched the lid, grabbed the box, and moved towards the window. Luckily, there was no noise indicating anyone heard her. She paused, taking a deep breath to settle herself before she continued.

Balancing the box in the window, she slid back out through the opening and hurried to hide the gem back under her clothes, squelching the light. Quickly and silently she carried her prize back to the wall.

Now, this presented more of a challenge. Scaling a stone wall was no problem, but with a box tucked under one arm, it would be near impossible. She pressed her free thumb to her forehead, thinking quickly.

Pulling a rolled strip of leather from a pocket on her belt, she took a deep breath and held it in anticipation before opening the lid of the chest. Expertly, she ran the strap through and latched it shut. It wasn't quite long enough to make this a comfortable solution, but it was long enough to drape over her shoulder, freeing her hands.

Beatrice smiled to herself. The stone of the wall was coarse and cool under her hands. The chest swung gently, knocking her on the backside as she went.

She had made it halfway up the stone wall when the soft rustling of padded steps hurried around the corner of the closest building behind her. Her veins turned to ice as the rippling growl of a large dog began to build behind her. She scrambled higher, her foot slipping in her haste. As the dog came upon the wall and jumped, its growl turned into a deep alarming bark in the night. She didn't dare look down, but she could hear the sound of claws on rock, and the lashing of teeth at her heels. A chorus of tearing barks began on the ground. She couldn't know how many there were. Couldn't bring herself to look. Couldn't waste the time.

This, of course, was followed by a renewal of the voices at the gate and hurried humanoid steps crashing through the compound. Only another foot and she would be able to slip over the edge of the wall and out of sight. "Hey, wait. Where are you going?" she thought she heard Malice shout at the guards.

By some divine grace she cleared the top of the wall, just before the Vipers reached her. Beatrice forced air into her lungs, slow and silent, trying to steady the shaking in her arms. Keeping as quiet as possible she began her descent. Her heart still pounded in her ears and her hands had begun to tremble, making the climb down more difficult. She looked down and found that in the dark, and with her adrenaline high, she couldn't tell how close she was to the ground. She closed her eyes for a moment, breathing in deeply.

"Beatrice?"

The voice startled her almost as much as the dog had, and she gasped.

"Ges?"

The voices inside the walls were a confused jumble, but one shout rang out loud enough for her to hear. "I don't see anything, check the outer perimeter!"

"Come on, Beatrice," Gespar insisted, and without further time to analyze the situation she began climbing again. As soon as she was within reach, she felt Gespar's hands on her waist, and let herself drop from the wall, guided gently down by his grip.

"What are you doing here?" she whispered, turning to face him now that her feet were planted firmly back on the dirt. 'A sight for sore eyes', was an understatement, though she knew in the back of her mind that his presence was just another complication.

"Getting caught by some Harbor Vipers, by the sound of it." The sound of quick footsteps could indeed be heard approaching around the corner. "Think we could run?"

Beatrice looked down the alley. The opposite corner was a fair distance from them with a tangle of hand carts blocking their path. She shook her head fervently. "How would you feel about a little misdirection?"

She could see his incredulous expression in the moonlight as he hesitated, running his hands through his hair.

"Alright," she muttered, "then we—"

In the space of a breath, the Viper sent to investigate came around the corner. The shadows would not be enough to hide them from view, but before he could spot them Gespar had pushed her back roughly against the stone wall. He pinned her with his body, a hand wound into her hair, pulling her close and tilting her neck, exposing it to his warm lips. A soft gasp escaped her. She quickly tried to convince herself it was caused by the shock and not the sensation. As his free hand found the curve of the top of her hip, her own hands moved upward. A motion that she had intended to be a gentle push to slow him down got jumbled in her mind by the soft feeling of his breaths on her skin and the persistent kisses he planted between them. Instead, she found herself grasping onto his armor, pulling him closer.

"Whoa there!" The Viper called out. Gespar paused, barely pulling back from her. The guard chortled after a moment. "You need some help?"

"I'm fine," Beatrice called back insistently, her voice catching in her throat.

"I wasn't talkin' to you, sugar," he snickered.

"Get out of here," Gespar ordered, his voice a low, threatening growl she almost didn't recognize.

"Alright, I get it. I wouldn't want to share either." The Viper waved a hand, still chuckling. "But some of the others around here might not be so understanding. You better move on if you plan on finishing what you started."

With that, the man walked back the way he had come.

"Did you find anything?" A voice called from further away.

"Just a couple of animals in the alley."

Gespar released her, turning away. "We better get out of here, quick."

Beatrice stood frozen, her back still pressed against the wall, stricken. "What in seven hells was that?"

"Misdirection. Like you said." His words were short. Impatient. "You're going to tell me that's not exactly what you had in mind?"

"I wouldn't say *exactly*, no!"

He sighed, gently grabbing her arm and coaxing her to walk down the alley in the opposite direction of the Viper. "I figured it would be better than your mouth, less intrusive somehow..."

Bee scoffed.

"Yeah, I guess it didn't feel that way. It worked anyway, didn't it?"

"Well yeah, it was great—" Beatrice floundered. "Great in the sense that it got the job done... meaning it worked. As a distraction. Obviously, it wasn't—"

They froze just short of the corner, as the sound of heavy steps drew them from their blundering conversation.

Before she realized what was happening, Beatrice was again shoved against the hard wall, jarred by the force of it. Gespar's hand cradling the back of her head was all that kept her skull from cracking against the stone. This time his mouth met hers, though he was notably less forceful than before. He moved gently, carefully, as if waiting for permission. Without thinking, Beatrice pulled him closer, moving her lips and lifting her leg to wrap around his hips.

If either of them remembered that this was an act of misdirection, it didn't show. They were so caught up in their charade that it took them more than a few moments of fervent kissing to realize that they hadn't been interrupted by the owner of the heavy step. As if this had occurred to both of them simultaneously, they paused, looking at each other with equal parts confusion and panic. The confusion being caused by the fact that they weren't currently being harassed, and the panic caused by the mutual feeling that they had just let something very secret slip in their haste.

"Hrrhem." Both feelings were chased away by the loud clearing of a large throat. "If you're about done we probably ought to move on."

In an instant, there were three feet of space between Beatrice and Gespar.

"Malice! We're done!" Gespar said quickly. "I mean, not done- it was just a distraction."

"Yeah," Malice nodded sympathetically. "You seem pretty distracted."

"No, not—"

"Come on, we've got to go," Beatrice interrupted, finding her voice along with some of her common sense.

The three hurried through the dark streets, putting as much distance between themselves and the Harbor Vipers as they could.

The weight of what had gone down that evening began to sink down upon each of them, but no one wanted to be the one to address the elephant in the room- the room being a wooden chest that Beatrice had handed to Mal so it would stop bouncing heavily against her hip as she walked. The elephant, a surprisingly ominous black stone.

Gespar, who had been eyeing the box for a few minutes, finally spoke. "You got it."

"We got it," Beatrice confirmed.

"How, exactly?"

Beatrice sighed heavily. "Malice caused a distraction. I snuck into the warehouse. Almost snuck back out too."

Gespar was quiet.

"I didn't realize that was something you could do. It seems like a fairly specific skill set." He paused. "Do you work jobs like that often?"

"Just cut to the chase." Beatrice bristled. She didn't want to have this conversation.

"You're thieves?" The word had fallen off his tongue like a bite of rotten fruit.

"Eck." She tossed a hand in the air. "People have needs. People have jobs that need doing, things that need acquired. That requires a 'specific skillset'. We happen to be pretty good at those jobs. We're like... Acquisition experts."

Malice snorted, and Beatrice promptly elbowed him in the hip.

"That's..."

"That's just the way it is." Beatrice stopped, turning on Gespar and jabbing a finger at him. "Those assholes had the stone. Now I have it. So, what is it you want to say?"

"I was *going* to say that it's amazing. *You're* amazing. You have proven that you have many skills, and there is a time and place for all of them."

"I bet I know which of those skills is your favorite," Malice muttered and was purposefully ignored.

"Yeah, well... Good." Beatrice turned away again. She hadn't been prepared for that answer. It made her cheeks warm. Suddenly she was very aware of the taste of his lips lingering on hers.

"If we had gone back there with the coin that Slone demanded, there's no guarantee they would have given us the stone," Gespar said.

"I'm glad you figured that out." She tried to recover, sprinkling a little more sarcasm onto the words than was necessary.

"And even if they had handed it over, technically you just saved the church forty plats. You've both been indispensable so far, and I would like to add twenty of that to your contract."

"Twenty more plats for getting you to Triad City?"

"How much was it originally?" Malice whispered. "Didn't really matter before, so I didn't bother checking."

"Forty total?" Beatrice pointedly clarified with Gespar.

He nodded.

"That's very... generous." Beatrice thought about this for a moment. "I think we've overstayed our welcome in Bay," she decided finally. "I think we should leave. Tonight."

"I agree, but I'll have to get my things from the Sea Drop."

"What about the animals?" Malice prodded.

"Hells, Mal? What about them?"

"No no. He's right."

"Sure. We'll just wait around until morning and go collect our livestock. That way, when the Harbor Vipers wake up tomorrow and realize they want to hunt us down and skin us at least they'll get the goat too."

"No, that's not what I'm saying. I think this is urgent enough that we can justify waking the liverymen." Gespar paused, considering a moment before pulling out a few coins and handing them to Malice. "Give him that to make up for the nighttime intrusion. I'll meet you outside the city. I won't be long."

"Be careful, Ges." Beatrice stopped him as he turned away. "The fewer people see us leave, the better."

He nodded, leaving them.

Beatrice and Malice headed quickly out of the city. It was closer to early-morning than late-night now, and the thick air was chilled by a damp breeze.

As they reached the gates, Malice spoke up. "Hey, Bee?"

"Yeah, Mal?" She answered more brightly than even she expected, still riding an adrenaline rush that had her feeling higher than the temple's belfry.

Malice held up the wooden chest that held the Shadowgate Stone cozily inside it.

"Oh."

Beatrice's mouth went dry. Her spirits fell from the belfry, right back down to the sloppy Bay streets. She stopped in her tracks. She looked around, half expecting a bell to sound or someone to leap out to claim the wretched thing.

"Well... shit."

"Yep."

"He just left it with us?"

"Yep."

"After we just snuck out and stole it from someone else?"

"Mhmm."

"And right after he sorted out that we're thieves?"

"I believe it was 'acquisition experts'."

"Gods, he's an idiot!" Beatrice threw her hands in the air as frustration boiled in to take the place of the elation that had just fled from her. "How did he make it this far in life? Does he think anything through?"

"I guess he just really trusts us," Mal said.

"Idiot!" Beatrice exclaimed, her voice peaking louder than was acceptable for the time of night. Mal began to laugh, big rolling laughs that bounced like boulders down a hill.

"What?" Bee glared daggers at him.

"Either he's wrong about us, or *we're* wrong about us."

"That's not funny!" Beatrice pressed her thumb to her brow. "That doesn't even make sense."

Mal evidently decided that it was time to start moving again, and Beatrice reluctantly followed.

"So," He let her stew for a moment before speaking again. "What do you want to do, Bee?"

She sighed, violently. "It's not about what I want, it's..." She stopped. Her brain had suddenly started churning again at the expense of her mouth.

"Well," She spoke again suddenly, her tone quite a bit more relaxed. "We can't just walk off with it."

"Can't we?" Mal raised a heavy brow.

"No. I've been thinking about it..."

"I can tell."

"And I think we've been looking at this the wrong way."

"Ya' don't say?"

"I *think,*" Beatrice spoke carefully now, "That we've found ourselves in a situation where we can have our cake and eat it too."

"Have our cake and kiss it too, more like."

Her forehead wrinkled in indignation, but she left the comment otherwise unaddressed. "We got forced into this mess, but at least we're getting paid... And we have an opportunity to get paid twice for this shitty job. Our big break just got bigger."

"Go on..."

"This guy *clearly* trusts us more than he should. Stealing from him will be a piece of...cake. So, let's do his job. Let's take this thing to Triad City, get paid, and *then* steal it. Then we get paid again. That's ninety platinum, if you haven't done the math already."

"Beatrice- " It was Malice's turn to sigh now. "If you really plan on going through with this, I think it's important that you hear me right now. The longer you put this off the harder it's gonna be."

"Didn't you hear me? The longer we're around the more he trusts our intentions."

"Right. That's not the point I'm getting at."

"Well, I don't see your point then."

Malice let the subject go, shaking his head heavily.

As they approached the livery yard, they paused. The house was nestled comfortably by the edge of the road. The dark, quiet inside could almost be felt pouring out of the windows. The yard and stables stretched out behind it.

"It does feel like a shame to wake them, doesn't it?" Beatrice asked, crossing her arms thoughtfully.

Mal grunted in agreement.

"How much coin did he hand you?"

"Two gold," Malice answered.

"I see." Beatrice nodded as she looked out over the darkened pastures with a glint in her eyes.

FIFTEEN

Lemry stood alone in the Inn's public hall.

He had always liked places like this. It wasn't perfect, or beautiful. The smells of the fire still burning in the hearth, live bodies, and salty old wood mingled in the air. It wasn't even particularly clean. The Bay streets were all dust and silt, the kind you could never keep off the floor. But it was the sort of place that was bursting with stories, bursting with *life,* and always hungry for more.

He was the only one still about when the Paladin returned. Probably the only soul awake in the building.

Fairchild was in a hurry. The man paused upon seeing Lemry, but then rushed through the room without a word.

Embarrassed, probably.

Only a few hours earlier the young man had made a marvelous commotion, banging on Lemry's door, waking half a dozen people, and looking like a proper mad-man.

"Where is she?" he had demanded, pushing past him into the room as soon as the door was open.

Watching the regret and shame building on Fairchild's face as he realized Lemry was alone had been a proper treat.

Gespar tripped over his words. "She wasn't in her room, I thought... I'm sorry."

"And if she had been here? What then, Paladin Fairchild?"

Gespar shut his eyes tightly until they wrinkled, and shook his head as though he had just realized where he was. "I didn't think that far ahead. Excuse me."

Lemry appreciated the honesty. "Have you checked with Malice?"

"I haven't. Thank you." The paladin bowed politely before turning to leave, but not before he could see the agitation on his face.

"Paladin Fairchild," the smooth cadence of his voice stopped him at the door, "What were *you* doing at her room?"

The Paladin turned back to him, hot cheeks and narrowed eyes. Poor child, he didn't even know.

Lemry grinned at him. "Nevermind."

Within minutes he heard Gespar hurry down the hall again, and out of the Sea Drop.

Presently, Paladin Fairchild came back from his room loaded down with more gear than it looked like he could manage. An interesting development, to say the least.

"No Beatrice?"

The paladin stopped, considering his response as though there was a right and wrong answer to the question

"She's safe," he finally answered. "Malice too. But regrettably, we have to leave earlier than expected."

"Oh, Beatrice. It seems she has a habit of leaving without saying goodbye. Send my regards."

Fairchild turned to leave, but paused once more. "If anyone happens to ask, I would appreciate if you didn't share information on our comings and goings."

"Of course."

"And.... Again, I'm sorry for my behavior earlier. Perhaps you wouldn't share that either."

"Of course." Lemry extended a friendly smile to the Paladin, and he slipped back into the night.

Lemry turned back to the fire, mulling over what came next. Things weren't going quite as he had expected with Beatrice Lemon, but there was no accounting for handsome young paladins.

This one seemed to be stealing his thief.

Sixteen

After a careful inspection, Malice determined that Darcy was at least as well-off as she had been when they had left her at the livery. Her hair was still glossy, her belly still round as a melon, and her eyes still bottomless wells of existential nothingness. Satisfied by this, he turned his attention to Beatrice.

She sat perched on the top rung of a wooden fence swinging the horse's lead listlessly - and thinking, he hoped. She could do with a good thinking spell. To encourage this he stayed quiet, petting Darcy's ears and watching for Gespar to come up the path.

When the paladin finally came in to view, he looked sidelong at Beatrice to read her reaction. There wasn't one. *Interesting*.

"Last chance," he pointed out, and she ignored him stubbornly.

As Gespar reached them, Malice couldn't tell if the tension in the air was imagined, or a byproduct of these two fools being in the same space again.

"There is my beautiful Beatrice," Gespar said as he reached them.

"Excuse you!" Beatrice leaped up, the wide-eyed expression she wore looked more like panic than anger. Her cheeks puffed out, pink as roses. "I don't know what you think is going on here but—"

"Oh," Sunshine feigned innocence, but his mouth twitched at the corner. "I'm sorry, you've misunderstood. I was talking to the horse."

"What are you playing at?" Beatrice scrunched her forehead into a suspicious scowl.

"Well, I was just thinking that Darcy has a name. A properly pretty name. And if the goat has a name the horse deserves one too, so she doesn't feel bad." He patted the horse's neck affectionately. "And Beatrice was the prettiest name I could think of."

"If this is your attempt at some misguided compliment, you've gone wrong. Frankly, it's insulting."

"To you, or the horse?"

"To me!"

"Aww, don't listen to her, Beatrice." He addressed the horse.

"You can't name your horse Beatrice." She crossed her arms.

"Well. I just did." He began fitting the horse with baggage and handing off some of the smaller items to be carried by Darcy.

Malice was thoroughly enjoying this. It was rare to find someone who could get under Bee's skin, and Sunshine was getting better at it with each passing moment. "You might as well try to see it as the tribute it is, Bee. Otherwise, you're going to have to spend the next twenty or so years insulted."

Beatrice began examining the amount of baggage the men were strapping to the animals. "Ges, what is all this stuff?"

He rubbed the back of his neck before answering. "I got us some proper bedrolls, a small tent, and some road rations."

"Seems like over packing," Malice pointed out. He wasn't blind to the way the topic made the Paladin uneasy. "There are at least three inns along the road between here and Central City, we shouldn't need half this."

"We won't be taking the road through Central." By the end of his statement, Gespar was wincing like he was braced to take a hit.

"What do you *mean* we aren't taking the road?" Beatrice was the one to ask (the woman, not the horse).

"We'll significantly cut down our travel time *and* our visibility if we take the path through the Wander Wood and cut directly to Triad."

"Oh." Beatrice nodded as if coming to a realization. "I get it, you're full of jokes this morning."

"Not a joke."

"You don't just take a shortcut through the Wander Wood," Malice agreed.

"You don't go into the Wander Wood at all unless you're looking for trouble... or you *are* trouble." Bee added, grumbling.

"That's superstition and bar stories. You've been listening to that storyteller of yours too much." His grin didn't quite land the way he wanted it to.

"Stories come from somewhere." Beatrice shot back. "If you're in such a hurry we'll just... hurry. We don't have to stop in Central. Or, we could even follow the coastline up. "

"Maybe you're right," Gespar sighed, giving in too easily. "Maybe we ought to take the long way around if you think we can't handle the forest."

"Good-" Beatrice had already begun to move down the path when she was interrupted by Malice.

"Of course we can handle it," he grumbled. "It's just woods."

Beatrice wheeled. "No." She pointed at each of them in turn.

Malice was well aware that the paladin had framed it as a challenge intentionally to get his way, but that somehow made it feel even more imperative that he take it.

"Well, it seems like Beatrice is worried it'll be too dangerous for us," Gespar lamented, poorly play-acting.

"Seems stupid to go around the long way, when you think about it," Mal said.

"I must say, I agree," Gespar admitted. "So, if you want to go through the Wander Wood-"

"I do."

"And *I* want to go through the Wander Wood...." Gespar was smiling at Beatrice, with the closest thing to wickedness that the golden boy could muster. "Then it's two against one."

"Fine. Fine." Beatrice gave in, assuming an air of indifference. "We'll go through the Wander Wood. I'm sure it'll be fine. But, when it isn't fine I want you both to remember this moment."

And so, as the sun crept out from its hiding place below the horizon and the dew began to sparkle on the ground, they came to a fork in the road and took the literal road less traveled, turning to the North.

Seventeen

A forest, generally speaking, is a sizable concentration of trees and other growth. It is a collection of many things. Framed by a clear blue sky on a cheery summer day, the Wander Wood was obviously and distinctly *one* thing. A solid object. There were the trees and the underbrush and the animals unfortunate enough to live within it, but it came together as one unsettling mass. Staring at the Wander Wood from any close distance was a bit like being in a room with a foul smell and knowing exactly where the stink was coming from. The birds sang in the fields, the breeze blew all around the travelers, and there sat the Wood, silent and still like it existed in a bubble.

As the road dragged them closer to the forest's edge the group slowed down. Gespar stopped for a moment, looking at the way the trees seemed to loom out towards them as they approached.

"Oh, no," Beatrice said, pushing on. "This was your idea. Get moving, Ges."

As they passed tree after tree, Malice was glad to see that the woods did not completely block out the sun as he had imagined. The way the light slipped through where it could in neat little beams spilling over the ground was rather pleasant. If something would just make a noise perhaps it wouldn't feel so damn unsettling.

"Not so bad, is it?" Malice asked, attempting to squash the silence.

Gespar stayed quiet, looking around them with every step they took.

"Maybe..." Beatrice sounded like she didn't mean that.

The feeling in the air was eerily similar to when they were about to be caught somewhere they weren't supposed to be.

A few minutes passed, the quiet around them unrelenting. It was broken by a *pat pat* on the dirt path, and Gespar speaking, concerned. "What's wrong, Beatrice?"

"Well, first of all, has anyone else started to think about what this place is going to be like after the sun goes down because I am not-"

"Not you." Gespar cut her off. He was gently petting the snout of the horse in an attempt to comfort her. Beatrice the horse was shuffling in the dirt, making breathy noises, and looking alarmed.

"Nered take you," Beatrice grumbled under her breath.

"What's got her spooked?" Malice asked.

"Maybe she's smarter than the rest of us," Beatrice said. "Or maybe-"

She was interrupted by a sound of snapping underbrush, and the approaching noise of feet in motion. All three of them produced their weapons in a hurry and tensed. It was only moments before they saw a shape weaving towards them out of the trees, and only a moment longer before they could work out that it was a man.

They could hear his heavy breathing, and all the little frightened grunts and squeaks he was producing as he ran, crashing through the woods, stumbling, and dripping with sweat.

"Son of a bitch." Malice growled, recognition sparking as the man came upon them.

The runner lurched forward, and finally seeing them in the path he cried out, first wordlessly and then between gasps. "Go! Turn around! Don't go in there!" He tripped, falling prone at Malice's feet. The wounds on the man's hands were fresh, still bleeding. The wounds on his ears were not.

"There's something in there..." As he whimpered, he finally looked up, and seeing Malice's fanged maw above him, he flinched. He rolled back, bloodied hands and clumsy feet pushing against the dirt to propel him backward, away from Malice.

"Grummy?" Beatrice asked. "That skeevy guy that was kissing Mess's ass?"

Gumby didn't correct her. Instead, he held his hands up over his head, shaking.

"What did you do to the kid?" Malice demanded.

Gumby clumsily scrambled to his feet and turned to flee. Two steps and he halted violently as if he had run into an invisible wall, and he stared deep into the depths of the Wander Wood before backing up and submitting to Malice, gurgling back sobs.

"You aren't going to run this time?" Mal growled.

"I won't go back... Won't go back in the woods." His voice came out somewhere between a whimper and a hiss. "At least I know all you're going to do is kill me."

"You gonna answer my question?"

Gumby found the capacity to laugh dryly in Malice's face. "You're insane. A wild beast, parading around like someone who gives a shit. No, I won't. I don't even-"

"Shut up." Malice drew back his hammer. Gumby cowered, his bravado failing with a whimper.

"Get up. You're coming with us. Back in to the woods, to Triad city. Then you're someone else's fucking problem."

"C'mon Mal, this sounds like trouble."

Gumby sobbed outright now. "Don't make me go back in there. They'll kill me in the capital, why won't you just do it now?"

"Because I just got the last of your friend's splatter off my hammer, and you're not worth the time it would take to clean it again."

Malice stooped, grabbing the small man by the collar and dragging him up to his feet. As soon as he released him, Gumby turned to flee, clumsy in his panic. He found Beatrice and Gespar standing in his path, their weapons still drawn.

"Your intentions are noble, but we can't trust him. We should bind his hands if we're taking him with us. He could be a danger to us, *or our mission,*" Gespar said.

"Do it then," Malice returned, hanging his hammer and moving forward on the trail.

"Well," Beatrice spoke, after what felt like the appropriate amount of silence. "Do you feel better now?"

"No," Malice answered.

It took a few hours for Gumby's frightened mumbling to quiet down.

As they moved further still into the woods Beatrice fell back to walk by Gespar, speaking to him in a hushed tone, "What do you think had him so crazy?"

"He wasn't exactly stable the first time we met him," Gespar pointed out. "And he's the only thing out of the ordinary we've seen so far."

It was true, for most of the day they didn't see anything unusual. They didn't *hear* anything unusual, at least in the sense that they didn't hear anything at all. All the pleasant sounds that usually would flavor a walk in the woods were absent. Only the occasional puff from one of their animals, and the sound of their own footsteps peppered the air. They might have been able to relax by now if only they could shake the unsettling feeling that they were being watched.

The more time they spent in the forest the heavier it seemed to grow, pushing on them in all directions. The otherwise deafening silence was sometimes punctuated by a snapping branch or an oddly isolated gust through the leaves, and the travelers began to gravitate closer together until they were walking almost shoulder-to-shoulder down the path.

Eventually, they came to a place where a large broken tree lay across the path.

"That's sort of odd," Beatrice said, tilting her head to the side.

"You're still frightened?" Gespar teased her. "Trees fall all the time in the forest."

"Sure. But look," Beatrice pointed towards the jagged broken end of the tree, the end that should have been the bottom. "There's no stump. Nothing. This tree didn't come from here."

"I told you." Gumby pulled on his ties in a fresh fit of worry. "I tried to tell you."

"Tell us then," Beatrice sighed. "What's out here?"

"It's the woods! They're alive, they follow us! Hunt us!"

After careful observation Gespar shook his head. "I'm sure there's a simple explanation for it. Let's just move along."

They left the path to lead the animals around. Beatrice didn't bother, climbing over the log and leaning against it on the other side to wait for the men.

Waiting alone in the path, Beatrice began to regret not following the menfolk. She thought about calling out for them to hurry up but she also didn't feel like listening to more comments on her bravery. Instead, she stared down the path ahead of them. *It must turn one way or another,* she thought, since the path that had been otherwise straight seemed to run into a cluster of thin, knobby trees ahead. She hoped it wouldn't become a pattern.

A twisting road meant a long road, and any longer than necessary in this damned wood was unwelcome.

At the far end of the felled tree, there was a sudden commotion as Darcy began pulling aggressively on her lead. The goat bucked and yanked, suddenly determined to turn-tail and run off into the trees. Malice squatted, attempting to calm the animal with pats and coos. "Easy there, Darcy. It's ok. Nothin' to be afraid of."

"What's gotten into that thing?" Beatrice asked, her attention drawn to them.

"Mmaaghaa," Darcy insisted.

"*I told you I told you I told you.*"

"Nothing," Malice assured her. "Just spooked. It's alright." He lifted the goat carefully in his arms to continue.

Beatrice rolled her eyes, looking back down the path. She blinked heavily, looking again. The path stretched out, straight ahead, running due-north as far as the eye could see. She was certain there had been a bend in the path. She took a step forward, trying to get a lay of the land.

"Argh!"

She nearly jumped out of her boots at the shout from Gespar. As she whipped around to look, her heart leapt to her throat. Gespar held the back of his neck and looked over his shoulder.

"*Dammit.*"

"Sunshine? What happened?" Malice sounded just as tense as Beatrice felt.

"Sorry, I'm fine. I must have caught my neck on one of these damn trees. I guess I wasn't paying attention."

He didn't sound convinced by his own words though.

When they were all back on the path Gespar let go of the wound, bringing his hand in front of his face to look at his fingers in the light. As he wiped the hand on his pants, Bee saw the mark it left behind.

"You're bleeding? Is it bad?"

"It's just a scratch."

"Bend down and let me see," she ordered. The demand was ignored.

"It's nothing. Let's move"

She shot Malice an exasperated look. *Are you going to help me out here?*

Malice shrugged. "It's nothing. Let's move," he mimicked.

The cracking and snapping of the trees seemed to become more frequent after that, sometimes sounding far off. Other times it was right at the edge of the path. The longer this went on, the more it made them jump, and the more inconsolable Gumby became. They were torn between their desires to keep moving, to make it out of the Wander Wood as quickly as possible- and the desire to stop and secure themselves before the sun went down. Perhaps it was stubbornness that kept them going as long as they did.

It had just begun to grow dark. While the thought had occurred to Beatrice to pull out the glowing stone around her neck, she hesitated to do so in front of Gespar. If it *was* an illegal artifact, he didn't need to know about it.

She glanced at him now, walking alongside her. He didn't seem to notice that she watched him, lost in his own world. She caught a glint of sweat dampening his forehead. He didn't voice any pain or discomfort, but she could see it in the way he moved, in the way he would wince occasionally. But he kept going. The stubbornness of it annoyed her. If he wanted to pretend he was unaffected, she could pretend not to notice.

Suddenly he stumbled as if his legs had gone weak underneath him.

"Ges!"

She moved to catch him, but he straightened himself on his own. He touched the back of his neck tenderly, wincing.

Beatrice frowned at him. "It's time we stopped for the night."

"We ought to cover as much ground as we can," he argued. "I can keep moving."

"You're freezing!" She touched his clammy face. "Mal!"

"Yeah, yeah. We're done for the night. I'll make a fire."

Malice and Beatrice worked together to start a blaze without going off the trail to find fuel. Forcing Gespar to have a seat and take off his chest plates, Beatrice ignored all of his insistence that he didn't need tending, and raising herself on to her knees she pulled back his collar to inspect his scratches.

There were two, side by side, short, and luckily not very deep. They had obviously bled but had dried hours earlier. She took a rag from her pack and wet it from her own water supply, before gently wiping the area. He flinched, despite her careful touch. It was swollen, but more alarming was the unnatural purple tingle around the cuts. It looked like poison in his veins. Deadly.

She tried to reason with herself that perhaps it was just a trick of the firelight. Beatrice swallowed her concerns, as Gespar wiped a fresh layer of sweat from his forehead. She opened one of her pockets, digging out the handful of yellow and orange flowers she had tucked away inside. She sighed and held out the wilted, crushed mess. "Will these still work?"

He nodded and reached to take them, but Beatrice pulled away. "I remember how you did it."

Beatrice crossed her legs, turning her full concentration to working the flowers into a paste. She tried to copy what she remembered Gespar doing.

"Watch her," Malice teased, watching her from across the fire. "She overcooks everything."

"Hey. Overcooked is better than undercooked," Beatrice shot back.

Despite her tone, she appreciated the banter. "You take a bite out of anything Mal gives you, and it's likely to bite you back."

"Maybe I ought to do the cooking from now on," Gespar laughed. But it sputtered out quickly, and his face went pale in the flickering light.

Bee caught the worried glance Mal threw her way, and as subtly as she could she shook her head in response. *It's going to be fine.*

"Alright," Beatrice adjusted her position to face the paladin again with the finished concoction in her hands. "Turn around."

"You don't have to do that."

Instead of arguing Beatrice stood up, walked around him, and began spreading the goo across the wounds. His shoulder tensed under her hand, and he sucked in a ragged breath. She flinched, afraid of hurting him. Only when his muscles relaxed, did she try again, more gently this time. Her fingers grazed his tanned skin, tracing the contour where his neck sloped into his powerful shoulders. Her mouth went dry. Gespar was hunched forward, his breathing steady and his posture relaxed. If her touch had lingered too long, he hadn't noticed. Finishing her work, she made him lie down, and he fell into a fitful sleep, almost instantly.

"He's gonna be ok?" Mal asked, keeping his voice down.

"I think so." She *hoped* so. He had to be. "I'm just not sure what's going on."

"And if he's not?"

If he wasn't... if she was honest, it would make their lives easier, wouldn't it? But that didn't mean she could stand the thought of it.

"You. Grumble. If I untie you so you can eat, do you promise to behave?"

"Let him starve." Malice growled, laying back on a bedroll by the fire.

"Well?" She pushed Gumby for an answer, and he nodded. Now that the sun was gone, the trees around them were kicked about by a steady breeze. Beatrice was grateful for it, despite the chill in the air. It made it easier to ignore the unnatural creaking and shrieking that had begun in the woods around them.

As Gumby ate he watched the treeline with darting eyes, looking like a rodent expecting a predator to appear.

"Did Mess do that to you?" Beatrice indicated the cut tips of his ears. Gumby remained quiet, nodding.

"Why?"

Gumby didn't answer, just kept looking around.

"Did you deserve it?" Beatrice pressed.

He looked up at her, silent, tears glistening in his wild eyes.

"He deserves worse." Malice spoke without lifting his head.

Maybe he did, but looking at him now, Beatrice regretted her words. Maybe he did deserve worse for his crimes, but what did that say about Bee and Malice? How different was a road bandit from a career-criminal, really? If he was scum destined for the dungeon, what were they? She was drawn from her thoughts by a sudden groan from Gespar.

"He's going to die, you know." Gumby's words were dry. His voice the steadiest Bee had ever heard it.

"We *don't* know that. He'll be fine."

"The trees got him... the woods will come to claim him. It will claim us all."

"Less talking. More eating." Malice sat back up, putting an end to the chatter with a glare.

That night Beatrice and Malice took turns staying awake, tending the fire and keeping an eye on the paladin's tossing and turning. It was the sort of night that stretches on endlessly, and just when they had begun to feel that they were trapped in an infinite bubble in time itself, the dawn began to creep in.

Eighteen

In the dewy morning, they waited as long as they could justify before Malice went to the paladin and gently shook him awake. "Morning, Sunshine. Ready to move again?"

"Of course," Gespar answered, but he struggled to stand. Malice helped him to his feet, and Beatrice insisted on checking his neck again. The scratches were still puffy, but the purple discoloration from the night before seemed to have lessened. Gespar however, still seemed weak. The dark circles under his eyes weighed heavily on his face.

"Do you want something to eat?"

"No, thank you." He packed his bedroll slowly, stopping several times to gather his strength.

"He's going to fall asleep standing up," Malice told Beatrice under his breath.

She sighed, then spoke. "Ges, we can all agree that we want to get through this damn forest as quickly as possible?"

"Yes?"

"If we make good time we could be out of here by tonight?"

"I believe so, yes."

"No offense, but you don't look like you're going to make good time today. Ride the horse."

He began to protest, but Malice cut him off. "She's right, Sunshine. It'll be better for all of us."

Being told firmly by both of them seemed to be enough to convince Gespar, who reluctantly pulled himself up onto the horse to ride alongside them. His head bobbed as they moved along, and he seemed to fall back into a sort of sleep at times. The horse handled it well, carrying her burden with a high head and a step entirely too jaunty for their surroundings. They didn't bother tethering Gumby to anything. His hands were tightly bound, and this deep in the Wander Wood he would do himself more harm by running from them.

In this manner, they did make good time, but as the afternoon set in and the trees around them showed no signs of thinning, they began to dread another night in the woods.

Gespar seemed to be coming out of his stupor, at least. He had even announced that he might try walking for a while, an idea that was met with disagreeing glares.

"You can stop sneaking looks at me like that," he told them. "I'm not about to drop dead."

Mal patted the horse gently on its shoulder. "Ah, nobody said you were. You just look so regal up there we can't help but stare. You're a distraction, Sunshine."

"All the more reason to come down."

"Do me a favor, and just finish out the day riding. You can walk tomorrow," Beatrice began to argue. Turning back, she saw that

Gespar looked slightly concerned, the horse seemed to have made the decision to stop on it's own. It picked up its front legs, stamping them down on the dirt again as if patting out a rhythm of warning.

A noise like a soft breeze started low and far in the woods. The travelers froze, listening intently. The sound began to grow until they were surrounded by the rustling of leaves as if all the trees had begun to shake.

They watched in horror as a shadow rolled out from the tree line before them, it seemed to separate itself from the larger darkness. Beatrice felt the hair on her neck rise as the sudden shock of fear hit her. Her muscles tensed, but she fought to keep her wits, to make sense of what she was seeing. As it came towards them, it became apparent that it was not a shadow, and indeed not even one entity. An uncountable mass of grey, mottled-looking spiders ran towards them, ranging from the size of a gnat to a plum. Bee jerked back, recoiling with a strangled yelp. As the swarm moved it grew larger, as more spiders ran from the trees to join the legion.

Her heart hammered in her chest. "What in seven hells," she hissed.

Her companions didn't answer.

"Bee," Mal called, tugging on her arm and freeing her from the paralyzing grip the shock had on her.

They hurried to back up, almost tripping over themselves. Malice grunted in frustration as the damned goat, against all logic, took a step forward. Before he could address the problem, a larger one arose.

Gespar called out, lowering his center of gravity just in time to avoid being thrown to the ground, as the horse turned abruptly and ran in to the woods, leaving the path behind.

"Mal!" Beatrice called. She drew her blade, though she wasn't sure what good it would do.

"I've got him!" And Malice ran into the woods after the horse and rider, leaving Beatrice alone with a horde of spiders, a goat, and a bound bandit.

"Hells!" Beatrice cried, retreating a few more steps as the spiders reached Darcy.

Gumby seemed frozen in place, either too scared or hopeless to attempt escape.

The swarm was as wide across as the trail now. Some began to crawl up the goat's legs, weaving through its hair, rolling over its back in sporadic grey waves. The goat never blinked, even as some of the arachnids crawled across its large black eyes and back around its face and neck.

Still, there were more, heading straight towards Beatrice. She took two more steps back before stumbling, falling on her ass in the dirt.

"Shit!"

The spiders reached her boots, and she began stomping furiously at any she could catch.

It wasn't enough, not even close.

Her cry turned into a scream and tore through the woods as the spiders began crawling up her legs. The itching, tickling sensation of hundreds of little legs began to incite panic. Beatrice swiped at her own body- brushing, slapping, willing it to stop. Fear had clouded her mind, and she had shut her eyes tightly, anticipating the swarm overtaking her face. She screamed again, suddenly terrified she would drown in the black, dark sea of the wretched things.

As a reflex, almost an instinctual action, Beatrice pulled the chain from her shirt, grasping it tightly. She had never been one to dwell on her mortality, but she couldn't help thinking now that this was a relatively shitty way to go. She wondered if maybe she ought to have stolen the Shadowgate Stone from Gespar after all... Maybe she ought to have kissed him a little bit more. Maybe, very probably, she should have listened to Malice more often. He was right more often than not, and *way* more often than she liked to admit. And maybe if she was going to die, it ought to hurry up and happen.

She opened her eyes in time to see the last of the spiders scurrying away, dispersing back into the woods. She was unharmed and so, it seemed, was the goat.

"Don't look so disappointed," she said to Darcy.

"How? How did you do that?" Gumby stared at her, bewildered. "Mess was right, you're blessed by some devil."

Beatrice quickly shoved the gem back into her shirt. "Don't be ridiculous. Who would bless this?"

She took a deep breath, trying to stop the spinning in her head.

"Which way did they go?"

"That way," Gumby pointed off into the distance, stepping closer. "Don't leave me, Beatrice."

"Yeah, alright. Stick close."

"What about the goat?"

"Shit." Darcy stared off into the woods. Beatrice looked at the animal, thinking for a moment.

"Oh no," she rehearsed. "Darcy is gone. Carried off by spiders. Real shame, am I right?"

"Uh... Yeah. Hard to watch."

She cocked her head to one side, then the other, considering it. "I mean really, I can't go dragging you with me," she told the goat, defensively.

Finally, she nodded to herself and turned to head off into the woods in the direction the rest had gone.

They moved as quickly as they could manage, with little attention to the direction they took. The shaking in the trees had stopped, and the eerie silence had fallen back into place. Dead underbrush crunched and crackled under Bee's feet as she moved. Beatrice took another deep breath, realizing she had begun to tremble all over. "No point being afraid now," she told herself. "I've already been covered in spiders, what could be scarier than that?"

As if testing her statement, a rustle in the brush to the left startled her. A few more steps and the chestnut horse came into view. "Dammit, Beatrice," she hissed under her breath.

The horse clopped haughtily in response.

To his credit, Gumby was almost as quiet as Beatrice, and he kept her pace with ease. Confident that she must be close to the others now and afraid of what she might find, she continued, quieter now, slinking through the trees. Normally slinking was one of her strengths. Now, she felt exposed. Every step seemed to go off like firecrackers in the underbrush.

It was Gespar she saw first, leaning against a tree facing the opposite direction. He looked over his shoulder as if watching for something in the woods. He looked very much intact and alert. Relief flooded her veins, settling her nerves.

"Ges!"

Her voice pulled him back around to face her, and the panic in his eyes caused Beatrice to stop mid-step. Gespar held out both hands towards her, palms out. Silently then, one hand still holding steady, he moved the other to his face, a single finger touching his lips.

Nodding at him as her heart began to pound, Beatrice brought her finger to her face. *I hear you. I'm quiet.*

He closed his eyes, and Beatrice watched as he took a deep, rattling breath. Looking at her again he waved her off, pointing back in the direction she had come from.

This again?

She rolled her eyes. He was still waving and pointing, and Beatrice was one wave away from just clomping over to him to ask what the hell was going on.

"Something is wrong," Gumby hissed behind her.

"Oh, really?" Her tone was biting, but she did pause for a moment.

Gespar's face was tense, his brow slightly furrowed and his eyes wide as he looked at her with a certain desperation. He was scared. Very scared.

As Beatrice watched, trying to work out what was going on; something moved behind the tree Ges braced himself against.

She watched in silent horror as a thin tree, no wider across than her leg, uprooted itself. The tree raised itself, until it hung four feet above the ground, creaking with the squeaking stress of wood pushed to its limits, dirt falling in clumps back to the ground.

The airborne tree moved slowly, purposefully forward, and then came back down to earth. It didn't drop with a crashing of splintering wood, but as if it had been set back down with all the awareness of a careful footstep.

She might have heard her name called, someone telling her to run. She didn't move. Something about seeing that the trees around her weren't tethered to the ground seemed to have rooted her to the spot instead.

In her peripherals, she became aware of another tree moving forward slowly.

Then two more.

Another.

Now the motion came from overhead. What had a moment before been just a part of the tangle of the canopy began to shift and separate. Branches from the wayward trees groaned as a vaguely round knot of foliage lowered itself. The mobile trees that served as its legs bowed out, the body came low to the ground, and Beatrice was staring, frozen, at four cloudy white eyes.

Gumby was making quiet wheezing noises behind her as if the air was sucked from his lungs.

"Back up," she whispered at him, "slowly."

She thought she heard the rustle of the brush behind her, but didn't turn to look.

The creature was something between a spider and a collection of trees, its body coated in mottled grey bark that looked tough as stone. Its legs grew gnarled branches that reached up and outward. It looked ancient and moved with the slow concentration of a creature that has been around forever and is confident that it will be around forever more.

A sort of menacing clicking sound came from the jaws of the creature. There was no heat, no dramatic spittle or growling aggression. Just cold menace.

As its face came closer, it occurred to Beatrice that maybe she ought to scream again. Its purple-tinged fangs clacked, inches from her face, its front legs raising threateningly.

No, Beatrice thought. *No point screaming after all.*

She brandished her blade, unsure that it would cut through the bark of this monster, but willing to make the effort. She braced herself. Still a shitty way to go, but at least it was better than a thousand of the little bastards.

She expected the blow to come from the front. Instead, a solid mass hit her from the left, knocking her down and pushing the air from her lungs. The snapping noise from the spider grew more agitated.

Looking to her left she saw Gespar on the ground next to her, catching his breath. He had knocked them a good six feet away from the striking distance of the beast, but it was already shifting, its long legs gliding through the other trees.

"Hurry! Get up!" Gumby begged them, squirming as though he could hardly bring himself to wait for them. He did though, waving frantically, urging them to move.

Gespar leaped to his feet, pulling Beatrice up with him. In a scrambling rush, they began putting distance between themselves and the creature. It wasn't difficult to do, and they were well assured of their escape until the trees around them began to shake again.

The leaves trembled, and the ground rolled. Ahead of them, in their path of retreat, Beatrice began to see the tree spider's smaller counterparts gathering again, building up, a sheet across the forest floor.

She stopped abruptly, pulling back against Gespar's grip on her hand.

"Beatrice?"

She shook her head, tugging backward again. "I can't."

She couldn't quite articulate exactly why she couldn't, or even precisely what it was she couldn't do, but she knew her legs simply weren't going to carry her back into the sea of spiders. She looked into his eyes, which glimmered back at her through a cocktail of emotions. Gespar dropped her hand, pulling out his sword and digging in his heels. Beatrice followed suit, grateful that she wasn't alone, guilty over holding him back.

The great spider was upon them again. It reared back, a sort of hissing noise issuing from its maw. Gumby wailed, moved to run through the small spiders, and then panicked. He doubled back, trying to weave around the creature's long legs. They creaked as it lunged toward him.

Whatever noise it made was drowned out by a much louder, more guttural sound. A growling, gurgling roar. Through the tangle of trees Malice came charging into view. His hammer was coiled for the strike as the monster had already begun to turn to face him.

He swung, making contact with the imperceptible joints of a leg. There was a sickening splintering noise, and the monster lurched. The injured leg was pulled up and inward towards its center, but the seven remaining were enough for it to complete its turn, with more speed than it had bothered using so far.

Malice stood steadfast, his teeth bared and his hammer held aloft as a dare. "Over here, you mossy bastard!"

The spider took the bait, lunging at Malice. His second hit stunned the beast for only a moment. It recovered and made contact with Malice's broad shoulder.

Beatrice screamed out as she watched the fangs graze the orc a second time. Running to the closest leg she swung with all the strength she possessed, her dirk bouncing off the thick skin, barely leaving surface damage. Malice cried out in pain but didn't buckle, already swinging again.

The spider reared back its front four legs, the closest thing to a scream the beast could muster echoing through the forest. The legs came slamming back down with a stuttering step before the thing scurried off into the depths of the wood.

Beatrice was at Malice's side before the spider was out of sight. "Mal! Are you ok? Let me see! Bend down, you big-"

"I'm fine," he assured her, but he did as she said. He squatted immediately, giving Beatrice access to the wounds on his shoulder. "Burns like nothin' though."

The wounds were strikingly similar to the ones Gespar had, except these cut through the surface of Mal's thick skin—more like knife wounds than surface scratches. The purplish hue was already spreading across Mal's shoulder, like smokey tendrils through his grey skin.

Beatrice's mouth went dry. "We've got to get out of here."

Gespar and Gumby hurried to join them as they stomped quickly back towards the path. The paladin looked over at Malice at the blood shining on his back. "It got you?"

"Mhff."

This seemed to put a halt to any conversation until they had found the horse, Beatrice stubbornly insisted that Malice ride it this time. He refused.

"I've already watched you trip over yourself twice, and it's only going to get worse. We've got to get out of here, and if your giant ass drops in the dirt, Ges and I won't be able to carry you far."

Malice hushed.

"It's the same thing that got the paladin." Gumby said, his face going a shade paler.

Beatrice nodded. "I think you're right. Look," Beatrice explained to Gespar. "The double marks, the purple color... I think that creature has some kind of venom. Only, Mal's wounds are deeper, the venom will be deep... And I don't have any more of those flowers to treat him with. I expect he's going to get very sick very fast... we need a healer."

Malice begrudgingly mounted the horse, who managed fine with the heavier load, though it had notably less pep in its trot. Gespar held tightly to the lead to discourage another sudden detour.

They made it back to the trail with no trouble. With some surprise (no one quite so surprised as Beatrice), they found Darcy the goat waiting for them right where she had been left. This is the way the party continued their journey through the Wander Wood, Beatrice leading the goat and walking closely alongside Malice and the horse, Gespar walking ahead. They didn't bother binding Gumby's hands again. It seemed cruel to leave him defenseless.

Before every little noise had been unsettling. Now it was downright terrifying. A branch would creak and the lot of them would jump to attention, spinning around, drawing weapons, anticipating doom.

Within an hour Malice had begun to slouch heavily. Two hours and the sweat poured off of him like mountain springs down a rocky slope. Three, and he was almost catatonic, bobbing and weaving on the back of the horse.

"We should rest." Gespar fell back, looking at Malice with a hardened concern.

Beatrice shook her head. "Not a chance. I'm not stopping until we're out of this damned wood."

"Rest would do him good."

"Sure it would, but it won't matter if we don't get him to a healer."

"Bee..."

She ignored him, marching ahead with her full supply of resolve. "Beatrice."

Still, she marched on. "Keep moving, Sunshine."

"Beatrice!" The urgency in his voice finally stopped her.

"I'm telling you-" she whipped around, finger pointed and ready to argue.

Instead, she watched helplessly as Malice's limp body slumped slowly to one side, falling from the horse and landing heavily on the ground.

NINETEEN

"**M**al!" Beatrice collapsed to her knees at the orc's side, shaking him with gentle persistence that poorly masked her growing panic. The sickly purple tinge had spread, coloring the skin around his eyes and mouth. "No, no, no."

"Look," Gespar reached out, stilling her hands, trying to offer assurance that he wasn't sure would matter. "It's labored, but he's still breathing."

"Do something!" Beatrice ordered.

Gespar could only look back at her with strain. What could he do?

"Do something!" she screamed this time, not just at him but at the whole wood and the world beyond it.

The forest seemed to hear her, and a small shudder rolled through the tree line like a wave.

"Bee, don't shout!"

She didn't care, he could see that in her face. She looked terrified and livid. Like she would cut him down if he didn't do something to save the orc. Like she would welcome the spider if it came down upon them now. Like she would gut it from the inside out if necessary. Gespar might have been afraid of her rage if the despair that caused it wasn't so apparent in her eyes.

"HELP!" She stood up, ignoring his pleas as she yelled into the evening air. She paced about them, helpless, and frantic, looking suddenly much younger. Gumby wrung his hands together, watching silently.

Gespar had no idea what to do. He wanted to help Malice. He wanted to help Beatrice. His heart ached for both of them. He was torn between shouting with her, and grabbing her to cover her mouth. Feeling for the talisman at his belt, he offered a silent prayer before undoing the golden button that held it in place and then refastening it to one of Malice's straps.

"What's going on here?"

The voice was unfamiliar. Male. It was authoritative and aged to a fine point, but not harsh. The source had appeared down the path. A tall, rugged man, with waved brown hair and a short dark beard peppered with white. The man next to him looked like an exact replica, de-aged by at least twenty years. There was no pepper in his stubbly facial hair, but still, he appeared older than Gespar. Or at least more worn.

Both men held sturdy-looking bows, ready to draw but pointed down at the ground. Gespar stood, his hand resting on the hilt of his sword. Beatrice didn't hesitate. "My friend is hurt. Please..."

The older man lowered his bow, looking at the group critically before putting away his weapon and stepping closer. "We have a healer in our village."

A wave of relief seemed to wash over Beatrice, her shoulders relaxing and her head hanging for a moment.

"Father," The younger man had come to Malice's side to inspect his condition. He wore a grave expression as he noticed the coloration clouding Malice's features. "It's the creature."

The elder sighed. "We'll do what we can, but we must hurry."

With the help of four extra arms, they lifted Malice carefully back over the horse's back, and hurried down the path with renewed energy. Almost immediately, they passed through a row of torches, carefully placed throughout the wood. They burned an inviting golden yellow. The line of them continued past their eyesight. It was the same yellow flame as the Church's shield fires, though that should have been impossible.

Graciously it was not much further until they reached the village proper.

Breaking through the treeline, they found themselves in a wide, expansive clearing in the wood. They passed between another row of torches, burning the same warm gold. The trail of torches wound around the clearing, forming a wall of light against the woods. A concentration of buildings lay at its center, hardly more than a dozen structures. The size and style of the houses seemed to vary. Some were built in the cozy northern style, with vertical planks and peaked roofs. A few were reminiscent of the Cestian style - flat, and square, and built with the profile taken into careful consideration, though the stones and mud that had been available in the Wander Wood gave it a very different feeling than the clean white and tan stones of Cestian.

They walked past a sprawling fenced-in pasture that, at first glance in the waning sunlight, Gespar thought was full of bears. Closer inspection proved that they were the largest hogs he had ever seen.

They reached a long wooden building and shuffled inside with some difficulty, caused by five people trying to carry one very large person through a very normal-sized door. They laid Malice in an empty bed, and Beatrice planted herself firmly at his side. The younger of the strangers promptly ran off, in search of the healer, the older explained.

"You had a close call with the creature of the Wander Wood?" he inquired.

Prompted by Beatrice's silence, Gespar answered the man. "We did. And only survived thanks to our friend here."

The man nodded. "It's a mighty warrior that can survive a run-in with the tree spider. We rarely travel past the firelight, and by the grace of the gods the creature doesn't either."

Gespar didn't know how to answer this. It seemed to him that it had taken a mighty warrior and a hell of a lot of luck, and even then, they hadn't gotten away unscathed.

"We don't get many travelers in our village, but we are glad to offer you what hospitality we have," the man continued. "I am Olesander. The man with us before is my son, Domlan."

Gespar shook his hand firmly. "We are grateful for whatever you can do."

It seemed like ages before Domlan returned with the healer, though in reality, it was probably mere minutes. The old woman that followed him in kept his pace, though each step that she took seemed to be an effort, as though she had to pull herself through the air for every inch she gained. In this manner she worked her way to Malice, inspecting his bare shoulder with a storm of tutting and hushed mutters under her breath.

Suddenly she spun around, the long black coils of her hair whipped lazily with her before settling back down. She opened a cupboard full of jars, plants, and all manner of items Gespar didn't recognize.

When she turned back to them Gespar got a good look at her face. It made him uneasy. Black soot smudged the area under her eyes, giving her an almost ghoulish expression.

"Start a fire," she ordered to the other occupants of the room. "Bring me water."

Olesander and Domlan scurried about to complete these tasks. Beatrice stood, rooted but not still. She fidgeted with her hands, wiping them on her clothes, pressing them to her face, knotting them together.

It was then Gespar realized Gumby stood in the corner, silent. Observing.

"Do you have anything like a jail in the village?" he asked Olesander.

"We've not had need, but there's a room in the old town center..."

"If we could take him there until we leave, I believe it would be better for everyone." He gestured to Gumby.

Olesander hesitated. "Bring him."

Gespar crossed the room, seizing the bandit by the arm.

"Beatrice!"

She hardly looked back. "Calm down, Gumby. Let them lock you up. It'll probably be the safest you've been in years. Don't give them a reason to be cruel and they won't be.... And if you *do* give them reason I'll drag you back into the woods myself and tie you to a tree."

He stopped struggling immediately, and let the men lead him from the building.

The dark of night was heavy enough on the village to prevent Gespar from seeing much more, but in a few glowing windows curious faces peered out at them as they moved down the path.

"When did you start taking orders from Beatrice?" Gespar asked Gumby in a low voice.

"As opposed to the orc that would see me hang? Or *you*, the Empire's servant?"

Gespar's jaw tightened. "I wouldn't expect you to cooperate with any of us."

Olesander directed them in to a long, low building with a pitched roof. The inside was dusty, and mostly empty. This place hadn't been used for anything in a long time, let alone the small lock-up in the back.

"Some of us don't have your title, Paladin. Or the Orc's strength. When you have little power of your own, you learn quickly who to position yourself close to for your own survival."

"Like Mess?"

"For very different reasons, yes."

"Forgive me if I don't trust your judgement."

"I couldn't care less. I have seen that woman cut down men that terrified me. I have seen her emerge from a blanket of spiders unscathed. You would do well to remember that neither of you faired so well in either situation."

Gespar didn't respond, letting Olesander lock the small man in the chamber.

"We'll bring him some blankets and water."

"Thank you. I know we've brought an unusual situation to your door with no information-"

"I don't need details. Your conduct will have to speak for itself. For now, go back to your friend. Can you find the way?"

Gespar nodded gratefully, and found his way back to Beatrice and Malice.

The next several hours were spent watching the old woman cleaning Malice's wounds. She prepared ingredients that even Gespar was unfamiliar with, tended the scratches, and sewed the wounds where they cut the deepest.

At one point her hand happened to graze the paladin's talisman hanging on Mal's leathers. Her eyes shot to Gespar, and she sized him up as he stared back at her. She looked carefully at Beatrice, who was oblivious to all but Mal. Then the old woman turned back to her work without a word.

Gespar observed this work carefully, but he watched Beatrice just as closely. She cycled between her fidgeting, holding on to Mal's arm firmly, assisting the healer in whatever small tasks she could, and sitting in the chair by the bed watching intently as the dark circles under her eyes grew and darkened just as the night itself.

Finally, the old woman paused, letting out a heavy breath as if she had been holding it for hours straight.

"Well." When she spoke her voice seemed to roll around in her throat. "That's all there is to be done tonight."

She eyed Beatrice slumped in the chair. "Go get some rest, child. I can't promise he'll recover, but he won't be dying tonight."

"I'm not going anywhere," Beatrice insisted, but her voice was hoarse with exhaustion

"Mm," the old woman nodded her wide head. "I see."

She crossed to the fire, burning comfortably in the hearth. She opened a kettle perched over the flames, stirring the contents with slow and deliberate strokes before replacing the lid, lifting it, and pouring the steaming liquid into a clay cup. "In that case, you had better have a cup of tea."

Her smile was crooked and kind, her deep-set eyes warm as she handed Beatrice the cup.

"Thanks..."

The old woman watched Beatrice take a grateful sip, then she turned to Gespar and winked. He smiled back out of polite habit, despite his utter confusion at the gesture.

"Now, I am going to rest." She held a hand up when Beatrice moved to protest. "If you want me up and about to tend him tomorrow, you want me to rest. Drink."

Beatrice obeyed.

"That's understandable. Please, rest yourself." Gespar bowed. "Thank you for all you've done, Miss..."

"Willow. And you're very welcome, Lad. There's a room in the back there with a few clean beds and a washing tub. You'll have to fetch your own water though. There's a well towards the center of the village and a clean creek runs east of here. Just don't go past the torch-line."

Willow snuck a glance at Beatrice, who sipped deeply with her eyes closed. "I expect the good man Olesander will arrange for someone to bring you something warm to eat in the morning."

Beatrice exhaled, setting the cup down on the bedside table.

"Good tea, dear?" Willow asked her.

"It was wonderful, thanks."

"Good, good."

The old woman smiled straight through to her eyes and turned back to Gespar. "You might want to carry her, Lad. She'll find her legs go jelly before the rest of her."

"What the hells do you mean?" Beatrice stood suddenly, her legs indeed gave out underneath her. She caught the chair, setting herself back into it carefully. "Whoa..."

"Yes, exactly. You're alright, but you best take it easy."

"You *poisoned* me?" Beatrice attempted to stand again. Gespar moved to her quickly, easing her back down with gentle hands.

"Don't be foolish. It's just something to get you to sleep. You need the rest as bad as the orc, and I can see clear as day that you don't intend to take it. And if *you* don't sleep, I doubt the young man will either."

Beatrice looked at him, surprise in her eyes, a question threateningly perched on her tongue. Gespar looked away. He couldn't deny Willow's words, and he sure as hell couldn't explain that to Beatrice.

"She'll be asleep within the hour." Willow told him. "Maybe two, if she's particularly stubborn. *Which it seems may be the case,*" she finished under her breath.

"Thank you," was all Gespar could think to say.

"You-" Beatrice glared at the old woman. "Who do you think you are?"

"I know, dear. I'm a terrible old hag. But, I'm the terrible old hag that's taking care of you and your friends. Now, goodnight to all of you."

And with that, Willow left them alone.

Beatrice sighed, rubbing at her face with both hands.

"Are you alright?" Gespar asked, kneeling next to her chair.

"Fine. I feel like my head might swim off, and my arms weigh as much as Mal's-" She stopped short, looking at Malice sleeping on the bed next to her.

His breathing was stable now, normal even, and although his eyes were still surrounded by deep purple circles, his skin was not as chalky pale as it had been earlier in the night.

"You big jerk..." she whispered to Mal, but all the anger had left her voice.

Gespar felt his heart in his throat as he watched her. Not for one moment during their short but eventful time together had she looked this vulnerable. It made him uneasy. He had seen enough to be certain that this was a woman that hid behind carefully built walls and whatever the reason for them, her walls were gone at this moment.

"How did you two meet?" he asked her.

Beatrice didn't look at him. Her gaze stayed on Malice, a hint of a smirk twinkled in her eyes for a moment as if she had recalled something funny. After a moment, it melted into a frown. He was certain she wouldn't answer.

"When I was young, just getting started, I used to run with a small crew in Beacon," she began.

Gespar scoffed dramatically, feigning shock. "Surely you weren't criminals!"

This caused her to roll her eyes, but at least she looked at him now, a controlled grin tilting her pillowy lips. It made her look a little more like herself.

"We were nothing more than glorified street urchins, running jobs around the city for coppers. We had fun though. My best friend, Vivienne Dupont... We were so much alike."

"I'm not sure the world could handle two of you."

"It couldn't, most of the time," she agreed. "Then, there was her brother, Penny. He was too clever for his own good. And there was Ramsey... Ramsey Galmen... We were..."

She shifted in her seat, her eyes closed heavily. "We were happy. Foolish, and rowdy, and full of shit. But we were happy."

Her eyes hadn't reopened, and after a long moment, Gespar was sure she must have been asleep, but she began again, her voice heavy and slow.

"We bit off more than we could chew. Took a job that sent us up north. We were supposed to acquire some urn from an orc camp. Turns out the 'camp' was a whole village, and they were on high alert."

She opened her eyes again, though they were heavy and distant. "We decided that the best plan was to split up. I would sneak through the camp and head for the urn, and they would each go to opposite corners and cause distractions. I did my part, but no distraction ever came. They left me. And I was caught by two dozen orcs, holding their damn urn."

She pushed weakly on the arms of the chair, to no avail. It took Gespar a moment to realize she was attempting to stand. "Easy, Bee."

He reached out and touched her arm. "You want to lay down?"

She nodded weakly. Gespar hesitated a moment, uncertain how to proceed. Finally, he stood, lifting her as gently as he could, with a few awkward resets, and an acute awareness of where his hands were placed. "You're heavier than you look."

"Watch it," she whispered, her voice as warm as spiced mead where it tickled his ear. She wrapped her arms feebly around his neck. Her whole body was as warm, and the way it pressed against him was an unwelcome reminder of the incident in the alley in Bay. The taste of her skin, the sweet sound of her breath catching in her throat. Gespar gulped, pushing the thoughts away. "You haven't mentioned Mal at all yet," he prompted.

"Right. The orcs threw me in this fenced-in pit. And there he was. Locked up for fooling around with the clan leader's wife."

"Malice? I wouldn't have guessed."

"He has a type. A type we don't run into often, luckily. You've heard of the tall, dark and handsome type? Mal has a weakness for *massive*, dark, and handsome. The beefier, the better."

"Noted."

Reaching the door to the back room that Willow had indicated, he carefully shifted Bee's weight to swing it open.

"But, I sized him up quick. Made a few comments about how it would take someone real impressive to get out of there. Bet him he wasn't the strongest in the clan. And, boom. We broke out of the pit, took out everyone that got in our way, got the stupid urn, and got out alive.

I promised him part of the pay for the urn, and he came back with me. By the time we got back to Beacon, I had talked him into sticking around. With him around, it would open up new job opportunities and the coin would flow for both of us. And it did, sort of."

Gespar laid her down on one of the beds, absentmindedly brushing her hair out of her face for her.

"And, what about your friends?"

Bee sighed, curling herself into a comfortable position. "I almost could've forgiven them for abandoning me. We all do things we aren't proud of when we're backed into a corner. But, when I got home, there was no regret for what they had done. Ramsey wasn't mourning. Wasn't heartbroken over losing me. He was warm and cozy in Vivienne's bed. Probably had been for years."

Her voice was cold and her face emotionless as she recounted the memory.

"You loved him?"

"I did. My mistake. We were going to catch a big break and move to Cestian. Live in one of those warm little coastal towns where all the colorful flowers grow.

After that, Mal and I made a point of getting the bigger jobs, doing better than them... *being* better than them. Turn's out he's a better friend anyway.

...He's all I've got."

She finished, her voice barely a whisper. The worry traced soft lines between her brow, even as her eyes closed. "Bee..."

He realized with more than a little relief that she had fallen asleep in earnest now, sparing him the impossible task of coming up with soothing words to try to ease her pain. He rested his hand softly on her cheek for an indulgent moment before retreating to a bed on the opposite side of the room.

He didn't realize how exhausted he was until he lay down. He should have, *could have*, been asleep almost instantly. Instead, he found himself thinking for another hour about these new friends. What would he do if Malice didn't survive? If this woman lost her one companion on his job?

He thought of Beatrice, listening to her soft breathing in the dark. This woman baffled him, but he was drawn to her like a light in the dark. She was so soft, and so far from it. She said so much, but never quite enough. She was beautiful and fearsome, divine and demonic.

What in seven hells would happen when they made it to Triad City?

TWENTY

When Beatrice awoke the next morning Gespar was still sleeping soundly on the other side of the room. She noted, with some surprise, that she had no headache, no drowsiness, no side effects at all from whatever the old hag had given her. In fact, she felt incredibly well-rested and clear-headed.

She couldn't help but watch the paladin for a moment before leaving him alone to rest.

She hastened out to the room where Malice slept. Quietly slipping through the door, she halted. There standing quietly at Malice's bedside was a small child. The girl leaned her elbows on the edge of the bed, peering with innocent curiosity at his face. Bee watched as the girl took a small finger, and reaching as carefully and slowly as a flower bending to the sun, she touched one of his fangs.

Beatrice didn't mind children. They were just small people, after all. And Malice was always so understanding and welcoming to them, just as he had been to that poor boy in Beacon. He would scold Bee if she gave the girl a hard time. But, she couldn't resist messing with her. *Just a little.*

"Good morning," Beatrice said loudly. The girl jumped twice her height, pulling her hand back to her chest. Her cheeks shone rosy pink when she looked at Beatrice.

Beatrice crossed to the other side of the bed, looking him over. He looked the same as he had the night before, breathing soundly but looking terrible. She wasn't sure if she should be relieved or discouraged. They stood in silence for several minutes.

The girl pushed her wild, golden hair out of her face. "Is he a monster?"

There wasn't fear in her voice, just interest.

"Nah. He's just a guy."

The girl looked slightly unconvinced, inspecting Mal's face more carefully.

"You've never seen an orc before?" Beatrice asked.

The girl shook her head.

"They look pretty different on the outside, but they've got the same sort of hearts on the inside. If you asked him, he would say I'm the one that looks funny," Beatrice smiled. "He's my best friend."

The girl pushed her hair back out of her face again, though it immediately fell back into place. She analyzed Beatrice with the keen, critical eye that only children possess.

"You're very pretty," she finally decided.

"Well... thanks."

"Dad says your friend might die." She looked back at Mal. "You must be sad."

"I must be..." Beatrice didn't give the comment time to land. "How old are you?"

"Five. But everyone says I'm a big girl already."

"I can tell," Beatrice agreed.

The front door of the building opened with a groan. Domlan came in carrying a basket with warm, pleasant smells wafting from it.

"Chammy, what are you doing in here?" he asked, setting the basket down. "Leave the poor folks be. Go play."

"She's alright," Beatrice assured him.

"Yeah, Daddy. I'm alright!" She pushed the wayward hair back again.

Domlan held his hands up in surrender. "I've brought some fresh bread and stew. I'll admit its leftovers from what I made yesterday and I'm not the best cook..."

"Don't sell yourself short. I'm sure it's fine."

Chammy giggled, shaking her head.

"Ah...Well, in any case, anything is better than nothing. Thank you, Domlan."

"You can call me Dom." He dipped his chin to her. "He's?"

"The same."

"Willow will be by shortly, though there isn't much to do now but wait. I'll tell you straight, ma'am. The creature of the Wander Wood doesn't leave many survivors. It's rare anyone makes it this far from the south edge of the wood. If they do it's usually not a happy tale."

Beatrice moved around the bed, acknowledging the words but finding nothing to say in response.

"Have you seen the farm animals yet? We have lots. We have more animals than people."

"Have *you* seen them?" Beatrice teased, pushing the hair out of Chammy's face herself this time.

"Didn't I tie your hair back this morning?" Dom asked her.

"Yeah, but I took it down. It was pulling."

Her father sighed. "Do you still have the ribbon, at least?"

She held up her wrist, where the ribbon in question was tied messily.

"I'll tell you what," Beatrice said. "You take me to see the animals, and I'll braid your hair for you. Deal?"

The little girl's eyes lit up with a grin. She nodded enthusiastically. Beatrice looked over Malice once more, squeezing his arm before she followed the girl out into the open air.

Chammy (short for Chamomile) became Beatrice's shadow from that moment. She spent a decent portion of every day being dragged around the village by the girl, being shown every inch of it in turn. Sometimes it was to meet one of the locals, who Beatrice found were as varied as their homes and in short supply. Within the first three days she had exchanged pleasantries with nearly thirty good, salt-of-the-earth folks, and Chammy proudly announced she knew everyone. She was no longer a stranger.

<hr />

Gespar didn't fare quite as well, perhaps because he was often left to sit watch over Malice while Bee was being paraded around the town.

He didn't mind it. Beatrice only began to recede into the vulnerable state she had been in that first night when she sat in silence by Malice for an extended time. As if she fell into her thoughts if she was still for too long.

He lived for the moments they would come to the room together, Beatrice teaching Chammy how to braid her hair, recounting for the thousandth time the tale of their journey through the woods, or listening to the girl read from an old book of Cestian folk tales.

Dom, who had been overly apologetic about his daughter the first day, settled down. In fact, he seemed to watch the antics of the woman and child as fondly as Gespar did. *And why not,* Gespar thought to himself. Hadn't it taken him less time to notice Beatrice's charms? She was a beautiful woman. Clever, kind, and stubborn in such an aggravating way that somehow against all logic it was captivating. On top of it all, what could more quickly endear one to another person than the affection of their own child? Not that Beatrice seemed to notice any budding affections, or that any were even made apparent. Still, Gespar had a feeling he could guess the man's thoughts with more accuracy than he had any right to.

The evening of their fourth day in the village, Gespar and Beatrice were sat down for a meal with their hosts. The spread was impressive for such a remote village. These people did well for themselves in the Wander Wood. There was an abundance of fresh vegetables. The crops here seemed to thrive, and they lost so little to pestilence, like the farms in the midlands always did. The meat came from the finest livestock they had ever seen, which they were told fell ill so rarely it was almost unheard of. There were sweets made from cream and fruit, drizzled with honey collected from the army of bees they kept at the outskirts of the village.

The things they couldn't make or grow themselves they acquired from their rare trips out of the woods, by trading the thick and sturdy silk they gathered from the trees for quite a high price. The northern edge of the Wander Wood was a half a day from the village they said, which was the best news Gespar and Beatrice had heard in quite a while.

As the conversation waned and the sun began to sink in the sky, Beatrice derailed the pleasantries to talk about Malice. No one was surprised, this was how it had gone every night.

"Has there been any sign that Mal is improving?" she asked Willow.

"You ask questions you already know the answer to."

"He's survived this long, surely the worst must be over? If he wasn't going to make it wouldn't he be getting worse?"

The old woman shook her head. "I don't know." But the look in her eyes said that she knew *something*. "He doesn't grow worse. He doesn't fade away. As if something were sparing him, *protecting him* from the worst of the venom." She caught Gespar's eye, her stare meaningful. "But he isn't getting better, either... as if he's in some equilibrium. None of us have any way of knowing how long it will last, or which way he'll go in the end. He could wake up tomorrow, or he could waste away from starvation without ever opening an eye."

Beatrice's face went red, her eyes were glassy. She nodded but didn't speak. Chammy reached over and patted her hand in the best attempt at comfort she could manage.

"The real question is, how long can you afford to delay your journey here? How long are you willing to wait?" Willow continued.

"As long as it takes." Beatrice answered shortly. "We aren't leaving him. That's not even up for discussion."

She looked at Gespar for confirmation. He avoided her gaze, unable to give the answer she wanted. They still had a job to do. An important one. The thought of that damned Stone, hidden away under the bed he'd been occupying, ate at his thoughts. They had to return it to the temple. *Soon.*

"We can't leave." She spoke directly to him now. "What if we left and-" Her voice caught in her throat. "What if we weren't here?" She finished, quietly.

The table had grown silent, blanketed by tension. "Let's talk about this later, Bee."

She stayed quiet.

"It goes without saying, I think, that you are welcome for as long as you need." Dom added, his cheeks flushed under his stubble. "Indefinitely, if that was something you wanted. I mean, you don't have to move on at all, if you don't want to."

Looks darted round the table.

"It seems some of us have things to think on, and things to discuss. Perhaps it's a good time to turn in for the evening?" Olesander chimed in, standing.

There was no argument, and the party dispersed. Gespar and Beatrice returned to the building that had housed Malice, walking in silence. Entering, Beatrice crossed the room and planted herself at the end of Mal's bed, looking at him intently, silently willing him to wake up.

"Beatrice-" Gespar spoke softly.

"You're really going to ask me to leave him here? Like this?" She didn't turn around.

"You know this is important Bee, I wouldn't even think of asking if it wasn't."

"And Mal isn't?"

"Bee, you know that's not what I meant. I don't want to leave him either. But you've seen the damned *thing*. I won't feel better until it's locked up somewhere safe."

Beatrice didn't respond.

"Mal would want the job done," he pointed out.

"Don't tell me what he would want." Beatrice turned on him now. "You don't know what he would want. You don't know anything."

She jabbed him in the chest with an accusatory finger. There was hurt in her eyes, and she was close enough that Gespar could see they were damp with tears that she refused to let fall. Without hesitation, he pulled her close, wrapping her tightly in his arms, and burying his face in her dark hair. "I'm sorry, Beatrice," he whispered.

She gripped his shirt tightly, and for a moment he thought she would shatter, that she would cry into his chest. He held her tightly as if it might hold her together. Gespar closed his eyes, breathing in the scent of her hair and praying that he could take away some of her pain. It was not a prayer to any god.

She shifted in his arms, raising her head and bringing her gaze to his, and her lips close enough that their breath mingled. Gespar couldn't think of anything but kissing her again. He fought against it, against himself, but found himself inching closer.

He couldn't. He would never.

And yet, his lips brushed against hers, barely, softly, like a whisper. His breath caught in his throat.

After a moment Beatrice stiffened, pushing him away. "Let go of me."

"Bee?" He stepped toward her, his brow furrowed in confusion. Her face was flushed, but dry.

She backed away. "Don't."

Her tone was sharp. Biting even, but he couldn't read the emotion in her eyes.

"Give me one more day. Leaving him is... Let me think about this. We'll discuss it tomorrow night. Can I have that?"

"Of course."

Without another word she walked out the door, leaving him standing alone, staring at Malice. Trying not to think of the darkness constantly fighting to escape the chest under the bed.

TWENTY-ONE

Beatrice wandered the village aimlessly, lost in her thoughts. Without intention, she found herself in the dimly lit town center.

"You alive, Gumbus?"

There was silence for a moment.

"I'm well fed. Moderately comfortable. And otherwise, I'm left alone." Gumby's voice came from behind a closed door with only a small window cut from the top half. She had to position herself to one side to see where he sat at a small table within. "It's like a fucking luxury vacation compared to some of the nights I've seen before. You were right."

"Well, I'm glad you're enjoying your stay. Appreciate it while it lasts. We'll be leaving soon."

"You don't sound like you're ready to move on." His voice wavered slightly, the casual curiosity in his voice sounding forced.

"Yeah well, we have business to get on with. Things we can't put off forever."

Gumby's eyes found her, his head tilting inquisitively. "I'm sure. And, the orc?"

"Recovering. Don't you worry, if he isn't ready to go on I'll make sure you find your way to Triad city."

Gumby's hands flexed against the table's surface. When he spoke again, there was a challenge laced in his tone. "You would leave him?"

Beatrice had heard quite enough. She didn't have to answer to Gumby, of all people. Especially when he was obviously trying to get a reaction. She turned away. "I'll leave you to luxuriate in peace."

"It must be very important, whatever 'business' you have with the paladin."

"Know when to quit."

"I'm not trying to guilt you, Beatrice. Making difficult choices is part of being a leader. It's not easy being a big hero."

Beatrice stopped, half way out the door. "I never claimed to be anything of the sort."

"Those that *claim* it rarely are. Do you want to be?"

"I want you to stop talking, Gumby."

The next morning Beatrice woke early.

She checked on Malice. No change.

Wandering out to the pastures, she watched Beatrice the horse grazing the damp grass by the fence. Walking further, nearly to the tree line at the far edge of the fields, Beatrice found Darcy. The goat stared into the woods, and Beatrice stared at the goat. The creature looked blank inside, nothing behind the eyes but the void. Beatrice tried it for a moment. She closed her eyes and attempted to clear her head. She tried to recall the last time she had made a decision based on logic, or right and wrong. She couldn't remember. Every choice she made seemed clouded by emotion—pride, or desire, or fear.

Chammy came skipping through the grass not long after.

"There you are, Bee!" She sidled up next to Beatrice, wrapping her little arms around the top wrung of the fence. "Will you braid my hair?"

"Only if you braid mine too." Beatrice smiled at the girl, but Chammy scrunched up her face.

"You look sad today."

"I am. A little," Beatrice admitted.

"Why?"

"You ever know you have to do something, but you don't *want* to do it?"

Chammy climbed up to sit on the top of the fence and began to messily braid Beatrice's hair. She was quiet for a long moment, thinking. Finally, she answered. "Every year at the harvest moon we take one of the giant hogs out to the woods and we leave it for the tree-spider. *I* don't like it because I think it's sad for the hog and his family. But Daddy says we have to."

"That is..." It was not lost on Beatrice that no one had mentioned this before now. "I guess that's a pretty good example of how I'm feeling, yeah."

"What do you have to do?"

"I think it's time for me to leave, but I don't want to leave Malice behind. And I have to leave him to do something *else* I don't want to."

"I could watch him for you. Until you get back," Chammy offered helpfully.

"You would probably be better at it than me."

They each turned around and Beatrice began to neatly and carefully tie back the girl's flaxen locks. "I should make you practice this yourself if I'm leaving."

"I can do it now. I just like it better when you do it."

The quiet of the early morning was heavy on the fields, and the air hadn't begun to warm to the sun yet. Beatrice noticed that Darcy had turned and was staring directly at them.

"What does the goat want?" Chammy whispered.

Before Beatrice could answer, the hissing sound of disturbed grass broke the morning silence. Beatrice turned with a jolt. Her relief at seeing it was only Domlan hurrying towards them was short-lived. She couldn't bring herself to call out to him or meet him halfway. She was frozen, her stomach flipping with a fear she dare not name.

He reached them all too soon. "You need to go back to the house."

It was all she needed to hear. Beatrice ran. Chammy moved to jump off the fence in pursuit, but Domlan caught the child in his arms, holding her back.

She wouldn't cry. Not yet. She braced herself for whatever she might find, preparing mentally and emotionally for what she was sure was heartbreak.

Bursting through the door of the house, Beatrice's mental preparations for disaster exploded in her face. Malice lay where he had been for days, unconscious and pallid, but breathing. Willow sat calmly in a chair at the far side of the room, looking little more than annoyed. Gespar, red in the face and fuming, stood in the center of the room, his sword drawn.

"What in seven hells is going on here?" Beatrice demanded.

Both of them turned to look at her.

"Go on then, tell her," Willow said.

"They're heretics. Demon worshipers."

"What?"

"She was attempting to use healing magic on Malice."

"Do you even hear yourself, child?" Willow asked.

"Healing magic? Is that possible?" Beatrice felt her pulse quicken.

"It calls on the realm of life and death."

"The realm of Din. The *demon lord.*" Gespar practically spat the words.

"Is it possible?" Beatrice asked again, "Would it work?"

"Beatrice!"

Willow ignored Gespar's outburst. "It might. I can't say. The lord Din's magic can heal when all else fails, but if it is truly his time to leave this world even a God's magic won't change his fate."

"I have seen firsthand the evil that demon magic puts in people's hearts. It grows *death* as much as life. She claims to heal today, but she might kill in the name of Din in her next breath!" Gespar shouted. "It is my duty to keep the Empire clean of such malevolence, and I will not let you use demon magic on this orc!"

"That is not your choice to make!" Beatrice raised her voice. "I don't give a damn who's magic she calls on if it saves him! If your Triad gods can heal him then, by all means, call on them instead!"

"He already tried that," Willow interjected, holding up a golden talisman baring the Triad insignia.

Beatrice looked to him for an explanation, which Gespar seemed reluctant to give.

Willow answered for him, "It's a paladin's secret weapon. A blessing from their patron. This one was bestowed by Vedett. It is a shield of sorts. Protection against many a threat. It kept our friend here from growing more ill, but only a boon from Din can truly pull him from the brink of death, back to the living world."

"Then do it."

"Beatrice, please!" He reached a hand towards her, desperation weighing down his words.

"Don't you 'Beatrice, please' me! You listen to me just this one damn time! I. Don't. Care." Beatrice drew close to him, her face mere inches from his, her eyes narrow and her voice piercing. "I don't care about your Triad gods or your empirical rules. I would break a thousand laws for Malice. If you're going to drag me off to some Triad dungeon, then *do it*, Paladin Fairchild. But you're going to have to wait until after the crime is committed."

Beatrice didn't look away, staring into his eyes- daring him. Begging him to see reason.

"The God's will not protect you, or these people from any wrath they invite upon themselves willingly," he warned.

Beatrice laughed in his face. "Is that a threat? Maybe the gods need to worry about their own protection if they want to fuck with me and mine."

Gespar's jaw clenched. Beatrice knew her words were trying, but she didn't care. She was surprised though when his response wasn't as biting.

"I can't just stand by and let this happen."

His shoulders fell, his voice quieter. His eyes had grown heavy with defeat. Maybe sadness, too, but Beatrice didn't have time to process the nuances of his emotions. Not until Malice was better.

"Then you had better wait outside." She stepped aside to punctuate her words.

Gespar stared back at her, but she could see his resolve as it cracked. He looked to Willow for a moment before sheathing his sword. "I hope you're making the right choice, Beatrice." And he left them.

As soon as the door was shut Beatrice let out a long, shaky breath, her bravado failing her.

"Don't be angry with the young man. A dog is only as good as the ones that train it." Willow stood, crossing to a basin by the bed, carrying a pitcher.

"He's a good man," Beatrice said, somewhat defensively. "Perhaps too pure and trusting, but his intentions are always good."

"Still sounds like a dog to me." The old woman scoffed and busied herself with the preparations.

"But he doesn't listen to his own heart, hell, even his own mind sometimes. If he doesn't start soon he's going to get himself in trouble."

Willow laughed a wispy laugh, like branches rubbing together. "Before it's all said and done, you *both* have to learn that lesson, child. Or we'll all be in trouble."

"What do you mean by that?"

Willow stopped, her ancient eyes digging deeply at Beatrice. "Have you ever seen the Gods' magic?"

Beatrice thought of the Shadowgate Stone, the living, grasping darkness and the uneasy feeling it left in the air around it even when the darkness was contained. Her hand reflexively grasped at the glowing stone under her shirt. "I have."

"Raw magic is like an idea in its purest form. The ideas of the One true creator. The Gods, as beings of the divine realms, have control over it, they are *made* of it. If it's pulled from the realms, summoned to our own, the earth absorbs it like a dehydrated field absorbs the rain. But if it's contained...it can be held on to. Set to a purpose."

"If it's that simple, why isn't the world flooded with blessed artifacts? Why don't we all ask the gods to bless all our things?"

"Because not just anyone can make the connection, can they? It takes the right plea, to the right god, from the right person. A high-cleric, a Cestian oracle, a very wise old woman who has devoted her life to such things... but, some people are just more connected to the divine realms, through raw emotion or some unknowable touch."

Willow poured the pitcher of clean water into the basin and closed her eyes. She sprinkled crumbled dry flowers that Beatrice didn't recognize on the water's surface, and muttered a prayer under her breath.

At first, nothing happened, and doubt settled in Bee's heart. She held her breath, willing it to work, pushing the doubt away. It *had* to work. It *would* work. The water stirred, as though the ground underneath them had shaken. It was only a small movement on the surface, but certain, and growing in intensity.

The water began to boil, deep rolling waves disrupting the basin. Beatrice realized with a start that she had taken hold of the side of the bowl, but she couldn't say when or why. She let go, as fine grey steam began rising from the tumultuous water. Willow blew the steam away, and instantly the basin calmed.

The old woman looked at Beatrice. "Fascinating..."

"You mean you haven't done this before?" Beatrice asked incredulously.

"I have."

"And this will work? It's going to bring him back?"

Willow considered the question before answering. She carefully scooped a cup full of the water. "I am optimistic, but I can't make promises. All magic has limitations."

"Sure, limitations. They only have the power of their own realm, right? A raw idea is powerful, but it's still only one idea."

"You aren't wrong, but that's not the whole picture. Today, we ask for healing. We ask Din's blessing to bring your friend from the grasp of death. That is his wheelhouse, after all. Life. Death. The space in between. But life is like a story, Beatrice. And every story must come to an end. If his story has come to an end, if it is truly his time... then even Din won't interfere."

"It's not his time." Beatrice insisted. "It can't be."

"I have a feeling you are right, child."

Willow carefully tilted Malice's head, pouring the water into his mouth and then holding it shut, coaxing it down. She then grabbed a clean cloth, wetted it in the basin, and began to gently soak the wound on the orc's shoulder.

Beatrice sat down, watching the healer's actions, clocking each movement. It was still early in the day when Willow stopped, turning away from Malice. "Would you like a cup of tea, Beatrice?"

"Not a chance. I don't accept tea from strange old ladies anymore." She narrowed her eyes at the healer.

"Want me to brew up something for the paladin? It might make him easier to deal with for the rest of the day."

"I have a feeling that won't be necessary."

"Fine then." Willow handed her Gespar's talisman. "You have good instincts, and something more. Trust in yourself."

Beatrice traced the engraved symbol in the metal and then tucked the thing away in her pocket. Willow left her in silence, and Beatrice turned all her attention to Malice, watching intently for any hint of change. The wait was excruciating and the silence maddening, but she did not watch in vain. A few hours passed, and Beatrice realized with an overwhelming wave of relief that the bruise-like color to Mal's skin was without a doubt receding.

She suddenly found herself exhausted by the weight of the morning and the preceding days, and relieved enough to surrender to it. Beatrice slowly slumped in the chair, falling asleep.

TWENTY-TWO

"**D**amned...Storyteller..." Malice slowly woke, groggy in the head, in an unfamiliar room, not quite sure what events had led to this moment. This must be something like a hangover, he imagined.

Beatrice was fast asleep in a chair close to him, curled into what appeared to be an incredibly uncomfortable position.

"Did you say something?" Sunshine was across the room, somehow managing to look more uncomfortable than Beatrice, despite his normal, upright seated position. "Mal?"

"Huh?" Mal tried to remember what he had even said, shifting himself to sit up in the bed as the paladin crossed to his side. "I dunno. I was having some sort of dream. I don't remember now."

Their voices caused Beatrice to stir. She opened her eyes, furrowing her brow. She looked as lost as Malice had felt for a moment. Her gaze settled on Gespar. Malice, just coming out of his mental haze, was still acutely aware of some tension between the two. Proving this theory, Gespar looked away from Bee quickly, and after another silent moment of watching the paladin's face, her eyes fluttered to Malice. She jumped out of the chair, tipping it to the floor with her momentum.

She grabbed his hand, squeezing it with a bit too much force. There was no crooked, smart tilt to her smile, no sarcastic remark. Only relief. *Must have been serious*, Malice thought to himself.

"How are you feeling?" Bee asked him.

"A bit stiff. But, otherwise? Fine."

"Gods, Mal! We thought you were- " Beatrice stopped short, shaking her head. "You're just *fine*?"

"Well, I guess I'm pretty damn hungry."

Bee rolled her eyes, but relaxed her vice grip on his fingers.

"I can fix that!" Gespar said. "I brought lunch."

"That was thoughtful," Beatrice responded simply, as Gespar brought out fresh bread rolls and a vegetable soup that seemed to have gone cold while he waited. Gespar didn't answer her, just nodded before taking a seat.

Malice took a large slurp from the bowl handed to him. "I think my sense of taste is broken. This tastes like nothing."

"That's just Domlan's cooking, I'm afraid." Beatrice laughed. Gespar didn't seem to find it funny.

"Domlan?" Mal repeated.

Beatrice and Gespar filled in the gaps, telling him the details of the time since they had come to the village in the wood.

"Sounds like we got lucky," was Mal's conclusion. "Sounds like some good people out there. Guess I've got some introductions to make."

Another tense look was exchanged by his human companions.

"There won't be much time for that." Gespar's tone was cold. "Perhaps I have to remind you, we have a job to do. We leave as soon as possible."

"Ges-" Beatrice sighed.

He shook his head, cutting her off. "I have been more than understanding, considering that you are hired help. *More than understanding.*"

"Oh yes, you've shown remarkable understanding, *Boss-*" Beatrice stiffened.

Malice saw the glare in her eyes, the way she pressed her thumb to her brow. Sunshine's words had struck a nerve. Whatever had happened between them was bubbling closer to the surface, and Malice wasn't sure if he wanted the details or not.

By some grace, before Beatrice could air whatever the tension was the door opened and a golden-haired child scurried into the room. Her small bare feet stopped short when she saw Malice sitting up in bed, examining him for a moment. She seemed to come to some sort of conclusion, crossing the room, lifting herself up to the edge of the bed, and throwing her thin arms around his neck in a clumsy embrace. Malice didn't move, unsure of how to react. The girl didn't seem to mind.

"I'm glad you're ok, Mal." She said, freeing him and dropping back to the floor by Bee's side. Her soft smile beamed at him, lifting her round cheeks under her eyes.

"You must be Chammy?"

She nodded happily.

"I hear you took good care of Bee and Sunshine for me?"

"Sunshine?" She giggled, looking at Gespar for his reaction. The paladin smiled stiffly, rubbing his palm across the back of his neck and shrugging. Beatrice huffed, amused. Their eyes met, and neither of them hurried to look away this time.

"I did," Chammy answered proudly. "You're best friends with my best friend, so that makes us best friends too."

"Makes sense." Malice agreed after a thoughtful look and a grin at the little girl.

"Oh, I was supposed to tell you that we're ready for supper at Papa's house."

"I am still hungry." Mal said, moving to get up.

"Maybe you should stay in bed a little longer." Beatrice's forehead creased with worry.

"From what you've told me, I've been in bed long enough. I feel fine." To prove his words, he swung his legs out of bed. His joints popped and creaked as he stood. Truly, he felt almost normal. The only evidence that anything had happened to him was a notable weakness in his left shoulder and what would be a very nice scar. Chammy grabbed his hand, gently leading him to the door. Beatrice and Gespar fell in line behind them, and the whole group spilled out of the wooden house into the village.

The walk to Olesander's home wasn't a long one but it was enough for Malice to truly appreciate the fresh air and the use of his legs. Chammy gave her account of the situation, which spared the group from making any more conversation.

The meal that followed was pleasant. Olesander and Domlan, while perhaps not as enthusiastic as Chammy, were genuinely glad to see Malice on his feet. A bottle of wine was brought out to celebrate. The one person from the story as he'd been told that seemed to be absent was the healer, Willow.

Amidst the food and drink, Chammy asked if someone would go out to play in the fields with her. None of the adults were keen, and Domlan urged her to go on her own but to be back in time for bed.

Between the good company and high spirits, it seemed like the gathering could have gone on all night. As the sun began to go down Gespar stood, summoning some authority when he spoke. "We must turn in. We have to get back on the road early in the morning."

This quieted the group.

"You're leaving already?" It was Domlan who spoke up. "Your friend has just recovered. Perhaps you should wait another day or so... to be safe."

"The safety of all those involved is part of my consideration, I assure you." Gespar's retort sent a new hush over them all.

Finally, Olesander nodded. "Perhaps you have indeed stayed too long already." He turned to Beatrice. "You have been gracious guests, and you are always welcome back here."

And, with an abrupt end to the evening, the three travelers were back on the village path to their borrowed home. Clouds had rolled overhead while they had dined. Darkness was beginning to settle over the houses, and indeed, the woods all around them were already blackened by night.

"So," Malice began. "Does someone want to tell me what's going on here?"

Silence from his companions was his only response.

"No? Just going to keep pouting at each other like a couple of children?"

"Mal-" Beatrice sounded exasperated. "We'll talk about it later. I promise."

"Perhaps some things are better left in the past." Gespar suggested.

"It's hard to say, without knowing what those things are." Malice pointed out.

"Quiet, both of you," Beatrice hissed, freezing where she stood. "Listen."

The hissing rustle of leaves, which had started as only a whisper, was growing ever louder. The woods all around the village had begun to stir.

As the shaking wood grew to a roar, the villagers began to step out of their homes, looking to the horizon for the source of the chaos. Some of them hurried back inside, and some began to murmur, adding to the noise in the air around them.

Willow could be seen, limping in an attempt to hurry towards them. "It's coming- the creature of the Woods."

Beatrice turned, running back to the house. Malice and Gespar followed close behind.

Inside, she found her blade and sheathed it. Gespar grabbed her arm.

"We need to leave, Beatrice. Now."

"*Now?*"

"I told you, these people have forfeited the protection of the gods. They have brought this on themselves."

"You have got to be kidding me." She whirled on him, the look of disgust so strong it made Malice flinch on Gespar's behalf.

"Beatrice, I cannot interfere."

"Why would you not help these people?" Malice asked, his brow furrowed in confusion.

"Ges," Beatrice was stern, but careful to keep her temper in check. "Whatever this twisted sense of honor is, I know you know in your heart that it's madness. You have to be better."

"It's not that simple."

"It is. It's not the gods that are here right now, it's us. And *I* will offer the protection that the gods will not. Sometimes we need divine intervention-" She glanced sidelong at Malice. "And sometimes we just need a good man."

Gespar hesitated, still holding on to Bee's arm. She sighed, and in a most unexpected gesture, reached out to place a gentle hand on the side of his face. "You are a good man. Please, just listen to yourself. Do what you think is right..."

The door burst open with a whack, and Domlan rushed in, his panic palpable instantly. "Is Chammy here? She hasn't come home."

Beatrice gave Gespar a final glance. With her own choice made and his out of her control, she ran out of the house. Malice located his hammer quickly, groaned slightly as he hoisted it, and followed her into the night. These people had done nothing but help him and his friends, he'd be damned if he didn't do the same for them.

TWENTY-THREE

As Beatrice scanned the village, getting her bearings, she heard Domlan yelling his daughter's name as he rushed between the houses.

"Where have you already looked?" Beatrice called to him as Malice caught up to her.

The sound of cracking wood echoed from the tree line out past the pastures, as a distant and high-pitched scream drifted through the air. Without a word Domlan, Beatrice, and Malice all broke into a sprint. Rushing through the fields, the sound of the throngs of the small spiders was all around them.

Beatrice felt her heartbeat grow faster, panic creeping into her bones as she thought of them. The memory of them crawling on her face, her neck... she pushed past the thoughts, using the fear to push her legs faster. The thought of Chammy's fear was more pressing than her own.

The sound of another pair of running feet behind them became apparent. The light of a torch grew about them as its carrier caught up and Gespar came into her peripheral view. It was enough to draw a small smile from Beatrice, and more than a little relief.

As they drew closer to the edge of the clearing, the monstrous spider came in to view. It looked even taller here, more distinguishable from the trees. More terrible.

"Stay back from it!" Gespar shouted at the group, holding his torch high in the air.

Sensing their presence, the spider lowered its body, its tree legs carrying it towards them with deliberate menace.

"Daddy?" The small voice came from the other side of the fence.

The tree-spider turned towards the new sound, but Domlan and Beatrice were faster, already hopping the fence and running toward the girl.

"What are you doing out here? Are you hurt?" Domlan grabbed his daughter up into his arms.

"Darcy was out here by the fence," Chammy said. There was a quiver in her voice as she spoke. She clung to Domlan. "She wouldn't run away. I had to make her."

The goat was certainly here, at the far end of the pasture, staring at the spider with a macabre interest.

The spider was lifting a long woody leg over the fence, creeping ever closer.

"Get her out of here." Beatrice spoke shortly, attempting to mask her fear for the child's sake. "Go!"

He hesitated only a moment before nodding and running back through the field towards the village. Towards safety, Beatrice hoped.

Malice, Beatrice, and Gespar stood shoulder to shoulder in the dark pasture, slowly backing away from the giant spider.

"Perhaps we should run too?" Beatrice suggested, hoping the idea might gain credibility if she said it out loud.

"We'd get away, but it might just go for the village," Malice pointed out. He lifted his hammer, not in his usual smooth swinging motion, but in two smaller heaves that seemed to take a great effort.

"This didn't go so well the first time," Gespar whispered.

"Mraah," Malice growled in some sort of disagreement. "I survived it the first time, what's another go?"

Beatrice gulped. She watched the spider, nearly upon them now, its cloudy eyes angled down and its purple fangs gnashing out in their direction. The Wood still shook and the field still hissed with the sound of the small spiders. Beyond that, it was quiet.

Very quiet.

"Shit." She cursed under her breath.

Their weapons had not been enough to hurt the damn thing before, like hacking at a barn with a butter knife. Even the leg that Malice had crippled before seemed to be functioning now.

Quiet, she thought again, her mind focusing on the bigger picture around them. There were no screams, no sounds of a commotion coming from the village, no panicked animals screaming in the barn.

"Mmgaaah," the goat yelled at her from its position behind the three of them.

"Shit," Beatrice said again. This time it was a realization, not a curse.

"They didn't bring this upon themselves, Ges!"

"I'm *here*, Bee! We don't need to go back through this right now, I understand! You were right, and I'm here!" Gespar waved the torch in an attempt to hold the creature at bay. It back-stepped slightly.

"No, I know. But think about this village. How have they survived out here? The spiders don't bother with them! They leave it alone and it does the same for them. They feed it a share of their livestock, and it clears other danger and pestilence out of the woods. *We* were the pests in the woods!"

"That's not good news for us, Bee!" Malice growled.

"Shit," she said again. Another realization. "Mal..."

"What?" He sounded as if he didn't want to know.

"You've got to give it an offering."

"Gumby."

"No, not Gumby. You know where this is going."

"No," he answered with clipped stubbornness.

"I know, Mal. I'm sorry."

The spider seemed to be realizing that the torch flames were not much of a threat to it, and it was growing braver.

"Mal, I will get you another goat. The best goat. *Any goat*." She was growing frantic.

"But this one- " His tone faltered, but he was holding on, shaking his head.

"Mal, please!" Beatrice was begging in a voice he'd never heard from her. It was pure, undiluted desperation.

"Mmgaaah," said Darcy, who seemed to be growing impatient.

"Dammit!" growled Malice, turning to the animal and dropping to a knee. He reached out, stroking one of its ears. "Look, Darcy. I'm sorry. I-"

The goat didn't seem interested in goodbyes and helpfully walked away, right towards the spider. They watched with bated breath as the goat trotted right up to the beast and bleated expectantly. The tree-spider swooped with lightning-fast reflexes, catching the goat in its grasp, its fangs sinking into the animal's flesh.

There was a sickening sound, like the popping of a grape, then a hiss, and a black boiling smoke began rising from the goat. It rose like a thundercloud over the tree-spider's head, rolling over itself in unnatural currents, and then it dissipated, blown away into the night air.

The creature seemed to take no notice and turned away, taking its carcass meal and creaking away back to the tree line and out of sight. The sound of a million little spiders rushing back to the woods rolled across the pasture like a retreating rain shower.

The three of them stood speechless for a long moment, staring after the spider.

"Just... for the record," Gespar asked. "No part of that was normal, right?"

"Not one bit," Beatrice answered.

"I think-" Malice added. "That I need some rest."

She took a moment to watch him. His chest was slumped forward with fatigue. The brief excitement had been enough to tire him out. She agreed that he needed more rest and was glad that he wasn't in the mood to argue about it. There was something else though. A subtle sadness in his eyes, a droop in his mouth around his fangs. He wouldn't give her a hard time about the move with the goat, but she could see that it hurt him. *Damn,* she really was going to have to replace it.

They walked back to the village with heavy feet. As they reached the little wooden house, Malice rolled his shoulder, grumbling under his breath.

"Do you have any idea what happened back there?" Gespar asked Beatrice. "That black smoke?"

"I'm not sure..." she answered. But, something about it had seemed oddly familiar. "You go on in. I'm just going to check on Chammy."

Gespar nodded. "Hey, Bee." He stopped her as she stepped away. "You were great. Again. You always are."

He stepped through the door, leaving her with that big bright smile that he wielded like a weapon.

Beatrice did check in on Domlan and Chammy, who were safe at home. Her real target, however, was Willow- who was waiting at the door of her clay and stone home as if she had expected her to come.

"All is well?" the old woman asked.

Beatrice nodded.

"And, the dog proved that perhaps he's better than the trainers after all?"

"You don't have to be hateful," Beatrice chided her. "You knew the spider was after us?"

"Basically."

Beatrice hesitated before asking her next question. "Did you tie some sort of magic to our goat?"

"Interesting. I certainly did not." Willow tilted her head, her eyes losing focus as if she were thinking of something very far away. "Would you like to come in for a cup of tea, dear?"

Beatrice nodded.

The inside of the old woman's home was a very particular sort of cozy. It was cluttered, though she seemed to have things organized in her own way- stacks of books on nearly every available surface, jars and bowls and baskets full of dried plants, rolled parchments, and asymmetrical melted candles that looked like they would very much be a fire hazard amongst all this dry clutter.

"Tell me what you saw," Willow posed, as they sat at a small round table.

"Well. We gave the spider Mal's goat... Do you have goats among your livestock, by the way? I'm in the market for a new goat..."

"Sheep, cows, hogs, chickens."

"Damn..."

"What happened, girl?" Willow asked impatiently.

"I think the goat's death released something. Something like demon magic."

Willow sat still. Silent.

Beatrice continued. "It was black. Ephemeral. Like the smoke from the healing water, or the tendrils of darkness from... Well, the other 'blessings' you can feel in the air. You can feel the darkness, feel the light, the life. This I could almost feel, but it didn't make sense. It was stronger, but I can't place what the feeling was."

"There's something else bothering you."

"The goat. It just marched right to its doom. Almost like it wanted to die... like it wanted to be released."

"Ah," Willow sat up, "Now *that* is something."

The old woman stood, crossing to a shelf and looking through a stack of books.

"The magic dissipates in our realm, and the divine beings are made of that same magic. It's very difficult for them to hold their true form in this realm. But just like the magic- if you can contain it in something of this realm..."

Willow found the book she was looking for and handed it to Beatrice with a nod. The Vessels of the Gods.

"Ok." Beatrice nodded. "Makes sense, *I guess*. But, you can't be implying what I think you are." She flipped through the book, a collection of tales of different people throughout history believed to be the gods in the flesh. "Mal's goat wasn't a god."

Willow shrugged. "Perhaps you are right. That would be madness, after all."

Beatrice bid farewell to the old woman, who sent the book with her. The night was calm now, as peaceful as if nothing had happened. The woods were quiet around the village, and the grass of the fields was still and undisturbed. It was beautiful in the moonlight. For that matter, it was beautiful in the daylight too. Beatrice would miss this place and the quiet way that life seemed to pass here.

She let herself inside and found Malice sleeping noisily in the front room. Gods, it was good to have him back. Whatever came next, at least Mal would be there too. She made her way to the back room, moving silently as she slipped through the door, with the intention of not disturbing the men. Gespar though, was already up, seated at the end of the bed. He looked up when she came in, and relaxed.

Neither of them spoke right away. An awkward tension filled the air.

"We still need to leave in the morning." Gespar finally spoke. He looked away when he said it, something like disappointment in his tone.

"I know," Beatrice agreed.

There was another moment of silence, as each of them looked everywhere in the room but at each other.

"Beatrice- "

"I know." She interrupted him. "Look, let's just get some sleep."

She promptly went about getting into bed, settled in with a candle, and began to read the book Willow had loaned her. From time to time she would glance over the top of the book at Ges across the room. She was certain he was lying awake in bed.

TWENTY-FOUR

"**P**romise you'll come back?" Chammy asked. She put on a brave face, blinking back the tears that stung her big, bright green eyes. Dom squeezed her shoulder supportively.

"Yeah," Beatrice agreed. "We'll come back some time. Make sure you take care of these old folks while we're away."

Chammy grinned, nodding. Beatrice smiled back, and then at Domlan. Malice ruffled the girl's hair fondly. Even Gespar exchanged respectful handshakes with the villagers.

Gumby waited, looking ill at just the thought of moving on. He had asked to be left behind, a request that was ignored.

And just like that, they were back on the path. Knowing the secrets of the Wander Wood only made it *slightly* less intimidating.

Beatrice the horse seemed to be the happiest to be on the move again. The time at the village had served her well. Her hair shone from the rest and the long days grazing in the fertile pastures. Now, she strutted down the path as pretty as a picture. The life of a paladin's horse suited her fine.

The sun was high in the sky when they broke out of the woods. Birds chirped, and the Grand Road that rolled between Central and Triad City rolled out before them like an invitation. There was a collective breath of relief from the group. Turning northeast, they continued, closer to Triad City with every passing moment.

The land this far north rolled more steadily in gentle up-and-down hills. The road weaved, sometimes around and some-times over. The mountains to the north were visible over the hori-zon. Their jagged peaks painted a crooked border between the land and sky. Clusters of forest still broke up the landscape around them.

In a few months, the air here would be crisp, the trees would turn from verdant green to golden orange. For now, though it was warm and bright and pleasant breezes made the traveling comfortable.

Gone was the claustrophobic weight of the woods and the un-canny silence. What didn't dissipate now that they were free, was the itching feeling that they were being watched. This had occurred to Beatrice not long after they left the woods. From the corner of her eye, she spotted an unnatural shadow in the trees. It stayed a good distance behind them and moved almost silently. Almost.

The slightest squint at Mal, and a subtle dance of her eyes from his to the woods, and the orc nodded at her. He was aware of it too.

They kept moving as if nothing was wrong. Tipping off their tail now would either result in a direct fight or the pursuer sneaking off. They would let the sneak believe they still had the advantage of surprise right until the last minute.

The afternoon saw them further north. The trees grew thicker along the edge of the road, and they began to veer in the direction of the Grey Sea, Triad City, and the Grand Temple.

"There." It was late afternoon when Gespar stopped them at the top of a hill, pointing out a gray shape glinting on the horizon. It was still distant, almost a day's journey, but visible. Gespar practically beamed, something like pride burning in his eyes, affection in his smile. Never had 'home' been a concept that Beatrice would have thought you could see by looking at someone but there it was, a man looking upon his home, his purpose... with the joy in his heart of knowing he would be back there soon.

It sprouted sadness in Beatrice's gut. She certainly felt relief when they returned to Beacon after a time away, but she didn't feel *this,* and returning to her childhood home in Central brought about almost the opposite reaction.

The more she watched him grinning contentedly as they walked along the more jealousy colored her sadness. Perhaps it was because if someone asked her where her home was she would have a tough time answering, let alone *beaming* about it. Perhaps, it was jealousy of a different sort. After all, if Ges looked so radiantly at a city upon his return- his cheeks dimpled by his boyish grin and the fondness written in his eyes- how must he look upon the woman that waited for him there?

Certainly more fondly than he would look at the woman who stole from him, Beatrice chided herself internally. She had let her thoughts wander well beyond the borders of her comfort zone. She groaned out loud as she realized where her mind had taken her- a place she found it wandering all too often as the days went by.

"Are you alright, Bee?" Ges reached for her arm as he asked, and Beatrice flinched away from the touch.

"Bee?" Now he looked at her with a raised brow, and his curiosity turned to concern.

"I'm ok, just... hungry."

"Maybe we should stop for the night. I'm tired anyway," Malice added.

"I have an idea." Ges lit up again. "Can you go a little further?"

Both agreed, with a certain amount of caution. When Gespar announced that they would leave the road here, they were even more hesitant, but his enthusiasm won them over, and they turned away from the trail, headed due-north through the trees.

Beatrice watched Mal as they walked. He did seem more fatigued than usual, and occasionally he would squeeze at his shoulder with his good hand. But otherwise, he seemed to be holding up just fine. She knew better than to ask him how he was. He'd say he was great regardless of the truth.

As the sky turned to gold they broke through, finding themselves upon the banks of a grand lake.

"High lake," Gespar told them. "I used to stop here with my friends every time we came back to Triad City. It's beautiful, isn't it?"

"Sure, if you like scenic views and gorgeous sunsets." Beatrice held back a smile.

His grin lit his eyes as he watched her. "Do you?"

"I do," Beatrice admitted, basking in the glow reflecting off the still waters.

"I could take it or leave it," Mal added. "I'm going to eat something."

Malice set about making a fire while the horse grazed lazily at a patch of grass.

Gumby sat a safe distance away, watching the orc with careful attention. Finally, as the fire sprang to life and Malice sprawled out next to the blaze, the man spoke.

"There was no child."

Beatrice looked quickly to Malice for a reaction, but the orc didn't even open his eyes.

"With the goat, I mean. There wasn't a child. We just found the goat wandering down the road."

"Doesn't change anything now. You're still the bandit trash we were hired to clean up. One count of innocence doesn't clear away your other crimes. You still deserve whatever you get in Triad."

"Mal!" Beatrice felt her throat go dry at his words. Her protest was too much for the *actual* topic, but it was too late. Malice and Ges looked at her, waiting for an explanation for her outburst. She couldn't agree with Mal on this point. If that were true, *once a criminal always a criminal,* if they were no better than their worst moments...

Beatrice felt all eyes on her, pulling her back to the moment. "Maybe we can talk about this."

"Talk about what, Bee? That was the job we were hired to do, you said you wanted to do it right."

"That's a job we were already paid for... and maybe there's more than one way to do it right."

"I'm not sure that's our decision to make, in a situation like this," Gespar said.

Beatrice shut her eyes, trying to block the voices in her head that were eager to argue. "Maybe not," she conceded. "Excuse me."

She wandered closer to the edge of the water, walking down the shore, attempting to clear her head. What did it matter, if Gumby was beyond redemption? If the only real difference between them was that he was caught like a rat in a trap that she was able to avoid? Beatrice knew who she was, *most of the time*. She had lived this life for years. The consequences were not new knowledge. So why was the feeling that she was trapped after all growing stronger by the day? Gespar came to her side, which defeated the purpose of her walk, but didn't displease her.

The pair stopped well down the shoreline, turning to watch the sunset over the lake. It was beautiful. Peaceful. Beatrice took a deep breath, trying to memorize the feeling.

"You were right, you know," Gespar said.

"You're surprised?"

"No. Not anymore." He laughed.

"What is it I was right about this time?"

"Me."

His tone grew slightly more serious, catching Beatrice's full attention.

"My choices. Where my responsibilities start and end... I serve to protect. What good is that if you begin stacking on conditions?"

"That's very wise of you."

"I told you I do what I must, and I strive to be the best at it. Perhaps it's time I start doing that on my own terms."

"And what might those terms be?"

"Well first, I am a paladin. Not a pawn. Not someone's dog."

Beatrice winced. "Paladin Fairchild, have you been *eavesdropping?*"

He smirked as he stared out at the lake. The sun soaked his skin in a warm glow. His face had been smooth the night they had met in Beacon. Now, the auburn stubble was growing thick. The days on the road, and in the Wander Wood shone on his face, but made him no less handsome.

"I am my own man, with my own convictions." He turned to face her now, his eyes searching her face as he brushed a stray lock of hair behind her ear. His gaze wandered somewhere over her shoulder as he went on. "I have my own mind, my own feelings. My own heart..."

He paused, his thoughts seemed to drift away for a moment. Beatrice found that she wanted badly to bring them back. She could practically hear her pulse pounding in her ears. Gespar's eyes moved back to her own. "Beatrice, there's something I must tell you, but please don't react. Not right away. Just hear me out."

"What is it, Ges?" Bee's voice came out breathy and rasping. He wound an arm around her, pulling her closer. Instinctively she reached out to grip his sleeve, trying to keep her hands from trembling. She couldn't stop her eyes from wandering to his lips as he came closer.

Leaning in so close that she could feel the warmth of his voice on her ear, he spoke. "There are two elves watching us from the trees. I think they've been following us most of the day."

Suppressing her initial urge, which was to shove him into the lake, Bee's eyes fluttered shut.

"Almost identical?"

"Yes!" The surprise in his voice was audible.

"Except one of them looks like he's got a stick up his ass?"

"What?" Gespar's eyes darted back to the trees for a moment. "I suppose I could see that, yes."

"Hells." Beatrice hissed, and wrapped a hand around the back of Gespar's neck, whispering quickly. "Alright, listen- their tactic will be speed, surprise, and using the fact that there are two of them to distract and confuse. I would rather not kill them, but... we'll see what sort of mood they're in." She released Gespar and taking a step back, she turned.

"I owe one of you lunch and the other a fat lip." She raised her voice enough that she was sure Malice would hear her downwind. "But, I'm sure you didn't come all this way for a sticky bun, so you must be looking for a fight."

She drew her blade and heard Ges do the same behind her. A moment later Dart and Paz stepped out into the open.

"What do you think you're doing, Lemon?"

"Working. What do you think *you're* doing?"

"We aren't here to fight, Beatrice. Just checking in. Boss's orders." Dart looked sincere enough, but the weapon in his hand made it difficult to tell if he meant it.

Paz made it easier. "Personally, I've seen enough. I'm here to slit your throat and take whatever it is this pretty boy of yours has."

"Wrong on both counts, Paz, but I'll give you a chance to walk away."

Malice was almost behind the elves now. Beatrice twirled her blade in an unnecessary, showy motion in the air.

"And miss the chance to cut the tongue out of your dull mouth? I think not." Paz lunged left and low, running at her with disorienting speed.

Dart had gone right, moving at the same time as his brother but he didn't make it far before he was snatched. Malice turned him roughly, growling in his face.

Beatrice planted her weight, holding her blade in front of her defensively. The elf was counting on her to break to the side- an attempt to dodge, but that would give him an opening. Instead, she faced him down, forcing him to slow his assault and strike her head-on.

"Help Mal," she called to Gespar. To her great relief, he followed the order without hesitation or question, allowing her to give her full attention to her assailant.

The twins wielded blades that were light, long, curved, and deadly. Her short blade was at a disadvantage. Striking at him once, Paz's block slid her blade out of the way at a wide-angle. She was forced to recoil quickly, jumping back to avoid the answering swing that would have cut her from shoulder to hip with little effort.

The lake grew deep much quicker than she would have guessed, and the minor retreat brought her in nearly up to her knees. The drag of the water around her legs slowed her down. Instead of trying to fight her way out, she stepped back, to the side. As she hoped, Paz followed her in. Beatrice smiled, throwing in a wink for good measure. Paz's problem, she was well aware, was his distaste for her.

He wanted it too badly, thought too little of her... she could play that game.

"Come on, Paz. Aren't we better friends than this?"

"Friends?" He struck at her again. "With a miserable, selfish wretch like you? Your failures belong to others, yet your success is always your own genius. People are stolen objects to you, the same as any target. You keep them as long as they serve a purpose- stroking your ego, keeping you alive." His swings became wilder as he chided her. "What's this one, Lemon? A bed warmer?"

Beatrice dodged another swing, more aggressive than the last but not the opportunity she was looking for. Not yet.

"It doesn't matter, does it? Because at the end of the day, when the coin outweighs their usefulness, you'll sell them off like everything else you steal." Paz's green eyes flared in the sun, and the shining curve of the blade glinted as he raised it high. "Just like that little crew you used to run with."

As Paz brought the blade down Beatrice didn't dodge. She didn't back away. Instead, Beatrice stepped into the attack, raising her arm with equal momentum to the elf's. She struck with her forearm, right at the hilt of the sword where Paz's fingers wound around the handle. He shouted in pain, the sword was knocked from his hand and fell into the lake with a wet plunk. In the same breath, Beatrice brought her sword to his neck, stopping just short of a fatal slice.

"Anything else you'd like to add to that, Paz dear?"

He glared at her, silent. She cautioned a glance to the shore and saw that Malice had Dart pinned and Gespar held him at the point of his sword.

"I don't want to kill you, Paz, but I will," Beatrice warned. "Go back to Claw and tell that fat fuck he can come kill me himself if he wants it done."

"What is your game, Beatrice?" Paz looked back at his brother and the others. "Why do you hesitate? When he finds out what you are, he won't stand by you. He *shouldn't*. The shining paladin, protect the lowlife thief? No. I hope he cuts you down himself and I hope I get to hear every detail."

Beatrice couldn't help but look to Gespar. She was unsettled to see that he looked back at her, his brow low and his stare deadly serious. Surely, he couldn't hear Paz's venom from that distance.... *Surely.*

She opened her mouth to speak, despite the lump in her throat. "I-"

She hesitated. Before she recognized how deadly a mistake this was, Paz grabbed her blade hand from the outside, shoving it away from his neck. Her arm pinned across her chest, he shoved her backward. Beatrice was plunged under the cold blue water with a violent splash. She grabbed wildly with her free arm for any hold to fight back but it was fruitless. The water burned as it filled her nostrils. A sound of wordless protest escaped her, and was lost in a storm of bubbles under the surface of the lake.

There wasn't space between the seconds to piece together her thoughts. If she had been able to think she might have been more tactful, saved her breath, but all she could manage in her state of panic was a frantic struggle. She shut her eyes tightly, now pulling at the hand holding her other arm.

The muted sound of shapes crashing through the water became more pronounced. She couldn't tell how close they were. Couldn't focus. The other sounds became indistinguishable from her splashing. Voices yelling above her could be heard, muted by the water around her. She was shoved, harder, further under before a scream pierced through the barrier around her.

Paz's hold on her was released, but in her panic Beatrice floundered, and unable to get her feet underneath her, she struggled to resurface.

Opening her eyes, Bee was blinded by glaring light. She stopped flailing, filled for a moment with the peace of surrender. *Death* she thought, *wasn't so bad after all.*

The next moment there were arms around her again, pulling her up. The light fell away, and Beatrice found herself lifted, pressed to a warm, firm chest and carried towards the shore.

"Bee?" As they settled on to the bank Gespar called to her, pushing her sopping hair away from her face and caressing her cheek. "Beatrice? Can you speak? Are you alright?"

"Fine." She sucked in air. Despite the stinging in her sinuses, Beatrice realized she was far from death. No water had entered her lungs, and she had already caught her breath. "I'm perfectly fine."

He embraced her, pulling her close to his body. Warmth pressed to the top of her head. Beatrice wondered for a moment if it was his lips. He adjusted to inspect her face closely, his expression still solemn. "*Perfectly* fine? You're sure?"

She nodded, and Gespar's brow relaxed slightly.

"Thank the gods," He muttered under his breath.

The gods.

Beatrice turned herself enough to reach her pocket and produced from it Gespar's talisman. It was warm to the touch despite the cold, damp chill that gripped her and clung to her clothing.

"Thank the gods, indeed." She held it out to him. "I forgot I had it..."

Gespar took the talisman from her, looking it over with surprise and a certain amount of reverence. "I'm glad you did."

His attention moved to her chest. "And this?" He reached out, lifting the glowing gem on its chain.

"That..." Beatrice looked at the small thing shining in his hand, feeling very much like an idiot. Of course, she hadn't seen the light of Din's realm, the stone must have come loose from her shirt as she struggled.

"It's realm magic. Illegal realm magic, touched by Crepus." Gespar inspected it, turning it about in his fingers before holding it up to look at her eyes in the glow of the stone. "It suits you though. Just don't let anyone in the Grand Temple see you with it."

He dropped it gently, a pinched discomfort on his face. He might be making an effort to let logic outweigh his previous feelings on what magic was condemnable and what wasn't, but she could see it wasn't happening without at least a little inner turmoil. Bee immediately tucked it back under her clothes before he had a chance to reconsider.

As Gespar helped her to her feet, she spotted dribbled blood staining the ground and leading from the lake to the trees.

"Where is Mal?" Beatrice didn't wait for an answer, hurrying to follow the trail of blood.

Gespar called after her, to no avail. She had hardly reached the tree line when Malice appeared, stopping her with a straight arm. "Where are you goin' with no blade and lookin' like a drowned rat?"

"Ah, shit."

The sudden realization that her dirk was lost in the lake turned her around, running back across the shore and splashing through the shallows.

"Bee," Mal called out. "The bandit ran off with the twins."

"Will they kill him?" Gespar asked.

"And miss the chance to hear about everything we've done since Beacon?" Mal answered. "I doubt it."

The three of them sat by the fire a short while later. Beatrice had found her blade with the help of the gem and now sat close to the flames in an attempt to warm and dry herself.

"How do we know they won't come back in the night?" Gespar paced the area around the fire, his eyes always looking back to the shadows in the trees.

Malice shook his head. "You cut up Paz pretty good. He would be useless in a fight now, and Dart won't come by himself."

Gespar stopped to consider this. "You know them well?"

No one answered. Beatrice wished she could see his face, but didn't dare to turn around. The words Paz had spat echoed in her mind. If this was to be a moment of reckoning, she wasn't prepared to face it.

"Why were they here?"

How the hell was she supposed to answer that?

With the truth, if the gleam in Mal's charcoal eyes meant anything.

"You heard. They know you have something valuable. Probably they hoped to get us on their side… or plant mistrust."

"Well, it's a good thing I already trust you explicitly."

Now Beatrice did spin around, looking for some sign on his face that he was serious. His smile was warm and sincere.

"Don't look at me like that, Bee." He laughed. "I *knew* others might come after the stone. It's not your fault you happened to be familiar with them."

"But, the things he said-"

"Bee." He cut her off. "The things he said were obviously said to distract you. If you were going to betray me, you've missed a dozen chances to do it already. Clearly, you're either *very* bad at this, or I can trust you." Gespar came closer. "You needn't worry. I can't be fooled that easily. I *do* stand by you. We have been through a great deal together, and I trust you with my life, Beatrice. Malice too."

This did not make Beatrice feel better. On the contrary, her insides began tying themselves into a heavy knot in her gut. She forced a smile to hide her unease. Malice looked at her with a raised eyebrow and a slight jeer. Malice, despite regular disagreement on a variety of subjects, had never judged her before. She hoped that the judgment she was sensing now was imagined.

Beatrice's sleep was restless that night, despite the gentle lullaby of the song toads croaking all around the shoreline.

TWENTY-FIVE

The weather was dreary the next morning, waking the travelers early and soaking them thoroughly before they were even on the move. Thunder echoed off the northern mountains, now visible on the horizon. They followed the lake for the first part of the day. The rain came down steadily, bringing the surface of the water to life.

They turned away from the water's edge, meeting back with the Grand Road. From there it was a long, straight shot to Triad City, cut through the rocky green landscape. The rain spurred them forward at a steady pace, and in relative silence.

As they drew near, the city began to loom over them. Triad City, the Capital of the Triad Empire, was the grandest and most sprawling city therein. She (because there was something strikingly feminine about the city), was built on the inclines and cliffs that kissed the Gray Sea where it met the land. The city rose and fell, tumultuous as the sea below it. Greystone stairs and sloped pathways carried the schools of people through the highs and lows. Even the slummiest parts of Triad city were nicer than most of Bay.

Gespar looked at the city warmly as they approached. "It's beautiful, isn't it? Have you ever been?"

"Only once. Only to the outskirts. For a job, on..." The Orc paused. "Cadence street, maybe?"

Gespar thought on this. "There is a Cadence Street, but you might be mistaken. I've never been there except in passing. It's a rough area, run by low-lives and-"

He stopped uncomfortably as he realized the implication.

"Yeah. That was it," Beatrice said shortly.

"My father brought me once when I was a girl," she added. "I grew up in Central, and this isn't too much larger. It's just another city. Just more buildings, and more people... But it felt like a whole different world somehow. I remember thinking we had gone into another realm."

Gespar smiled at her.

Their arrival in the city was inevitable and had begun to loom in Bee's thoughts in the way the thunder clouds loomed overhead. The buildings of the outskirts were visible, sucking the road ahead of them into the city. It wouldn't be long until it sucked them in with it.

A large inn lay by the road, two stories and dozens of windows staring out at them. There was no showy sign by the road, no artistic carving or clever name- just a board nailed above the door, with 'Roadhouse' painted in large white letters. Beatrice stopped, as they walked in front of it.

"Perhaps we should stop? Freshen up before we reach the Temple?"

Gespar looked at her quizzically, "We would be soaked again before we got there."

"I suppose you're right. It may be our last chance for a good drink though." She gestured at the roadhouse.

"I'm fine to keep going," Malice asserted.

"I assure you, you will be well fed at the Grand Temple. *And* well saturated if you wish. Come on, Bee. I'm eager to finish this."

"Right..." She relented, moving along down the road and into Triad city. A brief stop at the guard barracks to have Beatrice the horse stabled was the only delay she was afforded.

The streets were calm. Anyone who could avoid being out in the rain was tucked away safely indoors. The people who found themselves driven out to the streets stared shamelessly at the Paladin, the orc, and the young woman- all drenched, and heading toward the heart of the city.

The Grand Temple sat upon the highest shelf in the city, overlooking the sea at its southern face. It was a collection of three sprawling buildings. The central building was the Grand Palace, home to the Blessed Leaders, their spouses, and the other locally stationed Faithful. To the right was the Grand consulate, and to the left, the temple itself. The grounds were comprised of beautifully landscaped gardens, the likes of which had no business growing this far north. There was no denying its beauty. It was not only the heart of the city but of the entire Empire.

They were greeted at the doors of the temple by faithful guards, that bowed quickly out of the way as soon as they recognized Gespar.

"Welcome home, Paladin Fairchild."

It was a sentiment repeated by nearly everyone they passed as they moved through the hall, and there were endless people. Beatrice took in the sights of the bustling temple in silence as they followed Ges past the busy guests and servants, no doubt all preparing for the Triad Gathering. He stopped a cleric to inquire where he could find the Blessed Leaders. The cleric answered, peeking at Beatrice and Malice with polite suspicion. Gespar then led them up the wide fanning staircase to the Grand Throne room. Beatrice and Malice stopped at the large doors, exchanging a glance of mutual uncertainty.

"We'll wait here for you?" Beatrice asked, hopeful that this was correct.

"Nonsense." Gespar insisted, "We'll address the Leaders together." And he ushered them through the doors and into the throne room of the Blessed Leaders.

The room was longer than was logical or necessary. The walk from the doors to the far end was uncomfortable. Their boots on the stone floors echoed off the walls and high ceilings. At the far end, seven deep steps led to a raised platform with a long golden table and three imposing thrones. At the bottom of the steps, Gespar dropped to one knee, bowing his head low. Beatrice and Malice had stopped halfway across the room, standing back at what felt a safe distance.

"Paladin Fairchild." The woman seated in the center addressed him. "Have you been successful?"

"I have." Gespar held the small chest out in front of him. The woman beckoned him forward and he climbed the steps, placing it on the long table.

The white walls seemed to absorb all sound. The woman, Lady Lestra, figurehead of the Triad Empire, Blessed Leader of the temple of Sald, hesitated for a moment before reaching to open it. Her golden rings clacked against the wood of the box.

To her right, Arthur, Head of the Temple of Gerra, stood to get a better look. The third Blessed Leader, Diana, shifted uncomfortably in her throne. Beatrice tensed as the lid was lifted. Even though she couldn't see the Shadowgate Stone, she could feel its darkness in the air. Shadows darkened the faces of the three Blessed Leaders as they looked upon the stone.

After what felt like an eternity, Lestra shut the box.

"You've done well, as always, Paladin." Lestra's ghostly pale eyes turned back to Gespar. "We worried you wouldn't be returning to us. Diana was concerned she had lost a husband."

Beatrice snapped to attention, looking to the third blessed leader- Diana. The elven woman's pale skin flushed beautifully at her cheeks. Her long hair, so blonde it was almost colorless, flowed so neatly and prettily compared to Bee's dark curls. Her slender features, her soft face, her blue eyes- were all touched with perfect feminine beauty. She was gorgeous. *She was a Blessed Leader, for Gods' sake.* And she was the only woman Gespar Fairchild had ever laid with, and ever would.

Beatrice felt sick to her stomach. Every moment. The fond looks, the kind words, the stolen kisses- was thrown into a sharp new light. Beatrice Lemon was a damn fool.

"I had good help." Gespar's voice brought her back to the moment. He gestured back to them. "I present to you Malice Malacar,

Clan Killer, The Great Hammer wielder, Consulate mercenary, and bandit crusher. And... Beatrice Lemon."

The Blessed Leaders turned their full attention to the pair. Malice stood tall and proud, while Beatrice mustered every ounce of confidence she had left to keep herself from crumbling under their gaze.

"Very well." Lestra seemed entirely uninterested. "The consulate will sort out their payment. We thank you for your service to the empire. You are dismissed, mercenaries. "

Dismissed. Malice shifted, unsure of what to do.

"Come on." Beatrice moved towards the exit. "That's it. Let's go get paid."

As they walked towards the exit, business commenced at the table as if they had never been there at all.

"As you're aware, Paladin, the Triad Gathering begins tomorrow. There will be no further assignments until after the gathering is over... Instead of a full report on this mission, we will debrief now."

"I'm sorry-" Gespar responded, sounding uncharacteristically distracted. "I promised these two a place to rest for the night and a meal. They have served in such a way that cannot be repaid by coin alone."

Beatrice and Malice paused.

"Of course." It was Diana who spoke up, with the light and lyrical voice of a songbird. Her words were welcoming, but she looked at Beatrice and Malice with a frightening new level of interest. "We will house them in the palace and offer them the finest hospitality. They are welcome as long as they wish to stay. I extend to you, my personal invitation to the Triad Gathering as my honored guests."

"Thank you, my lady." Gespar bowed deeply to his betrothed.

"Very well," Lestra consented. "We will have rooms prepared while we finish our business and you finish yours. Dismissed."

Gespar turned to them, offering a friendly smile before turning back to the Leaders of the Triad.

TWENTY-SIX

"**W**hat are you thinking, Bee?"

They were wandering around the grounds in the warm afternoon glow. They had been to the consulate, received the largest payout they had ever earned with a shockingly low level of enthusiasm, and then found their way out to the Grand Temple Gardens.

"Well..." Beatrice sighed. "This Gathering, it's the big fancy party they have every year, yeah? Everyone will be preoccupied... Sounds like the perfect time to steal the stone and get out of here."

"Beatrice." Malice groaned. "What about Sunshine?"

"What about him? We have a job to do. This was the plan all along, remember?"

"And you don't have any conflicting feelings about that?"

"Let's pretend that I do." Beatrice held her face carefully, emotionless and calm. "What does it matter? He's a Paladin. His life is devoted to upholding the law, and I'm a *thief*."

"What if you weren't a thief?"

"Then I would be the middle child of a merchant, Mal. Not the Blessed Leader of the Temple of Beauty and Perfect Tits."

"I dunno, I think Arthur was the most impressive. He was massive for a human."

Beatrice crossed her arms, unamused.

"C'mon. What about Sunshine? You don't think there were any signs that he cared about you?"

"All the more reason for me to stay realistic here. If I stick to the plan, I'll be doing us both a favor."

Silence.

"So, let's just do what we came to do and get away from here. Far away... maybe to Cestian for a while."

"Fine, Bee. If that's still what you want to do by the ball tomorrow, then that's what we'll do."

A dwarven woman in a red and gold uniform approached them shyly. "Pardon, you are the mercenary guests of Paladin Fairchild and the Lady Diana?" She smiled at them as though she already knew the answer.

"That's us," Malice answered.

"Oh, good." She beamed. "I've been sent to bring you to your suite."

The dwarf led them inside the palace. The interior was breathtaking. The white walls were accented with glimmering gold patterns, and floors of shining marble and equally shining dark wood. They were led down echoing corridors and up spiraling stairs to a wing with its own sitting room, bed chambers connected by large double doors, and a long dining table with ornately carved legs.

Two human women waited for them in the sitting room.

"Now then, let's get you cleaned up before dinner."

The dwarf, Lara, herded them into a room with two claw-footed tubs. The air was scented with lavender, heavy and relaxing. The tubs were full of steaming water and bubbled over with luxurious soaps.

"In you get," Lara insisted.

Beatrice was hurried out of her clothes and into the hot water by one of the girls. She sank into the sweet-smelling bubbles, suddenly less bothered by any thoughts of what had transpired and what was to come.

One of the human girls gasped involuntarily as Malice stripped, and Bee sank low enough into her own bath to hide the fact that she was laughing at the girl's expense. She heard Mal groan as he slid into his own tub.

"I could get used to this, Mal." Beatrice lifted a handful of bubbles off the top of the water, examining the prismatic shine in the candlelight.

"You don't say?"

Beatrice shut her eyes, feeling too relaxed to fight. "They have tubs in Cestian, too."

"Hrmpph."

The women bustled back in after a comfortable soak, two of them pouring fresh hot water into the individual tubs. Lara came to Beatrice's side with a tray of soaps and delicately scrubbed her hair as if it were something precious.

It must have been more than an hour before they climbed out of the water, pruned but content. The ladies dressed Beatrice in a clean dress and attempted to put a silk top on Mal, only to find that it didn't fit across his shoulders.

Once they were dried and dressed, a Faithful guard came in to announce that Lady Diana had come to call on them. This spoiled Beatrice's relaxation a great deal, but she quickly plastered on the same gracious, welcoming face she had seen her mother use a thousand times during her childhood when stuck-up guests came calling.

Diana came into the room like a whisper, her long white dress gliding across the floor effortlessly behind her.

"Lovely." She spoke softly, looking at them with a subtle smile. "I hope the accommodations have all been to your liking?"

"Quite," Beatrice answered, matching Diana's syrupy sweet tone. "It treads a fine line though. If it was any *more* pleasant, I'm sure we would find it absolutely unbearable."

"Ah, quaint. I see why Paladin Fairchild likes you. He speaks *very* highly of you both, you know." Her blue eyes sparkled in the soft sunlight filtering through the sheer curtains.

"And we would do the same for him," Malice said, his eyes set seriously.

"He's a good man," Beatrice added, nodding her head in agreement.

"Oh, exceedingly good, I agree. He has earned every luxury that has been afforded and every honor he has been gifted. I am proud that he will be my husband when the time comes."

Beatrice wrinkled her nose. She bit her cheek. This was a perfect time to keep her mouth shut and move on, but she just couldn't help herself. Tilting her head, she smiled carefully at Diana. "When does the time come, if you don't mind me asking? Why the whole business with the vows of purity and betrothal? Why not just marry him right from the start?"

"How forward of you. I see you've been given more information than an outsider would normally receive." Diana's face didn't change. "To tie any Paladin into marriage, and send them out to serve the Empire would be a cruel distraction to them and their spouse. They serve with a promise of what is to come next and take vows as their own promise in return. Typically, they serve ten years in purity, unwed."

Perhaps though," Diana added conspiratorially, "I will marry him sooner. How could I help myself?"

"I'm sure I don't know." Beatrice responded with a cold smile.

"Look at you, though!" Diana came close, reaching out to touch Beatrice, feeling her hair and touching her face. Beatrice tensed, and Malice bristled beside her, seeing the change in her posture.

"You do clean up nicely, don't you?"

"I do."

"The Gathering tomorrow night will be a treat. Do you have a gown to wear?"

Beatrice deflated ever so slightly.

"Oh my, I would offer to let you wear one of mine, but I fear you're just a little too short and round for anything to fit right. You understand, dear."

"I do." She gritted her teeth, trying not to let the slight sting she felt show.

"Well, perhaps we can sort something out. For both of you." She nodded sweetly at Malice. "If you'll excuse me, I do have certain business to attend to. Please enjoy your evening, dears."

There was little to no time to talk between the time Diana left and when the servant girls returned with silver trays of food. Immediately, they began setting the table for their meal.

Without a word, Lara slipped a note in front of Beatrice's plate.

I regret that I am kept too busy to join you for dinner this evening, my friends. I hope they have made you comfortable, you deserve it. I will see you tomorrow. In the meantime, have an extra drink for me.
-Ges

Beatrice set the note down on the table, her mouth pulled into a tight line. She nodded to herself as if she had reached some conclusion, and began to eat.

"What's that about?" Mal gestured to the paper, and Beatrice passed it to him in silence.

"It's better this way," she insisted after he had read it and looked to her with all-knowing eyes.

"Not for me," Mal said. "I'll have to deal with your brooding when this is all over." He added under his breath.

TWENTY-SEVEN

Beatrice had gotten up early and dressed in the outfit Gespar had bought for her in Bay, intending to wander into the city to find something acceptable to wear for the evening. There were much worse ways to spend a morning, and after all, she had the coin for it. The problem was, she wasn't sure what *was* acceptable for such an event, and she wasn't entirely sure where to look for it.

In the end, it didn't matter. She was stopped at the end of the hall by a Faithful positioned in front of the staircase. "Pardon, miss. The rest of the Palace and grounds are off-limits... for preparations... for the Gathering."

The guard looked at the wall dutifully as he spoke.

"Well, that's alright. I was actually going *off* the grounds." Bee moved to step around him as she spoke, but the Guard sidestepped to block her way.

"P-pardon, miss. Sorry-" She could almost see him trying to think quickly behind big doe-eyes. "You would have to go *through* the palace to leave... So...."

"Oh." Beatrice stepped back, nodding at him sympathetically. "You're absolutely right. Sound logic, good man. I didn't think of that."

She squinted at the man, wondering just in passing how much trouble she would get in if she kneed him in the groin and ran for it. But this was a petty move by perfect, blessed, Diana herself, no doubt. If she wanted Beatrice and Malice out of the picture, acting out would only make getting rid of them too easy.

As Beatrice walked back towards the quarters provided to her and Malice, a stately-looking man came out of another section. He nodded at her in passing, his eyes lingering longer than was necessary on her frame before he walked importantly down the hall. Beatrice reached the doors to the suite, lingering a moment to watch as the man reached the staircase. She could see the Faithful hesitate a moment, his eyes darting to her for a split second before he stepped aside for the man to pass. The guard stepped back in to place quickly, staring at the wall again with impressive fervor. Beatrice was aware of the sheen of sweat on his brow, even at this distance.

"That was fast," Mal commented on her return.

"It would seem that we're under house arrest... 'palace arrest', I guess."

"You think they suspect us?"

"Of what? Delivering the stone to them just to steal it? I doubt it."

"Right, because only a mad man would do something like that."

"I think it's more likely that the Blessed Mrs. Sunshine hopes we won't attend the Gathering after all. She can't uninvite us, but she can make it very inconvenient."

"That's fine. If they don't want us there, we won't go. Doesn't really sound like our sort of party anyway."

"It's not. But we have to go. It's our one shot at diverting suspension. If people see us, talk to us, remember we were there- it'll give us deniability. And-" Beatrice added with a stubborn shrug. "If we show up dressed like this, we'll be all the more memorable."

As if by some divine intervention, Lara and her girls showed up shortly after midday with two large packages. The girls, Mimi and Shira, looked fit to burst, giddy over whatever it was they carried.

"We've been sent to help you get ready for the festivities."

"No need." Beatrice leaned back luxuriously in her seat, propping her dirt-crusted boots up on the expensive table. "We're pretty much ready."

"Well, that's fine." Lara took this quite well, smiling amiably at her. "But I've been sent with another letter for you. Perhaps you would like to read it before you decide that for certain."

Beatrice involuntarily raised a brow and took the letter. She unfolded it delicately, careful that her facial expression didn't change while she read it.

Bee,

Perhaps you have already been provided with a gown for tonight. If that is the case, please accept this as a gift. I saw it while out this morning and I couldn't help myself, it seemed to be made for you alone. I look forward to seeing you, whatever you decide to wear.

I didn't want Malice to feel left out, so I've sent him an outfit as well. It's not half as pretty, but the options are limited in garments that wide.

Yours, Ges

She lingered on the sign-off for a moment, her fingers brushing the page. Pulling herself from the words she turned back to the girls, her face carefully arranged into a casual expression. "Well, let's see it then."

Mimi, the slightly smaller of the ladies, hurried forward, grinning ear-to-ear. The girl placed the box on the table and carefully removed the lid.

"Oh, gods." Beatrice's cool façade fell away immediately. She stood to get a closer look.

Malice peered curiously from across the room, a smug grin on his face. "That Sunshine knows a thing or two."

Mimi nodded enthusiastically, the black hair piled in a knot atop her head nearly tumbling loose. "It's the prettiest thing I've ever seen."

Pretty, wasn't exactly the right word though. The gown was gorgeous- a work of art.

"Well then, standing here gawking at it won't get us anywhere. Let's get you into it." Lara began to shepherd them towards Beatrice's room. "Oh dear." She paused. "I almost forgot about the big one."

Shira, a tall and broad woman with ginger hair and a splatter of freckles, seemed to suddenly realize she had the other box in her possession, and froze. Her brown eyes went wide as she watched Malice cross the room to her, towering over her for a moment. Malice held out one large hand. "Don't worry. I can dress myself."

Beatrice once again had to remove the glowing stone, carefully tucking it away before the all-too-helpful women spotted it. The women meticulously helped Beatrice into the dress, taking much longer than was necessary. The preening and excited attention was most of the job. Shira, who seemed quite relaxed now that she had evaded dressing Malice, pulled Beatrice's thick hair into a neat braid. The style was finished with the golden pins that Gespar had thoughtfully sent along with the gown.

Beatrice looked in the mirror when they announced she was ready. Her hands smoothed the sheer fabrics, the deep blue of the night sky. It flowed down her body like water rippling over her curves. Spun gold glistened off the surface of the dress, sewn into hundreds of shining stars. It plunged low in the front and even lower in the back, belted with a golden band. Golden chains draped from shoulder to shoulder, kissing her skin with a cold touch where they rested on her exposed back.

"Look at that!" Lara beamed at her in the mirror. "I bet you don't even recognize yourself, eh?"

"Yeah," Beatrice answered agreeably, smiling back at herself in the reflection. It was a lie. She recognized the woman in the mirror, without a doubt.

"I think this shirt is a dud," Malice called from the other room.

It turned out that even the largest fine shirt Gespar had found didn't quite fit the proportions of a muscular orc, and Malice had nearly shredded it in his whole-hearted attempt to put it on.

"Oh, dear..." Lara looked at him, suddenly much more tired than she had been a moment before.

Malice was at least wearing the dress pants and the red sash tied around his middle section, although it was tucked in a messy tangle and he still wore his usual dirty boots.

"Well, I'm not sure what to do with that," the dwarf complained.

"I... I have an idea. I think I can sort him out." Shira spoke up, and hesitantly took Malice back to his room.

"And you, love? Are you ready for this?" Lara turned back to Beatrice.

"Yes," Beatrice answered. "Well, no. I don't know? I actually have no idea what to expect."

Lara looked like she had expected as much. "Well, think of it as a balancing act. They present an abundance of everything- food, alcohol, social niceties. You don't participate and people will talk. You have too much, and they'll talk even more. Eat a little, but don't fill yourself. Dance with anyone who asks, but never more than once. God knows you'll need the drink, but you shouldn't go through more than two the whole night."

"Sounds like a real fun time," Beatrice grumbled, deflating a bit at the advice.

Lara pulled a flask from her apron and unscrewed the lid with an expert flick before handing it to Beatrice. "Two sips," she instructed.

Beatrice obeyed, sucking air through her teeth after the liquid went down. "That's rough," she coughed.

"Dwarven spiced rum. It'll take the edge off and put a little color in your cheeks."

"I like you," Beatrice said approvingly. Lara winked back at her.

Shira stepped back into the room, her cheeks pink and her eyes tethered to the floor. "May I present Malice Malacar..." the girl hesitated. A guttural cough from behind the door spurred her on. "Clan Killer- The Great Hammer wielder-" her blush deepened to a beet red. "Consulate mercenary, bandit crusher and..." She paused. "And strikingly-"

"Aggressively," the cough corrected.

"and *aggressively* handsome orc," she finished.

Malice strutted through the door, flexing his chest in a manner that did indeed seem rather aggressive.

"Wow," Beatrice commented, supportively. "Not bad." And she meant it.

His boots were wiped clean, and the red sash came down across one of his shoulders, leaving half his chest exposed. A golden ring was slid over one of his fangs, drawing attention to his regal appearance, while accentuating his best qualities.

"Well now, that's much better, isn't it? Let's get the two of you where you need to be."

TWENTY-EIGHT

The sound of hundreds of voices met them halfway through the labyrinth of halls, with the undertone of cellos weeping a slow, sad song. Their help saw them down the grand staircase and into the wide-open hall. Lara pointed them towards the main ballroom and hurried back to the shadows. Among the crowds of elite nobles and church leaders, eyes and whispers were already directed their way.

Malice laughed, elbowing Beatrice playfully. "This fancy crowd doesn't know what to think of us. Just a couple of mercenaries, but we're still the prettiest bastards here."

Beatrice bit the insides of her cheeks to hold back a laugh and nudged Malice back.

Walking into the ballroom was like stepping into a dream. The ornate parquet floors would show themselves occasionally underneath the sea of feet and flowing gowns, like the sun peeking out from the rolling clouds. The ceilings were high, with more arches than they could count. The whole scene was lit by chandeliers ablaze with unnatural but beautiful golden flames. The people, all dressed in the finest clothing Beatrice had ever seen, glowed in the gilded light. In the center of the room couples danced, smiling and serene.

The rest congregated around the edges of the ballroom, engaged in more subtle dance. One wall was peppered with open doors, and people streamed in and out from the terrace.

It was all beautiful- gorgeous even. But Beatrice took it in only in passing as her eyes searched the wide room for a specific target.

At the far end of the room, three banners hung from arches. The first was red. Under the banner, Arthur, his high clerics, a husband and two wives, and a small congregation of other people all sat at a high table, laughing jovially about some unheard joke.

The center banner, white and marked with the Triad spiral, hung above Lestra. She sat in a tall-backed golden chair, watching the room with the eyes of a hawk. Her table sat empty.

The final banner was her target, golden yellow. Diana was a vision of ethereal beauty. Her long blonde hair was woven into a complex bundle, wrapped around the base of an intricate gold headpiece that pointed to the sky like a compass. A man sat on either side of her- one was a handsome human that looked to be in his fifties, the other was an elf nearly as beautiful as Diana herself. Both men looked perfectly content, a fact that annoyed Beatrice fiercely. A swathe of clerics sat around them, though they weren't having nearly as good a time as Arthur's bunch.

And there he was. Gespar Fairchild was the single most beautiful thing in the Grand Palace ballroom. His golden hair was neatly pushed back from his face, which Beatrice noted was freshly shaven. His clean jawline looked sharp enough to cut through the hearts of anyone that got too close. His clothes were the same formal uniform worn by all the paladins that evening, but his looked like it must have been sewn around his body.

The people around him were engaged in conversation, but Gespar looked detached. The drink in his hand was still and undisturbed, and his eyes wandered the room restlessly. As they landed on her, his smile lit up the surrounding area, overpowering the golden flames. Beatrice realized with a flutter in her belly that he had been searching for *her*. She tried to bite back her own smile and was barely successful while watching as he stood, excusing himself from the table.

He grinned at her and waved. They were simple gestures, honestly a little foolish. He looked so young when he made that face- youthful and gorgeous, and he was walking her way as if she were the only other person in the room. Beatrice failed one final attempt to push down the heat that rose in her chest and then in her cheeks. She raised her hand to wave back, but it was caught halfway up.

Beatrice looked in shock at the hand holding her own, and then at its owner. He was about the same height as her, on the stout side but objectively attractive. "Hatcher Townsed." He said, smiling at her.

"No, you must have mistaken me for someone else."

"No, my dear- *I'm* Hatcher." He kept smiling, oblivious. "And you are?"

Beatrice turned to Malice for support, only to find that he was surrounded by a group of Paladins of Gerra in their bright red uniforms, having a lively conversation. Looking back to the opposite side of the room, she was unable to see Gespar amongst the crowd.

"Beatrice," she responded, surrendering to the situation with a smile. "Beatrice Lemon."

"Beatrice Lemon." He tasted her name as it rolled across his tongue. "A lovely name for an *exquisite* lady."

"Yes, I have a horse named after me."

Either not hearing or not listening, the man plowed onward. "Would you do me the honor of a dance?" Beatrice noted that he had never lessened his grip on her hand.

"Of course." After all, they were there to be seen.

The dance was not unpleasant, nor was the one after that. She remembered Lara's advice and held to it strictly- accepting all invitations to dance, but never more than once. This wasn't particularly difficult to stick to, since there always seemed to be another partner waiting. Hours must have passed this way. After a particularly energetic jaunt with a Cestian royal delegate who seemed determined to move three times as fast as whatever music was playing, Beatrice found she needed a break- particularly one involving a drink and a moment's peace.

The drink was easy to find, there were literal stacks of them all about. Fine crystal glasses filled with red and white wines, Sunspot rums, and Cestian tonics. She resisted the urge to grab a glass for each hand.

The peace, on the other hand, was much harder to come by. In the process of finding it, she received three more invitations to dance (including another from Townsed), two introductions, and one inquiry as to who her father was. Eventually, though, she found herself out on the terrace behind the palace. People still strolled aimlessly about in pairs and small groups, but it was pleasantly quiet, and the fresh air was enough to bring her back to reality. Or, closer to it anyway.

The terrace stretched the full length of the Grand Temple grounds and was accessible from any of the three buildings. Beatrice drained the glass she carried and set it down on a bench before wandering to the far edge. There was no dividing wall at the edge of the terrace, only a few strategically placed statues of large stone hawks. Bee had expected to come upon a sloping hill down to the ocean, or steps even. Instead, she found that the stone edge of the terrace ended abruptly, overhanging an inlet that must be nearly fifty feet below. It made her stomach flip to look down at the sheer drop.

Lara had warned her against drinking too much for social reasons, but it was just as imperative to avoid a drunken stumble off the edge. If you took a misstep here (*or,* Beatrice speculated, *upset a blessed leader*) your only hope would be that the water below was deep enough to catch you and that the waves were gentle enough not to dash you against the rocks before you drowned.

She could see why it had been made this way though. The view was breathtaking, like looking out at the edge of the world. The Grey Sea lived up to its name, stretching out to meet the stars. The Triad harbors were visible to the south, and away to the east must have been the shores of Lorsen, though all she could see was ocean.

For a moment her mind settled on Beacon. Something in her wished that she felt a sense of homesickness thinking about it. Berta, the Knightcap, the familiar streets, they were all precious to her but her heart wasn't tied to the place. It wasn't tied to the city or the buildings or even the people there. It was tied to Malice, certainly, but he was with her everywhere she went. She never left her heart behind. That was perhaps why it was so easy to do what they did, to travel, to fight, to steal- to walk into any situation. But, perhaps if she had felt the mild ache of other ties, she wouldn't be so worried about how much of her heart she was about to leave behind in this place.

"Finally, I've been looking for you all night." As if summoned by her thoughts, Gespar sidled up next to her. "Enjoying the view?"

She looked out at the ocean, avoiding looking at him directly. "It's beautiful."

"It is." He answered, but she could still feel his eyes on her. He sighed before speaking again. "I fear I've made a terrible mistake."

"Just one? That's an improvement," Beatrice said. "What have you done, Good Paladin? Eaten too many of the tiny cakes?"

"I sent you that dress, knowing full well that you would be the most beautiful woman here tonight if you wore it. Now, everyone stumbles over themselves to meet you, and I'm not sure I can stand to watch any more of these men dance with you this evening."

"Well..." Beatrice turned away, trying to hide the blush in her cheeks. "That certainly is a problem."

"So, I'll just have to claim the rest of your dances for the night." He turned back toward the palace, offering his arm.

"I have been specifically warned about that sort of behavior," Beatrice teased, though she regretted it. "You get one, just like all the rest."

She looped her arm through his, and they headed back towards the ballroom.

"Well then," He leaned closer to her as if sharing a scheme between the two of them. "We had better make it count."

The postures and gestures that had felt so formal and meaningless for every other dance suddenly came to life. His arm at her waist, her hand in his, the close proximity... Beatrice felt each touch as they slowly turned about the room to the soft drone of the music. She watched the other couples around them to distract herself, and inadvertently locked eyes with Diana, still seated in her place of honor. The woman's expression was unreadable, eerie in its lack of emotion.

"You're quite good at this, for someone with your background," Gespar commented, lifting her hand over her head and pushing her gently into a turn.

"And what background is that?"

"Well, I only meant... A woman in your trade might not be expected to... I don't know." He finished lamely.

"I wasn't always in this 'trade'," Beatrice answered. "If you must know, I used to practice with my sisters. This is exactly the sort of dreamy scenario we used to stay up late chattering over." She finished with a faraway look in her eyes.

"So, what happens now?"

"What?" Beatrice was startled by the question, her mind still on girlhood fantasies of public proposals and stolen kisses in alcoves.

"The job is done, the stone is safe in the Temple...your contract fulfilled. Where does Beatrice Lemon go from here?" Gespar watched her face carefully. He spoke the question so casually, but his eyes burned with a weight that flustered Beatrice.

"Wherever the work takes me, I suppose."

"What if the work kept you here?"

"In Triad City?"

"Within the church. What if you and Malice signed on?"

"Sign on with the church for *what,* Ges?" Beatrice asked him. "Heroic thieving?"

"That's how we got here, isn't it?"

She rolled her eyes.

"It takes all sorts, Bee. Malice is already fitting right in." He gestured towards Arthur's table, where Mal was having an arm-wrestling match with the Blessed Leader himself. "And someone that can talk, sneak, *or* fight her way out of a tricky situation would be invaluable."

"So, I should join the ranks of the Faithful, because I would be the perfect tool for the Gods?"

"You should stay because you want to." Gespar tightened his grip on her, suddenly looking at her with a furrowed, serious expression. "And perhaps because I want you to."

A chill ran up her spine. Funny how the words she had longed to hear were capable of so much damage. "I don't know. If I stayed, I would get fat off of all these little cakes."

"Bee." He sounded frustrated. "Don't change the subject."

"Ges, I don't think this is the right time or place to talk about this."

To her surprise, he directed her away from the center of the ballroom, and breaking their dancing position, he pulled her by the hand through the door and down a long side-hall.

"Ges, I really don't think we should do this now." She protested, but he didn't turn around. He didn't even slow down.

At the end of the hall, Gespar opened a heavy door and pulled her into a room. There was a large table in the center of it, taking up most of the floor space. Dark wooden chairs surrounded it, and sideboards topped with delicate-looking vases lined the walls.

"There." He said, stubbornly. "We're in a different place, and we both know there's only so much more time."

"Time for what, Ges?" Beatrice crossed her arms.

"To have this conversation."

"About what?!"

"About you staying. Are you going to make me say it again, Bee?" Beatrice pressed her thumb to her forehead.

"I am asking you to stay. Because *I* don't want you to go."

"Why?" Beatrice whispered as frustration began to irritate her nerves.

"Why? Because you, me, and Mal work well together. You're my friends."

"Right. We are." She agreed, and let out a sigh. "So, say that hypothetically we stayed. We go out on jobs together? Do we become the Triad Empire's ultimate squad? And then one day Mal and I will sit in the front row at your grand wedding? And then we'll go on forever having meaningless conversations like this one, where we say everything except what we actually mean?"

"What do you want me to say, Bee?" Gespar stepped toward her. His voice was strained, and his lips were set in a frown. It wasn't a rhetorical question.

Beatrice felt her frustration reach a peak, burning hot enough to leave a hole in her chest. "I don't want you to say anything," she murmured, wrapping her hand around the back of Gespar's neck and pulling his lips to her own.

Like being blinded by a sudden flash of lightning, they were frozen in time for a single, precious moment. And then, the storm of their desires broke around them with a raging intensity. They couldn't kiss each other fast enough, or deeply enough. They couldn't grip at each other tightly enough, press their bodies close enough.

A deep rumbling sounded in Gespar's throat, something between frustration and pleasure, and he picked Beatrice up off the ground in one fluid motion. She wrapped her legs around him tightly, the sensation causing her to moan in response.

He set her gently on the tabletop, his kisses working their way down her neck as his hands found their way under the layers of her dress, caressing her thighs in a way that sent pleasant shivers throughout her entire body.

"I have never wanted anything so badly as I want you right now," Gespar whispered, his breath tickling her collarbone. His fingertips drifted over a sensitive area, and Beatrice sucked in a sharp breath.

"Ges-" It was as much a plea as an exclamation.

Gespar pulled back, looking into her eyes with a deeper intensity than Beatrice could have imagined, even in her wildest dreams. She pulled his face back to hers, kissing him roughly. The paladin began fumbling urgently with his belt, and Beatrice tightened her grip on his shoulders.

She tensed in anticipation, feeling him so close. Gespar pulled her body to his. "Gods, forgive me."

He kissed her again, but an ice-cold dose of reality was running down Beatrice's spine. He had whispered the words, so faintly that she had barely heard. But she *had* heard. And, now they wormed their way into her mind and took root.

"Ges..." When she broke their kiss to speak his lips moved elsewhere, continuing their hungry work.

"Gespar." She was more insistent this time, pushing him away. "Stop."

His beautiful brow furrowed in confusion as he stepped back. "I'm sorry." His face turned blood red as embarrassment and rejection set in. "I'm so sorry, I thought..."

"You thought right, Ges." Beatrice spoke softly, burying her face in her hands for a moment to clear her thoughts. "I want you too. Gods, I do. But that's just it. That's why I can't stay."

"Beatrice-"

"No." She interrupted him. "You know I'm right. I don't want to pine over a man that belongs to someone else. Maybe we could ignore this. Control ourselves. But we would both be miserable. And if we can't fight it, what then? I don't want to be the reason your vows are broken or the reason you lose what you are... I don't want to be a regret in your otherwise perfect history, Ges"

"I could never regret you, Beatrice. Not being with you, and certainly not how I feel about you. I think I-"

Beatrice cut off his words with a gentle kiss on his lips. "Don't say it, Ges. It'll make whatever comes next that much harder for both of us."

Beatrice climbed down from the table and stepped around Gespar, headed to the door. Her eyes burned, tears threatening to make themselves known, but she pushed them back with a deep breath.

"Maybe, I could leave..." Gespar spoke, but he sounded uncertain.

"What?" She froze, eyes wide and hand on the door.

Gespar gripped the back of his neck, a pained look in his eyes. He shook his head when he spoke again. "You're right. I understand why you can't stay at the Temple. So maybe the answer is for me to leave it behind."

"Is that even allowed?"

His voice was quiet. "No."

"What about all that you said about doing what you have to do, and being what you have to be? This is your *life*, Ges. Your home. Could you really walk away?"

"I don't know," he admitted. "I don't know, Bee."

She nodded and placed her hand back on the door.

"Bee." He caught up to her quickly, grabbing her hand as she made to leave the room. They exchanged a meaningful gaze. "Let's meet tomorrow. I'll think things over, and we can talk about it then."

"Sure, Ges." Beatrice squeezed his hand back, forcing a smile before she pulled free and slipped back out into the hallway.

Tomorrow... She wondered if he would hate her by this time tomorrow. Beatrice paused for a moment before heading back into the ballroom, taking a deep breath and pushing down the urge to cry. Then, resolutely she stepped back into the crowded party, determined to finish this once and for all.

It was unlike Mal to disappear when she needed him most, but multiple rounds of the ballroom and terrace turned up no sign of him.

TWENTY-NINE

A rthur Harrington's skin glistened under a layer of perspiration, the color of clay dirt after the rain. The handmaid, Shira, was jostled rhythmically by his thrusting. She muffled an indulgent moan and gripped the back of Malice's head. The three bodies moved in unison, and the orc growled his approval.

Sex, like most things in Malice's life, was a competition – a challenge to be won. It was entirely common for an orc female to choose her partner by laying with one suitor and then the other. Whoever performed better won the bride. Both at once though? It was higher stakes, immediate pay-off, *and* Malice thought, *a lot more fun.*

The door, locked for obvious reasons, was shaken violently.

"Mal?" The shout was immediately recognizable as Beatrice and followed with a slamming that he imagined was her small frame thrown against the door. "Mal!"

Malice pulled himself away from the tangle of bodies. He unlocked the door, and flung it open in a hurry, causing Beatrice to stumble slightly as she redirected the fist she had been about to slam against it.

Seeing his full body on display in the doorway, she wrinkled her nose and rolled her eyes. "Dammit, Mal! What are you doing?" As she diverted her eyes, they landed on the pair still rutting in the bed behind him. "What *are* you doing?"

Malice shrugged. "Enjoying the party."

She scrunched her eyes shut, pushing her thumb to her forehead. "Seven hells, Mal. Is that Arthur?"

"Does your friend want to join us?" Arthur called from the bed. "There's room for one more."

Malice considered Beatrice for a moment. "I wish you wouldn't," he said decidedly, not to be cruel. It was just a matter of fact.

"No, I don't *want* to, Gods!" She looked distracted, and somewhat dismayed by the scene.

"What is it, Bee?" Malice asked.

"I was going to say that it's time to go, but clearly you're in the middle of something.

"Go?"

"Go. Get what we came for and leave." Bee whispered, trying to move further from the doorway. Malice didn't follow her.

"You're still doing this?"

"Of course I am, Mal. We don't have a choice."

Malice squared his shoulders. "We do have a choice, and you're making the wrong one."

Beatrice gaped at him.

"You wanted to make it big, Bee. This is it. New work, new friends, maybe even a new life. Claw's men would have to work awfully hard to touch us here."

"Here?" Beatrice was exasperated.

"We could stay. We'd be good at it. It's good coin, and a home, and we wouldn't have to worry about winding up in jail on a daily basis."

"It's not that simple!" Bee exclaimed, before reigning in the volume of her voice again. "I *can't* stay here, Mal!"

Malice took a closer look at her now. Flushed cheeks, glassy eyes, the thin skin on her chest splotched with red. He stepped out of the room, mostly closing the door behind him.

"What about Sunshine?" He tried to speak more gently now, but Beatrice made it hard to be patient when she was like this. She wasn't listening. Not really.

"What about him?"

"You think you can bullshit *me,* Beatrice?"

Her eyes widened, and her brow knit together tightly. She stretched herself as tall as she could muster, puffing out her chest and glaring at him.

"We're taking the stone, and we're leaving. "

"No."

"No?"

"We shouldn't take it. If you do, that's on you. I won't stop you, but I won't help."

Beatrice looked stricken. When had Malice ever refused to help her? He knew how it must feel, now especially. Didn't change the fact that he was right, and she needed a kick.

Hurt and anger burned on her face. She turned abruptly and walked away from him, and he let her go.

THIRTY

After gathering her things Beatrice made her way out to the terrace. It wasn't wise to change out of her gown yet. It would be inconvenient to make a quick exit dressed that way, but she left the dress on to blend in, throwing her satchel over her shoulder. She concentrated on her task, shutting out any thoughts of Gespar and Malice. Guests still strolled the length of the terrace, and Beatrice blended right in.

She had a pretty good idea where she was going, thanks to Gespar. He had said the stone was safe in the Temple. Making her way to the far end of the grounds, Beatrice waited until she was certain no one was watching, and then snuck around the side of the building. The doors to the Temple were not locked, and the inside was just as bright as during the daytime thanks to the bright golden torches lining the walls.

Beatrice lifted her skirt, wrapping the fabric around her wrist and holding it aloft as she walked quietly down the halls. It was easy enough to find her way to the main hall, and luckily it was abandoned. She closed her eyes, trying to think of the best place to start looking. It obviously wouldn't be in the Grand Sanctuary for the eyes of the public to see, but she imagined the Blessed Leaders would want it near themselves.

To that end, she climbed the staircase to the Throne Room. The room felt even longer when it was empty. The three large thrones sat ominously empty at the far end, and as Beatrice climbed the stairs to the platform she paused for a moment before moving around the table and into the space behind. The same red, white, and gold banners lined the walls here, and five doors lined the three angled walls at the back of the chamber.

She could have easily tried all five of the doors, though it would have been time-consuming. Instead, Beatrice took a deep breath, trying to imagine what the layout of the temple might be, and which door most likely led to her target. Three of them were marked with the banners of their respective branches. But, it would probably be in neutral territory. The other two were identical, unassuming, unmarked wooden doors.

"There you are." Beatrice whispered somewhat uneasily, homing in on one of the doors. While one of them had a dim shadow around the edges, the other seemed to be leaking darkness- the opposite effect of the sunshine spilling underneath a door on a bright after-noon.

Beatrice cursed under her breath when she tried the door. There was no way the key to a room like this would be left unattended nearby.

She perked up as she flung her hand to her hair and gently felt at her braid, pulling loose two of the beautiful golden pins. She held them in her palm for a moment, admiring them. The heads were shaped like many-pointed stars. They were delicate, and beautiful.

It wasn't until then that she realized she hadn't thanked Gespar. She sighed, inserting one of the pins into the lock, and carefully used just enough pressure to bend it at a sharp angle. She inserted the other pin gingerly in behind the first, crooking the end before sliding it to the back of the lock. She leaned in close, closing her eyes and listening carefully for the click of metal on metal. A few moments later the lock released with a satisfying clack. She opened the door and stepped silently into the dark room.

Shelves lined the walls from floor to ceiling, stacked with books that looked ancient. Under different circumstances she might have stopped to admire some of them, but this was not the time or place to allow for such distractions.

The Shadowgate stone sat on a cushion on a pedestal, unsettling darkness wafting off of it like smoke. Beatrice swallowed, stepping towards it.

It was right there, ripe for the picking- not for the first time.

"Right..." Beatrice spoke to herself, urging herself onward. "There it is. Just reach out and take it, and this is all over."

She extended her arms, reaching for the stone, but found that the idea of actually touching it was unsettling. She hesitated, staring into the depths of the darkness. It was unnatural. Ominous. She could feel in her bones that there was something in that darkness that she was almost certain was better left there. Why would anyone want this damned thing?

Not for any good reason, certainly. The only good place for it was behind lock and key.

Why was she here?

"Ah, shit..." Beatrice hissed.

She had rebuked Gespar for not using his moral compass to make his choices, but she was just as guilty. Even worse, she hadn't let any vows or sense of loyalty control her actions. She had just been afraid. Afraid for her life, afraid of confronting who she was, and afraid of her feelings.

She didn't want this. She didn't want the money. She didn't care if Claw sent an army after her.

Beatrice Lemon knew what she wanted, and she wasn't going to get it by stealing this damn stone.

She turned back, pausing only a moment as if to confirm with herself that she wasn't going to take it. Then she slipped back out into the throne room, out the large doors, and down the stairs.

"Now what?" she wondered out loud, not entirely sure what this meant for her next move.

"Now what, indeed?"

Beatrice jumped as Diana stepped out of the shadows, a cold smile on her flawless face.

"May I ask what you're doing in here?" Diana purred, stepping closer to Beatrice.

"I needed some quiet... a break from the festivities. I thought a moment of prayer and reflection would be nice."

"In the Throne room?" Diana's smile didn't falter.

"Ah, no." Beatrice chuckled. "I got turned around."

"Of course."

Beatrice respectively bowed to dismiss herself and turned to hurry out of the Temple. She only made it a few feet away before Diana spoke again.

"It's going to tear my poor husband apart when he finds out what you really are."

"And what am I, *really*?" Beatrice took the bait, against her better judgement.

Diana's smile curled into a sneer for a split second. "A thief and a traitor, sent to steal from him by any means necessary. I wonder if he'll even bring himself to look at you when he hears of your betrayal."

"I don't have anything of yours, but you're welcome to search me." Beatrice spread her arms in a wide gesture.

"I didn't say you were a *good* thief."

"Okay." Having had enough of this, Beatrice dropped any false civility. "I haven't stolen anything, and you can't arrest me because you don't like me. Or is this about-"

"I don't know what has happened between you and Paladin Fairchild," Diana interrupted. Beatrice was disappointed by the lack of anger in her words. "Perhaps you've broken his vows- been a distraction. Frankly, I don't care. He still belongs to me."

"We both know he's better than that."

"We both know he's better than *you*. You don't belong here."

"And what if I don't want to go anywhere?"

"Well, luckily for me, I'm not the only one that wants you out of the way."

A shiver rippled across Beatrice's shoulders.

Two shapes moved in from the shadows of the hallway, and Beatrice cursed as she recognized them.

"Isn't this just like you, Beatrice? Making friends everywhere you go."

She spat her response, not bothering to try to run. "Fuck off, Paz."

THIRTY-ONE

G espar Fairchild was up before the sun, pacing in his chambers. He wondered, somewhat giddily, when he had last made a decision based on his feelings. He looked about the room. One wall was lined with bookcases, though there were more weapons on the shelf than books. A collection of swords, a handful of daggers, and one mace polished to a high shine. Tools to enforce ideals he had been taught, and had never thought to question.

A writing desk in the opposite corner had a box with correspondence from his father and brother and a few letters from Deacon. It wasn't even half full. His wardrobe stood open, full of uniforms and clothing that one could find in the wardrobe of any paladin in the Empire, except for the one civilian outfit he had bought in Bay.

There was little else in the room. He appraised it all one piece at a time, deciding if there was a single thing here that he couldn't leave behind. Nothing tempted him to stay.

And the job? His duty to protect the Empire? He thought of the village in the Wander Wood. Couldn't he protect those people just as well on his own?

He would be an outlaw. That didn't seem to burden Beatrice or Malice. The only person he'd ever known had defected was Carter, and no one had ever heard from him again. He had thought many times about what had befallen his friend, and why Carter had left. Was he still alive? Did his family know where he was? Did he take on a new identity? *Maybe* Gespar thought now, *maybe he'd met a beautiful woman and fallen in love.*

Gespar, with a sudden and decisive burst, went to his wardrobe and pulled out the civilian clothes. He stripped away his paladin robes almost ceremoniously and dressed in the unadorned outfit. He looked at himself in the mirror, standing tall. This was not Paladin Fairchild. This was Ges. He liked what he saw.

The hopes that carried him to his door were dashed as he flung it open. Diana stared back at him, four Faithful flanked her in the hall.

"Paladin." Her smile was gentle as she spoke, but the tension of all those in the hall set Ges on edge.

He bowed his head, partially out of respect and in part to hide the sudden surge of guilt he was sure would be visible on his face.

"What are you wearing?"

Though she wasn't more than an inch taller than him, Diana managed to look down at him as she spoke, taking in his appearance in a manner that left Gespar feeling uncomfortably exposed.

"Street clothes. I was going to take care of a few things in town." The lie came forth naturally, smooth and simple.

"Well." When she spoke, he couldn't tell if she was disgusted or amused. "You look so... Normal."

She moved to enter his chamber, halting her escorts in the hall with a wave of her hand.

"Your *errands* will have to wait. Lestra has called an emergency council and your presence is required."

"What's happened?" If he had been on edge before, the feeling stirring in his gut now was panic. This was anything but good news.

"I'm sure we'll be informed once everyone is gathered. You'll need your uniform. I'm afraid, I can't have my husband show up in the throne room looking like *that*."

She didn't move, watching him expectantly.

"I'll be along shortly." He bowed, hoping to dismiss her. His stomach churned with his unease and the desire to be left alone, to get away from here and find Beatrice and Malice.

Diana stepped into his immediate space, reaching out to trace the opening of his shirt. Her fingers were cold where they grazed his skin.

"Come now, Fairchild. You look tense. You've undressed in front of me before."

"It wouldn't be proper now, though."

"You were so enthusiastic then. So eager to please. Now you just seem... restless. We could remedy that. It's hardly indiscretion if you're promised to me already."

The memories from nearly four years past felt like another life-time. It was true he had thought it a blessing then. He had hoped to prove himself worthy of an honor he had only gained through the loss of a friend. He had relished the opportunity to explore the se-crets of a woman's body. A woman's touch. She was no less beautiful now. No less in *any* aspect. Yet she had no claim on Gespars heart, his body, and certainly not on his present thoughts. He stepped away from her touch.

"What if I didn't wish to be promised to you?"

Her eyes flashed for an instant before her face settled back to emotionless porcelain.

"Meaning?"

"What if I asked to be released from our engagement."

She was silent so long Gespar doubted she would acknowledge his words. Finally, she spoke quietly as though to herself. "Human men amaze me."

Without any change of countenance, or sign of her feelings on this topic, Diana crossed to the chamber door. "Of course, I wouldn't force you into anything you didn't want, but it's a serious request. One that will affect your family as much as yourself. We can discuss it further, but perhaps you should be caught up on current events before you make any final decision, Paladin. Make yourself decent and report to the Throne Room. I believe you'll find the topic to be *quite* informative."

With an almost silent clap of the door, she left him alone. Gespar found himself obeying the direction, though his intentions hadn't changed.

Informative was not the word Gespar would have used to describe the mornings report. *Heartrending, nauseating, unbelievable,* would have been more accurate.

Lestra was furious. He had seen her annoyed, impatient, even angry. This quiet, seething rage was so much worse. It was downright frightening.

Faithful Captain Gildred gave his report of the morning rounds in a shaky monotone that echoed from the walls of the throne room. Gespar stood at perfect attention. His face held serious and thoughtful, but his mind wandered.

He knew that all the facts pointed towards the same conclusion, but he still couldn't make himself believe the accusations. If Beatrice and Malice had intended to steal from him they would have done it long before now. He couldn't bring himself to mistrust them.

"And there were no disturbances in the outskirts..."

He couldn't forget the way Beatrice had looked at him. He had felt her feelings for him in the way she had pressed herself so close, and in the way she had clung to him so desperately. His cheeks warmed at the memory. If nothing else, that was real.

"And, no signs of our *departed guests?*" Lady Lestra droned on.

Wasn't it? More real than anything here, at least.

"Paladin Fairchild."

Something was wrong. They wouldn't have left him behind.

"*Paladin Fairchild!*"

Every eye in the throne room was on Gespar when he was drawn back to the moment.

"Yes, Lady Lestra?"

Everyone around him seemed to shift uncomfortably.

"I had just asked you, Paladin," Lestra spoke carefully, her jaw tight. "If you know where your mercenary *friends* might have gone."

"I haven't the faintest idea." Gespar tried to sound as collected as possible when he spoke.

There was no immediate answer, only another awkward silence and glances exchanged that he couldn't gather the meaning of. Finally, Lestra waved a thin hand broadly out at the crowd.

"Dismissed."

The gathered faithful, Paladins, and Clerics waited a breathless moment before beginning to file out of the throne room.

"Captain Gildred." She halted the guard captain with her voice. "Paladin Fairchild."

Gespar hadn't bothered attempting to leave yet anyway.

Once the room was emptied of all unnecessary bodies, Lestra turned her attention back to Gespar.

"What do you know about the thieves?"

A rush of thoughts filled Gespar's mind.

"They were skilled and pleasant to work with. They were an asset to the mission and I would recommend them for employment to anyone who asked."

Diana wore an expression of pure satisfaction as she watched, her nose held high as she looked down the stairs at him.

"I would trust them with my life," he added.

"Then your judgement is appalling and your trust worthless," Lestra spat.

"Who is to say they haven't left because their contract was complete? Do you have proof that it was them?"

"I caught the woman in the act," Diana interjected. "She attacked me, no doubt attempting to cover her tracks, and I only just escaped with my life."

"Bullshit." Gespar spoke without thinking.

"Excuse me?"

"If Beatrice Lemon had intended to kill you, you would be dead."

"Watch your tongue, Paladin." Lestra's voice raised now.

"It's alright." Diana raised her hand. "I do not blame my husband. I can guess that they were doting companions during your time together? Building you up, ingratiating themselves by any means. But for that sort, it's part of the job. Loyalty only extends as far as payment."

Diana paused, watching him as if soaking in the effects of her words. Gespar stood fast, hoping it would deprive her of some satisfaction.

"I forgive your naivety, husband," she continued. "Your willingness to trust is a strength, not a weakness. Some women simply know how to turn such things to their advantage."

Gespar's jawline tightened involuntarily.

"I do not doubt that Miss Lemon is such a woman, she knows how to turn many things to her advantage. However, I have full faith in both of them. I only see one side retracting false loyalties after it's no longer useful."

"Enough," Lestra decided. "Bring them in, *alive*. And get me that stone back. Send your five fastest on the road to Central," she told

Gildred. "Post watches on every road out of the city, and send men around to every inn and tavern you can get to."

"I'll send word to the Temple in Central to take similar measures," Diana added.

With that Gildred hurried from the room. Lestra and Diana stood, leaving the throne room together through one of the back doors. Gespar's rigid posture fell away, the shaking he'd been suppressing in his hands set loose.

This was wrong.

"You place more faith in these friends of yours than the Triad?"

Gespar looked up to see that Arthur had approached him, watching him carefully. He made the tactful decision not to answer. Arthur smiled, his unnaturally sharp canines flashing.

"Come to my chambers when you find a quiet moment. I believe I have something that will be of great interest to you."

THIRTY-TWO

"If we don't feed her, she's only going to slow us down."

"She's a dead woman anyway, it doesn't matter."

"Claw may want her alive."

"If he does, she'll wish we had let her starve."

Only one day of this and Beatrice was already tired of listening to Paz and Dart argue.

"Have you considered rock, paper, scissors?" she asked.

Paz lifted a threatening hand, only to have it caught by his brother.

"Gods, brother, is that necessary?" Dart released him with a jerk and a gaze of warning. It was going to be a long road to Beacon.

Gumby sat next to Beatrice, rocking gently on the ground. He wouldn't meet her eyes despite the several attempts she had made to speak to him.

Paz gave up, sitting in brooding silence.

"Would you like to eat, Beatrice?"

Beatrice wondered vaguely why Dart was still trying so hard to be civil.

"Sure," she answered, holding up her bound hands. "Untie me and I'll eat."

"Right, and then try to claw your way out of this."

"For what? I've been framed by the Empire itself. Where will I run to?"

It was true, she had nowhere to go. Perhaps no one to go to. Diana had made it quite apparent why she had thrown Beatrice to the wolves. What was still unclear was why she had handed over the Shadowgate Stone.

Beatrice eyed the chest that contained the stone, gathering her thoughts. Just because she had nowhere to go, just because Malice and Gespar might be better off without her, didn't mean she couldn't be the thorn in a few more deserving paws.

She waited until the twins were occupied with another argument to try her hand with Gumby again.

"How's life with the twins?" she asked. "Glad you ran off?"

"I saw a way out and I took it. Can you blame me?"

"Not at all. I'd like a way out myself actually." Beatrice held out her bindings hopefully. Gumby looked away. *Fine.*

"Let me give you a little advice." She lowered her voice, though they were unlikely to be overheard anyway. "If a way out is what you want, don't follow these guys back to Beacon. Claw is the sort you don't want to get tangled up in, trust me."

Gumby looked at her tied hands now, and Bee tried to look as casually bothered by them as possible.

"The way I see it," she went on, "the only real way out is that box, right there."

She had his attention now.

"The item in that box is worth more to the Empire than this lot knows. If I could get it back to Triad, I could clear my name and be set for life. Especially when I tell them Diana lied to them and gave it away."

Beatrice could see the man's brain churning. She was sure she had him.

"If I could get loose... If I could get a weapon, we could-"

A small stone made contact with Bee's shoulder, stinging where it hit and putting an abrupt end to her speech.

"What are you running your mouth about now?" Paz called, tossing another rock her way. This time Bee twisted out of its path.

"You know me, I just can't help talking about nothing at all."

"Don't encourage her." He turned his annoyance on Gumby. "If a serpent could talk, they'd call it Beatrice Lemon."

"And if a repetitive ass could talk, I would call it my brother," Dart said.

"It's always a fun time with you two. Why don't you just kill me now?"

"Good question." Paz mumbled.

"*Because,* Claw might not want you dead." Dart said.

Paz scoffed. "At least not right away. I hope he'll make an example of you first. Something gruesome."

"That does sound about right..." Beatrice agreed, with a pointed look at Gumby.

Gumby absentmindedly reached for his scarred ears.

The next morning, he was gone.

This was not the outcome Beatrice had hoped for, but she really couldn't blame him.

Every step they took further from Triad city felt heavier. It was the weight of a death sentence. Her own, and perhaps her friends' as well. Escape was the only thought in her mind, if not only for her sake, for theirs as well. Return the stone, save the day, and take back something she didn't have to steal.

An escape attempt then, Bee decided, and it might be the last chance she got. She took in the landscape around her. They were still on ground her companions had covered just days before. She looked to the men with her now, armed and alert. Paz showed the faintest sign of the injury Ges had inflicted on him at the lake, a slight favor to his right side. Dart carried the chest containing the stone. Though it was a nuisance it wasn't heavy enough to be a true burden.

She considered her own condition. Tied, weaponless, and slowed by the now ruined fabric of her dress wrapping around her legs. If she hadn't already been so put out by captivity and the metaphorical noose around her neck, she would have been heartbroken by the state of it.

She stopped in the path. She needed a moment to think. A way to stall. *Hells,* she needed a distraction.

"You don't plan on going through the Wander Wood, do you?"

"Why not? Your flighty friend told us all about your first pass through."

"Oh, good. That saves me the trouble. But I'll need to change clothes if I'm going to keep pace."

She indicated her satchel, carried by Dart. The twins considered her for a moment before reaching an unspoken conclusion between them. Bee was struck by a sudden pang of loneliness. She and Mal would communicate just like that.

"Here, by the road." Paz took the satchel, tossing it just off the path impatiently before coming to face her. His eyes burned hot as he cut her ties. "Try anything and I will gut you."

Beatrice opened her mouth to retort. Nothing came out. Struck by a sudden spell of vertigo, she closed her eyes. The feeling was familiar. Strong. Incoherent.

"Hurry up," Paz prodded.

Choosing to nod complacently instead of stirring him further, Beatrice searched his face for some sign. He showed no awareness of whatever had just struck her, but she could still feel it in the air, heavy and cold.

She turned away, stooping quickly to open her bag, searching the trees around them as she pulled loose her road clothes. There was nothing to be seen.

She exchanged the gown quickly for pants, and began haphazardly pulling her blouse on as she fumbled in a small pocket on her belt, looking for her gem, the Fire of the Depths. Her light in the dark.

An owl began screeching in a tree above them, shaking the branches as though it were being attacked.

The chain and the gem were gone.

"Looking for this?"

When she turned, Bee was startled to find Paz standing much closer than he had been a moment ago. He held aloft the chain, the stone glinting in midair. *Hadn't it been brighter?*

Paz stepped closer, something new burning in his deadly gaze. Beatrice quickly pulled her bodice on over her blouse, clasping the stays tightly and trying to look collected. Another step, and he had closed off what little space was between them.

"Here," Paz took the chain, reaching delicately around her neck to fasten it in place. "Wear it home, Beatrice. Leave it out for everyone to see, a shining example of everything you are. A lying, thieving traitor."

His long, graceful fingers traced the chain from the back of her neck, around to her collarbone. The touch lingered too long, setting Beatrice's instincts on fire.

"Get your hands off me." As she moved to swat his hand away, Paz caught her wrist, squeezing tightly.

"You prefer the soft men that coddle you? Like my brother. Like that Paladin." He twisted gently, causing her to bend to the motion. "Maybe you need someone to put a touch of fear in you."

Something was wrong. The electric feeling in the air was surging with enough intensity to turn her stomach. She couldn't decide between screaming, spitting, or laughing in Paz's face. She *did* feel fear, but a tinge of something wilder colored her emotions. Something beyond words.

"What the hell are you doing?"

Dart interrupted, his sword drawn and his posture tense. More birds began screaming in the canopy.

"Nothing you haven't thought of doing yourself, I'm sure."

"Clearly you have no insight into my thoughts then, *brother.*" The tension built with each word. "Let her go."

"Or what?" Paz twisted his grip on her further as he spoke, as if testing his brother's bravado.

"Have you lost your mind?"

In a breath, Dart reached to grab his brother's arm. Beatrice found herself released and watched, bewildered as the two elves turned on each other. As their tussle escalated into a full-blown fight, she gathered her wits, shoving her belongings back in her bag and pulling on her boots as quickly as possible.

"Shit..." She skittered about the area until she found the Shadowgate Stone's box. The guilt pulsed heavily in her gut as she ran to grab it, but her desire to get away was greater.

The chest held closely to her, she turned to flee, freedom all but guaranteed.

"Where are you going, Beatrice?"

With the words, an arm slipped around her neck, pulling her backward. Paz.

She couldn't see him, but she could hear the smile in his voice as he spoke in her ear.

"Misbehaving again. This seems like an awfully good excuse to dispose of you myself."

"I'll have to ask you not to do that." A new voice cut in, again out of her view. Beatrice felt Paz bristle where he held her.

"You'll mind your own business if you know what's good for you, stranger."

"Well, that's the trouble. This *is* my business, and here I am minding it, but *you're* in the way. So, you have five seconds to release the lady, or I will kill you."

Paz scoffed, turned to look at this newcomer making threats, dragging Beatrice around with him. She stifled the reflexive gasp that formed in her throat as she found herself facing Lemry.

Paz tightened his grip on her. "And just who in seven hells would you-"

Without a stutter or any other sign of struggle or distress, Paz went silent. His grip went limp, and Beatrice stumbled forward as the elf collapsed behind her. She could see immediately that the life had left his eyes.

"That wasn't five seconds." A tall, cloaked figure made himself known, stepping to Lemry's side.

Lemry shrugged, unbothered.

"How did you do that?" Beatrice turned her gaze away from Paz. The sight of him dead, even if he had been an ass, made her uneasy.

"Magic." Lemry bowed to her dramatically.

"And a touch of chaos." Added the stranger.

THIRTY-THREE

Gespar waited until late afternoon before making his way to the west wing of the palace, where Arthur and his spouses shared sprawling quarters on the top floor. He had never spent much time with Arthur or the servants of Gerra. They were a boisterous bunch, and the most inclined to bending the Triad's rules.

Now, bending the rules didn't seem like such a grave offense.

He climbed a wide set of stairs that deposited him in a short hallway lined with vacant armor on display and shining red banners. The hallway opened to a large parlor, designed for leisure and comfort- peace, not war. Large plushy seats, chess tables, a large piano, and multiple liquor cabinets crowded the space. More than a dozen people of varied races and affiliations lounged about the room. Hardly any of them noticed Gespar.

Arthur was among the numbers, deeply involved in a conversation with a small group. Gespar approached them, admittedly unsure of the situation. As he drew near one of the group spotted him. He recognized the middle-aged human woman as Arthur's first wife, Ophilia. She removed her full brown lips from the wineglass in her hand long enough to speak to her husband.

"Diana's pet is here."

Arthur turned to greet him, a satisfied grin lighting his face.

"Don't be unkind, dear. If I have any understanding of our situation, I believe he might resent being called Diana's 'pet'. And he did come to see us, after all."

"Which would anger Diana, no doubt. Forgive me for fearing her resentment more than his." Despite her words, Ophilia's tone was light, and she greeted Gespar by offering her hand and curtsying politely. "Welcome to the hall of Gerra, Paladin Fairchild."

She dismissed herself, pulling the other surrounding guests with her and leaving Arthur and Gespar to themselves.

"You keep plenty of company about," Gespar commented, as Arthur beckoned him down another hallway.

"War and Peace, Fairchild. To succeed in either requires friends." Arthur opened a door as he spoke, ushering him in to another room. "Luckily, you and I have friends in common."

"Sunshine!"

Malice's enthusiasm was contagious, and for the first time that day relief flooded Gespar's veins. He laughed as the orc thumped him on the back. It was short-lived however, as more questions sprung up, including the most prevalent question of the day.

"Where is Beatrice?"

"Probably pretty far off by now."

"You don't mean she actually stole the Stone?"

"Well, it sure looks that way."

Ges shut his eyes tightly, his fists clenching reflexively. "Was it your intention to steal it the whole time?"

"Our *intention*? That's a little fuzzy, but no. I would say we didn't intend to. Hell, Bee spent most of the time coming up with any excuse *not* to steal from you." Mal paused, as though weighing the words in his thoughts. "Were we *supposed* to steal it? Yeah, of course."

Gespar took a deep breath, trying to work through the flurry this started in his mind. *Why? Why now? And...* "Why are you still here? Why is she alone? The Triad is already hunting her, not to mention whoever was after us at the lake."

Malice shook his head, a pained expression drawing his face tight. "Maybe because I told her I wanted to stay. I figured she was being stubborn. In my defense, I really didn't think she would go through with it. Hell, I really thought you were gonna give her a reason not to."

"What is that supposed to mean?"

"Don't play dumb. She was goo from the moment she saw you, and you weren't much better. Like a couple of sexually frustrated pigeons cooin' around each other and then flying off spooked. I figured you would make some big scene. 'Stay with me, Bee.' 'Run away with me, Bee.' 'Kiss me on my mouth more, Bee'."

"That's..." *Hurtful. Rude. Uncanny.*

Instead of finishing the thought Ges pointed a threatening finger at the orc, who shrugged smugly. He turned his attention instead to Arthur. "You have nothing to say about all this?"

"It's not *bad*," Arthur admitted. "Though if you were trying to be persuasive you could've tried kissing things besides her mouth."

"I mean about the Stone! The theft!"

Arthur shook his head. "I have very little to say, except that it's dangerous and Lestra has plans for the Stone that would cast us all into the shadows. With any luck it will stay gone from here, though Lestra won't give up the hunt."

This was not what Gespar had expected to hear. Frankly, he wasn't sure what good his expectations were doing him anymore.

"That's where we come in," Malice said.

Arthur nodded. "Find the woman and make yourselves scarce. The farther, the better. Sun Spot, Cestian, anywhere. Take it to Lorsen and bury it in the ash pits. Just make it disappear."

"We..." Gespar brought his hands to his face. The information had landed faster than he could gather his thoughts. His emotions. This should change things, should change the way he was meant to feel. And yet...

"You can go without him." Arthur spoke to Malice. "He belongs to Diana as long as he's here, and she protects her own, even against her peers."

"That's his choice, but he's one of us now. I'm not leaving him unless he wants left."

"No." Gespar pulled himself to his full height. "I'm going."

Malice grinned at him.

"Then I suggest you don't delay. I'll see you make it off Temple grounds, and from there- " Arthur stopped short, tilting his head and squinting. "Shit."

"What?"

Before Ges had time to ask, the answer came in the form of rising voices down the hall.

"Stop! This is the Hall of Gerra, you have no right to go where you aren't invited." It sounded like Ophilia. "Arthur!"

Steps echoed down the corridor.

"Looks like we'll be fighting our way out." Malice hoisted his hammer, rolling his stiff shoulder and looking rather pleased at the idea.

"You won't make it down the hall," Arthur warned.

"Wanna bet?"

"Mal, wait!" Ges implored.

"There will be a time to fight, but it is not now," Arthur said. "Trust me, friend."

"Trust *me*. I won't go down without taking a few with me."

There was a banging at the door. "We are coming in under order of Lady Lestra of the House Sald."

"To what end?" Ges spoke in a hushed tone to Malice, trying to squelch out the fight already burning in the orc's eyes. "We won't do any good this way, and if we die here and now Beatrice will find a way to kill us all over again."

Mal groaned loudly enough it might as well have been a scream. "Then what do we do?"

The door burst open and a Paladin donning the white armor of Sald entered, Faithful streaming in behind him with weapons drawn.

"The Blessed Lady Lestra demands the companions of the thief be brought before her in the throne room." The paladin spoke to Arthur, giving a half-decent impression that he wasn't terrified. "And you as well, my Lord. For questioning."

Malice growled, still poised to attack. None of their options looked good, but Gespar was certain that buying time was the only chance they stood. As he had seen Beatrice do so many times, he looked at Malice with as much intention as he could muster, imploring him in silence. *Play along. Wait for a better opportunity.*

Malice snorted, releasing his hammer and letting it fall to the floor with a crash.

"Three on him, two on the paladin," the man ordered, and Faithful stepped forward to claim them.

As additional guards stepped forward Arthur spoke, his voice echoing off the walls. "Enough. We are going and require no assistance. I will not be led to my own throne like a prisoner. Any of you that lays hands on me will face the wrath of Gerra."

Gespar watched unblinking, as everybody in the room went still. Any primal urge he had felt to fight back had left him, and seemingly everyone else. The Faithful slackened their hold on him, bowing their heads low. Arthur stood tall and proud at the center of the crowded room, an energy rolling off him that Gespar could only describe as pure authority. His eyes flashed about the room, looking fire red for a moment as they caught the nearby light from the window.

Satisfied with the hush that had fallen, he gestured the Paladin of Sald towards the door. "Let's go then."

THIRTY-FOUR

Beatrice sat in the dimly lit Roadhouse, her thumb pressed hard to her forehead. The few hours of sleep Lemry had insisted they take had not been restful, and she was certain she didn't want to hear whatever was about to be said.

"Breakfast, my dear?" Lemry asked.

"Yeah." Beatrice figured she might as well get in a good meal if something bad was about to happen. "Lots. Eggs, sausage, coffee, and if they have any sticky buns get some of those too."

"As you wish." Lemry sauntered off.

Beatrice cautioned a glance at the stranger again, still to no avail. His hood hung so wide and low over his face that it hid him almost entirely, and every time Beatrice tried to catch a glimpse the man was always conveniently at just the right angle to hide him from view, or inexplicably she just couldn't quite focus on his features as if she were viewing him through water. Whoever he was, there was something familiar about him that she couldn't quite name. It wasn't his voice, which somehow was the single most *unrecognizable* voice she had ever heard. He sounded male, but that's about all she knew. His accent was unplaceable, and his tone rasping yet smooth.

She replayed their hurried journey back to the roadhouse in her mind again.

Lemry had eyed the chest she held hopefully. "Do you have it?"

"Have what?" There was only one thing it *could* have been, but Bee was nothing if not stubborn.

Her eyes found Dart's unconscious form lying on the ground. When she moved to check on him, Lemry held out a hand to stop her.

"That one will be fine. The Shadowgate Stone. Do you have it?"

Beatrice bristled. "How do you know about that?"

"Because, dear," Lemry answered, with a godly amount of patience. "I'm the one who hired you to steal it."

Beatrice couldn't bring herself to be shocked in the moment. She shifted the box in her arms and unlatched the lid.

The box was empty.

"So," Lemry sighed. "Does that mean you *don't* have it?"

The cloaked figure laughed merrily. "I *told* you she wouldn't. She's far too unpredictable for her chosen trade."

"Oh, sweet Beatrice." Lemry looked disappointed but not surprised.

Beatrice watched the mysterious stranger now with a glare. Lemry came back with food, which Beatrice promptly dug in to.

"Do you have to stare?" Beatrice stopped eating.

Lemry didn't look away.

"Just talk," Beatrice prompted him.

"Alright." He smiled at her, with sympathetic eyes. "You're certain the bandit has taken the Stone back to the Triad?"

"Almost positive."

"Beatrice, if we don't get that stone back, very bad things are going to happen."

"I've already been threatened several times over at this point. You'll have to try harder than that."

"I don't mean that something bad will happen to you alone. I mean bad things will happen to all of us."

"And our Paladin Fairchild will be at the epicenter," the cloaked stranger added.

Beatrice shook her head. "If I go back there it is for my own reasons. I won't steal your damn stone. It's back in the right hands."

"*Or* it's been placed directly into the wrong hands." Lemry presented this option delicately.

For the first time since she had met Lemry, his carefully sculpted smile disappeared. He turned to the stranger for a moment before going on. "Beatrice, there is something you need to understand about the Blessed Leaders."

"Is this going to be another half-assed bedtime story?"

Lemry ignored her. "They say the 'Blessed Leaders' are the Gods' own chosen to lead the Empire. That *may* have been the case at first. It may have been enough for the Triad Gods to be worshiped from a distance. But Arthur, Diana, and Lestra are more than just the God's favorites. They *are* Gerra, Vedett and Sald. They aren't mortal beings, they are three gods in mortal vessels. *The god's own chosen.*"

Silence permeated the space around them, and floating dust particles danced in the light that shone through the windows.

"That's madness," Beatrice said finally, though in the back of her mind she wasn't so sure that it was. "We spoke to them. Diana was a passive-aggressive bitch, and Mal and Arthur...." She trailed off, a pronounced frown tugging at her face. "How could you even know that? Even if they claimed to be the Gods, which they *don't*, how could you believe something like that?"

"My dear, I don't believe. I know. In the same way you know which person in a room is most likely to pick your pockets. Perhaps even in the same way you would recognize Malice if he came in wearing a funny hat and a velvet suit." He smiled again now, his eyes intently focused on Beatrice for her reaction. "I know because I know *them*. I know because I am of the same stock."

Beatrice stared back, unblinking. "Oh," she said plainly, as if she had just realized a very simple fact. "You're full of shit. There is a difference between storytelling and *lying*. You can't expect me to believe you're-"

"Din," He filled in for her.

A cold chill ran through Bee's veins.

"My true name is Din," he went on. "I am Prince of the realm of life and death. And I'm telling you, Beatrice, that getting that stone from Sald *is* a life and death situation."

"Prove it." Beatrice could barely raise her voice above a whisper.

Lemry—Din—sighed. He held out his arm, where the snake tattoo wound around his tanned flesh and caught its tail in its mouth. As she watched the snake began to move, crawling forward as if it were slowly consuming itself, but the slithering loop never ended.

"Is that supposed to impress me?" Beatrice said stubbornly, despite the dryness in her throat.

The cloaked stranger laughed again. "I like you, Beatrice."

He slid in closer to the table. With one sweep he pulled his hood over his head. What stared back at Beatrice was not a man, elf, orc, or any mortal race. His skin was blue, unnatural, and unfamiliar but beautiful. Beatrice found herself drawn to his eyes. They were *there*. He *had* eyes. But she couldn't quite see them, or at least her brain couldn't form a description of them that made any sense. They were endless pools of stars and time, shining at her from his face, making her feel small and insignificant.

He replaced his hood, covering the two small horns that grew from his scalp, and smiled at Beatrice. Canines as sharp as an animal's flashed at her.

"Nered is in his true form, not in a vessel. It's ideal, but not sustainable. The natural realm is like a divine void, and in our true forms, it sucks the power from us like a sponge. He won't be able to stay here long like this. He'll either have to return to his own realm or take a vessel."

"But the last one I was in was *such* a drag," Nered added. "It was a prison, not a tool, and I'm not ready to be cooped up again."

He smirked at Beatrice and for an imperceptible moment, she saw something familiar in the oblivion that was his eyes.

"You've got to be kidding me." She mumbled, pushing her thumb to her head.

"Is that a pun, Beatrice?"

"No, just run-of-the-mill disbelief. But it would have been a good one." Her eyes snapped up to him. "Why the hell would you be a goat?"

"I didn't *choose* to be. I was trapped in there by Sald. She wasn't happy with me."

He didn't show any signs of elaborating, so Beatrice shook it off.

"What does Sald want with the stone?"

"The stone draws darkness directly from the realm of light and dark, by opening a small portal between the two worlds. But the natural realm begins to draw the magic out. She would open it and leave it open until the natural world and the divine realms bleed together, creating something new. Sald is vindictive," Din continued. "This realm, in her mind, took her power of creation. The One creator made all the realms, the Gods, and the mortals. Sald has made nothing. She is the god of creation and destruction in name only. She wants to create something new, and her destructive nature won't be left aside."

"Fine." Beatrice pushed past this. It made her head ache and her hands shake and it was best left to muddle through later. "But why *us*? Why me? And why go through Claw instead of hiring us directly?"

"Well, because in your drunken ramblings- which are adorable, by the way- you confided in me that you weren't sure what you would do if Claw didn't welcome you back into the fold. I was trying to help. And as for why it had to be you?"

Lemry leaned back, crossing his arms as he looked at her. He looked rather pleased with himself.

"You see, the natural realm has one sort of magic the divine realms don't. Truly, there's nothing mystical, occult, or otherwise unnatural about it, but that makes it all the more mysterious." He leaned back across the table, waving his hand mysteriously in front of his face as he spoke. "*Signs.* Unmistakable omens, calling cards of fate. The magic of coincidence."

"I needed someone to acquire the Shadowgate Stone and who could be more suited to the job than the pair that had just stolen their opposite counterparts. The stones blessed by Crepus to draw out light otherwise unseen."

"Crepus has a flair for the dramatic," Nered added.

"So, Beatrice Lemon." Din's eyes were afire with enthusiasm. "Will you do it? Will you go back into the heart of the Empire, thwart the Gods themselves, steal the Shadowgate Stone, and save the world?"

"*And*, maybe sweep a certain Paladin in distress off of his feet?" Nered smirked at her.

Bee wished Malice were there.

She sat back, taking her time. Din wasn't the only one allowed to pause for dramatic effect.

"Yeah," she said finally, as if agreeing to a morning stroll. "I think I can manage that. But I can't do it alone."

THIRTY-FIVE

The Triad could learn a thing or two about taking prisoners from the southern bandits. The shackles that bound his wrists were rubbing him raw already. This, added to the inconvenience of simply being a captive once again, had irritated him beyond the limits of his patience.

In all his years Mal had been involved in countless bad plans, but this? This was worse. This wasn't even a plan. It was surrender.

On the far side of the throne room, Arthur was speaking to one of his own Paladins in hushed voices. When Arthur glanced towards Mal and Gespar, surrounded by nearly half a dozen Faithful, he held his gaze, tipping his chin up. Probably it was meant to be encouraging. Malice rolled his eyes, forcing a lung full of air out through his nose loudly. The guards around them flinched.

Usually when there wasn't a plan, there was still the same old skeleton to fall back on. The same main goal that every scheme fell in to place around. Protect Bee long enough for her to come up with a new plan. With no Bee there was no way out, and nothing to protect.

Well...

Malice turned his attention to Sunshine. The kid was taking being arrested by his own people incredibly well. Better than Mal had ages ago in a similar position. Sunshine stood still as stone, staring ahead with a thoughtful glare. Or maybe it was thoughtless. Maybe he wasn't taking this well at all. Mal couldn't tell, now that he thought about it. He missed Beatrice.

A door opened and the light, echoing click of female steps filled the air. Gespar shut his eyes, his chest rising and then falling in a slow breath. Sunshine didn't turn to look as Diana purposefully walked across the throne room. Her voice was as quiet and dry as ever, but somehow her rage still came through.

"What is going on here?"

And there it was. The urge to step in front of Ges and bare his teeth at the small woman. That was the plan then. Protect Ges until they found a way out. He could do that. Besides, if anything happened to Sunshine, Bee would be pissed. So, Mal stepped forward enough to make it clear where they stood.

Diana glared at him. Mal glared back. The woman didn't flinch, or even step back.

"Fairchild." There was the anger he would have expected. It leaked in to her voice for a moment, as she looked at Ges with the most pointed gaze Mal had ever witnessed. He was glad it wasn't directed at him. She went on.

"I will explain this *misunderstanding* to Lestra. When she hears that you were in contact with the mercenary in an attempt to find out where the thief has gone, I'm sure we'll be able to get you released."

"Except that's a lie." Gespar finally looked at the woman. "I was with Malice plotting to leave the church to find our *thief* and help her get far away from this place."

Diana's last thread snapped, but instead of the outburst Mal had expected she seethed with quiet wrath, her eyes burning almost literally. The guards gathered around them tensed.

"You foolish child, don't you see everything I've tried to do for you? I can't save you if your own survival instincts are stunted beyond hope."

"I see, and I'm grateful for your favor. But I've made my choice."

"And so you've chosen to throw your life away for a woman that's already dead?"

If Mal hadn't been shackled he would have grabbed Diana by her scrawny throat. "What the fuck does that mean?"

The anger fled from the woman's eyes, once again leaving her looking like a lifeless painting. She stepped away now, looking like she had suddenly grown bored with the conversation.

Ges pressed the question. "What do you mean 'already dead'? Did they find her?"

"Well... It's only a matter of time, isn't it?"

Diana walked away as briskly as she had come.

"Did they find her?" Ges shouted after her.

Diana was the only one in the long room that managed to ignore him. Every other set of eyes was on them now.

Malice met Arthur's gaze, and the man shook his head.

"They haven't. It's ok," Mal conveyed to Sunshine, but somehow the orc wasn't completely relaxed by the thought.

The tension jumped to new levels as Lestra entered. She was disturbingly calm as she came to stand by her spot at the center of the grand table.

The throne room fell silent. Lestra slowly looked over the hall, the Faithful, the prisoners, even her fellow Leaders. She took her sweet time about it, looking over every face for what felt like ages.

"You gonna ask us questions, or yell at us, or something?" Malice asked, causing a simultaneous clenching from everyone in the room.

"No." Lestra didn't seem angered by the question, although she certainly wasn't *happy*. "I imagine I know more than either of you at this exact moment."

"Lady Lestra- "

It was Diana that tried to speak, but she was quieted with a hand gesture and a glare cold enough to freeze flames. Malice noted this was the first time the emotion on the elf's face was readable. It was panic. But she shut her mouth.

"I would introduce to you a truly faithful servant of the God's. Some of you though, are already acquainted."

When Lestra summoned Gumby forward with a snap and a wave of her wrist the man scampered forward like a dog, and looked just as likely to start licking her palm. Malice wasn't surprised. He flamed with regret for not smashing the weasel's head in. But he wasn't surprised.

Sunshine wilted.

"You see, Gumbert has returned what was stolen from us." Lestra paused for reaction. Apparently, the stale hush and anxious stillness was what she was looking for, because she went on with pleasure in her voice. "And he's filled in the gaps in our understanding of the situation."

"Lestra, you can't-" Diana practically shouted, but was silenced with little more than a pointed finger.

"The woman, Lemon, was framed for the theft. Handed over to southern criminals. Along with the stone. He could not save the woman, but he has risked his own life to bring the Stone, so that it may not be used against us."

Fuck.

Malice shot Arthur a look, but the man was focused entirely on Lestra. All the warmth had fled from his face.

"Diana." Lestra drew out the name, almost singing it. "Would you care to explain why you've betrayed me this way? Betrayed the *Empire* this way?"

Now the hush was broken, the concerns and confusion of the few people there were made worse by the echoes off the long walls. Diana was braced against the long table, her eyes wild with the fear of an animal that hasn't decided if it should fight or flee.

"You have either forgotten our purpose or lied about it from the start, dear sister." Diana's voice shook.

"*My* purpose has never faltered. Make this realm in to something great and bring these half-complete mortal husks closer to divinity."

"I have been here too long, spent too many mortal lifetimes here, to watch you tear it apart." Diana stilled her shaking hands, taking a step toward Lestra with a new resolution. "The mortals don't need intervention or redesign, they need *protection.*"

"Enough." Arthur stood. He looked around for some way to stop the scene, or to calm the Faithful that watched with growing unease.

Lestra ignored them all, walking towards Diana. She smiled, a sharp and wild thing. Beautiful and well sculpted as the woman was, the expression was enough to turn Mal's insides soft with sickness.

"So, you feel it is your great purpose to stop mine?"

"If I must." Diana stayed in place, holding the taller woman's gaze.

"Leave us." Arthur shouted the order at Guard Captain Gildred, who seemed frozen in place. It was too late.

"Then you are a traitor and an enemy of the Empire, and of me."

One of Lestra's elegant elven hands closed around Diana's pale neck. Gespar tensed, as did a few of the other Faithful, but no one seemed able to move, or perhaps they weren't sure if they should.

Diana didn't struggle. She laughed, choking on the sound in her throat. She struggled to push words out through Lestra's grip. "Kill me then, show these people what a devil you are. I'll be back."

A strange thing to say, and stranger to hear. These uptight assholes seemed crazier the more time Mal spent around them. All their money and power and fancy shit-pots and they were no better than the likes of Claw. People were people no matter who they were, and people... Didn't start smoking when you choked them. Malice knew that from experience. But thick grey wisps were rising from Diana's skin.

"We'll see about that."

Lestra reached out with her other hand, but instead of doubling her grip on Diana's neck she grabbed the top of the woman's head.

As seemingly harmless as this ought to have been, the effect was immediate and violent. Diana's defiant attitude immediately changed to struggle. The pain was visible on her face even across the room. The grey smoke dissipated, replaced by the cracking hiss of wet wood in a campfire.

Ges flinched, stepping forward. None of the guards moved to stop him, so Mal took it upon himself to grab him. "Bad idea, kid."

He didn't judge the kid for looking away, most of the others already had. It was grim. But that meant that in the final moments, Mal was one of the few that saw Diana's eyes burst in to hot embers, blazing for just a moment before the woman went limp. Lestra let her fall unceremoniously to the floor.

The smell of sulfur and charred wood filled the Throne room.

"What did you do?" Arthur asked, so much quieter than he had been before.

"I *destroyed* her," Lestra answered.

"But she-"

"She's gone. Really gone."

Arthur sat down as though all strength had left him, his eyes empty with shock and confusion, as if the concept of death was new to him.

"This is the price of disloyalty," Lestra announced.

She was met with silence.

"You," She gestured to Gumby, who sat in a heap on the ground, tears shining on his thin face. "Come with me."

Her eyes landed on Malice and Ges. "Lock those two up. I've no patience for further disruption."

When the faithful grabbed Mal by the arm to lead them away he didn't struggle.

THIRTY-SIX

A thief and two gods approached the outskirts of the city.

"Is it too much to hope that you have a plan?" Beatrice asked, kicking a pebble in the path so that it skittered out ahead of them. She knew they had to go back. *Hell,* she wanted to go back. They had probably already delayed it too long. But she still didn't feel ready.

"Far too much, Beatrice," Nered answered. "What would you normally do?"

"Normally? As in how do I *usually* steal world-ending objects from crazed gods?" Beatrice thought for a moment. "The original plan was to steal it during the Gathering Ball. Everyone was distracted. I snuck right in, and back out. Well. Almost. Any chance you have some godly ability to go back in time?"

Din's grin didn't waver, but his brows creased subtly. "No god has power over time," he answered softly.

"But I am *quite* good at distractions," Nered added. Beatrice watched somewhat uncomfortably as his fangs glinted as he grinned.

"This sounds like a plan to me!" Din's enthusiasm was unmatched. "Nered and I will distract our brethren and you steal the stone."

"*And* find Malice and Ges," Beatrice reminded him, somewhat self-consciously. She suppressed the fear that her companions might not be glad to see her, that they would think she had left them behind intentionally. But they would listen. She would explain. And she wouldn't leave without them again.

She thought of Ges, and the uncertainty in his eyes when she had left him the night of the Gathering. When he knew the truth of the situation he surely would find his certainty. When she told him how *she* felt... when she told him how certain she was... *What*? What would it mean? For the immediate task, or the future? She didn't know, but she was willing to find out.

"Worried, Beatrice?" Din asked.

Beatrice flushed, realizing he was watching her intently.

"Not in the least," she lied. "Just... thinking. What's it like being a god?"

"What's it like being mortal?" Din returned.

She shrugged. "It just is."

"Exactly."

"But you have magic?"

"Some," Din admitted. "But mortal bodies weren't made for magic. I don't have much command over it in this form. Nered will have more raw power at his disposal, but it's like I told you before. He won't be able to sustain it."

"These vessels," Beatrice asked, somewhat hesitantly. "Do you make them, or..."

"Take them would be a better description. They were born of this realm, their own people with their own souls. It's a bit like moving into a house before the previous residents have left. They might go of their own accord, but sometimes they... linger."

"The man that was Lemry?"

"Made a deal with the Prince of Death. He had made poor choices, been cruel to the ones that trusted him. It brought about the end of his life before his time, and so in exchange for a little more time he gave me his body. I let him stay. In truth, there's a great deal of him in me now."

"Gods..." Bee muttered. "And the Blessed Leaders?"

"I imagine they were devout worshipers that gave themselves willingly."

"For the record, no one's allowed in here," Beatrice asserted, giving Nered an extra pointed glance. "I'm Beatrice and I'm staying Beatrice. There's no room in here for someone else. If anyone tries you burn this body to the ground."

"Noted."

"I prefer working with male hardware," Nered said.

Beatrice didn't need that bit of information, and it seemed like a good place to let the conversation die. She turned her attention back to the road ahead. A rather large patrol of Faithful moved in their direction, catching her eye. There was another. not far past them. She had been too distracted, but now her instincts came back in to sharp focus as she realized the streets were practically swarming with guards and Paladins.

"Shit," Bee hissed. "This is going to be harder than we thought."

"You can't sneak past them? I thought that was the point."

'Are you the Prince of Chaos, or smugness?" Beatrice answered.

The three stepped off the street, making their way closer to the side streets that ran between the buildings, musty and mostly abandoned. Bee watched carefully for space between the patrols.

"If we have to fight our way through the city one patrol at a time we won't make it." Din pointed out. "Seems like a good time for a new plan."

"Damn." Bee was struck with a sudden realization, she practically mumbled, "I have a new plan."

"Why do you sound disappointed?'

"I can't believe I'm saying this." Bee rolled her eyes. "What would Ges do?"

She looked to Nered, looking not just smug now but also genuinely pleased. Perhaps even proud. She realized, though it made her somewhat uneasy, that the Prince of Chaos and smugness understood her mind as well as her closest friends. Maybe better.

He smiled at her, his eyes twinkling like distant stars as he answered. "Something bold? Something simple? Like walking up to the guards, announcing himself and getting nabbed and...taken straight to the Temple."

"Exactly. We should do that."

THIRTY-SEVEN

G espar had never been in the jail. He had dropped a handful of petty criminals off to be incarcerated, but had never gone beyond the uninviting entrance. Most of the people he had been tasked with bringing in had chosen to fight rather than be brought here. He had thought it was a foolish choice to pick death over capture, but how long could he stay in this cell before he would make the same choice?

Light poured in from high windows, splashing against the door on the opposite wall and filling the small room with persistent heat even before noon. He supposed he should be grateful for fresh air, but it had made for a chilly night and an uncomfortably warm day. If it was intentional, it was needlessly cruel.

Malice had all but given up on talking to him a few hours prior. Gespar couldn't find much to say and instead sat on the low wooden bench, memorizing the spaces between the stone blocks in the wall.

The shuffle and squeak of leather boots echoed down the stairs and then the hall. Malice tensed. Ges didn't move, even when the boots stopped outside the door.

"I brought you some water."

The voice was somewhat familiar. Ges looked up long enough to acknowledge her presence. A Faithful guard he had seen plenty of times, a woman with fiery red hair and broad shoulders. He could sense her hesitation when he didn't move to collect her offering.

"I'll take it." Mal finally spoke in his place. "Thanks."

"Is he alright?"

Ges looked back at Malice now, finding that he was interested in the orc's answer.

"He's..." Mal hesitated, and in the silence Ges found his voice.

"I would be better if you let us out of this cage."

"You know I can't do that." The guard stepped back. He could tell she was uncomfortable, but perhaps there was doubt also. Doubt and fear.

"What I know is that things here aren't what they seem. If you won't let us out then do yourself a favor and leave. Get out of the temple. Hell, out of the city."

"What are you even in here for?"

Ges thought about this for a moment. "That's a good fucking question."

Mal let out a quiet laugh. It was enough to make Ges feel grounded in the moment, even if it was a rather grim one. At least they were in it together.

"I don't understand what's happening, but plenty of the clergy are still on your side, Fairchild. You've always been among the best of us, and we believe in you. Perhaps when things settle down they'll let you out and things can go back to normal."

"You know that's not going to happen."

She started to speak, almost certainly to restate her optimism, but she hesitated. Her eyes fell and a doubtful frown tugged on her face. Instead she gave a respectful bow. "May Gerra guide your sword. May Vedett shield you. May Sald craft your destiny well."

Gespar grimaced at the familiar words. "May we all learn to do those things for ourselves before it's too late."

The Faithful left them in silence.

Gespar stood with a loud sigh, stretching his limbs and rubbing at his face as though trying to wake himself up.

"So," Malice spoke with a forced casual tone. "This is pretty shitty."

"Yes, it is," Gespar responded.

"You wanna talk about it? I don't know how you felt about Diana, but…"

"I should be grieving, shouldn't I? It feels wrong that I'm not." Ges moved towards the windows as he spoke. They were too high to see anything but the sky, but it was something to look at while he thought. "Instead, I'm just angry. Angry at the Triad for portraying themselves as something they aren't. Angry at my family for being their lap dogs."

He paused, taking a settling breath before continuing. "Most of all, I'm angry at myself for never questioning what I was taught. I trusted blindly in what I was *told* was justice. I served it with every breath. Mal, I've *killed* people for demon worship because we're told it's too dangerous and volatile and self-serving. But they're all the same. Gods, demons, mortals… They're *all* volatile and dangerous…"

"Can be." Mal seemed to consider this only in passing. "But you know as well as I do that they can be pretty fuckin' great too. I wouldn't get too hung up on it, Sunshine. People are just people, Gods are just gods, and right now we have our own asses to think about."

Gespar took a moment to look at Mal. Aggressive and proud, coarse and undoubtedly caring Malice. He was right; and it calmed Ges's nerves. But as his thoughts settled in to a more stable pattern it wasn't his own ass he was thinking about.

"She's going to be alright, isn't she?" Ges asked.

Mal shrugged. Ges watched, somewhat guilty for even asking as the orc scratched at his bare scalp with both hands, shrugged again and then nodded, smiling convincingly at him.

Finally Mal sat heavily on the floor. "We'll have to get out of here to find out."

"Bee said you fought your way out of a similar situation before, so I guess it's not completely hopeless."

"She must *really* like you if she told you about that. She never talks about those days."

"Well, she was drugged."

"You drugged her?"

Ges rolled his eyes, shooting Mal a sidelong glance instead of an answer. He moved over, sitting on the ground next to the orc and picking up the waterskin the guard had brought.

"Did Bee tell you about the time we stole a badger from a monastery?"

"You're making that up."

"I wouldn't." Mal coughed a quiet laugh. "No shit. I think the guy that wanted it lives in Triad City."

"I bet it was Lord Westrin," Ges mused. "The man loves keeping pets. There was a rumor he keeps a miniature feathered dragon in his washroom."

"I believe it. You would be shocked what some people keep in their washrooms."

It felt like hours later that the sound of boots once again pattered down the stairs.

Ges hardly bothered looking up as the Faithful stopped at the door.

"Any chance you brought something stronger than water this time?" he asked.

The answer came clear and calm. Teasing, with a touch of amusement- the most beautiful response he had ever heard.

"Oh, you have no idea."

Thirty-Eight

Beatrice couldn't help but smile at the way they both jumped to their feet, practically tripping over each other as they rushed to the cell door. Gods, she was relieved to see them.

"Took you long enough," Mal scoffed, eyeing her through the bars.

"Yeah, well, I was a little tied up. I'm here now. You look pretty comfortable, though. I can leave you in there if you like."

"Open the door," Ges said.

"You're awfully bossy for a man in a jail cell." She stepped back, enjoying the opportunity to play with them for a moment longer.

"*Open the door,*" he repeated. Insisted, really.

His gaze was unwavering, his eyes dark, practically burning holes in her. Her stomach dipped as she took in his grave expression.

He hated her. He was pissed. The storm they had brought to town had destroyed his life, and he was *not* happy to see her. *Fuck.*

"Right," she said.

She fit the key in the lock and turned it with some effort. The door was hardly out of the way when he pushed past it. There was such forceful purpose in his motions that when his hands reached for her neck, her first response was a jolt of fear. Her arms went up reflexively. She thought to reason with him, though she had no idea what she might say. Any words were cut off at the source by his mouth pressed to hers, strong and unyielding. She softened at the touch, letting him pull her in as close as he needed her, gripping his arms. Gods be damned, this was all the magic she needed.

He broke the kiss too soon, leaving her mind blank and her arms weak. His hand stayed firmly on the back of her neck, pressing her forehead to his, his breath mingling with hers, deep and warm. She didn't want to open her eyes, didn't want to let this go yet. If they could stay another second, steal a few more moments...

Mal cleared his throat with a loud growl.

And they were back in reality, in the consulate dungeon. Ges pulled back, looking her over before smiling at her, that sunbeam smile.

"Hello to you too, Ges."

"So, you guys are just going to do that all the time now? All mouthy like that?"

In response, Ges gave Mal a pointed look before planting another quick kiss on her lips.

"You're ok?" Ges asked her, his eyes running a quick examination. "That armor- "

He lingered on the silver and red Faithful garb she wore.

"You don't like it? You're the one who wanted me to sign on with the church."

"Bee." His eyes narrowed, his brow falling into such a forlorn expression that she almost felt guilty. *Almost.*

"Relax, Arthur gave it to me so I could come get you. Don't worry, I plan on taking it off the first chance I get."

She threw in a wink for good measure, happily noting the effect. Ges went from sad concern to flushed cheeks in an instant.

"Gross," Mal said.

Despite his objections, Bee couldn't help but think he looked rather pleased with himself. It was one more thing he had been right about, after all.

"So, Arthur has decided to be helpful now?" Mal asked.

"I would say so. He went with…" Bee caught herself. Now didn't seem like the best time to explain that they were storming the Triad Temple with a band of gods. "With the others."

"Others?"

"Yeah, others. We've got quite the team. They've gone to cause a disruption at Lestra's little ceremony, which means we should probably make our own way there. We've got work to do."

Malice and Gespar looked at her resolutely, unwavering, waiting for their next instruction. More than anything, she wanted to take them both and leave as quickly as possible. But this wasn't something they could run away from.

With a sigh, she handed Gespar his sword and dropped Mal's hammer from where it hung on her back, glad to be rid of the weight. She then gestured for them to come, turned, and headed down the hall and up the stairs. They followed without hesitation. *Of course they did.*

"Apparently Lestra has been out on the terrace all day, and our theory is she may be waiting for sunset to start her big show. She isn't letting the Shadowgate Stone out of her sight, which is not good news for us, because we have to steal it. Before you ask, I don't have a plan. I don't know what's going on, and I don't know if we can pull this off."

"'Course we can pull it off," Mal grunted out and nodded his head, as though if he believed it, it would simply be.

"Right, just- " Beatrice paused as they walked past a pair of Faithful posted at the entrance. She nodded in greeting, not finding it difficult to keep a convincingly somber expression on her face. The guards stared but didn't speak, and they walked past at a steady clip, careful not to look back. "Just stay close and don't rush in to anything. We're only going to get one shot at this, and I don't think we'll be so lucky as to get sent back to your little cell if we screw this up."

They made their way around the corner, walking quietly through a narrow garden that led to the back of the palace grounds. The summer sun was high and hot in the sky, and the white roses scented the air heavily. It was also pleasantly quiet, only a soft breeze shaking the foliage.

"There's no one here," Ges said. "This time of year that's unheard of."

Bee held out a hand to slow them as they reached the back side of the building, scanning the terrace for a feeling of the current situation.

"It's almost empty back here too," she reported.

Almost empty, but there they were out in the sun, four gods facing off in the calm, lazy heat of a beautiful summer day. Din,

Nered, Gerra, and Sald. Lords of the divine realms. Gods with magic at their disposal.

She looked to Ges, her Paladin. Her golden hero. And Mal, her ruthless protector. They were brilliant, and strong, and worth a dozen lesser men. She was afraid, without a doubt. She knew this was something bigger than any of them had faced before. But below the surface, she was as calm as she was before any other job. She and Mal had made it through every challenge they had ever faced, and this would be no different. Bee was going to do whatever it took, *be* whatever it took to ensure that the natural realm was still ticking along this time tomorrow, and she knew her companions would do the same.

That didn't mean it was going to be easy.

Beatrice once again cautioned a look out across the Terrace. Lestra had brought her throne outside, turned to view the ocean. Beside it was a pedestal draped with a black cloth. Beatrice could tell without seeing it that it held the Stone. Lestra did have her back turned to them, at least. She faced the three other gods and appeared to be having a heated debate.

There were no structures to sneak around to get closer, no shadows to conceal them, and no crowds to get lost in. To reach the Stone would require a long, exposed walk across the grounds. To take it would require Sald's attention to be *completely* diverted. The gods on their side were keeping her busy for the moment, but would it be enough?

"We've got to split up. We'll come at them from this side, while you sneak around the long way and get the stone," Ges said.

"No." Beatrice shook her head adamantly, as though she could overpower the validity of the plan if she was stern enough.

"You have a better idea?"

"There are six of us and only one of her. We could charge her and overpower her."

"No," Mal grunted.

Bee blinked at him, not sure if she was more confused or frustrated. "No, we can't charge her?"

"We watched her burn a woman from the inside out. I think you wanna keep your distance."

"Shit." She closed her eyes, pressing her thumb to her head to speed up her thinking. "Fine. Be aggressive, but for fuck's sake, don't engage her. When you see I'm clear, just... run. Let the other three deal with the aftermath. We've got to get away. *All of us.*"

Their silent agreement made her uneasy.

"If you don't run, I swear on the Realms I will walk back over there and give her that Stone back."

Mal nudged her shoulder. "We've got this. Go, so we can get it over with."

Beatrice hesitated. It wasn't fear, just a gnawing feeling that there was more to say. Before she could decide what it was, they had left her.

THIRTY-NINE

Gespar admittedly didn't have much experience with theft. What knowledge he did have on the subject suggested that stealing an item right from under a person who had already proven they would kill for said item- in broad daylight no less- was not an ideal plan.

He crossed the terrace, Malice by his side. The orc's presence was comforting, at least.

"Mal," Ges said. "I'm glad to have met you, and I'm glad to call you my friend."

"Yeah, Sunshine, I love you too. We can get mushy about it later. Hell, I'll even have a beer with you if you can keep your mouth off Bee long enough to drink one."

"No promises."

"One more thing," Mal said, quieter now. "When Bee gets away, I'm taking a shot at the Lady."

Ges felt his mouth go dry, his apprehension turning to anxiety. "Mal-"

"Sending you away once was a kindness I will not extend again!" Lestra had taken notice of them now, raising her voice at them with dangerous impatience before addressing the others again. "You see?

The mortals are stubborn and ambitious, but they are helpless in this dead realm of theirs. In my new world, they might stand a chance."

"You're delusional. There might be nothing left of the mortals, *or us,* if you go through with this." *Is that Lemry, the storyteller?* Gespar squinted slightly, making sure his eyes weren't deceiving him.

The way they spoke of mortals made Ges's stomach twist uncomfortably. Arthur was with him, and a third...

"This isn't creation, sister. This is a mad experiment. Perhaps if you let us help you, we could create something together. Without tearing apart the Realms to do it," Arthur said.

Lestra shook her head violently. "I don't want *help*. I wouldn't even be using Crepus' damned stone if I didn't need it. I'm done talking. To all of you. You will just have to see my new world."

"Wait!" Gespar panicked as she turned toward the pedestal.

It didn't slow her, and the screech she emitted at the sight was otherworldly. The stone was gone. The cloth that had covered it lay in a dark puddle on the ground.

How? Ges's mind reeled. How had Bee gotten it so fast? So silently? Even knowing she was coming, he hadn't been aware of her presence.

"How many times must you play these same useless games?" Lestra fumed.

Before Gespar understood what had happened, he found himself prone and aching on the ground. He tried to piece together the sudden blast of air, the thunder of cracking stone, the flash of Lestra's ghostly eyes.

His ribs ached as he began to lift himself from the shattered stone of the terrace. All around them the ground was reduced to rubble, as though it had been crashed by relentless waves.

Large, warm hands found his arms. Malice. They stood together, finding their feet in the wreckage.

"It's time for you to run, Sunshine."

"Then let's go!" Ges pulled on Mal's wrist in vain.

The orc's eyes were on Lestra, his mind made up. "Someone's gonna have to stay, and someone's got to go. And I'm staying."

Ges didn't move. Each breath sent a sharp pain through his diaphragm, but he pushed the ache away, fighting instead with his contradictory instincts.

Another shock wave shook the ground, knocking Ges down once again, scraping the skin on his hands as he attempted to catch himself. If running was an option, the window of opportunity was closing rapidly.

"Mal!"

Beatrice's voice cut through the mental fog, sending chills down his spine. By the time he looked up, Bee was already back in the picture. Lestra was growling in anger, Beatrice on her like a rabid animal. Bee threw punches with all her might. The determination of a warrior, the form of a well-trained paladin. Her face was red, already beginning to sweat. Lemry cried out first, alerting Ges that the other men had also been tossed to the ground by whatever Lestra had done.

Mal let out a roar, certainly intending to draw Lestra's attention away. Instead, Bee's eyes darted in their direction for just a moment.

A moment too long. Lestra caught her arm mid-swing, snatching Bee off her feet. Ges shouted as Lestra pulled her in, stumbling in an attempt to jump up. He called her name again, his voice cracking in his panic, but Mal's voice overpowered his own.

He could see Beatrice's eyes, see her anger turn to anguish in an instant, but she didn't scream. A burning dread set in, an ache as though his own heart had stopped.

"That's enough, Sald!" This time the voice was Arthur's, and the name he used made Ges's head swim.

"Is it?" She turned to face Arthur, Lemry, and the stranger. "Don't you see? This proves I'm right. The mortals are mighty in spirit, but they are nothing. They are weak and helpless. Perhaps when divinity bleeds in to my new Realm, it will remake them as well. Perhaps then they won't throw their fleeting lives away for nothing."

Beatrice forced out a laugh with no joy to color it. "I don't do anything for nothing."

The words drew Lestra's full attention back to her captive, though in her moment of boastful glory she had already let her guard down for too long. Beatrice had gotten her dirk in her free hand, and she pushed it slowly, unyielding, in to the soft flesh between Lestra's ribs.

The woman released Beatrice at once, letting her fall to her knees on the ruined ground.

Instead of gasping or crying out, Lestra smiled as she wetted the fingers of her free hand in the blood escaping her wound.

"You idiot. You can't kill me. You can't *stop* me."

Her eyes began to burn like white hot flames. Gespar and the others watched, frozen as she reached out for something, Bee's satchel, and pulled from it the Shadowgate Stone.

"I hope you survive long enough to see this world crumble in the wake of my better one. I hope it destroys you. "

With a cracking noise, as if lightning had struck a massive tree at its heart, the darkness of the Shadowgate stone began spilling out onto the ground around Lestra and Beatrice. No longer frozen, Gespar found his feet. As fast as he could manage, he ran to them. He grabbed Bee, pulling her up. She worked with him allowing him to drag her away from Lestra as the inky dark poured forth.

Lestra laughed a victorious, fiery laugh, and in a final burst of white light she was gone, consumed by the darkness.

"Gods," Gespar muttered, retreating further, squeezing Bee's hand as he pulled her away.

"If there is any hope left, we must act now!" Lemry called to them.

"What in seven hells are we supposed to do?" Mal growled, meeting them and beginning to fuss over Bee like a mother.

"She's opened up a literal gate to the divine realms, and now it's leaking through like a hole in a boat. We could get to the stone and block up the hole somehow..."

The stranger came close as he explained, giving Gespar his first look at him. He was inhuman. Fearsome. The sight of him forced truths that Gespar had been trying not to believe in to reality. He looked away, staring in to the blackness in disbelief. Any hope that this was a dream faded away.

Beatrice squeezed at his hand again. He gestured into the void, where Lestra had disappeared. "She was really..."

"An asshole. Yeah," Bee answered.

He turned to Lemry, Arthur, and the other. "And you are-"

"Also assholes, I'm afraid," Lemry answered, smirking. "We can go over the details later if the world doesn't implode on itself."

Mal turned his heavy eyes to Ges. "You gonna be ok, Sunshine?"

"That remains to be seen." He looked down at Beatrice as he answered. "This isn't over."

As her eyes met his, he saw a stubborn flare in her expression and couldn't help but smile.

"That settles it then," Gespar announced. "I'll go in. I'll get to the stone and stop Lestra. It's been my responsibility all along, after all. I have served in the name of protection all my life. This is what I'm meant to do."

"Ges!" Bee began to protest.

"How do I stop it? The leak?" he asked the gods.

The way they looked at each other was not encouraging.

"I'm not sure," the blue one answered. "Touch it. Ask it to close. Will it shut. I don't know how, but you've got to try something."

"Brilliant." Beatrice spoke. "But how will we even get to it? How do we even know it's still in there? Can anyone even see in there?!"

Indeed, the darkness was growing by the moment. Large patches of the sky were blotted out by the shadows.

"There's no 'we', Bee. I'm going in alone."

"Like hell!" She crossed her arms. "I'm not leaving you again. If you're going, I'm going. Just try to stop me."

"What about me?" Mal asked.

"You can't go either. If something happens to me, who will look after Beatrice?"

"I already told you, I'm going too!"

"I was talking about the horse."

Beatrice pouted, punching him gently on the arm.

"As entertaining as this is, we don't really have the time for squabbling," Lemry interjected.

"Right. Then it's a good thing we've agreed that we're going in together." Beatrice looked at Gespar pointedly.

He had seen this look before. There would be no arguing with her now. She wouldn't back down. That was Beatrice, though, and he wouldn't have her any other way. He nodded.

"Right. If we step into that void, we have no way of knowing if we'll come back out?" He asked Lemry. *Or, not Lemry?* The elf, god, whatever he was- nodded back.

"Then we'll need just a second. Alone."

"We don't have long," Lemry reminded him, but the others stepped back respectfully.

The darkness had swallowed most of the surrounding area now. Gespar steeled his nerves and taking Beatrice by the arm, he led her away to the edge where the terrace hung over the sea below. They both peered out over the edge at the sheer drop for a silent moment before she turned to him.

"Is now really the best time for this?" She asked. Her cheeks were pink. He took in every detail of her face for a silent moment, trying to memorize the details. The soft curve of her jaw, the way her lips pursed slightly as she looked back at him, the anxious way her big eyes searched his own.

"If we're doing this, I want you to have this." He pulled the talisman off his belt and pinned it to hers.

She didn't argue and took his hands when he finished.

"I didn't bring you anything," she joked, trying to smirk at him. "Look at us. We started out tied up in a bandit camp, and now we're about to save the world... probably."

He looked at her, and finding no words, he pulled her into his arms. He stooped to bring his lips to hers, kissing her with every bit of the fire burning in his heart. He held her body to his, running his fingers through her hair, pressing her lips more tightly to his own. He drowned in the feeling, trying to make up for even a small portion of the kisses that they might not get after this moment.

Only when her breathing had grown heavy did he pull back. Her whole face was flushed now, perfect.

He moved his hand to her collar and, finding the chain about her neck, he hooked it with a finger, pulling the necklace from under her bodice and exposing the glowing stone. It burned brightly as if in spite of the growing darkness, casting opposing shadows against the black haze.

Beatrice reached out to place a hand on his cheek. Gespar closed his eyes for a moment, leaning into the touch.

"You can say it now," she whispered. "What you were going to say that night... If you're still thinking it."

Opening his eyes, Gespar looked at her, his heart breaking. It was bliss and agony. Everything he wanted, and the hardest thing to bear in this moment. He held the tears that burned at his eyes back by willpower alone, shaking his head at her.

"I can't. It would only make what happens next that much harder for both of us."

He regretted the sudden confusion that clouded her beautiful face, but Gespar tightened his grip on the glowing stone with one hand, and with the other he shoved her chest.

There was a moment of the slightest tension before the chain snapped. Beatrice looked at him with wide, terrified eyes, only reacting at the last moment. She reached out clumsily for him as her panic grew, but it was too late. He watched Beatrice disappear over the edge of the terrace.

He heard a scream from below as she fell and turned away. He couldn't dwell now.

"What in seven hells did you do?!"

Gespar braced himself.

Malice bore down on him with a rage that couldn't be put to words, grabbing him by the collar and lifting him off his feet. The orc snarled, spitting on his face as he growled his words, repeating himself. "What did you do?"

"We both know she wouldn't have backed down, but I couldn't let her go in there. It was the only way to stop her."

"Rgaah!" Malice's rage spilled out in with the shout, but he set Gespar down.

"I need you to go make sure she gets out of the water ok. She's protected, but it will only do so much. There's a path down to the shore at the far end, past the consulate building." He pointed the way out.

"So, you were getting rid of both of us?"

Gespar nodded. "Tell her... tell her I'm sorry, Mal. And take care of her."

"Take care of yourself, Sunshine. Saving the world is great, but you know she'll only forgive you if you come back." Mal hesitated a moment and then extended his hand to Gespar.

Gespar took the large grey hand in his own, their forearms twisted slightly. They exchanged a meaningful glance that spoke all the words there were left to say, and with a respectful nod, they released their grip. Malice turned and ran in the direction of the path to Beatrice.

Gespar took a deep breath, turning back to the heart of the darkness.

"You're a brave man," Lemry said, coming to stand by his side.

"Anything else I should know before I go in there?"

"Probably." He sighed. "But I don't know what it is."

"Who are you, really?" Ges asked, somewhat afraid of the answer.

"Din," the elf answered with a smug smirk.

Gespar nodded, finding it quite easy to accept.

"I suppose it's only right that you're the last face I'll see. The demon of death, sending me into the realms beyond..."

"Have hope. We don't know what may come to pass. After all, I'm the god of life as well. You can't have one without the other."

Gespar thought about this for a moment. He thought of Beatrice's stubborn face again, and holding the brightly glowing gem high in front of him, he stepped resolutely forward, plunging into the darkness.

FOURTY

B eatrice came to with a gasp.

She was jostled about, and as her eyes opened, her only view was of dirt and stone six feet beneath her. Her mind reeled, jumping back to her last memory to try to make sense, to place her in time and space.

Falling.

In her confusion, she screamed, her body contorting.

"Hey!" a deep voice rumbled. "Easy, Bee!"

She was swung downward, her feet placed on solid ground.

"You alright?" Mal bent down, looking at her face with narrow, concerned eyes.

Bee didn't answer, still piecing together the world around her. Her stomach retched. She doubled over, vomiting up a gut full of brine water onto the dusty path. As her breathing stabilized, she looked around her.

They stood at the edge of the temple grounds, now as dark as night. The swirling shadows clawed from the center of the terrace like hands seeking them out blindly.

"How long was I out?"

"Only about ten minutes," Mal answered.

Din and Nered watched with heavy-set eyes full of pity that she didn't want. Wouldn't accept.

"Where is he?"

The others were silent, suddenly much more interested in the stone beneath their feet than her or the raging darkness.

"Where is Ges?" she repeated, choking on the words in her panic and grabbing at Mal's shirt. Her chest was painfully tight, the dread so heavy her breath felt forced.

"He went in, trying to stop it."

"How?" she asked, horrified. "What will he do?"

Silence again.

"Where is my blade?" she asked. She would not sit by just because these menfolk refused to speak.

Malice offered the dirk to her, his eyes weary.

"The Paladin has made a sacrifice, Beatrice. He gives his life to save yours." Nered's voice was serious, but the ghost of a smile tugged at his lips. "You would deny him that?"

"He just wants to protect you, Bee," Malice said.

"Bullshit," Bee said. "When have we ever stood alone? Everything we have done to get us here, we have done together. If we're going to end this, it's going to be together."

"Give me your blade, Beatrice," Din interrupted.

"I don't think I will."

"It pierced Lestra, did it not? When she attempted to use her power on you?"

Bee nodded, holding the blade aloft, looking closer now at the blood that grew sticky on the blade.

"It carries some of her power. I believe we can set it to work for you. If you're set on pursuing your paladin, you will need every advantage," Din said. "Or do you prefer to run into the darkness with no forethought?"

She begrudgingly handed the thing over, watching as Nered and Gerra stepped forward.

"What do you expect to do?" Gerra asked.

"Set intention to it, the three of us together," Din said. "It's as she says. Alone, we may not be a match for Sald. But together we might awaken the power she left behind to turn it against her."

"It's unlikely to work," Nered said, grinning wickedly. "But, what a thrill it will be if it does."

He laid hands on the blade alongside Din. Gerra joined them hesitantly, setting his palm in to the congealed blood. At first, it seemed as though nothing was going to happen. A long moment passed and not one of them dared to speak, let alone breathe. Suddenly, with a hiss like a hot iron dipped in water, the blood began to bubble and burn. It heated to a glowing ember, and then just as quickly it solidified into golden plating along the length of her blade.

Din presented the dirk to her. "If you see her, you must kill her. As long as she exists, she will not stop. This will not end."

"You won't come with us?"

"This is your fight now. A chance for the mortal realm to prove its place among our own," Gerra said, watching them with proud resolve.

Malice stood a little taller.

"And," Din added, a tight tilt to his mouth, "if we enter the darkness now, it will be the same as entering the Divine realms. We would lose these vessels."

Of all the selfish asshole excuses. Bee didn't bother calling them out though. With little more than a roll of her eyes that she was sure they would see, she turned to face the black darkness.

"You ready for this, Mal?"

"If you are, I am."

They walked side by side towards the shadows, against every instinct that burned through her veins. As they reached the edge of the darkness, solid as a wall before them, they paused.

"This is crazy," she said.

Mal grunted his agreement.

"Who would've thought the likes of us would end up at the center of some shit like this?"

"Me," Mal answered.

She looked up to see if he was serious and was met with a deadpan gaze.

"I've been trying to tell you for years that we're worth more than you thought. This seems about right."

"You're out of your mind," Bee said. But she smiled, grateful for his madness, and his presence.

And with Malice next to her, Beatrice stepped into the enveloping dark.

FOURTY-ONE

It was worse than she could have imagined. Not only was any evidence of the light gone, but the warmth of the sun with it. A cold, wet chill ran through her, chased by a trickling of fear. She held her blade out in front of her but could not see it. Trying to peer into the depths that stretched before them, seemingly infinite, she could not see any sign that the darkness was broken. How could they proceed? What direction would they even move in? Was there anything in this void at all? Suddenly she was struck with a feeling that she would be trapped in this nothingness forever, alone until even her own being melted away into the darkness.

"Mal?"

"I'm here."

Thank the gods.

She reached out to her left, flailing into the empty darkness for a moment before her hand brushed against warm, tough flesh. With a breath of relief, she followed the arm downward to find the broad, rough hand. It closed around her own firmly, and hand in hand they stepped forward, further into the dark.

"You see anything at all?" Mal asked, his voice just as calm as ever.

"No. Nothing."

But, despite the blinding blackness, Beatrice had begun to feel as though the surrounding space was closing in. Unseeable, unimaginable things seemed to move around them, whispering like fabric in the wind, but never coming close enough to touch. Her feet grew heavier. More reluctant to move.

We have to find Ges.

A knot in her gut told Beatrice not to call out. Whatever moved in the shadows may not see them any better than they could. A shout now would make their presence known to any number of things. To Sald even.

But it was the only recourse she had. Bee swallowed the fear that lumped together in her throat, finding her voice. She called out Ges's name, and it echoed around them as though they were in a massive cavern.

No response.

"Ges," Mal shouted, louder than Bee could.

As the reverberations of his voice faded out, another replaced them.

It did not echo like their own calls. Instead, it was flat and quiet. A sob, or a laugh. Beatrice could not tell which, but she knew that it wasn't Gespar.

The cry seemed to be drawing closer, slinking towards them from behind.

"We're not alone."

"I know," Bee whispered back. "Just keep moving."

"That wasn't me," Mal grumbled.

She felt her heart rate double in an instant and fought back the urge to run blindly. They continued forward, holding true, she hoped. She didn't dare turn around, fearing that even in the complete darkness she would see what followed them.

And then the slightest glint of hope winked ahead of them, maybe thirty meters on. It started as nothing more than a single point of greenish white in the distance, but as they moved still onward, it grew into an unmistakable glow.

Beatrice couldn't contain herself any longer. She broke into a run, dragging Malice along with her. She thought she heard the tip-tap of light footsteps pick up speed behind them, but she hardly cared anymore, even dropping Malice's hand in her hurry.

Her relief was short-lived. The Fires of the Depths stone that Gespar had taken was still attached to its chain as it lay alone on the ground, casting a circle of light on the surrounding stone. But Ges wasn't there. She stooped to pick it up, and lifting it, she illuminated the space around her.

"Ges," she called again. Her voice caught in her throat. *Please.*

"Over here," Mal said.

She used the gem to locate him in the dark, not far away. He gestured to the ground at his feet before bending to pick up what lay there. The Shadowgate Stone. It swallowed his hands in its darkness as they looked at it.

"What the hell do we do with it?"

Beatrice stared directly into the darkness now, consumed by her own fear, barely hearing the swishing whispers of the shadows around them. She swallowed heavily, lost in the dark, without the slightest idea of what she should do. No plan, no knowledge, no way out.

And so, without another thought, she took the glowing stone in her hand, held it against the darkness until she found a crack in the surface of its dark counterpart, and she shoved.

A high-pitched ringing like the sound in a bad ear began instantly. It stabbed at their eardrums, seeming to only grow impossibly louder. Bee cupped her ears, doubling over. A few more seconds and Mal dropped the stone to the ground to do the same. As the infernal thing hit the ground, it crumbled to dust, like a dirt clot kicked on a path.

The darkness around them receded instantly, though they were not on the terrace of the Triad temple. They found themselves in a stony land still overcast with shadows. Some of those shadows seemed to flinch, temporarily taking the shape of some living creature before receding back into darker recesses where stone outcroppings created hiding places from the light.

Not twenty strides away, Beatrice spotted a familiar heap of armor on the ground and nearly cried out. Her vision tunneled and she ran to him, not noticing anything else. Stumbling the last few feet, she fell to her knees at the Paladin's side. Gespar lay unconscious and cold to the touch. She watched carefully for the rise and fall of his breath, but if it was there, it was weak. "Mal! Help!"

He was already next to her as she raised Ges's head into her lap, checking his limbs and face, feeling at his neck for a pulse. "He's alive." She could have cheered for the small win. "I don't see any blood."

"We have to get him out of here," she said, realizing that she had no idea how they were supposed to leave this strange place that smelled of soot and waste.

Malice nodded, lifting Ges with ease from her grip, and waiting patiently for some sign of where to go next.

"I think we came from that direction," Bee said. She hoped she was correct, though she didn't know if there would be a way out at all. Anything was better than sitting in wait where they were.

As she watched Mal carrying Ges over his shoulder a few paces ahead of her, Bee tried to fight back the feeling that this had been too easy. It wore into her bones, itching like a reflex. The hairs on the back of her neck stood, the feeling they were being followed returning. She doubted those shadow creatures would approach them in the light, however dim it may be. *Hopefully.*

But denial served no purpose. Even as she tried to calm her nerves, hell broke loose around them. A slate formation to their right exploded without warning, shattering with a clap and a rain of rocky shrapnel falling about them. She watched helplessly as Malice and Ges fell prone. Even as she cried out to them, she felt the stone pelting her own skin.

"It's as though you have set out to prove your mortal races have no hope." Sald's voice seemed to echo through the stale air. "I can't imagine what you hoped to accomplish in coming here. You shut the Gate, but it has only delayed my plans. And now you will die, for no other reason than I feel like killing you myself. I will destroy all those like you and start over. Hopefully, I'll create something with a survival instinct."

Bee found the strength to face Sald, but instead of the familiar ebony-haired woman, a creature unlike anything she had ever seen glowered at her.

The Divine Sald glowed, with skin like quartz. Where eyes should have been, white-hot flames licked out of the sockets, dancing across the contours of her face. She advanced on Beatrice without seeming to take a single step, towering over her with a fearsome scowl.

Beatrice's skin burned where Sald grabbed her around the neck, and she pawed hopelessly at the seemingly impervious arm. The flames of Sald's face flickered as her scowl turned into a mocking sneer. "It's more fun to watch you suffer than I had thought."

Sald lifted her off the ground, the pressure nearly collapsing her windpipe before she was flung unceremoniously through the air. Her back struck rock, the pain of the jagged surface tearing into her skin shot through her as she crumbled to the ground.

Righting herself proved to be an arduous task, but she pulled herself up to her knees, straining to ignore the pain that pulsated through her, begging her to stay down. Her blade had fallen by her side, the gold glinting up at her.

Sald crossed over to Malice and Ges laying sprawled on the ground.

"I see my brethren didn't bother coming with you. I wonder if they're afraid, or if they just don't care what the outcome is. Perhaps they just didn't wish to see their pets crushed."

As she spoke, Sald kicked at Gespar's form like he was a bit of refuse, flipping him to face upward before placing a crystalline foot on his rib cage. She applied an effortless pressure, and Beatrice's stomach churned at the wretched sound of a bone giving way. Hot tears stung her eyes. She was sure she heard an airy breath escape him and pleaded silently that it wasn't his last. Bee tried again to stand, clutching the hilt of her blade in her shaking hand. A hopelessness weighed on her aching chest.

Sald turned her attention then to Malice. "Look at you," she said. "Even the strongest of you is no more than an insect in the grand scheme of things. And yet you insist on your own importance."

The demon stooped, running a jagged hand over Mal's face. A fire lit in Beatrice, a rage hotter than any she had ever known.

"Don't touch him," she yelled. The low pitch and rolling ire in her voice sounded foreign in her ears. It almost reminded her of Malice's own growling baritone.

"Or what, little bug?" Sald laughed. "You'll poke me with your stinger again?"

"Exactly," Beatrice whispered. She propelled herself, pushing off the rocks at her back, forcing as much speed and power as she could into her legs.

With a shout as deep and loud as she could force from her chest, she lunged at Sald wildly. She would not submit without a fight. She would not let this wretch destroy them without feeling her wrath, and if she died here this day, it would be with at least a single drop of divine blood on her hands. Her dirk struck outward, aiming for the space where Sald's heart ought to be. Instead of making contact, Bee's arm was struck off course, and a stony palm hit her own chest, propelling her backward. The air was forced from her lungs as she landed on her back, the damage from earlier igniting fresh pain.

Bee struggled to restart her breathing, gripping tightly to the handle still in her grasp and praying to find another ounce of strength.

Sald came into view, standing over her for a moment before squatting and wrenching her shoulders off the ground to bring her to an upright seat. "You're brave, little bug. I'll give you that. But now you will die under my thumb. You'll die as you lived, as a thief and a louse. *You. Are. Nothing.*"

Sald wielded a single finger like a dagger, holding it up for Beatrice to see before finding the soft flesh about her ribs and driving the digit through her skin. Bee screamed, a sound unlike any that had ever come from her. Her mind struggled to free itself from the moment, but she fought with every breath to keep her wits, even as she felt the first knobbed knuckle stretch its way through the growing wound in her chest.

She sucked in a quick burst of air, painful though it was.

Beatrice Lemon may have been a thief. She may have been a thorn in the side of plenty of the folks she graced with her existence. But Beatrice Lemon was not *nothing*.

She did not have the strength or leverage to land a clean blow, but she mustered her strength to wheel her dirk upward, forcing it into Sald's gut.

The Divine simply looked down at her with disgust at first, hardly bothered by the blade stuck deep in her belly. But slowly the flames of her eyes faded from white to an angry orange. Smoke began to curl up and over the crown of her head. The expression on her face fell from rage to confusion. "You could never..."

Sald released Beatrice, causing her to cry out as the probing finger was ripped from between her ribs. The divine freed the blade from her middle, inspecting it as though it were the first she had ever seen, and then turning her gaze back to Beatrice. Her expression was void of emotion or any sense of urgency as she raised the thing. What was left of her flames danced in the reflection of the gold stains.

Beatrice braced herself for the end, determined not to scream again, if only to deprive Sald of that final victory.

But the god seemed to freeze in place. The last of the flames flared out, leaving only cavernous black eye sockets. Without so much as a breath, she dropped the blade to the ground at her side. Without warning, Sald shattered to thousands of pieces, falling around Beatrice, clattering like broken glass where they hit the stone ground.

Beatrice wished she could feel more relief. Really, she wished she could feel anything at all. She found instead that she was going rather numb, physically. Mentally. Emotionally.

It was done. They had ended it. She comforted herself with that thought as her vision grew narrower. As a different sort of darkness closed in around her, she thought of home.

Fourty-Two

She was enjoying a warm cup of tea when the crow arrived, landing on the banister and gently cawing.

Din smiled at her, offering to pour more. Beatrice considered, sipping at the rich, fruity remnants in her cup. It was pleasant, but she'd had quite enough. "That's all for now," she told him.

The crow called again, hopping a little jig as though it waited for something.

Their surroundings were pleasant. The endless forest that stretched around the castle reminded her so much of the Wander Wood, beautiful but daunting. The grand house itself was the finest she had ever seen, and the courtyard they sat in felt as though it had been torn straight from the page of a storybook.

The crow drew her from her thoughts, and she realized her companion was reading her face intently.

"You could stay. I would make you lady of this realm, give you eternal comforts... I'm quite fond of you, you know."

She rolled her eyes, and he chortled.

"It's lovely, but I've got other plans."

The crow grew louder, cawing and tittering persistently now.

"Perhaps someday then." He didn't seem disappointed by her rejection. Pouring himself another cup, he raised it in a casual toast. "I'll see you soon, Beatrice Lemon."

The crow went on shouting, stirring Beatrice's thoughts and drawing her back to consciousness.

FOURTY-THREE

Beatrice strained her eyes open, blinking against the morning light that spilled through the open window with the bird sounds.

Willow sat by the familiar hearth, sipping a cup of tea and watching her over the top of a book.

"Where are Malice and Ges? Are they-"

"Just fine, besides a few bruises. They're out picking parsley for me, and you'll leave them to it. They may be under the impression that it's to help rouse you, but truth is Dom offered to cook us lunch today. You'll want the parsley."

Beatrice relaxed against the headboard, closing her eyes for a moment.

"I suppose this is the part where you explain the spider got me in the Wander Wood after all, and everything since then has been a wild venom-induced dream?"

"Don't be ridiculous. You wouldn't want that anyhow." The old woman placed her book on a nearby table and stood with substantial effort and a few popping joints. "Cup of tea, dear?"

Bee shook her head. "What about our... other companions?"

"I suppose you mean Din, and Gerra, and Nered?"

"I suppose they're old friends of yours?"

"Quite. They've gone on. Gerra has an empire to sort out, and Din always enjoys being around for those sorts of things. Nered... well, he didn't say where he was off to. But I imagine you haven't seen the last of them. They'll turn up if you ever need them."

"If they need us, more likely," Bee mumbled, earning her a cackle from the old woman.

The door to the outside opened and heavy footsteps plodded in. Malice ducked on his way through the door frame.

"Where are my herbs?"

"Sunshine has them. Looks like there's no rush, though."

"Says you. I may keel back over without an immediate parsley tincture." She tried to look as stern as she could, but seeing him, it was hard not to grin.

"Don't you dare. You've been deadweight long enough." He was better at this than she was.

"*Deadweight*?" she scoffed. "I killed a god while your ass was unconscious!"

"Yeah, yeah. Don't let it go to your head."

Bee cracked, laughing at the absurdity of it. Mal came to the bed and lifted her clear off it into a rare embrace, squeezing the breath out of her.

She knocked on his chest, amused but stiff. "Put me down, you big bully. I feel like I've had a pike driven through me."

He relented, setting her gently back on the edge of the bed before taking both sides of her head in his massive hands for a moment.

"What is this?" she asked.

"Dunno, just..." he paused, shrugged, and patted her ears gently before releasing her. "You believe me now, Bee? We can do whatever the hell we want."

"Don't let it go to your head." She smirked at him.

There was a clatter as the door swung shut and a woven basket hit the floor. Beatrice met Gespar's gaze as he stood there, staring at her as though he was scared to move. He didn't seem to notice the groans and curses Willow threw out over the state of her herbs.

"They're fine," Mal pointed out. "They're still in the basket."

"You question an old witch's herb knowledge? They've been mangled. Ruined. Come, Malice, you'll help me gather more."

"I'm not the one that dropped them," he protested like a child.

"I'll take care of it." Gespar bent to retrieve the basket.

"No, you won't, you fool of a man!" Willow rushed across the room faster than any of them imagined she could. "Malice, with me."

He unenthusiastically complied, casting Bee one more glance. She smiled at him, and he huffed before following Willow.

"I'm not pickin' more of your damn herbs," he mumbled as they exited.

"Don't be ridiculous," the woman snickered.

The door shut once more, and silence filled the cabin. Where the hell had all the birds gone?

It felt like ages before Ges spoke, running a hand across the back of his neck. "I've thought a lot about what to say to you."

"Oh, a prepared speech. I'm honored."

"I can't apologize to you, Bee."

"Brilliant start."

She watched his eyes search her own. The distance between them seemed intentional.

"I'm sorry for any distress I caused you, of course, but I can't be sorry for what I did. I couldn't let anything happen to you."

"You're a piece of work, you know that? If you're set on some sort of chivalrous protection, next time stay with me. *Help me.* Don't push me off a fucking cliff." She hadn't realized how hot her emotions were running until her voice caught in her throat. He drove her mad. She had no business feeling the way he made her feel.

"Next time? You mean you aren't going to cut me down, or yell at me, or tell me to go away and never come back?"

She bit the inside of her cheeks to keep from smiling, raising a brow to look like she was considering the options. "Would you rather I told you not to come back?"

"Beatrice, my heart aches at just the thought. I will never leave your side unless you give the word."

Now she couldn't help but smile. "I'll keep that in mind."

His own smile broke out then, and if there was any part of herself that she had kept from falling, it was obliterated right then and there.

Ges closed the space between them, wrapping her in his arms and finding her lips like they were his home. She couldn't help but run her hands into his beautiful hair, and as he responded to her touch, his kiss deepened. She was consumed by a sudden hunger to feel more of him, to kiss more of him, *have* more of him. Her hands travelled from his head to his shoulders, caressing every inch along the way, pushing her body closer to his until he made that sweet, throaty groan. His arms moved to her waist. He gripped her tighter, lifted her, and suddenly the groan changed inflection. He released her in an instant, grabbing his side and righting himself with a wince.

"You're hurt," she said. *Of course he was, Gods.*

"It's ok, Willow says it will heal fine."

"It better." A thought wormed its way into her head. The thought of the future. "And when it does, will you go back to Triad city?"

"And let you and Mal have all the fun without me? Not a chance."

Epilogue

It was a quiet evening at the Knightcap. Relatively quiet, anyhow. A few locals sat around the fireplace discussing the word around town. Benny wasn't quite drunk enough to start playing the piano yet.

Beatrice Lemon sat at the bar, swirling an ale and growing impatient.

Mal and Ges were due back any moment, and while tonight's job had been about gathering information and shouldn't have involved any danger, she still hated being left behind. They had made the valid point that getting a city guardsman to open up about a romantic affair would probably be easier for them. Something about masculine comradery.

Fine. If it got them closer to figuring out who he'd given their client's heirloom jewelry to, let them have their boys' night.

Her head swiveled at the sound of someone entering. It wasn't them, just some middle-aged stranger with a delicate mustache and golden-brown hair shot through with the first signs of grey. She wouldn't have given him a second thought, but as the man walked up to the bar looking entirely out of place, she couldn't help but notice he was dressed a little too elegantly for this side of town.

She sipped at her drink, careful not to stare blatantly as the man removed his coat. He stood lost for a moment, looking about. With a chuckle, she realized he was expecting someone to take it.

Berta walked over, eyeing the full length of the man. He was rather attractive if she was honest. He was exceedingly regal, toned for his age, and had a facial structure that must drive the wealthy ladies wild. There was something oddly familiar about him.

"What can I do for you?"

Even Berta was less gruff than usual. Either she was curious, or just glad to see such a fat purse walk through the door.

"I'm looking for a man I have heard frequents your establishment, but I..." the man looked around the inn and chuckled to himself. "I believe there may be some mistake."

"Try me," Berta said.

"Are you familiar with Paladin Gespar Fairchild?"

Bee's heart jumped at the name, her ears suddenly burning. She took a sip of her ale to center herself.

Berta shot her a glance, clearly looking for some sign of whether she should be 'familiar' with their paladin or not. *Bless the old woman.*

Gerra had insisted that Ges keep his title, and all the trappings that went with it. Though he didn't serve a temple anymore. They were careful with their work, and in the four months since the incident in Triad City they had been very particular about their proceedings. In fact, they had only committed about two and a half crimes. Whoever this was, it was more likely their business with Gespar dated back to his legitimate days with the Empire.

"I may be able to help you, sir," Beatrice spoke up.

The man turned to her eagerly, though his eyes widened with some measure of surprise.

"But," Bee continued, "in this part of town it's very important not to give information without receiving some in return."

The man hesitated.

"Bee, you won't believe who we ran in to tonight." Mal's booming voice signaled her companions' return.

So much for playing this out.

Ges crossed the floor to her immediately, taking her chin in his hand to tilt her face to him, claiming a kiss before even speaking.

"Gespar?" the stranger spoke, his eyes now ready to pop out of his well-groomed face. He gawked as though their kiss had been an illicit act.

Ges noticed the man now, and oddly enough made quite a similar expression of shock. "Father?"

Well, shit.

"What are you doing here?"

"I would ask you the same thing! I have been looking for you for months! The Church could share no information on your whereabouts, no one had seen you in Triad since the accident at the Gathering!"

"I..." Gespar looked uncharacteristically pale, and unsure of how to respond. "I have been doing independent work across the Empire. My position as Paladin has been quite different since the *accident*."

"*Quite different indeed.*" The elder Fairchild looked at Bee with critical eyes, and she had to resist the urge to grimace back at him.

"I have been petitioning the Church to release you from service," he continued. "As my sole remaining heir, your place is within the Fairchild House. I must insist you come home."

"Sole remaining heir? What has happened to Phillip?"

"He has been missing for three months! His wife, Margaret says hoodlums took him from his own home! She was weeping about a gang of vipers. You and I both know Phillip's bad habits must have finally done him ill."

Ges's brow furrowed, and he shut his eyes as if to better consider the news. His voice was heavy with fatigue when he spoke. "Did you not report this to the city guard?"

"Of course I did, but Triad has been a mess. They said they would tell us if they found anything."

"Gods..."

Beatrice knew Gespar's family relationships were no more stable than her own, but the strain on his face was clear.

"Ges," she lowered her tone. "The *Harbor* Vipers might have business with a 'Phillip Fairchild'."

His expression hardened and worry glazed his eyes.

"Damn, does this mean we're going back to Bay?" Malice asked.

"*We* are returning to Triad," Lord Fairchild corrected, gesturing between himself and his son.

"That's not your decision to make," Ges said sternly, before turning his attention to Beatrice and Malice. "I have to do this."

"Course we do," Mal said.

"We have no way of knowing what we're walking in to…"

"What's new?" Bee asked.

She smiled as Ges relaxed slightly.

"If you'll excuse me, I believe I have some things to discuss with my father."

The Fairchilds found a quiet table on the far side of the room, and Mal took his seat next to her at the bar.

"Think he's still alive?"

"If he is he's not having a good time," she answered. She preferred not to think about it too much, at least for now. "How'd it go tonight?"

"As expected. Three drinks in he told us all about his lady Greystar. Her family is in Central city."

Just great.

"You said you ran into someone?"

Malice nodded. "Our old friend, Nered. Says he needs help with something."

Beatrice acknowledged by draining her drink. It was only a matter of time before one of them came calling, she knew. At least they paid well.

ABOUT THE AUTHOR

Kaitlyn Owenby is a fantasy author, a mother, and ~~a bit of~~ a nerd. She loves fantasy, science fiction, romance, and every mix-and-match combination of the three. When she isn't writing, you might find her playing video games, reading, or trying to keep up with her two boys

Other Books by Kaitlyn Owenby:

The Joke's On You (a rom-com novella)

Coming soon: From Stone To Stars